CONGRESS'S CRYPTOGRAPHER

A Novel of James Lovell
and the American Revolution

Advance Praise for *Congress's Cryptographer*

James Lovell is considered "the Father of American Cryptanalysis" by no less an authority than David Kahn, and William Friedman called him "the Revolution's one-man National Security Agency." His pioneering work as a codemaker and a codebreaker gave cryptology a singular role in the emergence of the new nation. He is a landmark figure in the history of American cryptanalysis and cryptography, and a model for present and future generations.
—John A. Tokar. Chief, Center for Cryptologic History, National Security Agency/Central Security Service

In *Congress's Cryptographer*, Jean O'Connor picks up James Lovell's story where her captivating novel *The Remarkable Cause* left off. Lovell is one of the "forgotten founders," but his story reads like a colonial *Imitation Game*, as Lovell both makes and breaks codes, playing an invaluable role in the diplomatic chess game played across the Atlantic with Franklin and Adams, and on the battlefield with Washington and Greene.
—Tim McGrath, author of the critically acclaimed biographies *John Barry: An American Hero in the Age of Sail* and *James Monroe: A Life*.

The extraordinary saga of James Lovell, which began in *The Remarkable Cause* as he moved from a teacher in a one-room schoolhouse to a British prisoner of war, continues in this splendid book as he develops his amazing cryptologic talents and endures horrific hardships during the struggle for freedom. Lovell becomes an unsung hero of the Revolutionary War who only now in 2024 is being recognized for his important role in achieving victory.
—Jane Lee Hamman, Montana America 250 Commission, Montana State Daughters of the American Revolution Regent 2016–2019, and sponsor of a revolutionary ancestor on the Pathway of the Patriots

Jean O'Connor immerses readers in the complex issues, intrigues, and decisions that faced James Lovell and his contemporaries during the 1780s. Based on extensive

research, *Congress's Cryptographer* vividly portrays the people and their courage, hardships, and resilience during the American Revolution.
—Beverly Ann Chin, Ph. D.
Professor Emeritus of English, University of Montana

Lovell is indeed a fascinating figure. Jean O'Connor makes good use of his story to narrate the larger political and military history of the Revolutionary War at a critical point. In lively and engaging writing, her account really brings Lovell and his friends and associates to life and captures the drama of the times they lived through. I found her interweaving of primary sources with O'Connor's version of his story quite compelling. All in all, *Congress's Cryptographer* is a terrific book, one that will, I'm sure, find an enthusiastic readership.
—Eliga Gould, professor of history at the University of New Hampshire, author of *Among the Powers of the Earth: The American Revolution and the Making of a New World Empire* (2012), finalist for the George Washington Prize

Congress's Cryptographer gives the reader a better understanding of the Revolution by looking at occurrences through the life and experiences of James Lovell, Congressman. Jean O'Connor's work personalizes situations and gives a human understanding to the events. The American Revolution involved people, not just major ideas and developments. *Congress's Cryptographer* should also be very interesting to people intrigued by how cryptography was used during the Revolution.
—William L. Kidder, author of *Ten Crucial Days: Washington's Vision for Victory Unfolds* (2018)

Jean O'Connor's second book, *Congress's Cryptographer: A Novel of James Lovell and the American Revolution*, is a continuation of the story of James Lovell, started in *The Remarkable Cause: A Novel of James Lovell and the Crucible of the Revolution*. Relying on primary resources from letters to the *Journals* of the Continental Congress, she offers a fascinating look into not only the importance of this forgotten revolutionary, but also the committee work in Congress. O'Connor offers a close-up look at several important figures: John and Abigail Adams, John Hancock, Samuel Adams, Benjamin Franklin, Thomas Jefferson, Henry Laurens, the Marquis de Lafayette, and Baron von Steuben. Many of the characters fight the war from behind their desks, dealing with the daily minutiae of Congress.

Perhaps the most interesting aspect of O'Connor's book is the portrayal of the epistolary relationship between Lovell and Abigail Adams. What starts off as a description of the role that John Adams played in Congress (information that Abigail craved, since her husband was too busy to write regularly) gradually turns into a real friendship. Lovell's role as a cryptographer was important to the Congress, and especially for George Washington. O'Connor includes images of actual ciphered-letters and cipher-keys in the novel. *Congress's Cryptographer: A Novel of James Lovell and the American Revolution* is both an excellent and unique addition to the historical fiction covering the American Revolution.
—Timothy Symington, frequent contributor to the *Journal of the American Revolution* and the author of *"Huzza!": Toasting a New Nation, 1760-1815*

About James Lovell: William Friedman [distinguished leader at NSA] called Lovell "the [American] Revolution's one-man National Security Agency." His pioneering work as a codebreaker and codemaker gave cryptology a singular role in the emergence of our new Nation. Leveraging Lovell's decrypts, George Washington knew of the approach of a British relief force and was able to warn his French allies, thus enabling a decisive victory at Yorktown. Lovell is a landmark figure in the history of American cryptology and a model for present and future generations.
—Press Release, National Security Agency, Central Security Service: Induction of James Lovell into NSA's Cryptologic Hall of Honor (2023)

CONGRESS'S CRYPTOGRAPHER

A Novel of James Lovell and the American Revolution

Jean C. O'Connor

MOUNTAIN PINE PRESS
ISBN: 979-8-9899009-0-9
ISBN (eBook): 979-8-9899009-1-6

Congress's Cryptographer:
A Novel of James Lovell and the American Revolution
© 2024 Jean C. O'Connor
All Rights Reserved

Cover Art by Steph Lehmann
Cover Image: "Philadelphia State House." Sarin Images / GRANGER - Historical Picture Archive

mountainpinepress.com
Helena, Montana

Published in the United States of America

"I was put upon a deciphering Business respecting
some of the intercepted Letters of Cornwallis…."
James Lovell to Nathaniel Peabody, 3 November 1780.

The National Security Agency and Central Security Service inducted James Lovell into the Cryptologic Hall of Honor, 2023, as a contributor of extraordinary means to the security and strength of the United States.

James Lovell, honored as "the Father of American Cryptanalysis," was self-taught in cryptography and cryptanalysis. He assumed responsibility for both designing ciphers to protect American communications and breaking those used by the British during the Revolutionary War.

By 1781, he had broken the cipher used by senior British commanders in America. George Washington thanked Lovell for data that enabled him to decipher a letter that sufficiently confirmed the dire circumstances of the surrounded British. William Friedman called Lovell "the Revolution's one-man National Security Agency." His pioneering work as a codebreaker and codemaker gave cryptology a singular role in the emergence of the new nation.

—*The Director, National Security Agency, presents the Public Service Medallion to James Lovell.*

TABLE OF CONTENTS

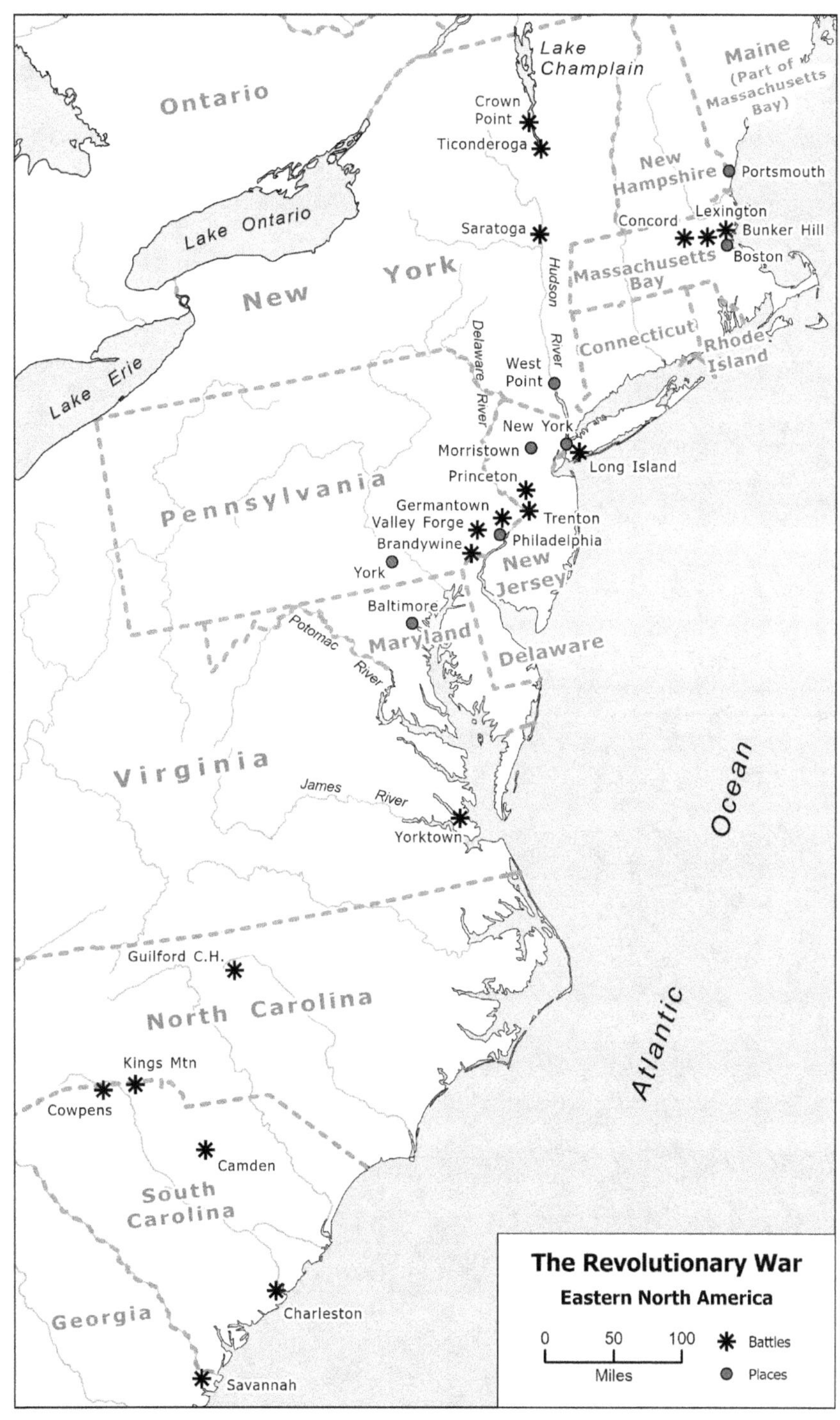

Map by Gerry Daumiller

Chapter 1

Congress in Baltimore

February 2, 1777, Sunday

The smell of sizzling pork crept into James's dreams as he lay in the narrow cot at the brick inn on the outskirts of Baltimore. He cracked his eyes open to see frost whorls riming windowpanes. Bare black branches creaked and whispered in a chill wind. He and John Adams had arrived at the meeting place of Congress, now moved from its home in Philadelphia to Baltimore for safety as General Howe's army pressed into New Jersey.

Across the room, Joseph Trumbull snored. *It is good to be with you again, my friend,* James thought. He had known Joseph since his days at Harvard. Now the commissary general of stores and provisions, his friend obtained food and supplies for the American army.

James reached for his boots, wincing at the stiffness in his joints. Hours, days, in the saddle. Weeks on horseback, after months of near starvation in prison. His body felt battered and sore. He let out a soft moan. Joseph Trumbull started, woke up.

"So, Congressman Lovell is ready to go again, eh?" he needled.

"Yes, before long. Did you get Jemmy and Johnny up this early when they stayed with you?" James groaned, tugging on a boot.

Joseph Trumbull chortled. "To pick the corn and hoe the beans? Much earlier, thank you. They must have been relieved when they moved to stay with another family in Cambridge."

James glanced affectionately at the commissary general. Jovial, ample in size, Joseph Trumbull had come to his aid while James had been a prisoner in the Boston Stone Jail, awaiting trial on charges of spying for the Americans after Bunker Hill. He had taken in James's older sons at his home outside of Boston, as the town was occupied by thousands of British regimentals.

"Will you be with Congress long?"

"I leave for business of my own in Hartford soon," Joseph Trumbull said. Trumbull's success at finding supplies for the militia, such as pork, beef, cooking kettles, and rum, had earned him General Washington's approval.

"I still can scarcely believe I am about to join Congress. Part of me expects to see that filthy cell in Halifax when I open my eyes," James said ruefully. "Nine months in the Boston Stone Jail and nine months in prison in Halifax leave their mark on a person."

"Aye. Congress is fortunate to have you, with your talents in writing, knowledge of French, and ability to speak the language."

"I can read and write cipher. Military and diplomatic matters sometimes require that." *A teacher at the Boston Latin School and holder of a graduate degree from Harvard, I have talents the country can use.* "And the salary as delegate from Massachusetts will help support my family."

He picked up the woolen coat Mary had cleaned for him twenty-four days ago when he left Boston, now grimy with sweat and horsehair, and pulled it on. His dark brown hair tied back with a silk ribbon, he stood, a trifle unsteadily, and felt the growth on his gray-streaked sideburns.

"I believe I am ready." *How could one ever be truly ready for such an undertaking as this?* he thought, as he followed Joseph Trumbull's large figure out the door. *Two or three dozen delegates in Congress, a handful of officers, and maybe five thousand Continentals and militia against the might of the British army. Add to those three commissioners at the court of France, there to bend the ear and with any luck the purse strings of the king. Dr. Franklin, the oldest, a respected scientist and public figure, well suited to represent his country. Arthur Lee, lawyer from Virginia, and Silas Deane, member of Congress from Connecticut. How could one make the odds work in such a case?* He was about to find out.

The well-kept inn was quiet. A fire crackled in the handsome hearth. A boy in a greasy apron muttered an apology as he squeezed past them bearing a tray of sliced ham and fresh scones.

John Adams sat at the long table in front of the fire, his round, cheerful face relaxed, his brown hair combed and tied. For a moment, James pictured him at the home of his brother-in-law Richard Cranch in Braintree, not far from Boston near the farm of the Adams family. There, on January 8, before he and John departed for Baltimore, James had dined with the Adams family. Abigail, John's wife, struck James as bright and knowledgeable. She was eager to converse about the events of the war, Washington's recent victories at Trenton and Princeton, and the difficulty of obtaining supplies and arms. Her dark hair, swept back to either side of her face, and her luminous eyes arrested him, lingering in his mind.

She listened with sympathy to James's story as he described his months in jail, imprisoned by the British for spying, first in Boston, then in Halifax, worried about his family's safety and not knowing when he would see them again.

"And you will now leave them, perhaps for a great length of time?" Abigail asked, her voice tinged with sympathy.

"Congress has invited me to serve," James answered. "I shall miss my family, but I am grateful to assist our cause while I provide for their needs." His gray-green eyes, light in color against his olive-toned skin, held her for a moment. Dark brows accented his lean features, lined by sideburns tinged with gray.

Abigail looked back at her husband with a depth of feeling that caused James to turn his head away. "I must rely on letters to keep informed about John's business and safety," she said.

"As I will remain connected to my wife Mary," he responded.

Abigail took his plate to serve him an additional portion of roast chicken. He saw the gallantry with which John Adams treated her and the special relationship that clearly existed between the couple. *John Adams realizes the treasure he has in his wife,* he thought.

He pulled up a chair by John Adams in front of the fire.

"Did you sleep well?" the lawyer asked.

"Well indeed, thank you. My joints will recover after these weeks of travel, given time."

Joseph Trumbull helped himself to food and passed the platter to James. James's first bite of smoky, salty ham awoke him to hunger and he began to eat in silence. John Turner, John Adams's quiet servant, joined them.

"It appears we have congenial weather. We will be in Baltimore a couple of days before Congress resumes," John said. His round cheeks glowed ruddy. Shorter than James, he appeared heavy, but James knew him to be sturdy as an oak, accustomed to cutting wood, mowing hay, tending to livestock.

James reached for a scone. "My wife Mary is Scottish, so she knows how to make scones even lighter than these." He thrust back the pang in his heart. Brave woman that she was, Mary had released him after her last embrace and smiled through her tears.

"Abigail works with our servant to strain milk, prepare bread, and see to Nabby, John Quincy, and little Thomas's breakfast," John said. "Being absent from one's family can be a hardship."

"I hope to make this absence a worthwhile one," James said. "I intend to dedicate myself to whatever work Congress sees fit to assign me. Mary will be able to manage the household, as she did during my imprisonment. As to my children, James, our oldest, has graduated from Harvard and joined a cavalry unit with the militia. Jemmy and Johnny are finishing their education and apprenticing to trades. Our younger six are at home in the care of their mother. Mary expects nothing less but that I will provide for our family."

"Abigail may take on more responsibility for the farm than she would if I were present, but change is necessary in these times. She must be content with my letters, as I must be with hers."

James allowed himself to relax. The warmth of the fire, the food, the realization that they had reached their destination, these all soaked into his tired body. For the first time he allowed himself to reflect on what a long and difficult trip they had completed.

The delegates had left Braintree, south of Boston, on January 9, nearly a month ago. Traveling through thick snow, they headed westward through Massachusetts to avoid British military activity around New York City and the possible presence of the enemy near the seacoast. The first night they reveled in the warmth of Dr. Sprague's home in Dedham.

They continued into Connecticut, slowed by fresh snow on the iron-hard rutted road. At East Hartford, four days after leaving Boston, they crossed the Connecticut River on the ferry, thankful for the ferryman's skill in avoiding chunks of floating ice. In Hartford, Commissary General Joseph Trumbull joined them.

After months in British jails, James found riding twenty-five miles a day in treacherous conditions extremely arduous. He managed to keep his seat on the bay gelding with more determination than skill.

Once on a sharp bend, he pitched sideways but righted himself, his breath coming fast. John Turner looked at him anxiously. "Are you all right?"

"Certainly," James answered curtly. Determined not to show weakness, he straightened in the saddle, though his head swam with the effort.

More than once, he glanced at John Adams with envy. The lawyer seemed to travel effortlessly. Of course, even before joining Congress he rode for days across Massachusetts to attend trials. He had covered the three hundred miles from Braintree to Philadelphia and back several times since joining the First Continental Congress in 1774. *He is no stranger to long rides.*

After the Connecticut hills, the journey became easier. Once, a thick fog enveloped them. The travelers had to pick their way carefully to avoid losing their way. On a day so cold the sun cast twin lights in the sky, John's horse lost its footing in a cavity in the road, nearly causing him to lose his seat and his temper.

Crossing the Hudson River at Fishkill, New York, had proven impossible, the ice treacherous. They turned north at Poughkeepsie, resting at private homes and inns. *Luckily, I had cash to pay for our lodgings. John and Joseph will reimburse me.*

Last night they finally reached the Susquehanna River and the ferry. The ferrymen tipped their hats to the travelers before bidding them Godspeed. The swinging sign of the inn, the Gray Goose, meant they had reached the outskirts of Baltimore.

"I suggest we join the Massachusetts delegation after Sunday meeting," John said. "Then we may look about the town and see Congress's meeting place, the Henry Fite house. The large building on Market Street has been our home since Congress moved out of Philadelphia on December 12, too close for safety to the British in New York."

"Indeed."

"Our presence in Congress is essential. The Committees of Correspondence united our states two years ago, but since then, Congress has been the governing body. We alone can requisition troops for the army, order clothing, ammunition, and supplies, authorize officers, and send emissaries to potentially helpful countries."

"How many delegates are there usually?"

"At least three from each state are required in order to conduct business. But with pressing needs at home, such as crops, sickness, and family emergencies, the number of delegates in Congress often dwindles to twenty-four." John shrugged.

"Yet, work goes on," James observed.

"It takes great dedication for the members to leave their homes, their employment, their families. Congress alone can guide the thirteen states to wage war for our freedom."

Joseph smiled agreement. The group was silent for a few moments, watching the fire flicker in the wide brick hearth, the sun dance through the diamond paned windows.

"Well, gentlemen, shall we head to town?" John stretched and rose to his feet.

"I'll prepare the horses," John Turner said.

"Would one of you settle the account?" the innkeeper asked, coming to the door and wiping his hands on his apron.

"I'll do that." James took out a small notebook from his coat pocket. Joseph glanced over his shoulder at the pages.

"What have you there?" he asked, pointing to a list of numbers and letters arrayed in a square.

"That is a cipher key. I create them when I wish to make writing secret to any who would show it unwanted attention," James answered. He glanced at Joseph seriously, his gray-green eyes calm.

"General Washington uses all manner of deceptions to keep his messages a secret to any who might intercept them, though I only know of his methods in a general way," Joseph replied. "It is likely that you will be able to help Congress with your knowledge."

"Sending messages securely is a constant priority," John said.

"I will be more than happy to teach others to use a cipher," James said. "I think it a great asset in delivery of sensitive information." He got to his feet and followed the innkeeper to the front room.

James counted out money to the innkeeper, met the others outside, and checked his saddlebags.

"Congress should be in good humor, given Washington's recent successes in New Jersey," Adams remarked.

"I wonder which delegates we will find?" James said. "Samuel Adams, Elbridge Gerry, Francis Dana, and John Hancock, now the president, all from Massachusetts—they should be there."

"We have one of the largest delegations," John agreed. "Work will go on, though perhaps not with sufficient numbers for a vote."

Flocks of sheep grazed in soggy pastures as the riders took to the road; flax rested in the moist ground, to be broken and swung by men and women come Monday.

The town of Baltimore lay along the Patapsco River, flowing into the north end of the great Chesapeake Bay. *It makes a pretty sight*, James thought. Homes and shops lined the hills by the river. Up the rise behind the settlement, the Presbyterian meetinghouse stood near a small Church of England. A courthouse, not yet finished, thrust tall rafters towards the sky.

At the meetinghouse, the travelers met up with the other Massachusetts delegates. James knew Francis Dana from his days at Harvard. The lawyer from Boston, his dark eyes flashing confidence, now stood firmly in the defense of liberty, following the failure of his trip to Parliament to mend differences. James greeted Elbridge Gerry warmly. The young lawyer, tall and energetic, had strongly supported the Declaration of Independence last summer. He shook hands with President John Hancock, dapper in a black silk coat with a white ruff, a wealthy merchant whose ships had smuggled goods taxed by the British.

Mr. Allison spoke from the square pulpit at the Presbyterian meeting, addressing his listeners with the text of the day, Joshua calling the people of Israel to take Jericho. *Appropriate for our fight.*

Out in the sunshine, President John Hancock turned to the others. "Congress has declared today to be a fast day. General Washington's forces dwindled to fewer than three thousand men over the hard winter. Those enlisted have commissions about to expire. We must increase our efforts to fund our army. Today, I suggest we leave the horses and walk through the town. You will appreciate its beautiful setting on the Patapsco River."

The group descended the hill, flocks of birds wheeling above. The air smelled fresh and moist—a harbinger of spring. They passed through streets lined with houses, greeting villagers. Shops stood shuttered for Sunday. In the busy parts of town, unpaved streets, muddy and rutted, trapped passing carriages in mire.

On Market Street at the western edge of town, they reached the Henry Fite house, sturdily built of red brick, boasting three floors of white-sashed windows and an attic set with dormers. The stately structure had been chosen for the temporary home of Congress in part because it stood a safe distance from the Baltimore harbor and the Patapsco River, should the British navy's ships threaten.

David Rusk, Patriot and Whig, welcomed them. "Your rooms are prepared for you this evening," he said, ushering them into his parlor.

"Thank you," John Adams said. "Tomorrow, we stay with Mrs. Ross."

"I intend to leave for Hartford in a few days," Joseph Trumbull said. "The army never stops eating." He shrugged and smiled at his little joke.

James turned to David Rusk. "I must excuse myself to deliver a packet of letters to Samuel Adams at Mrs. Ross's." He bowed slightly as he turned to leave.

A block away, Mrs. Ross, a severe-looking lady in a black dress, answered James's knock. "Mr. Adams's room is just to the top of the landing," she said in clipped accents, gesturing. James nodded his thanks and began the steep ascent, inhaling the smell of rose oil on the polished railing.

Samuel Adams enfolded his hand in a warm clasp of welcome. "Mr. Lovell. It is a pleasant sight to see you. Come in, come in." Tall, genial, Samuel Adams had been one of the main proponents of liberty for years, writing and speaking in the colony of Massachusetts in support of rights to self-government. He had helped form the Committees of Correspondence, adopted throughout the colonies to provide order during years of increased British oppression. He had guided the first Continental Congress to gather in Philadelphia, signed the Declaration of Independence, and served in Congress since its inception.

"I have these for you," James said, pulling from his pocket the packet of letters.

"It is most kind of you to deliver them. Here, please do take a seat."

James noticed the stacks of papers and books spread about the room. Clearly, the leader of the Sons of Liberty was comfortable with paperwork.

"Congress has such marvelous energy in Baltimore. Being driven from your home by the prospect of attack from a vicious enemy kindles the spirits. Like blowing on a fire with a bellows. Debates can often go on and on in Congress with no resolution. But here, we have managed to make progress, despite our poor showing in numbers. We have accomplished more in three weeks than I believe we have in Philadelphia in six months." He chuckled in appreciation.

"I look forward to learning of the group's success," James said. His eyes widened in curiosity.

"You will see how the business goes: committees, debates, resolves, considerations. Certainly, you will make a wondrous addition to our group. Your time in jail has, no doubt, solidified any apprehensions that you might not be wholly supportive of our cause."

James grinned. "I have no doubts as to the importance of our goals."

"We were most gratified to receive a visit from Colonel Baylor, aide-de-camp for General Washington. He delivered to us a letter from the general telling us of his success at Trenton on Christmas night. The audacity of our general! The timing!" Samuel Adams slapped his hands on his thighs in excitement. "Baylor brought us a silken standard from the Hessians that now adorns our mess hall at the Henry Fite house. The general took a thousand prisoners at Trenton. A few days later in early January we heard of the rout of the British at Princeton; now it appears Washington has recovered most of New Jersey and the British have retreated to New York."

"And General Washington and his army?" James asked.

"Are presently settled at Morristown, north of Trenton in New Jersey, for the winter. From the hills surrounding the settlement, the general can keep surveillance on any British troop movements across the Hudson River in New York City."

The older delegate drummed his fingers on the table impatiently.

"As support for Washington, and in view of our critical situation, on December 27, Congress voted to give the general almost dictatorial powers for a period of six months. He may raise sixteen battalions, three thousand light horse, three regiments of artillery, and a corps of engineers, all to enlist until the war ends. No more short-term enlistment. He may seize property he needs for the army and arrest anyone who refuses to take Continental money, such as uncooperative merchants. Without a strong army we have no country; if we do not give Washington the authority he needs, the British can ride right over us." Samuel's words echoed his impatience.

"And that, sir, is not going to happen!" James finished his thought.

"Certainly not. It is Congress's pressing job to raise the funds that Washington needs, by whatever means." Samuel stood up and shook James's hand. "We are most gratified to have you here."

"I am most pleased to join you. Good day, sir." James turned and descended the narrow flight of stairs. Back at David Rusk's he and the other delegates spent the evening talking over their hopes for the success of Washington's army.

The lack of money to pay the military or get supplies, despite Congress's issue of some $25 million in Continentals, was one of the foremost problems the group faced. James listened as the others talked, realizing he had much to learn. The Committee of Secret Correspondence had sent Connecticut delegate Silas Deane to France in the spring of 1776 with hopes the merchant could arrange for a loan to the United States from Louis XVI. Deane's mission was so secret that he had traveled without the knowledge of Congress, under cover of being a wealthy merchant from Bermuda, bearing a letter of introduction from Benjamin Franklin, already in France, who enjoyed great popularity with the French. Congress had yet to hear of any loans the French might offer.

But financing the war required funding on a daily basis.

"We could requisition the states again," John Hancock said. The faces of those present turned long at this suggestion. "However, we know that there is no real way we can compel the states to respond to our requests. We cannot tax. We can and will print Continentals. And we should hear from our representatives in France about loans. The funding issue is a thorny one that will preoccupy our time. On this thought, gentlemen, I bid you good night."

James stifled a yawn. Weary to the core, he made his way to his room, a small affair at the end of the hall on the second floor. He would do his best to be of help to the governing body of the thirteen American states.

February 4, 1777, Tuesday

On Tuesday, a cold rain splattering puddles in the road, the delegates made their way to the large brick building on the corner of Liberty and Market Streets. In the roomy hall, the polished plank floors and gilt-framed mirror gleamed. The smells of soap and bayberry hung fresh in the air, thanks to the women of Baltimore. A brisk fire crackled in the fireplaces at the ends of the long room. By ten in the morning, all delegates were seated, awaiting the beginning of the session. *About twenty-eight here*, he thought.

James looked about the meeting room, tall windows bathed in the gray light of winter. Quaker-built as a tavern, the space offered comfortable chairs. Adorning one wall was the Hessian standard captured at Trenton, woven with green and white silk with gold tassels, bearing a painted crown and a wreath. Washington's gift had no doubt cheered the delegates. A table for the president's use stood to one side.

"It was quite a d-d-day when we received the news of the victory at Trenton," Elbridge Gerry said, eyeing the captured flag.

Samuel Adams waved his arm towards the standard. "Before ordering over two thousand American soldiers to cross the icy Delaware river on Christmas evening, General Washington ordered his officers to read to them the first lines of *The American Crisis*, a new pamphlet by Thomas Paine. The words are, 'These are the times that try men's souls: The summer soldier and the sunshine patriot will, in this crisis, shrink from the service of their country; but he that stands it now, deserves the love and thanks of man and woman.'"

"Thomas Paine," James said thoughtfully. "His pamphlet *Common Sense* was well received when it came out in the early months of last year. Of course, I was in prison, so I did not see it until I returned to Boston. He has a way of speaking about the natural rights of men that appeals to people."

"It was very popular," Samuel Adams concurred. "*The American Crisis* is written in the same vein, encouraging folks to stand against tyranny. It must have emboldened the troops to hear the inspiring words before they set out to cross an icy river and march ten miles to surprise sleeping Hessians." He chuckled to himself.

"It is time we begin, gentlemen. It is ten o'clock," President Hancock said, taking his place. Nearby at a long table sat Secretary Charles Thomson. Tall, slender, efficient, Secretary Thomson's sharp eyes watched every movement. His pen recorded the proceedings as he gave orders to his two clerks, who sorted documents and copied correspondence.

"We meet during the day, adjourn for the evening meal, then gather in committees as needed," President Hancock said. Short of stature, his elegant black suit coat accented his fine features. "First order, we welcome new delegates to Congress."

James had been present for John Hancock's oration commemorating those who had died at the Boston Massacre. James himself held the honor of first giving the oration in Boston the year following the massacre, an event which became annual. He knew John Hancock from the Boston Latin School and Harvard. In the spring of 1775, Hancock was selected to attend the Second Continental Congress in Philadelphia, where he was elected as president for his prestige, wealth, and leadership experience. His was the first signature on the Declaration of Independence.

James rose to accept the smattering of applause when he was introduced.

"I believe you are fluent in French, are you not?" President Hancock asked.

"Yes, I both speak and write the language."

"Silas Deane in France has been referring officers to serve in Washington's forces. You may expect to serve on a committee to consider French officers who seek employment with our army. And provide translations for the communications of the French foreign minister, Count de Vergennes, who of course writes in French. Your services, sir, will be most appreciated."

"He can read and write a cipher, as well," Joseph Trumbull offered.

"Indeed." President Hancock's eyes lit up. "Your skill will be of use to us."

The business of the day began. Congress heard reports, appointed committees, authorized supply orders, reviewed petitions, and considered resolutions. Excitement over the success of Washington and the army spurred the delegates on in their tasks, while a feeling of urgency underlaid everything. If the body of men failed, if they did not retain the people's confidence, the revolution died. Only Congress could keep the country together and provide the necessary authority to conduct the war and support the army. Every man knew that, and, inspired by the victories at Trenton and Princeton, buoyed with hope for their army's success, they pressed onward.

February 7, 1777, Friday

On February 5, his second day in Congress, James was appointed to the Committee on Indian Affairs. *What, if anything, do I know about Indian affairs?* he wondered. The Six Nations of the Iroquois fought on the side of the British in the French and Indian War. That much he knew. On February 7, President Hancock announced, "Named to the Committee for the *Journals* of Congress, James Lovell and John Witherspoon."

James glanced over at Reverend John Witherspoon of New Jersey, the portly, energetic president of the College of New Jersey and Presbyterian minister.

"Your committee members are Samuel Adams, Richard Henry Lee, and John Rutledge," John Hancock said, moving on to the next item of business.

"What does the committee for the *Journals* do?" James asked Samuel Adams as the session concluded. *Surely the Journals were written by Secretary Charles Thomson?*

"When Congress orders a printing of the *Journals*, the committee reviews and edits them." Samuel Adams pulled a long face, as if to say the job were a tedious one.

James nodded. Secretary Thomson compiled the *Journals*. The committee saw to the editing and printing. *I can manage that.*

That night the delegates dined at the home of Mr. Lux, a merchant, ship owner, and Continental marine agent in Baltimore. The estate of Chatsworth lay at the end of a road lined with double rows of cherry trees. Servants in smart red and black dress ushered them to a candlelit table. *Probably slaves*, James mused. In Boston there had been very few slaves. Most black people there were free and independent.

During the meal, a succulent pork roast served with cherry cordial, Samuel Adams turned to James.

"I hear you are accomplished at reading cipher."

"I have some ability with it."

"How did you come by that knowledge?" Samuel asked.

"When I was young, I attempted several systems to write secret notes to myself. My brother John was always prying; this was one way to prevent that. I hit on an alphabet type of cipher. I recently read a publication titled *A Treatise on the Art of Deciphering and of Writing in Cypher with an Harmonic Alphabet*, published, I believe, in 1772. Are you familiar with it?"

"I am not."

"I purchased a copy and studied it. The art of writing in cipher has always inspired my curiosity. The author, Philip Thicknesse, points out that the practice of reading and writing itself is a wonderful invention. It enables ideas from a thousand years ago to be known to us just as ours may be known a thousand years in the future. He notes the use of alphabets to write messages that convey meaning. According to him, cipher began to be used thousands of years ago, perhaps with the Egyptians."

"Your knowledge will be of great use to Congress. Washington uses invisible ink for some dispatches, and cipher. So do the British. Sometimes the message is written very small and rolled up, to be concealed in a quill, a shirt cuff, even a button."

"Writing a cipher is a straightforward process," James explained. "Julius Caesar's was a substitution alphabet, where *d* is *a* and *a* is *b*, and so on. Messages written in a substitution alphabet can be difficult to read, but are not as complex and secure as messages written in cipher. There is another method where the words of the real message are mixed with the words of a fabricated statement in such a way as to make the actual message nearly impossible to recognize—that is, until the words are aligned in columns. Then the message is perceptible."

"The use of Black Chambers is common in Europe. There, all suspected correspondence is opened, read, and resealed for apparent innocent delivery," Samuel said. "Our ships sailing to France must often toss overboard packets of messages to our representatives. These may be pulled from the ocean if not sufficiently weighted. Messages written in cipher or other means of encryption provide additional security. We cannot be too careful." He finished his cordial and winked knowingly.

"The type of cipher I usually use," James said, "is similar to a Vigenère table. The encryption is based on a keyword, making it possible for each message to be tailored to the user. For example, if I were to write you that the keyword for the message would be the name of the host for this night's dinner, you would know it."

"Lux. How convenient."

"Yes. It creates a polyalphabetic system uniquely tailored to the user. The method of using a key, and of resolving the meaning of an encrypted message using a key, is described in the book I mentioned."

"It may be that you will have opportunity to use your knowledge of cipher," Samuel said thoughtfully. "You could be of great help to Congress."

"It would be my honor."

James thoroughly enjoyed the evening. In his room, preparing to rest for the night, he felt energetic, his work holding renewed purpose.

He took out paper, sharpened his quill, and wrote to Mary. He mentioned news that he could safely share. Letters containing sensitive information could end up printed publicly in the newspapers. And Mary did not require all of the details. Some news would upset her. She had enough to handle, caring for the family. He sealed his letter, sending his wishes for his family's safety and well-being, and placed it aside for delivery in the morning.

He woke in the night, drenched with sweat, his teeth clenched, his arms corded with tension. A vision of a dark, filthy cell lingered in his mind, the dungeon of a nightmare—slop thrown at him by a prison guard, boots bashing him in the ribs. A howl lingered in his mind, throbbing down the stone corridor. For a moment he wondered at the sound, full of pain and sorrow, then realized it came from his own throat. He sat up, tense from his feet to his head, shivering, and held himself still until he could quiet his breathing. *What was it?* A memory from his months in jail, crude and filthy, had come to him in a dream. He took slow breaths, willing himself to calm and acceptance. *This will not stop me*, he vowed. *My memories of such pain and misery will not affect me. I will persevere and be of service to my country, God willing. My absence from my family, my home, will prove worthwhile.*

His hands unclenched. Gradually the perspiration on his body dried, the cramps in his legs subsided, his vision cleared. He sank back on the pillow, exhausted, the trembling in his chest slowly gliding away like water settling in a shaken jar.

February 8, 1777, Saturday

President John Hancock unfolded a letter, frowning as he looked up from its contents.

"Robert Morris, of the Executive Committee in Philadelphia, received the enclosed dispatches yesterday from General Washington. He adds to what the general says of the want of money, that the last $200,000 we sent him is nearly gone. And he points out the need for horses and infantry for the army.

"Both Robert Morris and George Clymer send us a warning and request us to return." The president glanced severely at his listeners before he began to read.

> *This year will cost nearer forty million than twenty and*
> *where is it to be got if early and effectual means are not taken?*
> *We ground our present opinion of safety to this city on many*
> *recurring circumstances, but principally on the enemies' want*
> *of horses to move the necessary stores, provisions, forage,*
> *artillery and so on for such an undertaking.... They will not*
> *undertake such an expedition by water for they have not men*
> *enough to hold New York and attack this place at the same*

> *time…. We are convinced that your return here will give
> confidence to your army and credit to your money.*

"What do you say? Should we return to Philadelphia?"

Samuel Adams stood. "I move we do so. We can wrap up our business here this week and leave next week. The British threat to Philadelphia is gone, at least for this time."

Others nodded agreement.

"So be it," John Hancock said. "In addition, I move we send Robert Morris and the Executive Committee $300,000, via special post."

"Aye," the delegates responded. James felt a stir of excitement. They would return to Philadelphia. He would see the place where Congress met, where the Declaration had been written and signed. It would be a homecoming of sorts for some, but for him a joyous encounter with the city considered Congress's home.

At dinner that evening at Mrs. Ross's lodgings, talk turned to reports of the behavior of the British army moving south through New Jersey.

"They are like wild b-b-beasts, rampaging through the country," Elbridge Gerry said, his shrewd eyes narrowed. He stabbed a piece of sausage with his fork. "Whole families are murdered, farms are set to the t-t-torch, women are ravished."

"They take revenge on the people for their loss," John Adams agreed, chewing with little enthusiasm. "Sick and elderly people are turned out of their homes and left to freeze or starve."

"Our work takes on renewed meaning at such news. We must return our country to peace and stability, free it from the hands of these butchers," Samuel Adams said. "As capable as Robert Morris is, the most successful businessman and ships' owner in Philadelphia, he needs us to handle the duties of leadership. It is amazing that while we gathered here, Morris managed to get powder and arms that had just arrived at the docks loaded onto wagons and sent to Washington. The weaponry enabled the army's success at Trenton and Princeton."

"We do well to return."

February 10, 1777, Monday

In the evening, James and Colonel William Whipple walked to the tavern on Market Street. The colonel, a brisk, capable military leader, had been a successful seafaring merchant in Portsmouth, New Hampshire, making a fortune in trade with Europe, Africa, and the West Indies.

James knew William Whipple and his brother Joseph from Boston, though he had spent more time with Joseph, the younger of the two.

In the candle-lit tavern, over tankards of beer, he asked William Whipple, "You are still in the business of trade?"

"Yes, I am. Following years as a ship's captain, I went into partnership with my brother in the shipping business."

"And you signed the Declaration of Independence."

"It was a thrilling event. Those of us who believed strongly that British domination was not to be tolerated prevailed."

"I understand George Washington was a delegate from Virginia to the First Continental Congress before being chosen commander of the Continental Army," James said. "My stay in prison has left me with but a scanty knowledge of events in the past months."

"That is understandable. Yes, Washington's experience leading troops in the frontier during the French and Indian War, especially in the Ohio River Valley, recommended him. Not only that, but General Washington is commanding in appearance and believes in the cause of liberty. John Hancock wanted the position but clearly George Washington was the better candidate. It put Hancock's nose out of joint for a while."

"So, Washington led the Continental Army to New York, which had been taken by General William Howe after he left Halifax," James mused.

"And General Howe's brother, Admiral Lord Richard Howe, with his seventy war ships, joined him, making thirty-two thousand British troops in New York. The redcoats wanted to cut off New England."

"I understand that the fighting around New York last summer did not go so well."

"No, it did not. General Howe prevailed over Washington in several engagements. Washington and his forces were fortunate to escape and move into New Jersey."

"A difficult season," James said. *It appears our commander has apparently not always been successful.*

"Until the victory over the Hessians at Trenton, New Jersey, we had little to show for this year. Then, a few days after Trenton, General Washington captured Princeton, losing only five men and taking a thousand, as well as badly needed supplies."

"A much-needed victory," James said, nodding. "Truth to tell, I appreciate hearing of events that occurred while I was in prison."

"You will learn much. We are glad to have you."

"And the American army is now resting at their winter camp, I understand."

"Yes. General Washington keeps us informed of his needs and concerns."

Setting his tankard down, James assessed his companion, strong and knowledgeable. *Such as he would steer the country well.*

It was expensive to be a delegate, James realized. Daily his accounts added up—room and board, his horse's stabling and feed. At this rate, the funds he had remaining would not last long.

On March 1, all was prepared for their departure. The delegates settled their accounts at Mrs. Ross's boarding house. *Baltimore is inviting. However, I will not miss the muddy streets.*

Under blustery skies, John Adams, William Whipple, and James set out on March 2 for Philadelphia, John Turner trailing behind.

Chapter 2

Coming to Philadelphia

March 5, 1777, Wednesday

A painted sign at the inn proclaimed "The Boar's Head." Yellow light streamed from the windows, drawing the travelers like flies to honey. "I wanted to reach the next town, but this is as good a stopping place as any," John said, halting before the inn. James breathed a sigh of relief and swung his tired legs down beside his horse.

It had been three days since they left Baltimore. Early that morning they reached the ferry on the Shenandoah River near the border of Maryland and Pennsylvania. The frozen river stood choppy with hillocks of ice. Fifteen miles later, after a detour, they arrived at the ferry at Bald Fryar's and loaded their horses onto the ice-crusted craft. The rough crossing was precarious, with cold spray from wind-whipped waves wetting the iced deck. Colonel William Whipple handled his horse with the skill of one accustomed to riding, but James struggled to retain control over his mount. He was relieved when the crossing was over and they were once again on the road.

John dismounted and approached the steps of the inn. A weathered affair, peeled logs formed its first story, and half-timbers framed the second. He knocked at the stout door.

The innkeeper, a serious fellow with gray hair and a soiled apron, opened the door. "Wouldst thee have a room? And some roast venison?"

"That would be exactly what we want," John said. He dismounted and handed the reins of his horse to a cheerful young servant, then stretched his aching limbs.

"Quaker," John said, as they settled in front of the fire. "They make fine innkeepers and lay a good spread, but those I knew in Philadelphia—mostly dull as beetles."

"And they don't take with fighting," James said.

"Nor slavery."

"That is fine by me."

The venison roast with plum sauce lived up to the innkeeper's pride and before long the travelers were settled by the fire with cups of warm cider. The smell of pine smoke, roast meat, and pitch caulking filled the air.

"You notice we are served cider. Quakers don't drink, as a rule, yet I observed the broadbrims in Philadelphia drinking a toast," John said.

"I understand many Quakers are displeased with this conflict with Britain," James said.

"Indeed, they are. They generally side with Loyalists. Their allegiance is logical, as King George gave William Penn the land grants, and Penn offered them peaceful homes here. But they are shrewd businessmen, and they will support the side that lets them keep their homes and businesses, you may be sure of that."

"Very true," William said.

The servant brought them candles for their rooms. *He is about the same age as my own sons Jemmy and Johnny, fourteen and fifteen*, James thought.

With an effort he returned to their conversation. "The grand houses and estates in Baltimore—we saw quite a number of slaves there."

"Landed people in Maryland tend to live more as the planters do, owners living comfortably on the labor of slaves. Yes, there are more slaves in Maryland than we are used to seeing in New England. More than in Pennsylvania, as well," John said.

"Slavery is a curse which should be abandoned," James said, shortly. All occupations would be best pursued by freedmen. "I heard Benjamin Franklin thought that the Declaration was an opportunity to remove slavery from our country."

"Thomas Jefferson, as well, would have it so. Even though, paradoxically, he himself holds slaves. Yet the south would not agree to sign the Declaration with such wording in it, so it was stricken. We have other fish to fry. In time we will need to revisit and settle the question." William shrugged.

The comfortable fire blazed and the delegates relaxed. James felt the chill of the last days gradually ebbing and stretched out his feet toward the warmth.

"We may hear good news from our commissioners, Dr. Franklin, Arthur Lee, and Silas Deane, when we reach Philadelphia, though we must be careful not to make public news of any French aid that might be coming. The French want the British to remain ignorant of their informal connection with us," John said.

He stood and stretched. "Early to bed and early to rise. We ourselves should turn in; tomorrow will bring us to Philadelphia."

"Makes a man healthy, wealthy, and wise. How true," James agreed, remembering one of Dr. Franklin's aphorisms.

"Great talkers, little doers," William responded with a chuckle. "Let us find our room now."

That night, James awoke with a start. Something howled outside his window. *A dog? A wolf?* For a moment he was back in the jail in Halifax, prisoners around him in the large room groaning in pain or discomfort, the boards of the floor iron hard under his back. He could almost smell the vomit and refuse. He sat up in his bed, wiped beads of sweat from his brow, listened to the night. Whatever had made the noise had stopped. The wind rattled a shutter near the window, but that was all he heard. He breathed slowly until he was able to sleep.

March 6, 1777, Thursday

"Where will ye be going?" the innkeeper asked, as the group settled their accounts.

"Mrs. Sarah Yard's, just across from City Tavern on Second Street," John Adams answered. "We boarded there in the first session of Congress."

"The house has a good reputation," the innkeeper said. "Miss Lucy Leonard runs the boarding house for Mrs. Sarah Yard. It's just three or four blocks from the Pennsylvania State House. You'll find Philadelphia about twenty-five miles down the road."

James tucked his coat about him as he settled in his saddle. Frost shimmered in the morning sunlight, and the crust on the snow shone like a mirror. *If John Adams is tired, he surely doesn't show it. And Colonel William Whipple sits straight as a soldier on his mount, showing neither weariness nor discomfort,* he thought with some envy.

All about the riders stretched barren fields. In the distance a chimney threw a column of gray smoke up into the pale sky. As the hours passed, he looked about him, hoping to see signs of the city, but his gaze only met houses, farms, and stands of trees.

By noon they reached the Schuylkill River as it snaked around western Philadelphia.

"We will take the ferry," John said. "From there we can travel into Philadelphia. It lies between the Schuylkill and the Delaware."

At the ferry, the travelers waited while the ferrymen took on a cart of root vegetables bundled in burlap sacks. They loaded their horses and stood with them, admiring the ferrymen's skill as they guided the craft across the channel.

"We keep it clear of ice here, sir," one said to James, seeing his tense grip on his horse's reins. "No need to be concerned."

The city was still not evident as they made their way through the outskirts. Farms lay quiet in the afternoon sun.

Finally, they could see the spire of the Pennsylvania State House and those of churches. Shops lined the streets, their windows shuttered at the close of day.

"There's Christ Church," John said, pointing out the majestic white building at the corner of High and Second, its steeple reaching into the sky.

"The streets in Philadelphia are laid out starting at the Delaware River," John explained. "Water Street and Front Street along the river, followed by Second, Third, Fourth, and so on. The cross streets are named after trees: Pear, Apple, Walnut, Chestnut, and so on."

"I would call it a planned city, unlike the meandering roads that form our streets in Boston," James said.

"A good description," John agreed. "It is, in fact, the biggest city in the states."

A tall gentleman with a stylish black cloak and a tuft of pale hair paused at the corner to let the riders past. Catching his eye, John called out, "Is that you, Elbridge?"

A gleam of recognition passed over the man's alert, wry features. "Aye—hello! It is good to see you." Elbridge Gerry tipped his hat with a smile. His thin features and bright, perceptive eyes stood out amongst the passersby.

"We are bound for Second Street and Mrs. Yard's boarding house. Where will you be staying?"

"At present I have a room at City T-t-tavern. I will meet you at Mrs. Yard's tomorrow to make arrangements."

"Very good. 'Til tomorrow." John clucked to his horse and led the way down the street.

The travelers turned down Second Street and soon found Mrs. Yard's boarding house. They were greeted by a stout woman in an apron, dark dress, and layered pearl necklaces. A stable hand led their horses away.

"I am Miss Lucy Leonard, Mrs. Yard's business associate. Welcome to our home. Your room will be upstairs on the left." She motioned to a winding staircase. "I have had few guests here since Congress left. It is good to have you back! We will serve roast chicken and potatoes for our meal and discuss accounts later." Miss Leonard beamed at the delegates, her necklaces clinking. "Please do sit down. I must attend to the meal."

Wearily, the travelers sank into chairs by a brisk fire.

"It is my experience in Philadelphia that I spend twenty dollars a cord for wood and three pounds a week for board, including breakfast, dinner, and bed," John said, tugging off his overcoat. "Boarding a horse is expensive, also. I find it necessary to stretch the funds Congress provides us, as I am sure you will discover."

"Mr. George Duncan of Boston may offer us a more reasonable rate," William said.

"His wife is a friend of our family. By all means, we should inquire if he can house us," James said.

"He is a fellow New Englander," John agreed.

After enjoying an ample dinner, in his room James found letters, one from his wife. Mary told of baby George's teething, little Mary's efforts to knead bread, six-year-old Thomas's struggles with his alphabet. He responded, remembering her need for his support as she cared for the children.

And, he reflected, *a small benefit to being in Congress is that postage is free to delegates, so I might write as often as I like.*

"Independence Hall."
Courtesy of Independence National Historical Park,
U.S. Department of the Interior, National Park Service

Chapter 3

The Pennsylvania State House

March 7, 1777, Friday

Congress would not be in session for a few days, as there were not enough delegates present, so the following day James, William Whipple, Elbridge Gerry, and John Adams walked about the city. It was hard for James on such a pleasant day, snow melting, to realize that only a couple hundred miles distant a hostile force awaited the arrival of warm weather, possibly planning movement towards the home of the representatives guiding the country.

City Tavern across the street from Mrs. Yard's boarding house, three stories tall, looked the prosperous, genteel establishment John Adams had assured them it was. "According to Benjamin Franklin, it excels even eating houses in New York and Boston," John had said.

Just down the street, Christ Church's imposing steeple with its belfry and gilt cross dominated their view.

"When I was here in the First Continental Congress in the fall of 1774," John said, "I climbed to the top of the spire of Christ Church with Joseph Reed, at that time Washington's adjutant general. From there, one could see all of Philadelphia, down to the waterfront. It is quite a sight. Perhaps you will have the chance to take in that view."

A few blocks away on Chestnut Street between Fifth and Sixth the delegates reached the Pennsylvania State House, a tall, imposing red brick building, its evenly placed wings joined with colonnaded walkways on either side of the central two-story structure, wooden sheds attached to each wing for storage. A tall brick fence enclosed an open square behind the State House. Just last summer a committee of the Continental Congress had written and approved a Declaration of Independence in the stately building.

Elbridge Gerry, William Whipple, and John Adams had all been present when the Declaration of Independence had been written. Each had signed the document. James remembered reading the beginning of the Declaration ripped from a posting by a new inmate, when he was imprisoned in Halifax; shivers went down his spine at the memory, so thrilling the event had been.

"I imagine there was a celebration when the Declaration was first read," he said, staring in admiration at the handsome brick building.

"The city rejoiced with a military parade, the p-p-pealing of bells, and gunfire. Sheriff John Nixon read the Declaration aloud from a platform in the square behind the State House; after his reading, some in the crowd pulled down the king's arms from the State House c-c-courtroom and threw them on a bonfire," Elbridge said. He smiled at the memory.

John pointed to a smaller, classically formal structure a block and half east of the State House, in between Fourth and Third Streets. "That was our meeting place for the First Continental Congress. The home of the Carpenters' Trade Guild had a space large enough for our use. Massachusetts first recommended that Philadelphia host a Congress representing all thirteen colonies, after the nonimportation agreements, the closing of Boston harbor by the British, and the development of Committees of Correspondence by all colonies.

"The Library, with its excellent collection, is housed at Carpenters' Hall," John added. "And its long walkway makes a convenient place to meet and talk."

At the outskirts of Philadelphia, they reached the hospital, at Eighth and Pine. "Benjamin Franklin persuaded the Pennsylvania Assembly to donate funds to match those given by citizens to provide care for those sick or suffering with mental illness who could not afford to have nursing at home. Dr. Shippen is the director of the hospital. He is most learned, educated in London and Edinburgh."

A uniformed nurse greeted them and lead them on a tour of the facility. In a wing adjoining the main hallway, James winced at the sight of the lame and ill in rows of beds, some listlessly reclining in silence, others moaning in pain. Beneath them, cells housed the lunatics, whose cries and shouts echoed through the floor.

Near the Philadelphia Hospital stood the Bettering House, offering assistance, clothing, food, and medical treatment to the needy. The pleasant gardens surrounding the Bettering House were a stark contrast to the wretched individuals in the establishment, some of whom appeared to James as though they had given up hope. Many languished in crowded rooms.

Leaving the hospital and Bettering House behind, the delegates turned towards the city. "It is clear that citizens in Philadelphia have done much to improve the lives of the sick and poor," James observed.

He remembered that Mary had sought smallpox inoculations for herself and the family while he was in prison. She cooked daily for Dr. Joseph Gardner, Boston physician, during his imprisonment, and continued to do so. Dr. Gardner inoculated many in Boston against the dread disease.

"The city has also benefitted from the energy and inspiration of B-b-benjamin Franklin," Elbridge added.

James nodded. *Elbridge's stutter does not detract from his words, nor his ability to express himself.*

Returning to their lodgings, they paused at the deep, open harbor on the Delaware River to admire vessels loading and unloading goods. Here, trading ships arrived from the West Indies, bearing cargoes of sugar, rum from New England, and wine and textiles from Europe, as well as immigrants from Germany, Ireland, and other countries. William Penn's colony had offered a haven to individuals of different faiths and creeds.

The aroma of roast duck awakened their appetites as they entered Mrs. Yard's house. Miss Leonard glared at their muddy feet pointedly; James stopped to wipe his shoes on the mat.

That night he retired to his room, eager to relax. His feet ached from the miles on foot. *I would certainly appreciate new boots. Such luxuries will have to wait.*

On the Monday before Congress opened in session, James arranged to move to Captain George Duncan's boarding house on the south side of Walnut St., between Second and Third, where he joined William Whipple. Lucy Leonard's expression was dour indeed when James told her he was moving. James greeted the captain's wife as if she were an old acquaintance. She was in fact related to friends of his in Boston. When he was served fish chowder on the first evening, one of his favorite foods, he knew he had made the right decision. And these lodgings were cheaper than Miss Leonard's.

March 12, 1777, Wednesday

James brushed his best black jacket and straightened his collar. At length there were ample delegates assembled to allow Congress to meet. He and Colonel William Whipple walked to the Pennsylvania State House. The doorkeeper, a stout, friendly person, opened the heavy door.

Their footsteps clattered on the brick floor of the wide hall. On its far end an elegant stairway wound upwards to a second floor. "That is where the Pennsylvania Supreme Executive Council meets," William Whipple said, motioning up the stairs.

To the east of the hall, double doors opened to the Assembly Room, where the delegates met. On the west side, archways lead to the formal Pennsylvania Court Chamber used by the Pennsylvania Supreme Court. Entering the spacious Assembly Room, about forty feet square, James glanced at the tall windows on each side, curtained in green. Twin fireplaces flickered on either side of the president's table, at the front of the room on a slightly elevated dais. Corniced paneling framed the pale gray walls. Green baize cloth covered tables placed in a semi-circular arrangement faced the president, each appointed with paper and writing tools and set with sufficient Windsor chairs for a state's delegation.

At the rear of the Assembly Room a railing separated the back of the room from the front. This was the bar. The fixture set off a space for onlookers not part of the proceedings to observe, on the rare occasions when they were permitted. James walked past the bar and greeted Francis Dana, seated to the left, and shook hands with John Adams and Elbridge Gerry, nearby. The chair to the left of Elbridge stood empty; James found a chair there and settled to await the proceedings. Before long, perhaps twenty-five members of Congress had arrived and the room was abuzz with chatter. *Surely, more representatives will come to Philadelphia before long.*

"Later we can meet, perhaps at City T-t-tavern," Elbridge said.

Samuel Adams, at the front of the room, motioned to James to join him beside the tall, heavy-set Robert Morris, Executive Committee member.

"I am sure you are aware that James Lovell has joined us. His skills as organizer and writer, and notably his fluency in French, will be of service to us." Samuel Adams regarded James with assurance.

Robert Morris, Philadelphia businessman, owner of a fleet of ships, and member of the Committee for Secret Correspondence, nodded and extended his hand in a brusque gesture. "It will be a pleasure to have your services. You will find yourself at work straightaway." His serious face betrayed no hint of a smile.

"Of course. I want nothing else."

He bowed briefly to slender, energetic Secretary Charles Thomson. "Welcome to the State House," the secretary said, glancing up from his papers.

John Hancock called for order, startling them, and they took their seats. President Hancock introduced those who were new to Congress, including several attendees from Pennsylvania. He read letters from Generals Washington, Gates, and others from the last several weeks. Most pointed out various needs: ammunition, money for pay, supplies, personnel changes. He handed a request for cannon to the Board of War.

Samuel Adams stood. "The Massachusetts delegation proposes that Congress amend its requirement for a state to have but two delegates to be able to vote. This motion responds to the difficulty states have in sending three delegates for representation." To no one's surprise, the vote carried.

In the afternoon, Congress discussed and approved a loan to Rhode Island in the amount of $400,000, then agreed on a resolve recommending that state legislatures supply blankets for their quotas of soldiers, to be reimbursed with money from the United States for the blankets.

"And where will we g-g-get that, I wonder," Elbridge said grimly.

Postponing some matters and referring others to committees, the business of the day gradually wound down. As the light was fading, Congress adjourned.

That evening, James joined others at the City Tavern. Built just a few years before, the establishment on Second Street boasted rooms for eating and drinking on the first two floors, and rooms for accommodations on the third floor. A servant led them through the first floor, past the bar, offering the privacy of long woolen curtains, and upstairs to a long dining room, where they took seats under a brightly lit chandelier. James's eyes opened wide when he heard the menu for the evening: venison, roast pheasant, and duck, as well as creamed vegetables, sweet breads, and corn pudding. He chose a plate of venison in raisin sauce, and then at the last moment decided on a glass of port.

The evening concluded with toasts to the success of the army and to Congress's efforts to meet the needs of the generals. Reaching his lodgings late at night, the stars blanketed by clouds, James rubbed his head. Surely the headache he felt coming on was not due to the rich food. More likely it was the hours spent reading letters and reports. In his room, he wrote a letter to Mary, thinking of her managing the household on her own, describing for her the Pennsylvania State House.

March 13, 1777, Thursday

The following day, President John Hancock read a letter from British Admiral Richard Howe regarding exchange of prisoners taken by Captain John Paul Jones.

"Captain Jones has done well, I hear," James said under his breath to Elbridge Gerry.

"Extremely well. He was c-c-commissioned captain in our navy in 1775, as we were first organizing our small fleet of ships. Last year, Captain Jones c-c-captured some sixteen British ships in one passage."

Samuel Adams stood. "On another matter, our generals seem to find the number of foreign officers volunteering to be a problem. Officers from a number of countries, mainly France, have come to us offering their services. However, most can speak scarcely a word of English. Further, the positions they seek may already be filled by capable American officers."

"We must hold in high regard the ability and commitment of our American officers. I submit that the worst of the American officers will be better at working with our troops and understanding strategy appropriate to the terrain than the best of the foreign officers."

"Hear, hear," several said loudly. Applause broke out.

"Some French officers have excellent training and may even speak some English. But Silas Deane has promised an officer's commission to many. And what do we do when these officers prove unfit for service?"

"In defense of our purchasing agent, Silas Deane, may I say he has little else to offer in exchange for guns, ammunition, and supplies," John said, standing. "His duty is to arrange for loans or gifts of needed armaments."

"Yet we cannot permit this many foreign officers in our army," someone said.

"We only need those with engineering or artillery expertise," added another.

Samuel Adams shrugged his shoulders and sat down.

"To respond to these issues, I move we resolve that employment in the Continental Army be discouraged for gentlemen from Europe who do not understand our language." President John Hancock looked about the room. "Only those with mastery of our language and the best recommendations should be accepted. The Committee of Secret Correspondence will write our agents abroad to explain these conditions."

"Hear, hear! Yes."

"So resolved. You may take your seats."

"I move we have a committee confer with General Gates, the commandant of Philadelphia, upon the general state of affairs, now that we are back in the city," a voice said from the rear of the room.

"Agreed. Perhaps they might ascertain whether General Gates would consider returning to the post of adjutant general. Washington is in need of one. I suggest members of the committee be Daniel Roberdeau, Lewis Morris, Roger Sherman, William Whipple, and James Lovell."

James and the others chosen nodded their assent.

The day continued with a multitude of issues, some tedious, others critical, but each vital for the country.

That evening he met William Whipple in the front parlor at Captain Duncan's. The sea-faring merchant wore his formal military uniform of dark blue trimmed with gold.

"We are dining in luxury," James said, adjusting his silk scarf about his neck. His months in the British jails, existing on a diet of moldy bread and scraps, came back to him and he shivered. "Two successive nights at the City Tavern should be enough to please anyone." He glanced in the mirror, noted his dark hair secure in its black ribbon. *Excellent food and fine company appear to come with a commitment to Congress,* he thought. "Ready?"

"As ever," Colonel Whipple said, his smile jovial.

"You will like General Gates, I think," William ventured, as they turned down the block towards City Tavern, avoiding the sprays of water from a passing carriage. "He once served as an officer in the British army during the French and Indian War but retired from British service and bought a plantation in Virginia. When the war broke out, he offered Washington his services. With his extensive experience and military background, he was made adjutant general. In that position, responsible for procedures and records, Horatio Gates proved remarkable. At the siege of Boston, he organized the thirteen thousand militia who gathered to defend the city. And he related well to the rough, independent New England farmers and workers.

"But General Gates wanted a field command. So last June, Congress appointed him major general, replacing John Sullivan, commander of the retreat from Canada. This was after the failed attempt to take Quebec under Benedict Arnold and Richard Montgomery. Horatio Gates ended up in charge of the American retreat from Quebec."

"I knew the attack on Quebec did not go well," James said. He listened with interest. His knowledge of the event was scanty.

"The Americans struggled back to Fort Ticonderoga on Lake Champlain burdened with smallpox and poor morale. Gates's main objective there was to strengthen the American defenses, as the British had a sizeable fleet there. But the general came into conflict with Major General Philip Schuyler, commander of the army's northern department. I think the quarrel was personal, no doubt related to goals of supremacy. Schuyler is from New York, definitely of upper crust. Horatio Gates, despite his background, appreciates the common soldier. And he does not want to be second in command to Schuyler."

James nodded. "Generals can have powerful personalities."

They reached the front of the City Tavern and paused by the porch. William's words tumbled out.

"The conflict between the two was resolved by Congress limiting Gates's authority to Fort Ticonderoga and Lake Champlain, while General Schuyler retained command of the northern department. Last summer, Gates oversaw the building of an American convoy on Lake Champlain by Benedict Arnold. In an engagement last October, the American fleet was defeated, but fortunately the British drew back to await the close of winter.

"Then, Gates joined Washington in his winter camp at Morristown, New Jersey." William glanced about, but they were alone, so he continued in a low voice, his words hurried. "He questioned Washington's decision to attack at Trenton, admittedly a quick one. Rather than join Washington in the brief fight at Trenton, as General Washington had expected, he claimed illness, then left the army to visit Congress at Baltimore. Many think his choice to be cowardly. His explanation was that he would not hazard a foolhardy strike such as the one Washington led at Trenton. Then he pressed some in Congress to be made commander-in-chief, boasting of his military training and experience. There was, I believe, some support for him, but certainly insufficient for him to gain the appointment."

"A risky business, defying the commander-in-chief." James thought of the stalwart Virginian.

"Agreed. Congress then named him commandant of Philadelphia for this winter, a position of some authority given the British garrisoned not far away, in New York and New Jersey."

"I appreciate your explanation."

William gestured towards the door. "Shall we?"

"By all means." They entered the warm establishment. At the second-floor dining area, General Gates, in full uniform, stood at his table and greeted them with a cordial handshake, his hazel eyes and jutting jaw expressing frank openness.

Throughout the evening the delegates and the general discussed matters of training and funding the military. The general had much to share. James was wary of General Gates potentially advancing his claim as a superior to Washington, but he made no such implication. In fact, James found himself impressed with General Gates's considerate manner, his shrewd knowledge of events, and his unaffected manner of speaking.

General Gates explained his position that the northern theater for the Continental Army was of supreme importance. He would become general in charge of the Albany post; he laid out a plan of supporting officers for his staff. James noticed that Gates did not mention that at present General Schuyler of New York was appointed commander at Albany. *He must trust that Congress will approve his plan and put him in command over Schuyler.*

At an opening in the conversation, James asked the general, "Would you accept a request to assume the position of adjutant general?"

Gates turned an agreeable face to James. "I feel my service to my country best in the realm of military leadership. I have considerable experience and training."

Despite his cordial words, a hard flicker in the general's eyes gave James the sense he was determined to remain a commander. *He may not be amenable to suggestion, but he is impressive.*

Stepping out into the night air from the vibrant atmosphere of the City Tavern, the general shook James's hand. "We need more delegates such as you, familiar with the issues that drive our common goal." His hand gripped James's own with assurance. James felt flattered, yet at the same time sensed personal commitment.

Gates has an ability to connect, listen, and understand. And he prefers active roles in the army to administrative duties such as adjutant general. But it is clear that Congress has given supreme command to George Washington; Horatio Gates will have to flourish in his role as second.

March 14, 1777, Friday

As Congress gathered in the morning, clouds outside threatening rain, James found a group in conversation in the hall outside the Assembly Room.

"We have an unfortunate situation: Major General Charles Lee's arrest and imprisonment by the British in December," Samuel Adams said, his voice tense.

"What happened, if you don't mind explaining?" James asked. He had heard of the temperamental, uncooperative General Charles Lee.

"Major General Charles Lee is second only in command to General Washington. A former British officer, he is knowledgeable and well-educated. Washington has held him in high regard, renaming the fort on the New Jersey side of the Hudson Fort Lee in his honor, for Lee's role in the battle for New York," Samuel said.

General Wolcott interjected, "But General Lee has always been a hot-head. He served in the French and Indian war, where he pursued a military command in the Mohawk Valley. He married a Mohawk woman. For his extreme temperament the Indians called him 'Boiling Water,' a name that aptly describes his character. His preparation at military school in England makes him the best trained officer we have, with the possible exception of General Horatio Gates, yet his poor decisions have given General Washington and others great cause for complaint."

"And what about those dogs? You can't get near him without tumbling over a dozen filthy curs," said John Adams.

"True. His eccentricities are legendary. So is his pride. He chafed at being Washington's second-in-command ever since Washington was named commander-in-chief. His most recent decision has proven a recipe for disaster. When Washington was camped across the river from Trenton, he was expecting General Lee's arrival with four thousand troops. But on December 12, General Lee was arrested. General Cornwallis had sent out a British scouting party from Trenton to gather information about his whereabouts. They discovered him at a tavern owned by a woman named White. They arrested him and led him off in his nightshirt to prison."

"Poor timing to visit his lady love, I think," someone said. Laughter followed.

"The British celebrated his capture. Of course, General Washington was furious, and blamed Lee for his lack of caution," Samuel Adams said.

"Lee was placed under the custody of the provost. Congress resolved that General Washington send a flag to General Howe, offering Lee's exchange for six Hessian field officers. And, if that exchange were not accepted by the British, under the principles of retaliation, six officers would be detained in prison."

"However, General Washington protests that retaliation is not in our best interests," John Adams said with energy. "In his view, we need to continue as usual, exchanging one imprisoned officer for another. His displeasure with Congress's resolve is clear."

"So, we support retaliation, but General Washington does not," James said. *Why not? We are at war.* A clerk beckoned to the group, and the gathering broke up and entered the Assembly Room.

James settled himself and took his notes out of his satchel. *Apparently, though Congress valued General Washington, there were times when the group held different opinions than the commander-in-chief.*

President John Hancock opened the meeting with consideration of the dilemma posed by the British capture of General Charles Lee. He read aloud Washington's recent letters responding to Congress's resolve of January 6.

"In his letters to Congress, General Washington questions Congress's resolve that General Lee be exchanged for six Hessian field officers, or under the principles of retaliation six officers be detained in prison," John Hancock said. The president's expression was calm as he looked about the room. "Washington points out that the British have given General Lee a decent apartment, enabling him to live in comfort.

"As you know, it is the usual practice that prisoners when exchanged must be of equal rank and number. However, the enemy holds some three hundred of our officers while we hold but fifty of theirs. This imbalance threatens future exchanges.

"Washington's argument is that if we were willing to exchange six prisoners for just one, the principle of equality currently in practice would be threatened. And he points out that the present weak state of our army does not permit us to use the language of retaliation. In Washington's words concerning retaliation, 'prudence and policy require that it should be avoided.'"

James had been thinking hard about the problem. A vein in his forehead pulsed and throbbed; his hands balled into fists. He jumped to his feet. Before he knew what he was doing, the words were out of his mouth, sharp and bitter. "Why should we not employ the principles of retaliation? In fact, we are at war with an enemy, cruel and ruthless. Surely, we are compelled to keep agreements only if they suit our purposes." His words rang out in the abruptly silent chamber.

He sat down, aware all eyes were on him. A rush of rage swept over him; his thoughts blurred in a tumult. He came to himself and clutched his hands, white-knuckled. *What have I done? My anger at British arrogance in dictating terms of imprisonment has overcome my rational thinking, if only for a moment. I know what it is to be held for many months in a British prison, the object of curses and abuse, fed barely enough to keep a body alive, praying for an exchange. My anger at British injustice overcame me, if only for a moment.* He took a deep breath and looked about the room, guarding himself against a further outburst. *I must be more careful.*

To his relief, Reverend John Witherspoon, president of the College of New Jersey, stood. "I too believe that agreements made between states at war must be honored only as long as they serve to be beneficial."

"I do not think we should abandon agreements with the enemy, as these from time to time may be in our best interest," a delegate from North Carolina said thoughtfully. "However, in this instance the British are reluctant to exchange General Lee, contrary to the agreement, and therefore the general understanding regarding exchange of prisoners should be considered void."

The discussion continued throughout the day. James took heart that no one criticized his impulsive stand on behalf of firm statements by Congress. By the end of the day, all had participated in the deliberation.

"Gentlemen, we conclude that General Washington be informed that the resolve of Congress of January 6 stands. General Lee may be exchanged for six Hessian field officers, or a similar exchange, or we will keep six enemy officers in prison as long as General Lee is kept."

"Hear, hear," many agreed. James joined in. Perhaps Washington did have reason to question threatening the British. After all, if he engaged in retaliation, the British would likely treat captured Americans with even less humanity than they did at present. Starvation, exposure to the elements including bitter cold, and lack of medical treatment were all forms of cruelty the enemy practiced on prison ships and warehouses in New York. Yet Congress, in holding this resolve, expressed a firmness that James felt well conveyed their leadership.

"Thank you. We will inform General Washington that our resolution stands," John Hancock said.

The president shook his head at the doorkeeper, Andrew McNair, who stood with candles in his hand, ready to light the space. "Thank you, Andrew, but those will not be needed. We will take up business tomorrow."

James returned to Captain Duncan's, chagrined at his outburst. His sudden reaction must have been associated with his terrible experience in prison. For some time, violent dreams had wakened him from sleep, plunging him into a state of agony. Memories of cruel guards, the taste of moldy bread, the ache of sleeping on cold floors were as fresh in his mind when he struggled to awaken as if he had just again experienced them. He thought over his quick response to the suggestion that war was more a matter of following the rules in a prisoner exchange than a conflict to be won at any cost. Yes, perhaps. But he needed to be on his guard, lest his emotions carry him away at some future point.

The three Duncan children, playing outside the house, reminded him of his own, and he thought of little Thomas, Charles, and George with a rush of feeling. He brushed off his worries and determined to write to his family later.

That night he reviewed his notes. Congress had spent at least two days on the policy of exchange of prisoners, including the dilemma posed by the capture of Major General Charles Lee. And the issue was not yet settled. *Is it any wonder that people say Congress gets nothing done? That we are just a group of politicians who spend their days arguing while the country is in peril?*

Those of us in Congress, sometimes so few that we must postpone meeting altogether, do disagree. Yet we know how important is our business. We must fund an army, though we have no power to tax. We must reward our soldiers and officers to keep their services, though we have limited means to raise funds. We can request the states provide ample funds: some will raise money and some will not. We can print more money, but this causes inflation and the devaluing of our currency. We can call a lottery and some will invest, hoping to reap great reward. We can lean on our foreign friends, relying on our agents in France, with the goal of establishing at least one ally in this war. Those are our choices, and while our options are limited, we must make the best we can of them and work towards a successful end.

He rubbed his aching head, then blew out the candle and collapsed in bed, mercifully falling into a deep, undisturbed sleep.

March 19, 1777, Wednesday

"We have the minimum of nine states represented, gentlemen," President John Hancock announced. "Congress is in session."

"Better than the last two days," James remarked under his breath to Elbridge Gerry, who nodded.

The morning's business saw consideration of petitions and reports. President John Hancock read a letter from Dr. Benjamin Franklin written in December, a few days after his arrival in France at Nantes near the western coast. The venerable agent of Congress would travel to Paris. From his joyous reception, he predicted he would be well received at court. He also noted preparations for war being made all over Europe; he felt sure the confrontation between Britain and France would soon break out into armed conflict.

"As you know, many soldiers and officers arrive here from Europe, most from France, to volunteer for the American army," President Hancock said. "While the idea of helping a country to gain liberty appeals to many and offers them a chance to oppose England, the long-time foe of France and Spain, many also seek their own advancement through employment in the military. Contrary to what one might think, these volunteers often pose a problem for us, especially in view of the complaints we receive from the generals at Morristown. The foreign officers, some of whom have excellent experience and training, some but minimal, arrive bearing credentials and letters of recommendation to Congress. However, they lack understanding of the war and the Americans whom they wish to command. Language is often a barrier to communication. Reports from Morristown are that the French officers cause serious conflicts with the American officers, and though a few prove valuable, particularly those with knowledge of artillery or engineering, most pose more difficulty than they are worth.

"While it is true that some are serving us well, others clearly are not suitable to be part of the United States Army." The president set his papers down and folded his hands in resignation.

James and the other delegates listened silently. The problem of foreign officers volunteering was thorny.

"The Committee on Qualifications of Applications is in charge of assessing the officers who apply to us for positions. I suggest we change its name to the Committee on Foreign Applications and appoint three to this committee: James Lovell, Thomas Heyward, and Daniel Roberdeau."

James stood to acknowledge his appointment. He glanced over to see Thomas Heyward of South Carolina, slender, dark-haired, and Daniel Roberdeau of Pennsylvania, proportioned like a giant.

"And it is my understanding that Mr. Lovell is fluent in French. I suggest he chair this committee."

"*Oui, merci,*" James responded, with a slight bow.

"Your abilities will be an asset to this committee. You will interview prospective candidates who wish to serve in the army."

"I understand there are those who arrive with recommendations, even contracts, given them by Congress's agent Silas Deane," James said, a question in his voice.

"Those recommendations pose a unique difficulty." John Hancock nodded. "Silas Deane successfully obtains cargoes of supplies and arms from the French, unofficially, as they have not entered into a state of war as our ally. But what does he have to offer the French? No money, though we can from time to time arrange loans. When the French officers come to him, he feels he must respond positively to their requests. He does not wish to offend or antagonize them."

"Perfectly understandable," James agreed. "But then, it is all the more important that we interview these candidates, ascertain their value to the army, and if necessary, state in polite terms our refusal of their employment."

"Consider, if you will, this offer of service from Monsieur Faneuil." President Hancock took a folded paper from those set before him and handed it to a clerk, who brought it to James. "Mr. Lovell, you will interview this French officer, then write a report with your recommendation as to his service. Those of us who have little knowledge of French can only estimate his potential benefit to our army, though his demeanor is most earnest."

"I will be glad to do so," James responded, taking the paper.

"Thank you. Now to other business. Washington's letter states his concern that he has fewer than three thousand soldiers in Morristown fit for duty and their service is set to expire at the end of the month. He requires an additional $200,000 for his paymaster. Finally, he wants regimental surgeons to be offered sufficient reimbursement for their skills and work.

"And in Morristown, the Continental Army has endured one of the worst winters on record, snowfall at times reaching the height of a man's head. But even so, the commander is working on discipline and training his soldiers. We must support him and provide the funds he needs to attract new recruits."

"Gentlemen," Robert Morris broke in, "I would have you recall that when this conflict began, Congress had no clear idea of the needs of an army. The militia served as they pleased and left as they pleased; they might serve for a month or six weeks, then depart as they saw fit, and none could stop them. With improvement in the regulations and systems now adopted by Congress, we should see a stronger and more dependable army."

Murmurs of assent rippled through the delegates.

"I would add," Robert Morris continued, "that the general has achieved success this winter despite the problems of maintaining an army. Wintering at Morristown, he has confined Howe's army to Brunswick, killed and taken between three and four thousand of their men, and apprehended four or five hundred horses and wagons, as well as stores and clothing. As a result, the enemy has suffered a lack of provisions and discontent among their troops, if not desertion.

"Were we to require enlistment of a year, or preferably until the end of the war, we would strengthen the Continental Army and provide the trained fighting force Washington needs," Robert Morris continued, his voice charged with determination. "It takes time and rigorous training to transition a green farmer who has never fired a shot in anger into an efficient fighting soldier. We must change the period of enlistment of our recruits."

The heavy merchant from Philadelphia sat down, his face flushed.

"Thank you for your recommendation regarding enlistment. We will take that up at a further time," John Hancock said. "And thank you, Mr. Morris, for reminding us of the successes as well as the needs of Washington's force. In addition, gentlemen, we need to think of all possible ways we can gain funds to assist our commander-in-chief."

We are what Thomas Paine writes about, James thought as Congress adjourned, *in crisis. And we must support in ways large and small our commander-in-chief and our soldiers, despite the difficulties.*

March 21, 1777, Friday

James handed his report from his interview with Monsieur Faneuil to Secretary Charles Thomson. The elegantly dressed French officer, his uniform and plumed helmet imposing, had fidgeted nervously as they visited in the evening at Clark's Inn across from the State House. *He is most eager to please, but his English is barely sufficient for him to order his food. How could such an officer, trained in a military academy in France, understand the rough, practical Americans whom he would have to command?* Most Americans in the army were farmers or tradesmen, with little military training and less respect for foreign ways. In truth, there could be no success for such an officer in the struggling American army.

Monsieur Faneuil had expected James to pay for his meal, then explained with some embarrassment that he had spent all his savings to buy passage to America. He admitted, his eyes downcast, that he had no funds remaining to return to France. James remembered seeing a letter from the agent Silas Deane among his recommendations. *Surely the Frenchman had been misled by our agent.*

He prepared his report carefully, working long into the evening. His eyes burned; his head ached. He blotted the ink on his signature late at night.

In the morning, James took his seat, grateful for the warmth of the twin fireplaces at the front of the Assembly Room.

"Congress will come to order," President John Hancock said. "We will begin by considering the French officers who hope to be granted a position in the American army. Thank you, James Lovell, for your report on your interview with Monsieur Faneuil. You indicate that our military would not benefit from his acceptance."

James nodded. "I will be interviewing other French officers," he said, with as much cheerfulness as he could muster, remembering the list he had received.

President Hancock's face twisted in thought. "Gentlemen, the last thing we want to do is offend these officers who have come with real intent to serve. Their country's friendship is vital to us. We know shipments of arms and clothing are on their way to us. If we are to have an ally in this war, it will more than likely be France. We must cultivate this friendship and do nothing to dissuade it. While we cannot provide employment to all, we should give officers such as Monsieur Faneuil a statement that the officer was given an expectation of employment by our agent and that no dishonor was intended in refusing their service. Would you agree?"

"Aye," was the answer.

This will help, James thought. "Monsieur Faneuil said that he paid for his own passage to the United States. With embarrassment, he told me he has no more funds with which to return home. I recommend Congress grant him three hundred dollars to travel back to his home."

"Agreed," John Adams said. "Silas Deane is able to procure goods for us, though all he has to offer in exchange is potential employment in the military. But we should caution him to be less enthusiastic in accepting these officers."

"We should see fewer French officers coming with expectations of employment," John Hancock said, nodding. "Gentlemen, are we agreed?"

"Aye," was the response.

James met up with John Adams as they left the State House. Head down against the wind, they trudged to their lodgings at Captain Duncan's. James glanced at his friend. "What likelihood is there that the British may advance on Philadelphia?"

"The enemy would have to first evacuate New Jersey in order to advance to Philadelphia, as they cannot both hold Philadelphia and maintain the troops in New Jersey." John Adams quickened his steps to keep pace with James's longer legs. "But Loyalists in New Jersey would be frantic if the British withdrew, fearing the revenge of the Patriots, who are their neighbors. And if the British took Philadelphia, they would require a strong naval presence to hold it. Yet they could not spare many ships from their position in New York.

"I believe they will not attempt to take Philadelphia without reinforcements. This is contrary to the fears of our military leaders, who think the enemy may advance on Philadelphia for its wealth and central position. But I think even if they did take it, they would find it a conquest they would be forced to relinquish, as they cannot keep two divided occupations at once."

James took a deep breath. He hoped his friend was right. The thought of the British attempting to take Philadelphia was an ogre lurking in the dark. "It is true their navy is far superior to ours, but they deploy it to keep New York." The threat to Congress of their very lives did not always seem to him as a real possibility. But in reality, they would all be in danger of arrest, even execution, should they be captured. "John Paul Jones may be equal to several British captains, yet the American navy is a David in comparison to the British Goliath. But I agree, to divide their fleet between Philadelphia and New York would not, I think, be in their best interests. They may be reluctant to make the attempt."

James and the committee arrived at City Tavern to confer with Major General Nathanael Greene, who had brought a letter from General Washington authorizing him to explain matters essential to the well-being of the army.

Seated at a dining table in his lodgings on the third floor, General Nathanael Greene impressed James with his air of energy and confidence.

"Thank you for meeting with me," the general said, formal in his blue and buff Continental uniform. "General Washington and I need to inform you of several matters that will benefit our army. These relate to the exchange of prisoners, the pay of aides-de-camp, and the pay and supply of the army." A servant quietly entered the room, served steaming food from a nearby tray, and left without speaking a word. General Greene took a bite of the roast pork.

In the silence that followed, James spoke up. "May I inquire as to whether the officers often use a cipher to permit sensitive messages to be sent securely?"

"Yes, we are familiar with various cipher systems." General Greene's face kindled with interest. He set down his knife and fork. "General Washington has used one or more from time to time. It is important that the person for whom the message is intended should have the correct cipher alphabet and know how to use it.

"We have apprehended more than one traitor by a knowledge of cipher. We arrested Dr. Church, for example, who was one of the most trusted of the Sons of Liberty. His pregnant mistress was captured with a ciphered letter to the British. Unfortunately, Dr. Church destroyed his other papers before we could uncover the extent of his traitorous activities."

"I have knowledge of a polyalphabetic cipher system that does not depend on a specific cipher alphabet."

"Do you indeed." General Greene looked thoughtfully at James. "Your method may be helpful to Congress."

"The system uses a keyword. It is flexible, tailored to each use."

"The use of cipher alone can indicate the writer seeks to convey intelligence. It is not to be used lightly. We also use invisible ink," General Greene continued, picking up his fork again. "However, one must have a supply of a certain type of white ink and a reagent that will cause the invisible letters, often written between the lines of a regular message, to become visible.

"But to the business at hand." Greene began the discussion of the needs of the army. At nearly midnight, the meeting broke up.

March 24, 1777, Monday

"Do the members of the committee charged with visiting with General Greene have a report?" President John Hancock asked. It was nearly noon. The stack of letters and requests that Congress had considered made a considerable pile on Secretary Thomson's desk.

"Yes, we have one," William Whipple said, standing. "First, General Greene explained that one of General Washington's concerns was the exchange of General Charles Lee. The committee suggests that General Washington exchange the prisoner in the manner that seems to him most advantageous. In future, Congress should permit all commanders to use their own best judgment in such matters." He listed the other matters brought forth by General Greene.

Those present voiced their agreement.

General Greene sat in Congress throughout much of the day, listening with stern attention. As the delegates adjourned, he passed by James's seat, his slight limp from a stiff knee noticeable.

"Thank you for your report," General Greene said.

"No need to thank me. Our united efforts are essential in this cause."

Greene agreed and scratched his head. "Permit me, but are deliberations in Congress always this long? It seems to me efficiency would dictate a shorter, less circuitous route for decision making."

James smiled. "Yes, always this long. In fact, to include all in the conversation, often much longer."

Nathanael Greene shrugged and made his way out, clearly tired and annoyed.

James and John Adams returned to Captain Duncan's in the early dark, the first stars bright in the clear sky.

"I am surprised that Congress granted Monsieur Faneuil three hundred dollars to return home," James said.

John Adams smiled. "We can show sympathy, on occasion."

That evening, climbing the stairs to his room, James stifled a yawn and paused to stretch his aching back. His work for Congress might not be the same as that of an officer in the army, but his service was no easy matter.

In his room, he lit candles, then wrote letters and jotted notes, thinking over the day's work. At length, the wind came up, rattling the window. He blew out his candles and fell into bed, weary and tired.

Hours later he woke. His heart raced; sweat poured from his body despite the chill air. He threw off the suffocating covers, sat up, and gulped the night air. The dark shadows enthralling him gradually faded to the familiar contours of his room. He forced himself to take deep, even breaths, until his heart calmed and his breathing slowed. What had caused the terror to return, unbidden? The thought of the Hollis Street Jail in Halifax, near starvation, illness threatening, rose up, and he shivered. His experiences in that filthy place would not shrug off so easily. But he must continue with his work. He had no time to reflect—certainly not to indulge in self-pity. He thought about Mary, the children, their progress in reading or helping their mother. He pictured them in his mind, growing and learning. He hoped they had enough to eat. With these more peaceful thoughts pushing back the dark, he lay back down and, before long, fell asleep.

A few days later, James confided in William Whipple his opinion that in the coming weeks his work for the Committee for Foreign Applications, especially interviewing the French, would lessen.

William looked at him in disbelief, then chuckled.

"Don't you know that once you are part of a vital service for Congress, you will be involved in it as long as that service is needed? At the rate we have seen French officers coming to volunteer, they will not stop soon."

James frowned. "Interviewing them and writing reports take up most of my evenings. I hope for fewer officers arriving."

In fact, foreign officers continued to arrive. For days, James's time outside Congress was spent visiting with those seeking placement in the United States Army. It would take weeks, possibly months, for Congress's resolve requiring agents to send only those officers with the best skills, including command of English, to reach Europe. Meanwhile, Benjamin Franklin, Silas Deane, and Arthur Lee continued to recommend applicants to serve in the American army. Many candidates he felt compelled to turn away. They were simply ill prepared to work with the American army.

In this work, Captain Duncan's lodging proved a great help. For a small additional sum, the officer he needed to interview could eat with him at his residence. Most seemed grateful for the invitation and the meal. He turned over these charges to Massachusetts and received compensation. Yet the constant writing and late nights were arduous.

Mary's letters arrived regularly. Cheerful, they said little of her own feelings, focusing on the children and home. James rubbed his eyes after yet another short night. *My part in this war is to attend Congress, pursue my duties, and send money to my family.*

March 31, 1777, Monday

"We have good news today, gentlemen." John Hancock turned to the secretary. "Kindly hand me the letter from Dr. Franklin, Silas Deane, and Arthur Lee."

He unfolded the ivory pages. "Sent from Paris on January 17 of this year, the American Commissioners write that on the 28th of December, just days after arriving in Paris, they attended an audience with his Excellency the Count De Vergennes, Minister for Foreign Affairs for King Louis XVI.

"They gave De Vergennes their commission for the proposed treaty of commerce, a statement of our present situation, and a request for ships of war. They are in the process of expediting several vessels bearing artillery, arms, ammunition, and clothing to aid our forces. The people of France are enthusiastic for us, while all of Europe, except Portugal and Russia, wish us well."

The delegates broke out into loud applause. For some moments the sounds of cheering and stamping of feet filled the Assembly Room.

President John Hancock cleared his throat and waited until the applause died down. Then he continued, his voice rising in conviction. "The wealthy in France are so desirous of helping us that they offer us a loan of two million livres, to be repaid without interest when we have obtained a peace. Though the court of France cannot at this time sell us ships, the Farmers General, wealthy aristocrats who collect royal taxes and act as patrons to a variety of causes, have agreed to provide us with cargoes of arms, ammunition, and other supplies. In exchange, Congress will send them twenty thousand hogsheads of tobacco, to be purchased in Virginia and Maryland.

"At this time, gentlemen, we must keep this knowledge secure. Until we have a firm, written alliance with France, we are still on edge. Statements outside this room must not reveal these understandings. Do I make myself clear?"

"Perfectly," responded several. The room quieted.

John Adams stood and walked towards the president, a paper in his hand. "If I may?"

"Certainly."

"The *Mercury* from the port of Nantes has arrived at Portsmouth, New Hampshire, with thousands of fuses, barrels of powder, gun-flints, bales of woolen clothing, and other supplies." He held up a gazette.

Clapping and stamping of feet followed.

"Much needed," John Hancock said, with a broad smile.

Congress took up more business. Two more members were selected for the committee for the *Journals* of Congress. James glanced towards them with approval. He had found the work demanding enough. Reading over Charles Thomson's notes and marking the margins with small dots where sensitive matters were recorded, reviewers indicated statements that should not be published before the transcripts were turned over to the printers. It was tedious but vital work to permit secure reports of Congress's proceedings.

Leaving the Pennsylvania State House that day, tired but thrilled at the news of France's aid to their cause, the delegates were in a celebratory mood. "Shall we meet at the City Tavern for a drink?" John Adams suggested.

"It is certainly an occasion to celebrate, so, yes," James said. "France's encouragement requires a toast. But a quiet one," he said, looking at John Adams meaningfully. "Until we have their assurance in a formal agreement, we cannot be too careful."

"Agreed, my friend," John said. "I will share some information with Abigail, knowing she is careful and cares greatly about my business and welfare. She undertakes the burden of our family on her own and deserves my frankness."

"I must say, though I write Mary as regularly as any man would in the absence of his wife, I keep my statements about our affairs to a minimum, knowing she might not understand our concerns. She trusts me to make decisions to our greater benefit." *What it would be like to have a wife that understands the issues we grapple with? Mary, wise though she is in the ways of running an efficient home, would choose to leave such considerations to me. Abigail Adams, on the other hand, reads widely and understands many matters with which her husband is concerned.*

"I do trust Abigail. Her wide reading compels her to seek information I can share with her. I write her as often as I can, though heavens know that has not been enough of late."

"The information you send Abigail must be vital to her," James agreed. "Even as my letters to Mary are important to her," he added.

John nodded. "Let us celebrate this news. At present, French aid seems our only hope to prevail in this war." They reached the City Tavern and mounted the steps to join their friends.

Chapter 4

Sabers Rattling

April 7, 1777, Monday

Major General Philip Schuyler drew the eyes of all as he took his seat near the front of the Assembly Room. Formal in his blue and buff uniform with gold epaulets, the New York general's expression was tight as a lid. A hush of apprehension spread among the delegates. Appointed to Congress from New York earlier in the year, the general had not yet attended.

Philip Schuyler, commander of the northern army, was one of the first four generals appointed by Washington. But from the conversation James and other members of Congress had with General Horatio Gates a few weeks ago, it was clear that Gates assumed Congress would appoint him commander of the northern department.

The two generals had managed to work together when General Gates had been commander at Ticonderoga the previous year, but rivalry pulsed between them. In James's view, it would be best if both were given satisfactory appointments. Ironically, he reflected, on this very day General Horatio Gates had left Philadelphia for Albany, there to proceed to his post at Fort Ticonderoga.

General Schuyler had written letters to Congress criticizing their decisions, a course of action that had met with stern disapproval. Perhaps this was the reason for the clenched jaw, determined frown, and calculated look of calm that James now saw.

"Good morning, gentlemen," President John Hancock said. General Schuyler stood, waiting to be recognized. John Hancock nodded. "Please proceed, General."

"Mr. President," General Schuyler said, standing, his gaze steadily focused on John Hancock, "I request a committee of Congress be appointed to look into my conduct as commander of the northern army of the United States. Certain charges have been made against me in letters from this body that must be cleared. I await Congress's pleasure before assuming another command."

His voice even, John Hancock responded, "We will look into the matter. I will see to it that Congress appoints a committee to review the charges. Thank you, General." The president did not flinch, as he glanced at Schuyler, then back to the stack of papers arrayed before him for the day.

General Gates is expected to work with General Schuyler, James mused. *Schuyler expects Congress to clear his name and solve their conflict. I wonder what Gates's solution would be.*

April 11, 1777, Friday

James took a deep breath of fresh air. With an effort, he turned from bitter memories of his captivity to the tranquil Delaware River before him.

He could almost imagine he smelled the ocean, some one hundred miles down the channel. The grim thought occurred to him that farther down the Delaware and past the Chesapeake Bay lay the port of New York, where Lord Howe's army geared up for a transport of troops, their objective most likely Philadelphia.

Turning to John Adams at his side, James said, "Washington wrote he would send covert exploration into the enemy's quarters to obtain intelligence. A woman bringing eggs to sell could return with new insights and never be suspected. Or a farmer with a load of cabbages might gain enough information for a report.

"And Washington enclosed a letter from an applicant, Le Chevalier Count of Vrecourt, which I reviewed. He is a native of Luxembourg and served as captain of engineers and artillery in the French army during the Seven Years' War. He should be employed, even if he doesn't know our language. Washington has no engineer at all at present with the army. An interview is unnecessary, as he arrives with sufficient recommendations."

"Congress should approve the Count of Vrecourt's appointment," John said. The two began walking slowly back to the town, savoring the fresh air and lingering sunset.

"General Washington's letter mentioned that according to accounts from Brunswick, the British were cutting timber and stripping boards from buildings, possibly to build berths on transports," James said. "The general suspected their destination would be Delaware Bay."

"And they have sixty-three transports wooded and watered to take on men, fitted with brass cannon. Also, thirty-two flat bottomed boats to form a bridge."

"His report should put us on defense. General Gates is currently en route to Albany. He will remain there until needed at Fort Ticonderoga. I trust his decisions, I believe."

"But according to information from the commissioners, Howe is more likely to act against New England. General Carleton might come from Canada to Fort Ticonderoga. General Burgoyne, who commands ten thousand men, may invade

Virginia and Maryland. The bridge preparation noted in Washington's letter may be a feint."

"We must pursue all avenues of defense. At least, at this time Congress has representatives from all thirteen states," James said. He glanced at the sun, descending into the clouds. "It is time we return for dinner."

April 16, 1777, Wednesday

"Here is the crux of the matter. How, gentlemen, are we to wage a war without an army?" President Hancock held up a letter. "Washington provides reports from ten states indicating meager enlistments. Officers leave for business or pleasure, men do not return from furlough, and quarrels over rank or money are perpetual.

"Despite our concerns about a standing army, leading us initially to depend on volunteer militia for short terms of enlistments, last fall we recognized the need for a stable force. We resolved that each state raise regiments and arm and equip them."

President Hancock's voice rose. "A year ago, Washington expressed his deep regret that General Montgomery died in trying to take Quebec. Montgomery knew his troops were preparing to depart, their terms of service nearly ended, so he tried to storm the walls of Quebec. His rush to employ his troops before they abandoned their positions ended in disaster. An army cannot be driven by the terms of enlistment of its members.

"General Washington accepts free blacks, even boys, into the military. Still, his numbers are not adequate. We need to encourage the states to fulfill their quotas as required in Congress's resolve and consider all possible ways to support the army."

A lengthy discussion followed this statement. It was clear to James that without Congress's leadership, the states would not make sufficient efforts to provide for the military. Yet Congress could only advise and request. For the country's success, those in the governing body must do their utmost to ensure adequate recruits and supplies for the army. *Each day we work to that end.*

April 19, 1777, Saturday

James met the other members of the Committee for Foreign Affairs, Thomas Heyward and Robert Morris, in the hall outside the Assembly Room as Congress gathered.

Robert Morris extended his large hand to James. "Welcome. You will be an asset to the committee's work."

"I suspect I have been chosen for my knowledge of French, but I am hopeful my skills in cipher may also be of benefit. We must follow the practice of those in Europe, who encode their sensitive writings to safeguard them from hostile eyes."

Robert Morris was about to speak when a slender young man, aspiration written large on his face, approached. He clutched a set of journals in his hands.

"I am Thomas Paine," he said, extending his hand.

James shook his hand. *What is he doing here?*

"I am the new secretary for the Committee for Foreign Affairs. I wondered if you would meet this afternoon." Paine's words tumbled out.

"I believe so, after Congress adjourns. And you?" James said, turning to Robert Morris. Morris nodded agreement, as did Thomas Heyward.

"Very good. I will arrange for a meeting place for us." Paine whirled and left.

"The author of *Common Sense* will be our secretary? How unusual. Perhaps he wishes a position."

"No doubt. The seventy dollars a month will serve him well as he reads statements attacking monarchy and tradition in taverns. The people love him. But perhaps he also wishes to read our correspondence. I would be somewhat wary of him, at least for now." Robert Morris shook his head doubtfully.

They entered the Assembly Room and took their seats just as President Hancock called the meeting to order.

April 21, 1777, Monday

James found himself listening with interest as President Hancock turned to the Articles of the Confederation, a document which would establish the government in more stable form. Congress had not discussed the Articles since he had been in attendance.

"When did Congress last consider the Articles?" James asked Elbridge Gerry, as President Hancock stepped aside to confer with an aide.

"Last summer," Elbridge answered. His shrewd eyes gazed at James over his hawk-like nose. "Completing the draft of the Articles hinges on three issues. Originally, in 1774, when Congress first f-f-formed, the idea of one s-s-state, one vote was accepted. Now the larger states with the bigger populations want more representation. Another s-s-stumbling block is whether the expenses of this war— and you know we are creating a huge debt—should be shared by each state on the basis of their total population including s-s-slaves, or just their free population."

"I imagine those in the north think population should include both free and those enslaved, as that would require the southern states to pay a larger share of the debt," James said thoughtfully.

"Quite so, and those in the s-s-south think the reverse. The third issue which Congress has yet to r-r-resolve is that some states, such as Virginia, have no boundary to their western lands, so they would like to claim the vast expanses west of their p-p-populations. These are termed landed states. Others, such as Rhode Island, are clearly bounded by their charters. These states want C-c-congress to assume ownership of the western lands so as to be able to s-s-sell lands in the west after the war to repay the national debts."

"That sounds like a good plan to me. I am sure those in Massachusetts would agree."

"But getting Congress to agree on these issues has not been easy. Thus, the Articles are still in d-d-draft form." Elbridge turned to see President Hancock standing to speak.

The president cleared his throat. "Today we will hear from the new delegate from North Carolina, Thomas Burke. I believe Mr. Burke has a suggestion to amend the Articles."

Thomas Burke, a heavy-set Irish man, stood. In a loud, rough voice, he said, "With due respect to this Congress, setting all guidelines for the states in one document will never do. Each state must be empowered to devise such laws as will best answer for the interests of that state. Therefore, I propose we adopt an article stating the following." He held up a paper and read: "Each state should retain 'its sovereignty, freedom, and independence, and every power, jurisdiction, and right, which is not by this Confederation expressly delegated' to Congress."

To James's surprise, agreement on this article came fairly rapidly. *It seems the states are concerned they will lose their rights.* He glanced at John Adams, who shrugged his shoulders. *After all, the states must work together.*

April 28, 1777, Monday

"Gentlemen, we will have official reports soon of the arrival of the *Amphitrite* in Portsmouth, New Hampshire. The *Amphitrite*, sailing from the French port of Lorient three months ago, follows the *Mercury*, arriving last month from Nantes." President Hancock looked about the room expectantly.

Huzzas echoed throughout the Assembly Room. Though not publicly, as they did not choose to confront the British, the French were coming to the aid of the Americans.

"The stores on the *Amphitrite* include brass cannon, thousands of arms, hundreds of tents, bales of clothing, blankets, tin plates, ammunition, and powder. In addition, there are at least twenty-two officers and ten other service personnel, all of whom come with credentials and letters of recommendation from Silas Deane."

More applause followed. James felt a prickle going down his back at the thought of more officers from France. He sighed. *Perhaps some will be suitable for service.*

Chapter 5

Parlez-vous Anglais?

May 5, 1777, Monday

James set down his notes and turned to Colonel William Whipple, seated across the room at Robert Duncan's. "I have taken the liberty of writing to General Gates."

William looked up from his newspaper. Behind him the setting sun cast a rainbow through crystal candlesticks onto the finely worked rug.

"The state of affairs for New York is critical. At Albany, Gates was startled to see troops unfit for duty, cannon missing, and the treasury empty. We have resolved to send him support.

"Then to the west stands Fort Ticonderoga, old and run-down. It has fewer than a thousand troops. We will move that garrison to Mount Independence, on the east side of Lake Champlain. On higher ground, Mount Independence commands the district."

"What did you write to General Gates?" William's expression was serious.

"Since the situation in New York is critical, many feel that one man alone can keep the country united and prevent the spread of British loyalists. They hold that General Schuyler must be the chief of the northern department at Albany. I thought it well to let General Gates know how the wind blows."

"You did him a favor there," William answered.

"Meanwhile, we find that Burgoyne is sailing to Boston, or possibly Rhode Island, with ten thousand Germans and three thousand British. He may then join Howe in New York. And then the plan to cut off New England would be a reality."

William smiled grimly and picked up his gazette again.

May 8, 1777, Thursday

"I understand members of the Committee for Foreign Affairs have information for Congress that arrived on the *Amphitrite*." The president looked about the Assembly Room. Reverend Witherspoon, portly, energetic, stood for the committee.

"We have the invoices of the military stores carried on the *Amphitrite* and the *Mercury*. A couple dozen officers also arrived on the *Amphitrite*. Thomas Conway is listed as the colonel commandant. Major General Du Coudray arrived on the ship as well. On behalf of Beaumarchais and Silas Deane, he was the one who chose artillery and military supplies from French arsenals to outfit the ships."

Reverend Witherspoon shuffled his papers and cleared his throat. "All officers bear letters of commendation from Silas Deane and agreements made with him regarding their service with the United States Army."

"Excellent," President Hancock said. "Mr. Thomson, please give the list of officers to James Lovell, chair of the Committee on Foreign Applications."

James looked at William Whipple, seated nearby. "More business for the translator, I have no doubt," he said in a low voice.

"We endeavor to please," William said with a quiet chuckle.

Following pay requests for supplies, President Hancock called for the Committee for Foreign Affairs to report on privateers acting as ships of war. Robert Morris, standing for the committee, spoke of the benefits of enlisting privateers as adjunct navy ships, his voice raised in enthusiasm.

Under Secretary Jacob Rush approached James, the list of foreign officers in his hand.

"Mr. Lovell, I request you copy this list of officers arrived on the *Amphitrite* for Secretary Thomson and retain the original. I trust you will assess their language skills."

"Thank you. I will see to it," James said, placing the list in his satchel. His never-ending stream of foreign officers to interview flowed in abundance, at least for the foreseeable future.

May 22, 1777, Thursday

"The first item for our consideration has been a matter of debate for several days. Major General Schuyler, you are hereby directed to proceed to Albany and take upon yourself the command at the northern department." President Hancock glanced in the direction of Philip Schuyler.

General Schuyler bowed. His penetrating eyes lit with fierce pleasure. Applause rippled through those assembled, the New York delegates loudly stating their approval.

James thought of his friend, General Horatio Gates. Conferring the commandant's position on General Schuyler meant Gates could either serve under Schuyler or return to the post of adjutant general with Washington. He could only imagine the ire this would cause the ambitious general.

Requests from the Committee for the Treasury for funds followed. Then came the decision to print five million dollars of Continental bills, to be backed by Spanish gold or silver, as well as instructions to the printing press as to which plates to use, and the signing and dating of the bills.

"And are we confident we have sufficient gold and silver in securities to support such printing?" James asked William.

"No, but we are confident we need the currency. As long as we can meet our payrolls and obligations, we can and will print bills," William answered, his voice tired.

May 30, 1777, Friday

"The Board of War has concluded its meeting. But what keeps you?" John said.

James motioned to the stack of letters on his delegation's table in the Assembly Room. "I wrote to General Washington, sending him the list of officers lately arrived on the *Amphitrite*. Each is highly desirous of achieving elevated rank. Thomas Conway, colonel commandant, heads the list and speaks English adequately."

He frowned. "Remember the problem of foreign officers in our army. Many of our Continentals would grumble at having to serve under them. Yet some have skills we need greatly."

"Very true," John said. "And one must consider the learned Philippe Tronson Du Coudray, French artillery officer." He rolled his eyes expressively.

"To be sure." James smiled. "*Mais oui*, we have all heard of his amazing abilities. The man is never silent. Most unfortunately, he brings a contract with Silas Deane announcing he will be major general in charge of artillery. What was Deane thinking? What about the American officers managing artillery positions quite professionally? Generals Greene, Sullivan, and Knox would be mortally offended at the mere thought of having Du Coudray in charge. That contract presents a delicate problem of relationship with a country with which we need to remain on good terms. But seriously, just what to do with Du Coudray, I do not know."

"Perhaps we can void his contract in some way—carefully, of course."

James took a breath. "Today, the Committee for Foreign Affairs wrote to the American commissioners, recommending that they ignore the news in the London papers, as the British ministry hears the real news from their officers, but in the papers they print what they like for the people."

"Ah, yes. British papers carry letters as if written by General Washington, fabricated to show him filled with doubt and fear. An underhanded hit, to manipulate the public's beliefs through untruth. But it grows late. I must leave you," John said, rising.

"I have more work to do."

"Your new situation is proving comfortable?" John asked.

"Quite suitable. Robert Duncan felt the house was crowded, so as Mrs. Cheeseman's rates are reasonable, Colonel Whipple and I have determined to make the best of it."

"It is said Mrs. Cheeseman, mild though she may appear, has buried four husbands and is quite ready to take on a fifth." John smiled and stood. "I leave you to your efforts. Good evening."

In his room, James searched and found in his papers a letter to the Honorable Doctor Franklin he had started a few days ago. He had begun by greeting the distinguished representative of the United States in as polite and deferential a manner as he could muster.

He felt it was time he explained a cipher system for diplomats. It was imperative that sensitive messages be transmitted to Congress's agents in Europe securely. Too often letters were captured by the enemy, stolen at sea when vessels were taken, or, if the letters were thrown overboard, retrieved from the waters. He would describe not a polyalphabetic substitution cipher, a variant of which was called a Vigenère cipher, but a simpler system, based on an alphabet square.

Picking up his pen, he wrote the numbers 1–27 from top to bottom on the left-hand side of the paper, then again in the middle, from top to bottom, and finally on the right-hand side of the paper. *Using three columns of the numbers will help the eye to track*, he thought. Starting with *a* at the right of number 1, he wrote each letter of the alphabet in a column from top to bottom. For the number 27 he placed the ampersand symbol. Then he began filling out the square, writing the remainder of the alphabet to the right of letter *a*, skipping over the "1" he had written in the middle of the page after the thirteenth letter, and continuing on to the end where he wrote the ampersand. For the following line he began at the left with the *b*, finished the alphabet, again skipped the number 2 in the middle of the page after the thirteenth letter, and placed the *a* at the end of the line just before the final "2." He continued with the square but completed just part of it, relying on Benjamin Franklin's knowledge of the cipher to finish it.

As explanation he wrote, "Three lines of figures help the eye in making angular reference. By continuing 'til the square shall be complete, each letter of the Alphabet will be referrable to every figure of the 27."

Then for good measure he provided an example. "Powder & Ball are already sent to the amt. ordered, and Cannon as directed will be shipped by May." He then wrote his example using the cipher: "14.8.23.14.27.21.12.2 are sent to the amt. ordered, and 27.14.1.12.8.14 as directed will be shipped by 23.25.11."

As he finished his directions for Benjamin Franklin, he imagined it to be like a thistle. As a thistle bristled with protective prickles, his cipher would guard the information it contained. *I will just use that analogy to describe it.* "Should this letter arrive unbroken in its seal; we may draw advantage from the Thistle." *There*, he thought, folding and sealing the letter, *that should be sufficient to have the good doctor up and running with a cipher in no time. So much depends on useful and accurate information being shared by those in diplomatic channels and those waging a hard-fought war.* Confident in the usefulness of his cipher, James left the State House, his empty stomach rumbling.

Hon.^d and dear Sir

    I catch up my pen in haste: but, it is not that circumstance which makes me omit prefatorial apology, in this attempt to draw You into a literary correspondence. Difference of age and other differences vastly more important vanish, when I consider our relationship as "Friends to America". And, I am conscious that the service of these United States is the only motive prompting me at this time to an act, otherwise, egregiously vain.

    Letters to Congress have been too often cast into the sea by the bearers of them, when in danger of being taken by the Enemy, in consequence of directions given by the Writers. The last unfortunate instance was where, M^r McCreary was bearer for the Honble Mr Deane. I think the great ingenuity of that young Gentleman could have found means to preserve a packet in the chase & his after captivity, if he had been emboldened by any consideration to make tryal, under contrary orders. I wish to lessen the necessity of such directions as have been heretofore given, on like occasions.

You have practised modes of secret correspondence. I submit the annexed plan to your judgment. Having gained it by accident, I am satisfied myself that it is sufficiently inscrutable to warrant the attempt of preserving packets of importance thro' the risques of captivity.

Should this letter arrive unbroken in its seal, we may draw advantage from the Thistle. Should it arrive under dubious circumstances, you may use the Alphabet; and, by one of your ten thousand ready devices, may communicate to me a new Key-Word.

The Secret Committee doubtless give you all proper history. I am too young in my present service to know the just limits of communicating those subjects which are most interesting to your Heart.

I am
With great & sincere Esteem
Your very humble Servant

James Lovell

Hon.ble Doct.r Franklin

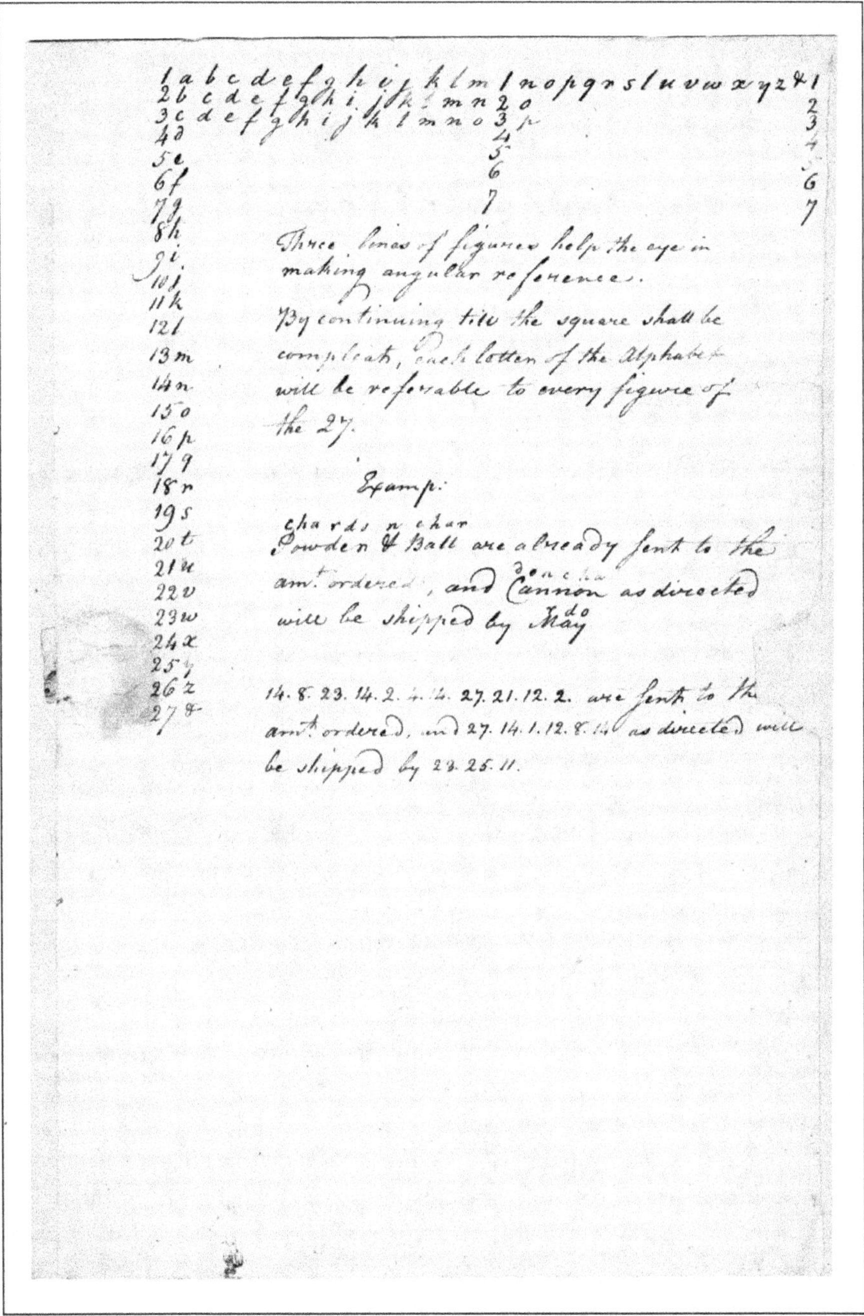

"James Lovell to Benjamin Franklin, after May 24, 1777."
American Philosophical Society

Chapter 6

The Problem of Foreign Officers

June 8, 1777, Sunday

"I had a marvelous adventure today, travelling down the Delaware River to inspect batteries and obstructions the army has erected to prevent the enemy from coming to Philadelphia by water." John Adams wiped his forehead and took a seat in Mrs. Cheeseman's sitting room. A warm breeze flowed through the open windows.

"Did you reach Fort Mifflin?" James asked. His legs twitched with inactivity; his duties were leaden weights.

"We went about ten miles down the river to Billingsport. Our three boats, including General Arnold, and General Du Coudray—perhaps you have heard of the eminent French artillery officer?"

"Ah, yes. He of the amazing talents but not as of yet the elevated position he so dearly covets. He writes letters to Congress so frequently that Secretary Thomson can recognize his handwriting from across the room." They both chuckled.

"Yes. At Billingsport, the Pennsylvania militia set up *chevaux-de-frise* in the river to obstruct enemy ships from their passage up the channel. They are constructed of massive logs with heavy timbers affixed like branches, extending some fifteen feet or so across. The militia sink them with boulders to form a barrier resting below the surface of the water."

"Effective at blocking enemy ships."

"At Red Bank on the Jersey side, Colonel Bull showed us floating batteries, then gave us dinner—roast wild turkey—and afterwards ordered his regiment on parade. An impressive spectacle. We are well prepared to stop a British advance by water, I believe."

"The defenses sound formidable. Howe has not made a move."

"Yet intelligence indicates the possibility of an advance. I must return to Robert Duncan's. I owe Abigail a letter and can scarcely write her as often as she would like." John stood up. "Don't let those foreigners wear you out. Good night, then."

56

"Good night," James said, with a sigh of resignation.

June 9, 1777, Monday

"Gentlemen, we have before you a letter from General Henry Knox sent by General Washington. General Knox takes great exception to a recent action of Congress." President Hancock sighed and glanced at the thick packet in front of him. "We might have known that foreign officers arriving with contracts guaranteeing them positions in the army of the United States with dates of service extending back to previous service in France would cause a problem."

"Be more specific, if you would, Mr. President," a delegate urged.

"To be blunt, General Knox expresses great dismay concerning Congress's resolution of May 31. Our resolve gave officers of artillery arriving on the *Amphitrite* rank in the American artillery according to the dates of their French commissions. General Knox states that it is unfair to the American servicemen, many of whom have been enlisted for three years, to give these officers a superior rank." President Hancock scowled at the letters and drew a deep breath.

"General Knox is as fine an artillery general as we could wish," Benjamin Harrison said, disbelief in his voice.

"We are in agreement. And the commander-in-chief states that to place these French officers over those who have worked diligently to raise the men to proficiency would be unmilitary and unjust. They cannot even communicate effectively with the Americans.

"I would support General Knox's suggestion that all we can do reasonably is to give the French officers commissions as of their date of service to the American army. Therein, of course, lies the rub. Shall we offend and possibly alienate a foreign power of which we have great need?

"For now, Congress's resolve ranking the French officers according to the dates of their French commissions must stand. Meanwhile, the Board of War will consider the concerns raised by General Knox and agreed upon by General Washington." John Hancock picked up another letter and smoothed it out.

James groaned inwardly. All his reports on the French officers seemed to make little difference. *How can I improve the situation? As chairman of the Committee for Foreign Applications, I could write to Benjamin Franklin explaining that the many contracts offered to foreign officers cause Congress a problem. As senior statesman, surely Franklin could provide guidance to the others. I will risk it.*

President Hancock continued. "You must know that General Washington provides reports from New York indicating the enemy may make an expedition by water in the near future. Intelligence from one Enoch Willis states he worked on one of fifty vessels outfitted for the transport of horses with water and hay. It is rumored that they are to go to Philadelphia. Another report indicates the transports were to take on British troops in New York, along with bundles of fascines, to go to Boston or Philadelphia. We cannot know at this time, gentlemen, which way the advance may come, but we will do our best to prepare in case we must move."

And I sold my horse, James thought, his muscles tensing. *In case of sudden need to abandon Philadelphia, I would be hard pressed to travel. I must be on the lookout for a horse, though I surely hope it does not come to that.*

June 18, 1777, Wednesday

James awoke with sweat beading on his forehead, his light summer bed covering tangled and thrust to the floor. He sat up, heart pounding. The dream had been all too real, a sense of foreboding and fear palpable and heavy, a huge stone crushing him in his sleep. A suffocating smell of rancid meat and refuse hovered at the edge of his memory. *What had occasioned this terrible nightmare?* It had been weeks since he had suffered such torments. His dream was already fleeing: *who had been imprisoned?* He cringed as the memory of rude insults pelted him like grapeshot.

No, I had a vision of the past, nothing to fear, and I am all right. He swung his legs out of bed and looked up at the window. The moon shone steadily down on what was a perfect summer night, not a breath of wind, a hint of cloud at the horizon, the stars brilliant in the quiet sky. Yet he was breathing hard, his hands clenched, his stomach taut with distress.

James got up and sat for a moment in the chair at his bedside. He waited while his heartbeat returned to normal. The pain he had just experienced might have been brought to life by today's turmoil. If Congress's actions had been effective, surely today should not have happened. Yet it did.

General Gates had arrived at Congress and received admittance into the Pennsylvania State House. At his appearance at the door, William Paca of Maryland demanded in loud tones to know what Gates was doing, but he had responded firmly that he had intelligence of importance to communicate.

Once inside, the general seated himself with dramatic pose in front of the assembled delegates. He was splendid in his full uniform, yet almost visibly trembling with rage. There was a moment of quiet, as though all realized they might be witnessing the calm before the storm. James noted that the general's eyes did not for a moment rest on him, as if he denied the existence of any friendship among those in the gathering.

General Gates took a sheaf of notes from his pocket and held them out. When every eye was on him, he began in a cool tone, asserting he had spent years in the service of his country. He listed the reforms he had introduced at Ticonderoga as befitting his appointment. As the general's voice began to rise, scratchy with fatigue but carrying loudly in the large room, William Paca forcefully demanded he be ordered to leave. William Duer of New York seconded the motion and soon there was shouting all around, Gates's voice ugly with harsh protests regarding his ability and merits for office. As others chimed in, the discord heated. Finally, the general, in a rage, stomped out of the Assembly Room.

James felt clearly the division in Congress in the confrontation, more than at almost any other time. Those from the more conservative southern and middle states, led by New York, had taken the upper hand. New England, earliest in the fray against Britain, had not won this time. Yet he knew General Gates to be an effective and competent general. To James, the sight of General Gates storming out of Congress was more than disheartening. The general had lost his composure in a bid for supremacy; his actions left a sour taste in the mouths of all present. James could only hope that in time his position in the United States Army would reflect his abilities. For now, he was sorry for his friend. He regretted the day had come when the general turned his anger on the governing body of the United States.

He sat for a while in the quiet dark, letting his mind and body rest. Though he missed his family, he must continue here. His good friend Colonel William Whipple had left for his home in Portsmouth, New Hampshire, to enter the army. His friend Joseph Trumbull, commissary general, surely had his own difficulties, yet he persisted with his work. James shrugged off the nightmare, calmed by recognizing its source, lay back down, and as the soft wind blew in the open window, fell asleep.

June 23, 1777, Monday

Elbridge Gerry pulled up a chair near James at the Pennsylvania State House. Loud voices echoed from the hall. "The New Jersey militia has s-s-successfully forced the British out of New Jersey."

"Excellent news," James said. He looked up to see the president take his seat at the front of the room.

President Hancock raised a hand for attention. "Washington sends a letter from General Schuyler at Saratoga, requesting help for Ticonderoga. He has no information about Howe's movements.

"General Schuyler reports that he has interrogated a spy, William Amsbury. American troops captured Amsbury on the east side of Lake Champlain and took him to General Arthur St. Clair at Fort Ticonderoga, who sent him to Saratoga. There, General Schuyler interrogated him on June 15.

"Amsbury at first did not come clean with information, but when threatened with execution, Amsbury explained that a judge in Montreal had sent him to carry a canteen with a false bottom to Major General John Sullivan. Schuyler opened the canteen and found a message attempting to persuade General Sullivan to defect. The spy said that General John Burgoyne was expected in Montreal in a few days along with seven thousand British and Hessian troops and several hundred Indians and Canadians, as well as ample provisions."

The congressmen drew in their breaths at this news.

"General Burgoyne is expected to march south from Quebec with his troops to Fort Ticonderoga. Schuyler requests reinforcements from General Washington, in addition to supplies," President Hancock said, his voice clear in the hushed assemblage.

James drew in his breath. "Ticonderoga is vital for defense," he said to Elbridge. "Ethan Allen of the Green Mountain Boys told me while we were in jail at Halifax about his capture of the fort two years ago with Benedict Arnold. It was considered a great prize."

President Hancock continued. "We will refer the letter of General Washington with its enclosures to the Committee of Intelligence. Any threat to Fort Ticonderoga should be prevented, if at all possible."

June 24, 1777, Tuesday

"Our commander-in-chief has a way of working at the enemy's positions that often turns in his favor," Samuel Adams said. "His letter today described the evacuation of the enemy from Brunswick."

The delegates from Massachusetts sat about the maple table at their evening meal at Mrs. Cheeseman's lodgings.

"In fact, he employs Fabian strategies, so-called after the Roman general Fabius, retreating and waiting, then striking only when an optimal opportunity arises. Consider Trenton and Princeton," James said.

"Yet we look for more from Washington," said John Adams.

"How go the interviews with the f-f-foreign officers?" Elbridge asked, turning to James.

"In truth, I drink of a bottomless cup. I find many who are not capable of conversing in English. Though they come with testimonials to their previous action, I cannot endorse their success in our army without a command of our language."

"And what would that most promising officer from France, Monsieur Du Coudray, propose for his position?"

"I see you have heard of him. He is by his own account highly talented and would make a fine officer." James pursed his lips in disapproval, but his gray-green eyes glittered in amusement. "Yet we also must tread lightly when we discourage his interest, as he comes so highly recommended. It is a delicate situation."

"That much is clear," Samuel agreed.

"I fear that Silas Deane is no clairvoyant when it comes to French manipulation or flattery," James said. "Now, the Baron de Holtzendorf bore excellent credentials. He nodded eagerly when I asked him about his knowledge of English. Yet when I requested an explanation of his training in the Prussian army, he struggled to put any of it into words. I am afraid I got a bit upset with him."

"You got upset?" John asked mildly.

James gritted his teeth. "I must admit it. If I recall correctly, I may have said to the baron that I wished the devil would have drowned Mr. Deane a thousand times over before he ever came to France. If I had my way, all the French officers who had come to our shores would board a large vessel and return to France."

The delegates burst into laughter. James smiled apologetically. "I am not usually so irate, I can assure you. But in my experience, the most ignorant American officer who has served well since the beginning of the war is worth far more than the most skillful foreign officer."

Mrs. Cheeseman, her hair piled high, looked in the door to see what the amusement was, then withdrew with a coquettish smile.

"Baron de Holtzendorf seemed disdainful of service that would place him in a learning capacity if he were recommended to the American army. Yet I think that is just where he belongs. I found myself ill from long hours on Sunday, and I must say, these Frenchmen have used me quite up."

"We may have to abandon Philadelphia," John reminded them.

"I have no horse at present. I do not know how I would manage."

"There are Quakers nearby who do not s-s-support the war effort but who keep horses. I would inquire of them," Elbridge said. "I b-b-board my horse at my lodgings."

"Very good. However, I do not believe we will need to leave Philadelphia. General Washington may bottle them up in New York."

"To liberty and the health of our forces," Samuel said. All held their glasses high before drinking in solemn agreement.

Chapter 7

First Independence Day

July 1, 1777, Tuesday

"A couple of days in bed and I am better," James said, tugging his tricorn hat down tight.

He and Elbridge Gerry walked to the Pennsylvania State House, wind whipping branches and driving rain. It did not feel in the least like July.

"Unusually f-f-fierce," Elbridge said. A torrent of water gushed down the cobblestone street. "You should know that yesterday in Congress the t-t-topic of the New Hampshire Grants came up. This land to the west of New Hampshire wants to be independent. Their s-s-spokespersons stated that since the United States declared itself independent of Britain on July 4 last year, neither New York nor New Hampshire could claim them. But the spokespersons were misled, thinking all they had to do was to petition Congress to have their own delegates seated."

"It seems a complex situation," James said. "Independence Day is this Friday."

"Congress plans to devote that day to f-f-festivities."

"As we should."

At the Pennsylvania State House, President Hancock read a letter written in March from commissioner Arthur Lee, now in Spain. "Arthur Lee assures Congress that the Spanish crown pledges friendship and trade with the United States, but no offer of funds as of yet."

By afternoon, James felt chilled despite the fires in the twin fireplaces. The storm outside rattled windows and blew iron-hard drops against the panes. *Is this July? If so, the weather is most unseasonable. Is it an omen? Though I don't believe in omens.*

At length, the president called for the draft commissions that the Committee for Foreign Affairs had prepared for the new commissioners in the courts of Vienna, Berlin, and Tuscany.

"William Lee of Virginia will go to Germany and Prussia, Ralph Izard of South Carolina to Tuscany. The instructions for both diplomats call for them to recognize Benjamin Franklin as chief commissioner, inform the countries of the independence of the United States, cultivate friendship, and if possible, enter into treaties of friendship and commerce." Thomas Paine bowed and handed the drafts to Secretary Thomson.

To James's relief the commissions and instructions passed with little comment. *After all, they are the same as those given to Benjamin Franklin and Arthur Lee. If we don't have one Lee too many in the group, all should be well. What would it be like to live in Europe, make the acquaintance of foreign diplomats, and speak for the United States? Interesting, no doubt, but not for me.*

As Congress adjourned, the storm continued to bluster. James and Elbridge made their way back to Mrs. Cheeseman's, guarding every step.

July 4, 1777, Friday

Congress did not consider an observance of the first anniversary of the Declaration of Independence until July 2. They planned to celebrate by enjoying a meal together. Military displays would follow. A sermon would be appropriate, but it was too late to arrange for one. Another year, perhaps.

In the morning, James and Elbridge walked to the river.

The day was sunny and bright. The storm of a few days ago had passed, leaving broken branches and scattered leaves. Crowds lined the docks, the mood festive and cheerful. A band played while merchants hawked fresh buns and popped corn for sale. Large galleys, Continental vessels bristling with cannon, and small boats slowly processed down the river. All, including the splendid new frigate Delaware, fluttered with the newly authorized flag of the United States and those of France and Spain.

At one o'clock in the afternoon, the men on the ships ordered themselves into companies, some on deck, others climbing the tops and yards. Gunfire rang out. Shouts and cheers went up from the ships and those watching.

The Marine Committee and President John Hancock assembled at the dock and boarded the twenty-four gun ship the *Delaware*. They stood at attention while the frigate let fire a discharge of thirteen guns, their boom echoing across the water. People held their breaths while the sounds died away, then gave a great cheer. Thirteen shots resounded from the other vessels in the river. The reek of gunpowder billowed up. As the president and those accompanying him returned to the shore, three cheers went up from the boats in the river and the crowds lining the way.

James was thrilled at the commemoration of this one-year anniversary. He imagined his wife and family joining the celebration at home, listening to a band and speeches at the town common, church bells ringing and ships firing their guns.

Following the display at the river, James and Elbridge joined Congress for dinner at the City Tavern.

A regiment from nearby Fort Mercer crowded the street in front of the tavern, waiting in formation to salute dignitaries. Near the door, the Hessian fife, bugle horn, and drum band that had been captured at Trenton, dressed in their full regalia, played cheerful tunes. The group appeared delighted to be joining in the festivities. Delegates, the president, and town officials filled the establishment.

James and Elbridge settled at a table on the second floor. Out of the corner of his eye he saw a serving woman with a white cap covering red curls, bending over to pour water. Across the room, she smiled and curtsied, then vanished. She reminded him of Mary, some ten years ago. His heart skipped a beat and went on.

Toasts in honor of the country proclaimed good will. Some offered speeches for fallen officers and soldiers. Waiters in white aprons presented to Congress a dessert of flaming cherries especially created for the occasion. Drink flowed abundantly— Madeira, port, Chablis, and rum.

The noise and confusion, voices raised in excitement, was deafening. As some rose to leave, James and Elbridge made their way out into the fresh air outside. The clatter of hooves announced two troops of light horsemen from Maryland riding to camp down Second Street. A company of artillerymen from North Carolina trooped after them. At the common the artillerymen displayed their maneuvers and fired for the enjoyment of the crowd. The sun grew low, and the evening turned fair and pleasant. As they were about to leave, John Adams greeted them.

"Would you care to join me in a stroll through the streets?"

"I would," James said. Elbridge declined and turned towards his lodgings, as James and John set out.

"I trust your health is improved," John said.

"I am better. It was a rough bout, but rest has made all the difference."

"See there—and there." John pointed out candles in the windows of houses along the street. In fact, as evening approached, nearly every house had a lit candle at a window. Gatherings appeared around bonfires on street corners. From the waterfront, fireworks sent colorful sparks flying into the night.

"I believe our celebration to be successful." The air cooled as stars came out.

"If General Howe had been watching from an unseen window here, or his master, either would have been most distressed. We show ourselves proud of our accomplishments," John said.

"And proud we will remain, God willing." James gave a sigh of relief.

"With that, I shall retire." He bade John Adams good night and returned to his lodgings.

Weighing on his mind was the matter of French officers, particularly the situation of Du Coudray.

But while we question his suitability, the four engineers who arrived this week, trained in the royal Corps of Engineers, should be in the army, not wasting their time in Philadelphia waiting for approval. Further, Congress's agents must understand that a perfect understanding of our language is not the only criteria for acceptance into our army. Congress's resolution requiring a command of our language never suggested that.

Of the diplomats in Paris, only Benjamin Franklin might understand these matters. Silas Deane would take umbrage at criticism of his actions. Arthur Lee seemed to frequently disagree with the elder statesman. Late though it was, James decided to write to Benjamin Franklin. Perhaps future unwise contracts could be avoided. He settled himself at the small table in his room and took out paper, the new moon a bare sliver in the night sky. *And like the moon we are new too*, he thought.

> *Philadelphia, July 4, 1777*
> *Sir,*
>
> *I think it my duty as an individual to communicate to you some information which you may not perhaps receive in a more formal or authoritative way.*
>
> *The treaties made with the Chevalier de Borre, Mr. Du Coudray, and others have given infinite trouble, being inconsistent with each other, and all of them, except the one you signed with four engineers, inconsistent with the honor of the American officers, who, though not formed in regular standing armies, have the most just claims from their services since this war commenced.*
>
> *Though we have now a standing army for three years or more during the war, yet the genius of the people of these states is far from relishing the thought of having foreigners placed in the highest trusts. The merit of Brigadier General Knox is great and he is beloved by his corps. How then could Mr. Du Coudray's treaty fail to create the greatest confusion among our Officers of Artillery, since honoring it would place Mr. Du Coudray above Brigadier General Knox? But this is not the only problem. Many of our major generals would also be placed under Mr. Du Coudray, should his contract be honored. The four engineers also, who have at length arrived, do in the most preemptory manner state they will not serve under this Chief of Artillery and any engineer who is not like them of the royal Corps of Engineers.*

> *Mr. De le Balme may, however, be useful as Inspector of Cavalry which cannot disgust our other officers.*
>
> *Mr. Holtzendorff is a fresh embarrassment in every respect. I very much fear from these examples that a resolve formerly passed in Congress respecting French officers who do not understand our tongue will be construed into a general practice for those who do. The resolve was never intended for that end; and I assure you, Sir, nothing is more dreaded than such a construction. I will not multiply words, but conclude by assuring you of my most sincere esteem as, Sir, your friend and most humble servant*
>
> *James Lovell*

He set the letter aside. The image of the serving woman he had seen at the City Tavern earlier in the day came to him, appealing and cheerful. He resolved to write his wife a letter, though the night watchman had cried midnight at least an hour before. *I must do what I can to keep up her spirits, and mine as well,* he thought, taking out another piece of paper.

July 7, 1777, Monday

"Gentlemen, we have received letters not only from General Sullivan and General Knox, but also from General Greene. All express disapproval of Congress's granting Monsieur Du Coudray a commission as major general with the date of August 1776, which would place him above the three generals. Further, they request permission to resign, if Congress grants Du Coudray a commission." President John Hancock looked about the room, a worried frown on his face, a stack of letters in his hands. A storm of protests broke out.

"Does this not speak to collusion, Mr. President?" John Adams asked.

"Assuredly, as all three letters are written at camp in Middle Brook on the same date, July 1." The president glanced down at the letters, perplexed.

"And does this not threaten the confidence of other nations in Congress's authority, if our generals defy our ability to honor a contract?" Samuel Adams asked.

"We did authorize Silas Deane to make agreements with foreign entities for the good of our country," President Hancock said.

"Further, now we are placed in a delicate position. We cannot question Deane's authority to make contracts without seeming to be goaded by the arguments of our generals," John Adams pointed out.

"Our generals must not doubt the authority of the civil powers over the military," Samuel Adams said.

A thought occurred to James and he stood. "If the generals chose to take the appointment of Du Coudray as an accomplished fact, why did they not just ask leave to retire, rather than write letters in appeal?" He sat down to a smattering of applause.

"Indeed," President Hancock said. "They clearly are attempting to wield authority here when none can be granted."

A pause followed, then a buzz of conversation.

President Hancock spoke, cutting through the exchanges. "We must send copies of these letters to General Washington. He must inform the generals that Congress considers these letters an attempt to influence their decisions and an attack on the liberties of the people. The officers should apologize for these dangerous challenges. If any are unwilling to serve their country under the authority of Congress, they may resign."

Applause broke out. "Hear, hear."

"So resolved," President Hancock said. He handed the offending letters back to Secretary Thomson as disdainfully as if passing a piece of offal.

"We have trouble to the north, gentlemen." The president waited until he had the attention of all. "At our last meeting, on Saturday, July 5, we heard from General Arthur St. Clair at Crown Point Fort on Lake Champlain. The British vessels and Indian parties he observed proved to be the advance of a larger attack. On Saturday, he wrote that seven vessels of the enemy had come up to Crown Point Fort. He does not think he has sufficient troops to defend Ticonderoga unless the militia come. He will abandon his post, since his two thousand troops will not be able to counter Burgoyne's eight thousand British and Hessian troops advancing from Quebec. That is, if the intelligence gained from the spy Amsbury proves correct. We wait further information from Generals St. Clair and Schuyler."

"General Schuyler never considered that Burgoyne would come in force to Fort Ticonderoga," Reverend Witherspoon said, his broad forehead puckered with concern.

"Apparently not. In fact, he thought Burgoyne likely to head east or join Howe at New York."

"It would be a dark day indeed if that fort were to fall," Reverend Witherspoon said.

"Most true. We will await further news."

That night, after hours of writing letters, James considered the three engineers who had arrived on the *Amphitrite* with Monsieur Du Coudray. The fourth of their company had remained in the West Indies temporarily due to illness. The three engineers brought with them a treaty made with the commissioners in France. *But*

theirs is not just any treaty. Doctor Franklin and Silas Deane placed them under contract by direct request from Congress. In December of 1775, Congress had asked the Committee of Secret Correspondence to obtain the services of four royal engineers, schooled by the most reputable training in Europe. Their service would be invaluable to the American army. James decided to recommend the Chevalier Duportail be given the rank of colonel, Monsieur de la Radière that of a lieutenant colonel, and Monsieur de Gouvion that of a major of engineers. Further, Congress must be informed that the treaty specified their payment from the day they signed the contract.

Feeling well prepared for the following day, he placed his reports in his satchel.

July 11, 1777, Friday

President Hancock rose to his feet, his face taught, his wig untidy. The delegates regarded the president with some curiosity. *His appearance is quite uncharacteristic of our dapper president.*

"We have important news that concerns us all, but particularly the Board of War," President Hancock announced in a grim tone. "General Schuyler reports that General St. Clair has abandoned Fort Ticonderoga and Fort Independence. He does not know where St. Clair is."

James imagined he heard every man there draw in his breath. Then several outbursts punctuated the quiet.

"Did not General Schuyler come to assist St. Clair?"

"Then St. Clair's predictions which we reviewed a few days ago proved correct."

"What is the strength of the enemy?"

President Hancock looked about the room. When silence returned, he continued. "General Schuyler writes to the commander-in-chief that the enemy has great strength and plentiful supplies. He requests reinforcement from Washington, including tents, ammunition, horses, entrenching tools, and a good engineer or two."

"St. Clair must have been wholly unprepared," Samuel Adams said, dourly.

"Apparently. Washington says that our Continental levies are so deficient in number that the militia must be called out. He suggests to Congress that General Arnold would be capable of leading a spirited defense and should set out from Philadelphia."

"Could we conclude that General Washington thinks Arnold will be successful where St. Clair and Schuyler were not?" Benjamin Harrison asked shrewdly.

"That depends on where Schuyler is at present. I would withhold criticism at this time. At any rate, this is a matter for the Board of War to consider. I move we turn this correspondence over to that group."

"And what of General Howe?" someone asked. No one answered.

July 17, 1777, Thursday

The day turned hot early, the dew dissipating as the sun rose. Andrew McNair, doorkeeper, opened the tall windows of the meeting room at the Pennsylvania State House to permit air to enter, then closed them as the delegates gathered. It would be all too easy for curious or unfriendly ears to hear the conversation of those within through open windows.

"We have before us, gentlemen, a letter from the artilleryman Monsieur Du Coudray, imploring us to permit him the position in the contract given him by Silas Deane. He reports his financial situation to be precarious and urges our prompt response." President Hancock glanced at the papers in his hand with a sour expression.

James stood. "Mr. President, I remind you that on July 2, over two weeks ago, I placed before Congress the original contract between Silas Deane and Monsieur Philippus Charles John Baptist Tronson Du Coudray, adjutant general of artillery. On several occasions we have not come to a conclusion regarding M. Du Coudray's service. We need to determine a placement for him.

"His contract represents that he should be the officer in charge of the four royal engineers, though he has neither the experience nor the education for such a position. The mere thought is repugnant to the engineers. Their treaty with Doctor Franklin and Mr. Deane is unique, as it represents the one and only agreement with any foreign officer initiated by Congress. Monsieur Du Coudray is likely an effective artillery man, but hardly an engineer, much less an officer capable of overseeing royal engineers. Mr. Deane allowed himself to be led astray when he wrote the contract. In my opinion, we must not honor it."

James sat down and glanced across the room at Benjamin Harrison. The Virginian was silent, scowling in disapproval. Each time the Committee of the Whole had brought up the contract with Du Coudray, Harrison had requested more time to come to a conclusion. *How many times had this happened? Three? Four?* He wasn't sure.

"Mr. President," Secretary Thomson said, "permit me: Examining the record, I find that on multiple occasions we agreed that the contract between Silas Deane and Monsieur Du Coudray should not be honored."

William Duer stood. "Our resolve of July 12 stated that since Silas Deane had no power to enter into the agreement which he made with Monsieur Du Coudray, we are not bound to it."

"Consider too, his contract gives offense to our valuable generals, who have expressed their opinions on the matter in no uncertain terms," President Hancock said in brusque manner.

James stood again. "Mr. President, the committee charged with communicating with Monsieur Du Coudray has visited with him. He understands Congress's resolutions. He still awaits our determination and a placement in service."

"Apparently, off the record, Monsieur Du Coudray is too valuable to let go and too great a liability to employ," Benjamin Harrison grumbled.

"Precisely. But how should he be placed? I move we appoint two more members to the committee to suggest a proposal, those being Robert Morris and James Wilson," President Hancock said. "James Lovell will return to Monsieur Du Coudray his original contract as he requested. The committee will meet at their earliest convenience and inform Congress of their suggestion. All in favor?"

"Aye," some delegates said. Others merely nodded, with little enthusiasm, James noted. *This matter had gone on long enough.*

He stood, report in hand. "Mr. President, may I speak regarding a final request?"

"Certainly."

"This is from Baron de Holtzendorff, who bears a treaty made with him by Mr. Silas Deane." He handed the translation of the treaty to President Hancock, who looked it over without enthusiasm.

"We can only honor so many treaties, unless the individuals bring skills of great merit. Would you recommend the Baron de Holtzendorff to our service, Mr. Lovell, from your interviews with him?"

James shrugged. "The baron speaks some English, though his lack of the language appears to be on the whole a deficit. While he is wholly unacquainted with Americans and their ways, he seems prepared to remedy that. He seeks an office of high rank, but I would recommend that placement at a lower rank would give him opportunity to learn with fewer responsibilities." *And he could pretend to a greater share of modesty,* James thought, remembering the stiff, arrogant baron. He pursed his lips and held back his words. "He appears suitable."

"I recommend he be employed but only at the rank of lieutenant colonel," John Adams said. "His pay may begin from the date of his contract, last November."

"That seems acceptable. All in favor?" President Hancock said.

"Aye."

"I will convey your decision to the Baron de Holtzendorff," James said.

He sighed as he returned to his seat. *The baron does lack a command of English, but he is willing to try to improve. As for how much good he may do our forces, at least as a lieutenant colonel he cannot do much harm.*

"General Washington writes that he is at camp near the Clove, north of New York and west of the Hudson. He states he has received intelligence that on Sunday, seventy of the enemy's ships came down to Sandy Hook near Amboy, south of New

York, but he does not know if the vessels took out to sea. He will remain where he is until he knows what General Howe's real intentions are."

The room was quiet, the delegates listening closely.

"We have received the first message from St. Clair since he abandoned Ticonderoga to General Burgoyne. The general was not captured, nor was his army taken. He is in desperate need of provisions and will proceed east to Fort Edward or Saratoga, or else Bennington."

"I can imagine those lads hacking their way through forests, hungry and eaten alive by mosquitoes," James said under his breath to Elbridge Gerry, who nodded.

"Losing Ticonderoga to Burgoyne may not be as critical as we thought," John Adams said. "We lost Forts Washington and Lee and are no worse for it. If I may be so bold, Howe and Burgoyne will not be able to meet this year. If they did, we would pull all our forces together and counter the assault."

"Many agree with you," President Hancock said, looking about the room. "The sacrifice and effort of our determination is unchanged."

The delegates applauded. *Truly, it is both a privilege and a duty to serve in Congress,* James thought. Despite the long hours and constant demands, he was thrilled to be part of the work.

July 26, 1777, Saturday

President Hancock's voice rose in alarm as he read the commander-in-chief's letter.

"'The bulk of Howe's navy, about one hundred and twenty ships, has left New York. Their destination is unclear." He looked up, dismayed. The congressmen waited in silence. He began reading again. "'But I have thought it my duty to inform Congress of these facts, that they may give orders to the militia to hold themselves in readiness to march on the shortest notice in case Philadelphia should be their object.'"

Exclamations of disbelief and alarm rippled across the Assembly Room. James glanced at the startled faces of his fellow delegates. They turned to their business, thoughtful and not a little apprehensive.

Settled in his room for the evening, James opened the window. The heat was stifling. He should write to General George Washington about the engineers. They had great potential benefit for the army. General Washington appreciated communication, as he demonstrated by his frequent letters. *He would welcome information I could provide him. And I owe him my gratitude. I would not even be in Congress, had Washington not freed me from a British prison, authorizing my exchange.*

His letter turned out to be very long, he realized, taking out his fourth sheet of paper. Yet he wished General Washington to realize the benefit the engineers would be to the army. He concluded by apologizing for the length of the letter.

He folded up the general's letter, and, taking out more paper, he wrote to Henry Knox, Washington's chief artillery officer, introducing the Chevalier Du Portail. *Knox must realize the valuable asset Du Portail will be.*

July 28, 1777, Monday

"Due to the necessity of protecting Philadelphia from possible approach of the enemy by water, the Marine Committee requests the provision of ten fire ships for the Delaware River," John Adams said.

A clerk tapped James on the shoulder. "Will you come with me, please? There are some gentlemen outside who wish to speak with you. They say they have an appointment."

"Robert Morris said that there would be some French officers reporting," James said with a sigh, rising to follow the young man out the door.

Outside, in the yard of the Pennsylvania State House, stood a group of men, dusty and road-worn. As James approached, a sharp-featured, slender young man stepped forward, his hand extended, his smile bright. Those standing behind him gazed at James, their expressions apprehensive. James shook the young man's hand and introduced himself in French.

"I am Gilbert du Motier, the Marquis de Lafayette," the young man said, in passable English. "With me are the Baron de Kalb and his aide, as well as several other officers. We have travelled from France with secret approval from the French government to assist your army." He smiled broadly back at James, apparently delighted.

James's first reaction was alarm. *More French officers, unasked for, unsought, and doubtless bringing more problems? And did we not refuse Baron de Kalb an appointment in March, despite his long service in France?* He glanced at the dignified baron, who returned his look in a determined and stern manner. James recovered himself and tried to be polite, though despite himself his words tumbled out harsh as gunfire.

"Gentlemen, have you any authority from Mr. Deane? Forgive me, but we have had so many officers who have come from France, some who pretended to be engineers but were not, others who came with testimonials which proved to be fabrications. Monsieur Du Coudray arrived with artillerists who had never even seen service. The only instruction we sent was to Mr. Franklin, a request for some engineers, and these at length did come. It seems French officers have a great fancy to enter our service without being invited. Last year we needed officers, but now we have plenty."

He bit his lip, struggling to keep down his anger. *How dare these imposters show up to offer their services and provoke trouble?*

The Marquis de Lafayette stepped back and looked at James kindly, even thoughtfully. His voice mild, he said, "Monsieur, we have no desire to intrude on your service. But due to our strong affection for your country, because of the experience which we bring, the many miles we have travelled by sea, by carriage, and on foot to come to your Congress, we request you consider our placement, as we have only the good intentions for your country and its success. You should have our papers that I gave to the president of Congress yesterday." He paused and his face brightened. "As for me, I request no payment for my service. I only wish to join in your cause, for which I have affection as though it were my own. I cannot speak for my fellow officers," he gestured towards the group, "but for me that is my desire."

Somewhat taken aback, surprised at the humble yet confident tone of the young Marquis, James answered, his tone more moderate, "Congress will consider your offer. I will look through your papers and meet with you tomorrow. Thank you for your patience. For now, I ask you to wait. Please return tomorrow in the afternoon. I will meet with you then."

"Most certainly, Monsieur. *Bonne journée.*" The Marquis bowed cordially, then motioned to those with him to leave. Some looked back at James with startled looks, muttering to their friends. *He must be about twenty years old. So young to be leading such a group. But what else can I do? With the difficulty the surplus of foreign officers has given us, many of whom only seek profit, I can hardly welcome this new group with immediate acceptance.*

The Marquis glanced at James. "*Merci.* We look to conclude this matter within a day or two." Motioning to his companions, he left.

July 29, 1777, Tuesday

At an opportune moment, James stood. "I received yesterday a group of officers recently arrived from France. I will review their credentials and meet with them later today. The leader of the group, a young officer who says he is the Marquis de Lafayette, told me it is his desire to serve without payment."

The delegates were silent, considering this statement. Then Samuel Adams spoke up. "A most unusual request. You should interview the Marquis and discover what he had in mind. Then we could decide on his offer."

Robert Morris added, "Please do meet with the Marquis. Convey to him Congress's apologies for being unable to immediately accept him into our service, but explain we have had a surplus of foreign officers apply lately."

"Yes, I will," James said. "And I will give him our apologies for being somewhat circumspect regarding acceptance of those who come, even with credentials and contracts from Silas Deane."

That afternoon, James read the letters and contracts brought by the Marquis de Lafayette. The young French nobleman's credentials appeared to be in order.

He and Thomas Heyward met the officers outside of the Pennsylvania State House and invited them into the Assembly library. Tired and anxious, their faces creased with worry, the group stood stiffly and uneasily in the crowded space. The Marquis de Lafayette seated himself with James and Thomas at their table. He faced them with calm determination.

"We understand you have travelled a long way to offer your services." Thomas smiled encouragingly.

"*Mais oui,*" the Marquis de Lafeyette answered. "I obtained the contracts from your agent Silas Deane, arranged for the letters of recommendation, and purchased the ship for our departure. My dear wife gave me her leave to seek a place with you. Permission from our king for us to come to your assistance was about to arrive, but I left before it reached us." He smiled engagingly. James wondered how willingly that permission was granted, if at all.

"You must know that America has inspired me from the beginning. The moment I knew she was fighting for her liberty, I loved her. Her cause is mine, that of civil liberty. I met your agent William Carmichael in France, assisting Silas Deane. What he told me of America's struggle moved me to come to her assistance. I carry a letter of introduction from William Carmichael for General Washington. My friends are in agreement. They also have a desire to serve." He motioned to the quiet officers standing nearby.

James and Thomas Heyward exchanged glances. *So young—the Marquis might not be twenty years old. But so confident and self-assured.* He was unusual, James realized. Indeed, he felt his defenses against allowing the Marquis to join the army crumbling.

"What placement did you want for rank?" Thomas asked.

"My training and experience would qualify me at the least for major general," Lafayette answered. "But you need not assign me the rank. I have written a statement which explains my intentions and goals. Please assure me you will read it aloud to Congress. I have made sacrifices for this cause, and therefore I have the right to ask to serve without pay as a volunteer."

James took the paper, noting its stamped seal, and said, "By all means, I will read your statement."

"This is a most unusual request, you must realize," Thomas said. "Are you sure you are volunteering and have no desire to receive pay or rank?"

The Marquis nodded his head vigorously. "*Certainement,* it is my desire. Please inform Congress of my wish. I also hope to find places for my friends." He motioned to the officers listening anxiously nearby. "This is the Baron de Kalb, who served with me at Metz on the staff of the commander, the Count de Brogli. His contract specifies he should be a major general." Baron de Kalb, an imposing, dignified officer, bowed formally. His dark eyebrows nearly met as he regarded James in determination.

We have already read the excellent credentials of Baron de Kalb and declined him an appointment. He avoided the baron's direct gaze and turned to the lively Marquis de Lafayette.

"And this is my associate the Vicomte de Mauroy." He motioned to a young officer nearby, listening wide-eyed to every word. The Marquis then introduced the other thirteen officers.

"Very well," James said. "We will share your statement with Congress and inform you as to their decision."

"Excellent. This is what we ask," the Marquis said. He stood and bowed to both James and Thomas Heyward, who returned the gesture. With a brief smile, he motioned to his company. "*Laisse nous partir*, let us go."

Throwing backward looks at James and Thomas, the officers followed the Marquis de Lafayette out of the Assembly library.

July 30, 1777, Wednesday

"The movements of the enemy are of gravest concern to us, as you know." President Hancock's face was a wall, tense and stern. "Howe has two hundred and fifty sail off the Delaware capes, his destination unknown. The states of New Jersey, Delaware, and Pennsylvania are all in immediate danger."

Is it possible that Howe's presence along the Delaware cape is yet another feint? James wondered. Perhaps if he drew Washington into the area near Philadelphia, the British general would turn and set sail for New England, intent on cutting it off.

Concerned about the northern department, Congress resolved that Major General St. Clair, the commander at Ticonderoga and Mount Independence, be directed to report to headquarters in Philadelphia for questioning.

At a suitable moment, James rose.

"Thomas Heyward and I interviewed the Marquis de Lafayette yesterday and are prepared to lay before you the unusual nature of his request. He and those with him bear contracts from Silas Deane. The Marquis also bears letters of recommendation."

President Hancock nodded. "Please continue."

"The group arrived in June in Charlestown, South Carolina, then travelled to Philadelphia, covering most of the journey of some nine hundred miles on foot. However, travel seems not to have dampened the spirits of the Marquis. He is a nobleman of considerable wealth, a respected officer in France; he purchased the ship that brought the group to America. His desire is to assist the American cause. He left his wife to come to America."

James read aloud from the Marquis's note. "After the sacrifices that I have made in this cause, I have the right to ask two favors at your hands: the one is to serve without pay, at my own expense; and the other, that I be allowed to serve at first as a volunteer."

The delegates were silent at first. *Stunned*, James thought. Then Samuel Adams spoke up. "An unusual request. I recommend we agree that the Marquis de Lafayette should have the rank of Major General. He should serve without pay or compensation, without a command or a promise of one."

"I agree. His determination, his youth, his enthusiasm suggest he has the right to serve in this capacity. America needs friends," President Hancock added. "Are we in agreement?"

All nodded assent. "Aye."

"I will inform the Marquis of Congress's decision. Thank you."

July 31, 1777, Thursday

"General Washington has reached the outskirts of Philadelphia to the northeast at Coryell's Ferry and crossed the Delaware with General Greene's division. We have just received intelligence that the enemy's fleet of two hundred and twenty-eight ships has arrived at the capes of Delaware, leaving no doubt that the city of Philadelphia is the object of their attack." President Hancock fixed his gaze on the assembled delegates.

James felt a sinking sensation in his heart. *Surely, we do not have to abandon our position? The danger might yet be averted. I still do not have a horse.*

"It is imperative that we inform the assemblies of Delaware, Maryland, and New Jersey that they send any available militia with all possible speed to assist in the defense of Philadelphia," John Adams said. His face was solemn.

"I will write them this afternoon," President Hancock said. He turned to James. "It is my understanding that General Washington will be in Philadelphia this evening. Should the Marquis de Lafayette desire to speak with the general, he might find him at City Tavern."

"I will ensure that he is informed," James said. Compared to other French officers he had interviewed, Lafayette clearly stood out for his energy and passion. "Also, I will interview the officers who came with the Marquis. We may have a place for them."

Though, it is also likely we do not have a place, language barriers, funding, and lack of appropriate credentials being what they are.

It was hard to believe that Washington's army was camped only a few miles from Philadelphia. Walking to his boarding house, James could see no unusual disturbance in the streets. That evening at Mrs. Cheeseman's, he was about to settle into his chair to read over the letters and contracts presented by the newly arrived French officers when John Adams knocked on his door.

"General Washington is dining at the City Tavern," he said, opening the door at James's request. "Would you care to join me there? You might without fear of interrupting him make his acquaintance."

James stood up and shook his friend's hand, his movements brisk. "Thank you, yes. I will accompany you to City Tavern."

The first floor of the City Tavern was crowded with army officers and soldiers. On the second floor, General Washington was seated at a round table under a chandelier. Dressed in his uniform of blue with buff trim, Washington was a much larger person than James had thought him to be. Across from him sat the Marquis de Lafayette in a clean, though plain, jacket. The Marquis smiled at James when he recognized him.

John Adams motioned to James. "Your Excellency, this is James Lovell of the Committee for Foreign Affairs."

"General Washington, I am delighted," James said, extending his hand. General Washington stood, revealing his height and solid stance. He towered over both James and John Adams. *Yet he has a grace about his movements that is striking.*

"And of the Committee on Foreign Applications," General Washington said, shaking James's hand. "I have appreciated your communications."

"It is an honor to make your acquaintance." James bowed. "I owe you much for your service and your kindness to me. For now, I would not keep you from your meal—or your company."

"Thank you. Indeed, we have much to discuss. The Marquis here," the general motioned to Lafayette, "is enamored of the American cause. He may prove to be most helpful. We are discussing how he can best serve our army. My good wishes," the general said, nodding to James and resuming his seat.

At a table on the first floor, James and John enjoyed a cup of rum. Having General Washington and his army close by was a relief. The likelihood they would have to evacuate Philadelphia seemed far away. Congress's work would go on.

Chapter 8

Dear Madam

August 21, 1777, Thursday

In the middle of the afternoon, an express rider, sweaty and covered in dust, knocked on the door of the Pennsylvania State House. The young man handed over a thick packet to Secretary Thomson.

"Beg your leave, but General Washington desires Congress be informed of the contents herein posthaste."

"Much obliged." Secretary Thomson shut the door and walked to the front of the meeting room, where he presented the packet to President Hancock.

President Hancock skimmed the contents of the letters. He handed them to John Adams and turned to the assemblage.

"Gentlemen, we will adjourn for two hours, to reconvene at five o'clock this afternoon and consider messages just arrived from General Washington. The Board of War will remain with me during the recess."

Promptly at five o'clock, the delegates returned, in a buzz of conversation. *What now?* James wondered. The Board of War, James noticed, did not appear overly serious or concerned. In fact, John Adams was smiling from ear to ear.

"Maybe we will learn what the British fleet is doing," James said in a low voice to Elbridge Gerry.

President Hancock stood. "Gentlemen, we have letters from Generals Schuyler and Lincoln, giving us an account of the Battle of Bennington. Excellent news worth celebrating. Through great bravery, General Stark and his militia have saved the day."

"Stark? The New Hampshire general who agreed to command only if he could do so under militia rules, not those of the Continental Army?"

"The same," Elbridge answered.

John Hancock's voice was exuberant. "In July, as we know, General John Burgoyne led some eight thousand enemy troops south from Lake Champlain to Lake George. We think Burgoyne's plan was to join Howe, cutting off New England.

78

But his army moved slowly in the heavily forested country. Also, St. Clair's men felled trees across the road as they left, further slowing Burgoyne's progress.

"Burgoyne sent Hessians, Canadians, Loyalists, and Indians to Fort Bennington in southern Vermont to confiscate provisions, including cattle, horses, and carts. But Brigadier General Stark met them with his New Hampshire militia. He captured or killed the force." President Hancock looked up from the letters, his smile infectious.

"This is exceedingly good news for our forces. We should publish General Schuyler's letter in handbills," Samuel Adams said.

"Yes!" the delegates agreed, breaking out in applause. *Victories are so few and far between*, James reflected, clapping his approval.

August 28, 1777, Saturday

James returned to his lodging with an ache in his heart. *Whatever is troubling me?* Though he was engaged in vital business, playing an important part, tremendously busy, he missed his family. He felt like a cog in some enormous machine, functioning but not cared for.

He had moved back to Robert Duncan's boarding house some days earlier. Mrs. Cheeseman was planning to visit her sister in the country; she thought the approaching war unsettling. He was grateful when Robert Duncan again offered rooms for him and Elbridge Gerry.

He needed to review his notes and translate letters in the quiet of his room. The evening sun sank into a brilliant sunset; the birds chirped outside his window. His letters from Mary rested in a neat bundle on a side shelf, their words about home, the business of the family, and the daily struggle to obtain the necessities of life and care for the little ones speaking to his heart. The letters aroused his sympathy for his wife and concern for her condition.

Yet, he wanted something more. A friend, perhaps, who would understand the complexities he must deal with on a daily basis. Vaguely, he felt uneasy. He could not expect Mary to understand the political difficulties of serving in Congress, of speaking for principles while recognizing the opinions of others. Mary's concerns were and always had been those of her family and her community, for which he was grateful. Yet he wanted someone who might understand the issues he dealt with daily.

He remembered what John Adams had said a few days ago about his wife, Abigail. She had been through quite a trial in July, according to John, losing the little baby she had planned to name Elizabeth. John said that she had been unwell, had had a shaking spell, even a premonition that the baby might have been stillborn. It must have been a terribly hard event for her to endure.

Abigail might know Mary, or might meet her. Both women had to bear so much, raising families on their own without the help of their husbands. *Women have to assume roles unusual for them in these times. Both Mary and Abigail deserve respect and consideration.*

He remembered the neat, well-mannered Abigail. She interested him. She was certainly a unique individual, well-read, and informed about political matters. According to John, she understood all he shared with her. Just the other day, John Adams had commented to James that if Howe had a wife as smart as his, she would have put him in possession of Philadelphia a long time ago.

He remembered the map of the Chesapeake and Delaware Bay area he had seen in the Pennsylvania Library. Beautifully drawn, it had presented the entire bay and river system between New Jersey and Pennsylvania, all the rivers and tributaries labeled. A thought struck him. He could copy that map and send it to Abigail. It would help her understand the references made in the news to the movements of the British fleet. She would understand more about where her beloved John lived. She had been under a tremendous stress, lately, after losing the baby. Mary, fortunately, had never had to undergo such a trial. He knew John sent Abigail newspapers frequently. Perhaps she would appreciate the map of the area that was now the focus of the British army. He resolved to prepare a copy of the map for her and send it to her. It would be a friendly gesture. He sighed as he picked up the letters he must read and translate.

August 29, 1777, Sunday

When Congress adjourned, James made his way to Carpenters' Hall, the small, formal building to the east of the Pennsylvania State House. He crossed the parquet floor, his footsteps echoing. On the second floor in the library, he found the book with the map of the Chesapeake and Delaware Bay area, pulled it from the shelf, and placed it on one of the tables. He took out his writing materials and began the laborious task of copying the detailed map.

His artistic ability lent itself to his work and he began to enjoy it. Larger, more important bays, such as the Chesapeake and Delaware, he labeled in a large script. Smaller rivers and tributaries he carefully identified in small, neat writing. For towns he drew little buildings. The task took him a couple of hours. When he was done, he surveyed his rendition. Yes, Abigail would be able to read the map to locate any rivers, bays, or tributaries, as well as major settlements referenced in the newspapers. John would never have time to copy such a map for her. His friend would probably consider his task a helpful gesture. Now he had to write her a note.

He freshened his quill, took out a clean sheet of paper and ink, and composed his message, the long rays of the sun illuminating the quiet space.

August 29, 1777

Dear Madam,

 More than likely General Howe will waste his time this fall between the Chesapeake Bay and the Delaware River. I have copied for you a map showing the part of the country to which the newspapers will frequently refer. I know you give unique attention to the concerns of America in this present struggle.

 This is not the only trait I admire in you, though I will not mention others. I should apologize for any offense my presenting this map to you may cause.

 It is true I could have given it to your husband. But, I could not easily have told him, to his face, that your having given your heart to such a man is what, most of all, makes me yours, in the manner I have above sincerely professed myself to be.

       James Lovell

There, he thought. *I have told her I admire her because of her husband, which is the truth. That is all,* he told himself.

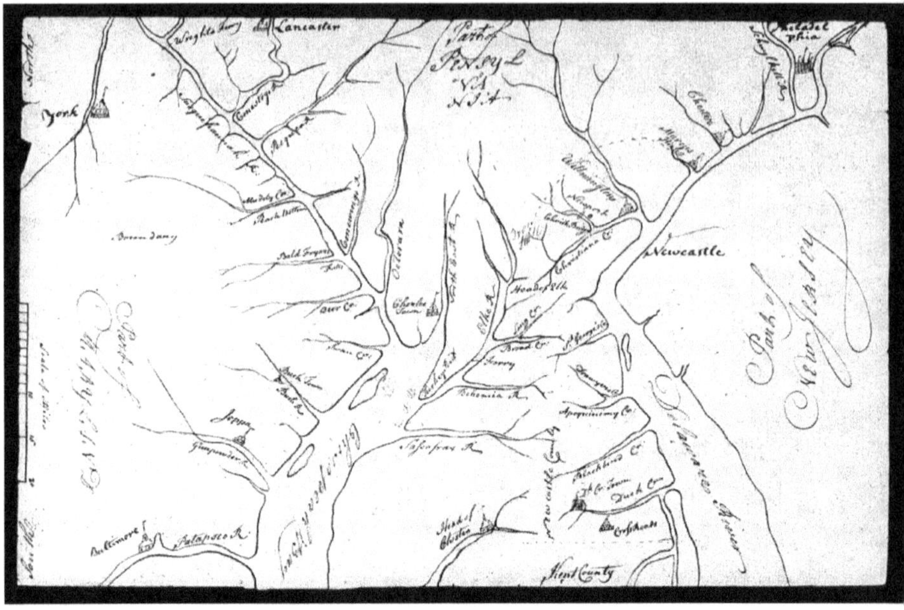

"James Lovell's Map of the 'Seat of War' in the Fall of 1777."
Enclosure, James Lovell to John Adams, 29 August 1777.
Massachusetts Historical Society

Chapter 9

Escape to York

September 8, 1777, Monday

"Are you ready?"

"More than ready." He patted the bundle of papers he carried in his satchel. "I conclude we simply do not need the services of the Baron de Kalb and Viscount de Mauroy."

John Adams bowed slightly to James as a compliment to his work. A fresh breeze lifted the air on their walk to the Pennsylvania State House.

"If I could be home on a day such as this," John said, as the two strolled along the brick walkway, "I would enjoy a lunch made from our fresh produce. Beans, carrots, lettuce—all would be served. What I can afford here cannot compare. How difficult it is to make ends meet on the funds Congress can pay us! I will be sending my servant Turner home today. That will spare me the cost of his room and board."

"My wife would never understand how expensive it is to live here."

"The produce of our farm seems a luxury to me now." John glanced at James. "But I should not complain."

"I have just heard from Mary that she can scarcely find bread for the family. I suspect some merchants in Boston are not above making excess profits in these days."

John nodded, his expression sour. "I wish our army would advance—attack, rather than avoid." He paused on the walkway outside the Pennsylvania State House, his round face flushed with energy. "Washington has a great body of militia, more arriving each day, and a grand Continental Army as well. But the Fabian methods he seems to use—evasion rather than confrontation—only prolong the war. Supplies are so limited. If Stark were in command of the northern department—there we have a stalwart, determined fellow."

"Our soldiers are resolute and hardy. Think of the difference in the two forces. Both our army and that of the enemy are exposed to fever and sickness. At Head of

Elk, morning and evening fogs create unhealthy conditions that sicken General Howe's troops. But our soldiers sweat off fevers, go on as if nothing has happened." James felt proud of the American soldiers, persistent in the face of danger and shortages of food and supplies. They were surely their country's best hope. *And though I am not a soldier, my part, too, is important,* he reminded himself.

"We should be proud of them." John scowled. "Perhaps Washington is right not to risk his army. Yet the Continentals should be able to prove that Burgoyne will run from a fierce strike."

"I agree," James said. "Action is needed." They entered the State House, the Assembly Room quiet.

James settled himself in his chair. "My work on the committee to produce the *Journals* of Congress is at length making headway," he reflected. "I think I could recognize Charles Thomson's handwriting amongst that of thousands."

"Surely a complete record of Congress's work will be important in days and years ahead, though at times our considerations seem tedious," John Adams said with a smile.

James felt a flush of pride. Despite the threat of war hanging over the day, their work went on.

September 12, 1777, Friday

"Your excellency, wake up!"

Sharp knocks beat a tattoo on his door. James scrambled to his feet, grabbed a housecoat, and flung the door open. A messenger, scarcely in his teens, stood there, his face pale and anxious.

"You are needed at the State House right away," the boy said. "President Hancock's orders."

"Thank you," James said, shutting the door. It was still dark outside. *Could it be the city is under attack?* He threw his clothes on, reached the street, and joined Elbridge Gerry.

At the Pennsylvania State House, President Hancock paced near his desk, glancing at the delegates as the room filled up. His unpowdered hair and his rumpled coat showed his extreme haste.

By six in the morning most of the delegates had gathered. The doorkeeper, wide-eyed, shut and locked the door. All turned to the President.

"Thank you for your attendance at this hour," President John Hancock said, standing at the front of the Assembly Room. "We have pressing news from two sources, a letter of yesterday from General Washington's military secretary and another from the general himself. Following an engagement at the Brandywine Creek, General Washington reports his troops withdrew, leaving the enemy in possession of the field. He states that due to a lack of intelligence he was unaware the enemy had crossed the creek at a ford some six miles above his forces. The division under General Wayne and the light troops under General Armstrong were compelled to retire after severe conflicts. General Washington believes his loss of men to be not very considerable, though seven or eight pieces of cannon are ruined."

The delegates' faces turned serious. James thought of the Brandywine Creek, just a day's ride from Philadelphia, running with blood, and the men that would never return home. He gritted his teeth and looked over at John Adams, nearly scowling in his intent focus on the president's words.

"Do we know the extent of the damages to our side?" John asked.

"At this time, no. The Marquis de Lafayette, whom you know rides with General Washington as an aide, was wounded in the leg. General Washington has drawn back his forces to Chester."

There was silence for a few minutes. Then James Wilson, Board of War member, said, "I suggest we give General Washington's letter to the newspapers. Let everyone read about this battle."

"Agreed. Gentlemen, this has been a serious encounter. As it is so near Philadelphia, we must be looking for more news, as well as more information about the casualties. For now, you have as much intelligence as we have received. I suggest we recess for a couple of hours to allow time for refreshment, and then reconvene."

James glanced at Elbridge and nodded. Together they walked back to Robert Duncan's boarding house. The war had moved closer yet. He could not help but wonder, uncomfortably, *will it be at our doors before long?*

September 15, 1777, Monday

Congress met each day over the weekend. The executive council of Pennsylvania was ordered to remove all linens, blankets, shoes, spirits, and other necessaries for the army to secure places outside of the city, in case of invasion by the enemy. All public bells were to be taken down, as they were too valuable a source of metal to be lost.

Reports drifted in that American losses at Brandywine were far more deadly than Washington first indicated. Many soldiers had lost their blankets in the battle, so Congress asked towns in the west of New Jersey, said to have plenty of blankets, to send them to Washington's army.

At the Pennsylvania State House, James met John Adams.

"Philadelphia seems silent; people are keeping close to home. Even the market is at a standstill," John said, motioning to a nearby chair for James.

"With Howe some fifteen miles away, it is not surprising that folks are cautious about venturing out."

"The approach of the enemy threatens our safety. Yet if Howe takes the city, does that harm the cause?" John shook his head in disbelief.

"I think not. Remember, yesterday we resolved to meet at Lancaster, should danger here threaten."

"Have you a horse?"

"A Quaker establishment near the market was more than happy to oblige."

"Howe has caused great anger among the people. Reports are that his troops plundered hen roosts, private homes, and cattle in their path from Elke River. The Quakers especially are greatly disappointed as they were promised security for their property."

The meeting room filled with delegates, readying for the day's business. James put his hand on his friend's shoulder.

"Surely good news will be with us before long." He took his seat with others of the Massachusetts delegation.

"Gentlemen, we have before us a letter from Monsieur Du Coudray requesting that he and others who traveled with him to this country from France fight in the American army as volunteers," President Hancock said. Someone sighed audibly. Everyone knew of the French artilleryman's lengthy efforts to join the American army.

"Has not Monsieur Du Coudray been assisting General Washington in drawing up potential plans for barricades and other fortifications?" Samuel Adams asked.

"That is my understanding, though to my knowledge the general has had no need to use the plans as of yet," President Hancock said. "I recommend we agree to accept Monsieur Du Coudray and his companions as volunteers, with Du Coudray to serve as inspector general of artillery and military manufactures. All in agreement?"

"Agreed," the delegates said, raising their hands. One or two grumbled, "At length Du Coudray gets his way." No one, however, objected to the vote being carried.

Other business followed. Towards the middle of the afternoon, the conversation turned to the need for another major general for the army.

"What of the Baron de Kalb?" President Hancock said.

"The Marquis de Lafayette does speak highly of the Baron de Kalb. However, he is on his way to a seaport in South Carolina, told to return to France," James said, standing. "Perhaps he can be recalled. We could send a messenger to stop him."

"Very good," President Hancock said.

"Would it not be wonderful if the French were to b-b-become our allies," Elbridge said to James under his breath.

"That day may come."

September 18, 1777, Thursday

A stiff wind rattled the windows at Robert Duncan's boarding house. Rain battered the panes, a constant drumbeat.

The hearth stood cold, unlit. James glanced at Elbridge, moodily pacing boards in the sitting room. The Duncan family had left in haste a couple of days ago. Robert Duncan apologized, saying the delegates might remain at their lodging.

"Imagine how muddy the L-l-lancaster road must be, should we need to evacuate." Elbridge stopped his pacing to consider the floods of water swirling in the streets.

"It was more than ill fortune that caused the loss at Brandywine last week. Certainly, knowledge of the enemy's intentions on the right wing of our army was wanting."

"That seems to be the case."

James looked out the window at the bleak clouds, then back to his friend. "Was it not an irony that just when Monsieur Du Coudray had received his commission as inspector general of artillery and military manufactures, he was drowned the following day?"

"The day before yesterday. The Schuykill s-s-swallowed him up, and his horse. They were crossing on the ferry to join the army. Had he not been mounted and in the s-s-saddle at the time, both might have survived."

"Du Coudray was highly regarded by the other French officers," James said. "Yet he caused the outrage of our generals. In fact, though I had nothing personal against the artillery officer and would not wish his demise, I agree with John Adams's private words, that in this circumstance we are saved much altercation."

"He was buried at the Romish church, I b-b-believe."

September 19, 1777, Friday

A harsh knock pounded on his door, waking James from a deep sleep. He sat up in alarm, his heart thudding. *What time is it? It must be after midnight. Perhaps two in the morning.* He got up and opened the door.

A messenger, dripping wet, stood in the doorway. Behind him hovered the servant in his nightshirt, his mouth agape. "Sir, I bring an urgent message from President Hancock."

"Please, proceed."

"President Hancock has just received word directly from Colonel Alexander Hamilton that the British army is in possession of the ford and could be in Philadelphia by morning. All members of Congress are advised to proceed directly to Lancaster, with no delay."

The messenger's words tumbled out, so great was his excitement.

"Good man. Thank you," James said, shaking his hand. "Best be off. I will let Elbridge Gerry here know and I will notify John Adams."

He knocked on Elbridge's door, awakened him and gave him the news, then dressed, putting on his stoutest coat, heavy boots, and warm scarf. He thrust his pocketbook deep into his coat pocket. In it he placed all the cash he had, as well as some valuable lottery tickets he had just purchased for Joseph Whipple, and correspondence he was working on. Thanking heaven he had arranged for a horse, he returned to speak with Elbridge.

"I am going to wake John Adams. I will meet you on the road."

"Very g-g-good. I am nearly ready."

At the nearby stables, James saddled his horse and hastened out into the dark, the rain lessened but the wind moaning. Thick clouds scudded over the moon.

John Adams was startled to be awakened but immediately got up and dressed. He walked down the hall and aroused Henry Marchant of Rhode Island. James waited while they hastily prepared, then all set out on the road to Lancaster, their horses' feet sloshing in the mud.

They saw no signs of an approaching army, or indeed any alarm along the way. The rain let up towards morning. A dairyman waved at them, milk jugs clattering in his cart as he drove. A shepherd with a flock of sheep bade them good morning as they passed a field, the sun rising behind clouds, grass jeweled with rain.

James's thoughts raced ahead. *Surely, the city would not be besieged in just a few hours. There should be a day, perhaps two days, before the British actually enter Philadelphia.* He had left behind items that would be of help to him. He could return, retrieve some mail, and pack some clothing for the days ahead.

The rain had ceased as they reached Bristol, where an innkeeper welcomed them. "Oh, we have several from Congress here already," the innkeeper said, motioning them into a paneled room where a fire blazed. At a broad table, John Hancock and several other delegates were enjoying a breakfast of eggs and sausage. James and his fellow travelers gratefully joined them, pulling off their wet cloaks.

"I have been thinking," James said. In fact, he felt it would likely be days before the British approached Philadelphia. The recent rains, moreover, had swollen the Schuylkill until it would be some time before the army could safely cross. Besides retrieving clothing, he should ensure the safety of the *Journals.* Thomas Paine had left the city with all Congress's vital correspondence to transport it to Trenton in a sloop. William Houston, deputy secretary of Congress, had carted other papers out of the city in casks. And an assistant auditor had hauled out the treasury books, papers, and money. These would be in Bristol, where the delegates planned to take them on to Lancaster. But the printed *Journals* of Congress? Surely, he should check that these too had been taken to a secure place.

"I believe I will return to Philadelphia, perhaps just for a day or two. I should check that the *Journals* of Congress are safe. I also plan to collect some mail I am expecting and pick up clothing and personal articles. I could do the same for some of you, if needed." He looked about at his colleagues.

"Heavens, yes," John said. "Do check on the *Journals*. As to clothing, I would appreciate you picking up some of mine."

Colonel Richard Henry Lee wiped his chin. "I have a bundle of clothing in my room which I would be most grateful if you would retrieve." Several others echoed the request with their own.

"I will do my best to get your articles for you," James said. "And you?" He turned to Elbridge.

"I intend to go on to R-r-reading, where I have acquaintances. Please do speak with Lucy Leonard. I am missing some articles which I l-l-left at her house last I was there, including my s-s-spurs."

"Do return safely. As for us," John said, "our charge is to convey the papers of Congress to safety, those of the Secretary's Office, the Treasurer's Office, the War Office, and so on, papers even more valuable than our own safety. We will leave here and travel through Trenton, Bethlehem, Reading, and so on. We make a wide circuitous route to Lancaster to avoid any encounter with the enemy."

James recalled the wagons he had seen outside the inn, covered with canvas and guarded by vigilant soldiers. He nodded.

"We shall see you in Lancaster," John said, shaking James's hand.

"Godspeed to you all. I will visit with Lucy," he said to Elbridge.

He left the delegates and returned down the road to Philadelphia. The morning was quiet; the skies hung low with clouds. He reached the Pennsylvania State House just after noon.

He found the *Journals* safe in the nearly empty Pennsylvania State House, those for 1775 and 1776 resting in multiple boxes. Congress had ordered over two hundred of each volume, the plan being to distribute them to the states, but so far, the distribution had not taken place. James assessed their bulk. *How am I to have these transported out of the city?*

He decided to ask the printer, Robert Aiken.

Robert Aiken opened the door to his shop, startled to see James. Somewhat reluctantly, the portly printer agreed to help transport the *Journals*. Just as the two were leaving, Robert Aitken's wife, a large woman in a dusty apron, came out on the steps. Waving her hands vehemently, she said, "You are going nowhere. Your daughter is with child, she is due at any time, her husband is gone to the service, and you are not leaving us on our own."

Robert Aitken shrugged. "I suppose you are right. You'll have to find someone else," he said to James.

"But whom could I ask?"

"I do not know." Robert Aitken turned and shut the door in James's face.

Disturbed, James spun about. *Not the printer, then. Perhaps the paper supplier.*

He set off to find Frederick Bicking, whom he knew to be a reliable businessman. Fortunately, he found Bicking in his shop. A slight, balding fellow, he opened the door nearly trembling in a stance of defiance, as if prepared to hold off any number of redcoats.

"What can I do for you?" he asked, a look of relief on his face when he recognized James.

"The *Journals* of Congress: I need them to be transported out of the city for safety. Robert Aitken says he cannot help, so I thought of you. It would take a cart," James said.

Bicking considered for a moment. "I have no cart, but my neighbor, John Roberts, is a miller and drives his cart regularly into the city. He is an honest fellow— a Quaker. He has Loyalist tendencies, you understand, but for a price I am sure he would be dependable. You know how Quakers are."

James shifted on his feet. *What if John Roberts proved untrustworthy?* Yet he had no choice. His contacts were few. Certainly, Bicking was honest, and if he thought John Roberts would be responsible with the *Journals*, he would have to trust him.

"Very well. Will you see John Roberts today?"

"I expect him before long, as I ride with him."

James produced his purse and gave Frederick Bicking twenty dollars; it was all he could provide. "I want the boxes in the Pennsylvania State House taken to John Robert's farm and buried securely. They are located upstairs in the east wing. This must be done this evening. Can you do this and help him bury them?"

"I can." Frederick Bicking seemed relieved to realize what James wanted.

"Very well. Thank you. Congress expects to be at Lancaster, so before long we will contact you to arrange for the *Journals'* delivery there. We rely on you," he said, shaking Bicking's hand.

"And do see to it that they are well buried. Oh, and one more thing. The type sets that William Bradford used to create the first printings of the *Journals* should still be in his shop. Please stop by and get those as well."

"Yes, sir," Bicking said. His pinched, pale face brightened with a smile. "Glad to be of service."

James left the paper shop, hearing the tinkle of the shop bell as he shut the door. It was late in the afternoon, and he suddenly realized his exhaustion. *I must rest.* He reached his lodgings and found the house empty. It took him no time at all to fall asleep; when he awoke, a couple hours later, he was refreshed and starving.

The meal at Bondford's Coffee House revived his spirits greatly. From an officer sitting near him he learned that Commodore Hazelwood had attempted an attack on some of the enemy's ships in the Delaware that day, but the ships had turned and fled. The officer also said that General Washington had crossed the Schuykill and was camped not far from Philadelphia. No plans for a battle seemed imminent.

At the counter, James reached into his pocket to locate his pocketbook. To his horror he found that it was empty. He searched his pocket's depths but came up with nothing. His heart racing, he frantically hunted all about Bondford's Coffee House, retraced his steps, and summoned one of the maids to help him, but found no trace of his pocketbook. *I must have met up with a pick pocket. This is a calamity. What evil genius tempted me to return here? All I had was in there, $260, and the letters as well.*

He searched outside the establishment, then strode down to the wharf, his face fiery with rage. It occurred to him then that not only had he lost all his money, but the fifteen lottery tickets belonging to Joseph Whipple as well. In disbelief, he retraced his steps. The pocketbook had been in his coat when he left his lodging, he was sure of that. Some vile, tricky individual had swiped it from him, perhaps at Bondford's Coffee House. He walked up and down the wharf, returned to the tavern, looked at all the walkways, checked the bushes. *Did I drop it?*

A hoarse voice interrupted his endeavors.

"Be you looking for this?" A workman dressed in a shabby black coat held up a small almanac dangling from a leather strap.

James spun around. "Let me see." He took the article from the man and examined it. "Yes, this is my almanac. It was fastened around my pocketbook. Where did you find it?"

"Down there, on the wharf. I was walking with a light horse man who was carrying a pocketbook with this attached. After we parted, I found this almanac lying on the dock near the water."

"Where can I find him?" James asked, his voice rising.

"Oh, you canna find him. He has ridden off over an hour ago, by what way I know not. He has gone, no mistake about it."

"Thank you," James said miserably. He took the almanac and turned to go back to his lodging. "If you see him again, you can find me at Captain Duncan's home."

"I will, sir, but I know he is nowhere around. Not that one," the workman said with a scowl.

What will I do about the lottery tickets? If the thief sold them, anyone who buys one will be out of pocket if his number wins, as the ticket will be checked and he is not the owner. The possibility of purchasing stolen tickets could well ruin the lottery. Oh, what convinced me to return to this city? I am at my wits' end. The tickets—and my money. How am I to get funds for my family?

James hurried back to Miss Leonard's boarding house. He should at least attempt to give Elbridge's request to Lucy Leonard. He found Lucy and Sarah Yard sitting on their porch, enjoying a glass of sherry.

"Please have a seat, Mr. Lovell," Lucy Leonard said. She retrieved a cup from inside her home and poured a stream of ruby liquid into it.

"You are most kind. Thank you." James took long swallow of the sherry, then a deep breath. His mind cleared, he found himself telling the women of his sad circumstance. "And to think I did not need to come here. Though I have been able to find a safe place to secure the *Journals,* and for that I am grateful."

"It is an ill wind that blows no one good," Lucy said, shaking her head sympathetically.

"I suppose. I came to deliver to you Elbridge Gerry's regards and inquire if you know the whereabouts of his wallet and his spurs."

"Oh, the items that nice young man left here. I think I know what happened to his belongings." She leaned over to Sarah Yard, who smiled knowingly and took a sip of sherry. "The servant of Mr. Marchant, he more than likely took both. And his wife sold them. We have our suspicions," she said, wagging her finger.

"Oh yes, we do," Sarah Yard said. She shook her head in disapproval. "He is a sticky finger, make no mistake about it."

"Yes, indeed," Lucy Leonard said. "But," she added, with a gesture of dismissal, "I would do nothing about it, make no effort to locate the items, as that person's wife is about here still and will no doubt destroy or abandon the items rather than have them found."

"Yes, it is a sad state, but you can do nothing about the loss. Nor can that nice Mr. Gerry."

"I see," James said. "Well, it is a day when pickpockets and cutpurses have prevailed. I will say no more. Good evening, ladies. I thank you for your refreshment and for your company." He stood, shook their hands cordially, and left. The long day was catching up to him. Still in a turmoil as to what to do with no cash to send home, he returned to his lodging.

He passed the night despondent and cheerless. Surely this trip was doomed to cause him pain from the start. He never should have come.

September 24, 1777, Wednesday

For four days, James checked the post for the letters he had expected. A packet did arrive from the Hague, dated June 11, but Congress's agent Dumas had nothing of great importance to communicate, though he indicated both the French and the

Dutch were waiting to offer their support until the Americans had freed themselves by their own efforts.

From soldiers in the tavern, he learned that General Anthony Wayne's division, ordered by General Washington to keep surveillance on the British as they advanced towards Philadelphia, had been surprised a few days ago in an attack near midnight at the Paoli Tavern, about a day's ride away. A messenger reported that Wayne's troops had sustained fire at close range with more than two hundred casualties. Many met their end at the bayonet. Others were taken prisoner. James shuddered to think of the treatment those groaning with wounds or thrown into prison stockades would endure.

Less than a week after he had returned to the city, an officer stopped him in the street, his horse flecked with sweat and mud. The enemy had crossed the Schuylkill and were marching towards the city, scattering American militia in front of them. "I will leave at daylight," he told the officer.

To his surprise, Peletiah Webster, the postmaster of the army, knocked on his door in the evening and urged him to take $200—money that belonged to the state of Massachusetts. Though James knew he had no authority to take the money, he did so, considering it an advance much needed. He thanked Peletiah Webster heartily. *I can be grateful, for either I take this now or I should return to Boston, penniless, to find another position with which to support my family at home.*

Peletiah Webster also asked for his help. One of his nieces who had been employed in Philadelphia by a wealthy family now sought to return to her home in Bethlehem. She was ready to leave in the morning but had no one to accompany her. Would James be willing to see her safely to Bethlehem? He agreed, told Peletiah he would meet the young lady in the morning, and shook the postmaster's hand.

He gathered the clothing he had collected for the various members of Congress and stuffed it into his saddlebags, placing any correspondence that had arrived on top. At first light he would be gone.

Chapter 10

Victory at Saratoga

October 2, 1777, Thursday

It was October 2 by the time James reached Congress, now assembled in York. He took the same circuitous, one hundred and eighty mile route that John Adams and the other delegates had to avoid any possibility of meeting the enemy, finally reaching the quiet community of Lancaster. The first couple of days he rode with Peletiah Webster's niece, a young lady of perhaps eighteen, and found her company very pleasant. Twice they were stopped by British patrols. James was able to state himself the escort of young Mathilda, and the patrols questioned them no further. He heard later, passing the American army, that four lieutenants had been arrested by the British on the same road, so he had much to be grateful for. He left Mathilda with her family at a farm in Bethlehem, thinking of his own children.

Reaching Trenton, he rested two days at the inn, shaken by a spell of fever, sweating and coughing for hours under thick quilts. Eventually, the Quaker innkeeper's administration of tea with honey and warm compresses brought him back and he sat up, rejoicing in blue skies for the final days of his journey and newly aware that there were some helpful aspects to Quakers after all.

As he was paying his bill at the inn, the innkeeper told him of the battle that had just occurred outside of Philadelphia. "At Paoli's Tavern," the man said, pushing back his spectacles and wiping his hands on his apron. "More of a massacre than a battle, they are calling it." He grimaced. "The British attacked General Anthony Wayne's battalion, taking a thousand men. They made use of their favorite tool, the bayonet. A cruel and nasty thing, war."

James shuddered. "I heard of that attack before I left Philadelphia. The number lost is even greater than was first reported." He shook the innkeeper's hand, grateful for his help.

He was wary of unfriendly faces everywhere but found none. In fact, the countryside seemed at peace, farmers tending their fields, women gathering vegetables. He found the Lancaster Courthouse empty, or nearly so, except for an elderly servant clad in black who informed him that Congress had gone on to York after a one-day stay in Lancaster. The next day he reached York, a town of about two thousand on the far side of the Susquehanna, a safe distance from a potential threat. The brick courthouse commanded the town square. Next door under russet oaks stood a tavern, the upper story half-timbered, the lower constructed of hewn logs. A number of the delegates sat there at a long table, the door opened to the fresh air.

"Glad to see you, James," Elbridge said, moving over to offer James a seat. "Welcome to the Golden Plough T-t-tavern. You look ready to return to b-b-business."

"I am pleased to find you," James said, sitting down. The delegates passed pitchers of cider and plates of bread, cheese, and sausage down the table, enjoying the repast.

"Down the street is a boarding house run by Mrs. Henricks," Elbridge said. "She may have room for you. John Adams, S-s-samuel Adams, I, and several others are lodging at the large house General R-r-roberdeau has rented."

"I have been successful in bringing your clothing and other goods. However, not your belongings," James said, turning to Elbridge Gerry. "Lucy Leonard says don't waste your time trying to regain your stolen spurs, as they are probably long passed on to other hands, but do warn John Adams's friend Mr. Marchant concerning his servant. He was likely the thief."

"Thank you for your efforts," Elbridge said. "You are back just in t-t-time; we are about to t-t-take on the Articles of the Confederation, again."

"I am more than happy to be back," James said. He drained his glass and looked about at his fellow delegates.

"You may obtain fodder for your horse and other supplies from the commissary general of provisions," John explained. "And you have to pay for such goods."

"I took my own carriage when I left the city," Henry Laurens said. The rice planter from South Carolina apparently did not lack for funds. "At Bristol I was called upon to take with me the Marquis de Lafayette, who was wounded in the leg at the Battle of Brandywine. I left him at Bethlehem to recuperate at the inn."

James looked around at his companions. *How long might Congress make its seat here?* "It seems likely that General Howe will remain in Philadelphia this winter, while our army rebuilds."

"General Burgoyne's plan is to join General Howe, if he can," John said. "Ever since he reached Lake Champlain earlier this summer, he has been maneuvering to meet up with Howe and cut off New England. He forced the evacuation of Ticonderoga and our retreat to Albany. Yes, John Stark obtained victory at the Battle of Bennington, but Burgoyne made gains by taking Freeman's Farm, near Saratoga, on September 19, though at a high cost in casualties."

"We heard that General Gates argued with his s-s-subordinate, General B-b-benedict Arnold, during that conflict," Elbridge added. "General Arnold disagreed with Gates's orders. They exchanged s-s-strong words. Following the b-b-battle, Gates removed Arnold from command."

"An evil day for me as well, September 19. I returned to Philadelphia to retrieve clothing and goods, then my pocket was picked by a light-fingered thief. I did retrieve your clothing," James said, gesturing to Colonel Richard Henry Lee and Elbridge Gerry.

"We appear to be safe here," John said, standing. "General Daniel Roberdeau, delegate from Pennsylvania, is expecting me. I hope your accommodations at the boarding house down the street prove acceptable. General Roberdeau and his two sisters are kindness itself."

He found the boarding house, a vine-covered, two-story affair a few blocks from the courthouse. Mrs. Hendricks, the landlady, looked him over and at once offered him lodging, her weathered face crackling with pleasure. Round, short, she led him up the stairs, puffing slightly with the effort. In her thick German accent, she said, "Here, you sleep. And here," she pointed down the hall, "Reverend John Witherspoon." Short and stout, her dark hair piled on her head in an absurd bun, she fingered the long chain she wore, her key ring dangling from its end. "My room," she said, pointing to the end of the hall, "there. I appreciate quiet in my home."

"You may be assured of that," James said. "I will be working most of the time." He noted the unpainted wood lining the hallway. "Do you have stabling for my horse?"

"*Nein.* The stable is down the street. Breakfast, dinner, downstairs. In the *stube*," she gestured.

Stube? James wondered. Aloud he only said, "That will be fine." *Any port in a storm,* he thought. He would have to sell his horse. It was unlikely he would travel any time soon. He wondered if Congress coming to York had presented an economic opportunity for the thrifty Pennsylvania Germans.

James climbed the creaking stairs to his small bedroom. *Before long I may have occasion to regret the lack of a fireplace here.* The house had but one chimney, set in the center, a characteristic of German homes. The chimney heated the upstairs just enough to keep water from freezing. He set down his writing tools, threw cold water on his face, and lay down. Before long he was asleep.

In the night he awoke, startled. He sat up, sweat beading his forehead, his heart thumping like a horse in a race. *Again?* It had been weeks since he had found himself suddenly jolted from sleep, his mind chasing phantoms. He had been running, running—just where he could not remember. Like a hare before the hounds, he had dodged British pursuers, papers flying from his hands despite his desperate attempts to secure them, his stomach reeling at the loss of his pocketbook. He took a deep breath, resolved to regain calm. *Just a dream.* But he sat for some time, 'til his breathing evened, 'til the pounding in his head lessened. He wrung a cloth out in cold water, placed it on his forehead, and lay down, his heart slowing.

When was the last time I thought about my wife? He wrote her every week, if at all possible, sent money regularly, and remembered his children in his letters. Mary's red curls had faded to gray when he last saw her; her laugh came less frequently; her hands were roughened and cracked from cooking and caring for a family. Aside from the few weeks he had been home after his release from prison in Halifax, they had been apart for over two years. Now she had taken up the burden of raising their family, while he had joined Congress. Their lives had altered. Mary was strong, committed to her family, and able to handle difficulties as they arose. He sighed and wiped his forehead with the cool cloth. *War has many casualties*, he reminded himself. His own overwork would not cause his.

"York County's First Courthouse."
From the collection of the York County History Center, York, PA

October 8, 1777, Wednesday

"In truth, my hand is all but completely worn out from writing," James said to Elbridge. "As Mr. Paine is not here yet, I am doing all the writing for the Committee for Foreign Affairs." The two sat at the Golden Plough Tavern by the fire in the evening, enjoying a tankard of beer before retiring to their rooms. The chinked log square room was nearly empty, except for a couple of townspeople playing chess near the door. Through the diamond windowpanes they could see the wind ripple grass in the town square like waves on the sea, bringing a hint of coming winter.

James gestured to an iron box, about two feet by three feet, that protruded from the whitewashed wall of the tavern. "What is that?" he asked.

"That is a jamb stove. On the other s-s-side of the wall, it opens to the large kitchen hearth. The servants put coals in the iron stove so it heats this room. A local c-c-contrivance of German origin, I understand." Elbridge nodded at the stove, its sides impressed with scrolls, flowers, leaves.

"Had Congress the power to tax, we would be less dependent on the good will of nations across the seas. Meanwhile, General Gates and the northern army held their own against General Burgoyne last month at Bemis Heights, again demonstrating Gates's capability and that of his commanders."

Through a window Elbridge watched the lamplighter raising his pole, lit wick flickering on its end, setting a lamp aglow. "Then there was the engagement at G-g-germantown."

"General Washington writes that his advance to the northwest of Philadelphia at Germantown, four days ago, was an utter failure, but apparently one that was occasioned from deep fog rather than any fault of his own. He attempted to attack General Howe's troops camped outside of Philadelphia. The men could scarcely determine who their own forces were and whose were the enemy's. They retreated despite the general's attempts to rally them."

"No doubt the s-s-smoke caused by cannon and muskets worsened the fog. I understand not many men were taken," Elbridge said, turning from the darkening window to the candlelight within.

"Yet the loss of the Delaware River, coupled with the occupation of Philadelphia, makes one wonder what new advantage the enemy might soon possess. Now the Northern Army, under General Gates, gives us confidence.

"General Gates's army is strong and gaining in reinforcements every day. And an aide of General Gates states that the testimony of prisoners, deserters, and American troops who have escaped capture by the enemy concurs that the enemy lost possibly one thousand and two hundred men—killed, wounded, or missing at Bemis Heights. General Burgoyne himself suffered a rifle-ball in his shoulder. Their provisions are severely lacking. In a word, their situation is growing desperate. Before long, we may be able to proclaim success over Burgoyne and his forces."

"Such v-v-victory would be good news, indeed," Elbridge said.

"I believe I will retire to my room," James said, rubbing his temples. He drank the last of his beer. "Our day does not end at four in the afternoon. A good rest might help."

"I could use a qu-qu-quiet evening, as well." Elbridge Gerry stood and shook his friend's hand.

October 18, 1777, Saturday

The morning of October 18 dawned fair and clear, the deep blue sky a harbinger of a crisp fall day. James arose early to complete some letter writing. Wearing his jacket, he was tolerably comfortable despite the chill.

By nine, he joined Reverend John Witherspoon for breakfast. Reverend Witherspoon had lost his son in Washington's attempt at Germantown. James accepted his fellow boarder's quiet with sympathy. Mrs. Hendricks brought in plates from the kitchen to the stube, which turned out to be the other room downstairs, warmed by a jamb from the kitchen fire. Apparently, it was a common fixture in Pennsylvania German homes.

With a squint and a perpetual pout in her expression, Mrs. Hendricks placed the plates before the delegates. *Potatoes again*, James thought, and glanced at Reverend Witherspoon with a forced smile. She specialized in potatoes, they had realized. They had whipped potatoes with gravy for dinner, potato hash for the occasional noon meal, and potatoes with sausage for breakfast. Perhaps a Pennsylvania German specialty, though more than likely Mrs. Hendricks was having to scramble to find food. York was not a large town, and the influx of dozens of people who came and went—Congress, officers, soldiers, merchants—must put a drain on the town's resources.

He left the boarding house soon after breakfast and was pleased to encounter Richard Henry Lee of Virginia on his way to the courthouse. He fell into step with the tall Virginian, now a member of the Committee for Foreign Correspondence along with Benjamin Harrison. It was he who had initially made the motion to declare the states free and independent from Britain during the First Continental Congress.

"Our request to several states for clothing for the army can't be too strong. In truth, our soldiers are desperate for clothing, blankets, shoes," James said. He coughed, a dry, rusty rattle.

"Our states need to supply those articles," Richard Henry Lee said. His voice rose over the clatter of a cart carrying pumpkins and squash. The driver, a black man with a tri-corner hat, clucked at his donkey. Richard Henry Lee motioned lightly towards the man with his left hand, the one missing four fingers—the result of a hunting accident. He kept a black silk cloth wrapped around it. "Surely not a slave," he said quietly.

"In these parts, it is unlikely."

"Slavery is an abomination," Richard Henry said. "At the very least, we need to outlaw the trade. At best, it would be abolished. I must admit, I have slaves who work my plantation or who are employed in skilled crafts. One cannot be profitable in growing rice without them. But years ago, I presented a motion for the Virginia House of Burgesses to eliminate the trade, and I have continued to support that change."

"I agree. In my mind also it should cease." They reached the York Courthouse, the door of the formal brick building standing open like an invitation, and entered the square courtroom. A dozen delegates were there, arranging their papers and visiting. John Hancock sat at the front of the room at a table raised on a platform, talking with Secretary Charles Thomson and his assistant.

Five tables, each covered with a green cloth on which were placed writing utensils and a candle, stood to either side of the president's table. Several wooden round-back armchairs were arranged at each. To the rear of the room stood rows of benches for those attending a trial. Steep stairs in a back corner led to an upper floor. There was no fireplace, a fact James had noted on his first day there, but a handsome ten-plate iron stove was positioned in the center of the meeting area, decorated with scrolls and medallions, its pipe extending to the wall at one side of the president.

Richard Henry took a seat in the armchair near to James. "What did you think of the change Congress made yesterday to the Board of War?"

"Three permanent members, assisted by clerical staff, should be more effective than several members of Congress whose time is divided with other duties," James said. He looked about the room at the number of vacant seats.

"Yes, we are down to scarcely two dozen," Richard Henry said. "The problem of desertion is not limited to the army."

"Even our president wishes to be absent. It surprised me that John Hancock a couple of days ago requested a leave of absence from Congress and the presidency."

"He has been most dependable and consistent, leading during many a crisis for over two years."

Benjamin Harrison entered the room and seated himself beside Richard Henry, smiling a greeting to James. "It appears the ship has sailed," he said, indicating President Hancock, who stood to open the session.

In mid-morning President Hancock startled all by announcing he had an important message to share.

"Gentlemen, we have received notice of vital information," President Hancock said. Samuel Adams, who was about to bring up the Articles, sat down abruptly. "General Gates reports to us in a letter of the 12th of October that what he characterizes as a warm and bloody fight broke out on October 7th at Bemis Heights, near Saratoga, at the same place as last month's conflict. General Gates's divisions carried the field, capturing some of the enemy's defenses, forcing General Burgoyne to retreat.

"Gates regrets to inform us that the gallant General Arnold, fighting even though he was relieved of command, owing to the disagreement he had with General Gates, suffered a musket ball to his leg and was further injured when his horse was felled by a shot and landed on his leg. General Lincoln also had a leg shattered by a musket ball. General Gates reports that General Burgoyne wrote him a note stating he left his whole hospital, some three hundred wounded soldiers, in Gates's protection. Mark you, Burgoyne has neither the resources nor the provisions to attend to his own wounded."

President Hancock looked up from the letter and glanced about the room as if to emphasize the plight of the British general.

"In addition, General Gates reports that as the British retreated, they burned all the houses before them, including buildings and mills that belong to Major General Schuyler." The delegates drew in their breath and mumbled in outrage at this act of unnecessary spite.

"We look forward, gentlemen, to more information from General Gates. It would appear he has the enemy on the run." There was the hint of a smile on President Hancock's pale features.

"Excellent news," John Adams said. The delegates applauded.

At four in the afternoon the meeting broke up. "We await the next move from Gentleman Johnny Burgoyne," James said.

"The Foreign Affairs Committee should meet later to write to the American commissioners and share the excellent news," Richard Henry said quietly. James nodded agreement.

"Like a game of chess, it is," Richard Henry said. "Only with more deadly and far-reaching consequences."

October 20, 1777, Monday

"So, what do we think happened?" James said to Elbridge Gerry. He took an empty space on the bench at the Golden Plough Tavern. Delegates filled the dining area, all talking loudly about the exciting news reported by the chairman of the Committee of Safety at Albany. General Burgoyne and his whole army had surrendered to General Gates. Elbridge gestured to John Adams and thrust a forkful of potato into his mouth.

"The news we r-r-received seems authentic," he said, speaking around the potato.

"If we just had official word," John said to Richard Henry Lee. "Not even a line from General Gates as of yet, and no statement from General Washington."

"For now, all we have is the letter Cornelius Harnett received from the Albany Chairman of the Council of Safety." Richard Henry glanced at the delegate from North Carolina, seated to his left.

"Yes. The account we received relates the surrender of General Burgoyne and his whole army on the 14th of October, though we do not have the particulars as of yet. In celebration, General Washington ordered thirteen cannon to be fired, while the bells in Albany rang for hours." Cornelius Harnett looked quite solemn, but his eyes twinkled in excitement.

John cleared his throat. "I would feel greatly relieved if we had word directly from General Gates. Surely the general can trouble himself to inform us of such a momentous event," he said. He stabbed his cabbage with displeasure.

James helped himself to ham and potatoes, his mouth watering. A gathering at the tavern such as this was unusual, the delegates generally too busy for unofficial meetings. A barmaid filled tankards, then disappeared into the small bar in the corner.

"If this is true, it would be the best news we could possibly receive," James said.

"A toast to c-c-courage and success," Elbridge Gerry exclaimed, raising his glass.

We will be back to the Articles tomorrow, God willing, and looking for the arrival of an official statement of General Gates's success.

October 31, 1777, Friday

The rain had finally abated. A cold wind drove streams of muddy water along cobblestone streets and mucky paths. The boarding house developed a leak in the roof in the upstairs hall; water had been dripping into a bucket outside James's door. The servant, a crusty older fellow with unkempt gray hair who stayed in the unheated *kammer*, a room on the ground floor, and the landlady kept up their long-standing feud over whether the servant should climb the shingled roof to repair the leak. The old fellow, who spoke with a thick German accent, built the fire in the kitchen each morning. Even so, the house was cold enough that James shivered while hastily dressing. Meanwhile, the cook took ill. Mrs. Hendricks turned out tough biscuits and overcooked pork, a scowl on her face.

To escape the cold and begin his work, James arrived early at the York Courthouse. The servant smiled at him, whistling and piling split logs onto the fire in the iron stove. With a twig broom he swept the nearby area. *About the same age as my son Johnny*, James thought, and took a seat near John Adams, already at work.

"We have yet to hear directly from General Gates of the surrender of Burgoyne. Such a lackadaisical performance I have never encountered. It is enough to make one lose patience," John sputtered. He slapped his papers down with audible disgust.

"Surely, we will soon. I wonder what could be keeping the news."

"It was ten days ago that we heard from General Washington, who forwarded to us General Israel Putnam's letter announcing the surrender and enclosing Governor

Clinton's letter with intelligence that on the evening of the 14th, the capitulation was signed. General Burgoyne and his entire army became prisoners of war.

"In celebration, General Washington presented a *feu de joie* for his troops. Have you ever seen one? It is quite a sight. The brigades line up, then blank cartridges are fired from one end of the line to the other and back, all in succession. Very martial and inspiring."

James nodded approval, imagining the sight.

"Between us," John Adams said, "I am grateful it was not Washington who delivered this victory. It is enough that we have heaped such praise on him. Yes, our commander-in-chief is capable, but he is not the only general in the Continental Army. We need to avoid the suggestion that he is a savior, deserving idolatry."

"I am glad you say this. Whatever reason has caused the delay in General Gates delivering information, he is deserving of recognition."

"Just so," John agreed. The door opened and several delegates filed in. "We begin. The Articles await."

The first Articles bound the Confederation together in a league of friendship, each state having one vote, James recalled. *We have approved the first through the fifth articles. The fourteenth article, the powers of Congress, which we discussed for three days this week, is not yet completed. The sixth, giving the central government the sole power to declare war and requiring each state to maintain a militia, has been hung up on questions of wording. Perhaps today we will finish those discussions.*

Secretary Charles Thomson stood. President John Hancock had left the assembly two days before, after a final farewell speech. Secretary Charles Thomson would conduct meetings until Congress chose a new president. The secretary called the meeting to order and led the group in prayers. He then motioned to a young messenger in military dress standing near the door, looking nervously about the room, his blond whiskers shaggy. *Possibly*, James thought, *our visitor is all of twenty years old.*

"Allow me to present an aide to General Gates, Colonel James Wilkinson. I believe he has a message of importance for us."

Colonel Wilkinson cleared his throat, as if apprehensive, and glanced about the room. His voice surprisingly strong, he said, "From General Gates to the Congress. The capitulation of General Burgoyne and his troops, and a letter from General Gates." He stepped forward and held out a thick packet, bowed slightly, and retreated a few steps, as if wishing to be out of sight of the assembled delegates, all eyeing him with interest.

"And we are just now receiving it? It has been two weeks. Unbelievable," Samuel Adams muttered.

Secretary Thomson took the packet, opened it, and read aloud General Gates's statement. The general presented the Convention of Saratoga, by which Burgoyne surrendered himself and his whole army to the American general's hands. He noted that the enemy troops were now under guard, marching to Boston, on their way to return to England. General Gates added he felt the event was the more glorious since it was achieved with little loss to the army of the United States.

"And we have a copy of the capitulation, signed by General Burgoyne," Secretary Thomson said. He held up a packet, splashed with sealing wax. "For the review of the Board of War." He handed the document to John Adams, whose smile of pleasure lit up his face, but who glanced in quick disapproval at the aide to General Gates.

"Thank you, but we have questions regarding the state of the army and that of the enemy," John said. "Are you prepared to answer them?"

Wilkinson stammered, then regained himself. "Not at present. I have not had liberty to arrange my notes, so if you will give me until tomorrow, I will be pleased to entertain any questions you might have."

"Certainly. Tomorrow it is," John said, returning to his seat with the packet. He paused and turned back to the secretary. "On this great and momentous occasion, it is only suitable that a committee be selected to consider recommendations for the states for a day of thanksgiving and celebration." He looked about the room.

"Hear, hear," several agreed.

"The ayes have it. Do we have suggestions for a committee?" Samuel Adams, Richard Henry Lee, and Daniel Roberdeau's names being offered, they were chosen.

"What say you? Should we extend Congress's thanks to John Hancock?" someone asked.

"He did his job. Like any other entrusted with that position. Congress needs to remember that his office, like all public offices, must be undertaken with the zeal and attention which it requires," a voice answered.

"I move that it is improper to thank any president for discharging the duties of the office," a third voice said.

After two votes, the resolution carried. *We can always offer our thanks as individuals,* James thought.

"We agree it is improper to thank the president of Congress, at least officially, for merely doing his job. So, liberty is upheld," James said to Elbridge, as the afternoon concluded.

"So be it." Elbridge shrugged.

The day's business concluded, the delegates prepared to return to their lodgings or to meet for committee work. Richard Henry rose from his chair and crossed the room to speak with James.

"The Committee for Foreign Affairs should meet this evening to write to the commissioners and offer the momentous news. Surely this victory will change the minds and hearts of the French court. We can hope for more assistance, maybe even an open commitment."

"And we are the committee, so we will meet and draft our letter," James said in agreement. "Our office is available."

"The law office of James Smith, on South George Street near the Square," Richard Henry Lee said.

James thought of the small room allotted to the Committee for Foreign Affairs. Private, it nevertheless was at times interrupted by outbursts from the Board of War, assigned to the larger room in the same building. It was cramped, smelled of tobacco and old papers, and frequently unheated. "First, a bit of refreshment?"

"A drink is in order," Richard Henry said, with a smile.

**"The First County Courthouse and Adjournment
of Continental Congress at York, Pa., November, 1777,
on the Reception of the News of Burgoyne's Surrender."**
Library of Congress

Chapter 11

A New Board of War

November 1, 1777, Saturday

"This is delicious," James said with approval.

His host's sister laughed, her glass beads swinging. "Apple crumble makes a fine conclusion to a meal."

He was pleased to accept the invitation to dine at General Roberdeau's home. John Adams had been praising the general's hospitality since they came to York.

The room smelled of roast beef, cinnamon, and roses. Dried floral arrangements in porcelain urns flanked the hearth.

"I look forward to returning to Philadelphia," Ann Clymer said. "I open my home there to boarders since my husband passed away. My house is not far from the State House. And I miss my grandchildren."

"Perhaps I might inquire as to a room at your house, when we return," James said.

"I would be more than happy to accommodate you. Now, you must excuse me." She turned with a swish of her skirts.

"General Howe may not remain in Philadelphia long," John said.

"I understand that Howe and his troops are eating all Philadelphia has in its stores and ransacking the countryside for produce. Meanwhile, our naval captains on the Delaware prevent the British from resupplying their provisions. We think that before next summer they may be forced to abandon their hold on the city."

"That would be good news. Did you hear Samuel Adams's jest directed to Colonel Wilkinson?"

"No, but I would be glad to hear it," the general said.

"Samuel suggested Congress should vote the colonel be presented a horsewhip and a pair of spurs." John smiled at the joke, while the others laughed. "The nerve of that young aide. Keeping such important information from the governing body of the country while entertaining himself along the road."

Daniel Roberdeau gestured to the glass decanter near James. "Please help yourself to rum. I am in the business of producing and shipping it."

James poured himself a cup, admiring the amber liquid, and passed the bottle across the table.

"Before the war, my distillery in Alexandria was turning a profit. Now, my investment in privateers not only offers me a return in goods, such as sugar, rum, and cocoa, as well as thousands of pounds of British money and silver coins, but makes an excellent stumbling block to the British navy." Daniel Roberdeau set his cup down with an emphatic gesture.

A child's voice sounded in the stairwell, punctuated by the clatter of a falling object.

"One of my sisters will be seeing to her," General Roberdeau said, with an anxious look at the door.

Muffled sobs and footsteps echoed in the hall.

"How many children do you have?" John asked.

"Four, none older than fourteen. A boy, the oldest, then three girls. It is a great responsibility. Since my wife died last winter, having my sisters with me has been a relief."

"I cannot imagine my own children without their mother. You must be grateful to have your sisters here," John said.

"With their help, I can continue service in Congress. And my business ventures allow me to contribute substantial sums to Congress. Also, I have another proposal. Our army stands in great need of lead for bullets and ammunition."

"What do you suggest?" Richard Henry Lee asked.

"There is lead to be mined in western Pennsylvania. If I could finance finding a good vein of lead and set up a mine, it would greatly benefit the war."

"Excellent idea," James said. "Lead is vital to our armaments and in scarce supply."

"There are the problems of the Indians and the Tories," John said.

"It may require a small force to protect the mine from Indians, to say nothing of Loyalists," Richard Henry Lee observed.

"I envision just that sort of thing."

"And Henry Laurens is now president of Congress?" Mrs. Clymer asked, returning with a pitcher of water.

"Indeed, he is. He is the vice president of South Carolina, a man of order and efficiency, who has travelled and traded in Europe," James said. "All but he himself voiced their support in the affirmative to vote him into office."

"And we settled on a day for an official thanksgiving for the victory at Saratoga over Burgoyne's forces," John reminded the group. "It will be December 18, giving us time to send out a proclamation of a day to offer thanks."

"Let us raise a toast to the victory at Saratoga and further victories to come." All stood. James was once again aware of how large Daniel Roberdeau was. *He is at least a head taller than I am and twice as heavy.*

"We should not allow Burgoyne's troops to return to England before this conflict finishes, no matter what the capitulation says."

"We are in agreement there," General Roberdeau assured him. "We should not permit those boats to sail."

November 10, 1777, Monday

James glanced at the letter on the corner of his table, a single sheet written in a distinctive elegant hand. He felt like the magpie he had seen once, eyeing a shiny silver button, stepping towards it with delicate, mincing steps, head cocked to watch for interruptions, eyes focused on the prize.

He had postponed reading Abigail's letter since receiving it a few weeks ago, as he was busy with many affairs. She had written to him in response to his letter of the end of August, in which he had enclosed a carefully drawn map of the battle-contested area of the Chesapeake. Tomorrow, John Adams would return to Braintree for a visit to his family and could take his letter to his wife. *With all the letters I write regularly, why is this so difficult?*

No interloper into her private affairs, he thought of her as a friend. Certainly, that would meet with John's approval.

He picked up her letter and unfolded the delicate paper. In it, she wrote of her extreme dismay when she saw it was addressed to her from a member of Congress, from a delegate she knew to be a friend of her husband. "Ten thousand horrid ideas" had rushed upon her, fears for her husband's safety. When she finally summoned the courage to open his letter, she could not even read it right away. Eventually, the map James had created for her fell out, and she realized the purpose for his writing. Only then had she been able to read his letter.

"Your professions of esteem, Sir, are very flattering to me. No person possessed with common humanity can be an inattentive unconcerned spectator of the present contest," she stated. *She alludes to the war's constant presence in our lives. And she states her gratitude to me for my suffering, a reference to my trials in prison at the hands of the British.*

Finished, James set the letter down. *Truly, our part in this conflict, the "present contest," as she calls it, totally consumes us, takes us from our families and loved ones, and keeps us constantly agitated, afraid of the news of tomorrow and yet looking forward to it. At least she did not take offense at my writing.*

With a sigh, he took up his pen and wrote a short letter to Abigail, expressing his concern for her and sharing congratulations with her on the joyous news of Saratoga. He carefully stated that with this letter he hoped to provoke no disagreeable alarm for her, as he had done with his last letter. He apologized for causing her fright, stating his letter was intended to be "a well meant but indiscreetly-managed compliment from one of her admirers." He closed by assuring her of his affectionate esteem.

I want her to think well of me, and thus I must speak to her of my high regard for her. John Adams is her husband, that says much for her, even if she had no other admirable qualities. But add to that the excellent particulars that she is well read, manages her home, farm, and family on her own, and holds the respect of her husband—surely those attributes indicate an individual of taste, distinction, esteem.

From a conversation he had had with Elbridge Gerry the day before, James knew that before long Congress would formally invite John Adams to be commissioner to France, replacing Silas Deane, who would soon be recalled. Elbridge had told John of the plan, and John had assured him that likely he would accept the post. *So, John will be traveling before long to France. I will write to Abigail to reassure her of his safety and send her news in his absence, since I receive all the news, and likely will read far more of his writing than he will have time to write to her. Unless of course she travels with him, in which case I can still be of service to her—and to him.*

He smiled to himself, folded and sealed his letter, and set it aside to give to John Adams in the morning. His friend would be pleased that he would be able to keep Abigail informed in his absence. Having Abigail Adams as a correspondent seemed a marvelous prospect.

November 15, 1777, Saturday

"Are we ready?" James looked up from his stack of papers at Richard Henry Lee, just entering the door at the York Courthouse. An icy wind swirled snow through the open doorway. The tall Virginian entered and stamped his feet.

"To my knowledge, yes, as my weary head attests." Richard Henry Lee placed his satchel of papers near his seat and removed his coat. A fire cracked and sputtered in the stove. The young caretaker briskly arranged a stack of split wood in a brass container. Through the tall windows black branches whipped in the wind, under a gray sky.

Two days ago, their committee had made minor adjustments to the wording for Article Four, which secured free travel and commerce between the states for citizens. They improved Article Twelve, in which the Confederation accepted the war debt incurred before the passage of the Articles. Finally, as part of Article Nine, they had finalized Congress's right to settle controversies regarding the boundaries of the states. The committee had given their work to Secretary Charles Thomson, who wrote out two final copies of the Articles of the Confederation. Yesterday, the committee had reported to Congress the results. And last night, the committee had reviewed the Secretary's neatly written final copies.

"And today's the day," James said with a long sigh. "We will approve the Articles of the Confederation."

"Then we expect that all the states will ratify them," Richard Henry Lee nodded. "Have you the draft we discussed of the circular letter to accompany the Articles when they go to the states?"

James selected a page from his stack of papers and held it up. "Here it is. Just under the Articles." He read aloud.

To form a permanent Union, accommodated to the opinion and wishes of the delegates of so many states differing in habits, produce, commerce and internal police, was found to be a work which nothing but time and reflection, conspiring with a disposition to conciliate, could mature and accomplish.

Richard Henry eyed the document with approval. "We have done our best. We may not be as General Gates, who rightly received a commendation from Congress for his success at Saratoga, but our successes are vital, be assured."

The door opened and Henry Laurens entered, followed by a number of delegates. They stamped their feet and removed outer wraps as they took their seats. Henry Laurens, tall and dignified, greeted Richard Henry and James with a smile and strode to his table at the front of the room on its raised platform.

James glanced up at the map of the colonies tacked to the wall near the president's table. *Thirteen states. Would the Confederation unite them more fully?*

"Congress is in session," announced the president. Henry Laurens turned to Secretary Thomson, who passed him a letter. The room became quiet as the delegates stopped their conversations to listen.

"First on our agenda today, gentlemen, is the request from General Washington contained in his letter of the 11th. Chief Engineer Duportail, commander of all engineers in the Continental Army since July, is in charge of the defense of the Continental troops, including the use of *chevaux-de-frise* and embankments. General Washington recommends a promotion for Duportail, from colonel to brigadier general. The Chevalier Duportail has served with distinction, his experience and knowledge invaluable."

Henry Laurens glanced at the delegates. "We will take up the promotion of Duportail in a couple of days, when time permits."

"In General Washington's letter of the 11th," the president continued, holding up a page, "he states the distresses of the army due to want of clothing and blankets. The general explained that seizing supplies from the local people near his encampment only causes bitterness. Therefore, he requests that Congress address the states as to fulfillment of their quotas as early as possible."

President Laurens looked up from the letter at the members of Congress. The delegates, scarcely twenty in number, shifted uneasily in their seats.

Richard Henry Lee stood. "We resolved to inform General Washington that months ago, Congress requested the commissioners in France provide clothing for eighty thousand men. We have heard that we may expect that shipment before long."

Samuel Chase of Maryland added, "We also agreed to remind the general that Congress passed a resolution giving him powers to take provisions and other articles for the army and in exchange provide certificates."

"Yes, but these actions seem just what the general is loath to do." President Laurens looked about the room solemnly, his fingers touching in an arc as if summoning patience.

"We have requested the states supply clothing, blankets, and other needs for the army. I move we resolve to send an extract of General Washington's letter of the 11th to nearby states, urging their immediate response." Eliphalet Dyer of Connecticut glanced shrewdly at the others.

"I am in agreement. Are we in favor of the suggested resolve?" President Laurens said.

"Aye."

"We have before us today, gentlemen, our final work on the Articles of the Confederation. Are the Articles complete?" he asked the committee members.

The three committee members stood. "They are," James said. "The details we discussed are added and the language finalized. The circular letter is drafted, as well."

"Then I will ask for a vote. Gentlemen, please respond aye or nay to the approval of the Articles of the Confederation."

Nearly in unison, the delegates responded "Aye."

"Then if we are in agreement, we will ask Secretary Thomson to prepare thirteen copies, one for each state, to be sent out with the circular letter. We will expect the states to approve the articles, though it may take them some time to do so, as they are considerably tasked with needs as of late."

An understatement if ever there was one, James thought. *Yet we have made progress. Compromise on the manner and form of the Articles, for certain. Each state will have one vote on matters in Congress, still the sole legislative body. Each state will raise funds for the use of the central government. The Articles unite us in purpose and goals.*

"We have more business for today. Three foreign officers, French, have applied for positions. One, I understand, Lafayette has endorsed. Let us turn to their consideration," President Laurens said.

James picked up his report from the Committee for Foreign Applications. He thought briefly of John Adams, on the road to his family. For a moment he wished he too was on the road home. Then he pushed the thought aside and began his report.

November 21, 1777, Friday

The Golden Plough was crowded with congressmen. Some stood in a corner, tankards in their hands; others jostled one another for room at a table. A couple of townspeople sat near the iron jamb stove. The room smelled of wood smoke, tobacco, and cinnamon. As James passed, he heard one of them, a bearded workman with dusty clothing and a barrel-like chest say, in a thick German accent, "The longer the lot of them stay, the more my pockets are lined. With the action —or lack of it!—from their army, they'll be here a long time."

His companion laughed and was about to respond when he saw James's gaze directed to him. He smirked, and said, "Come on, then. We're done here." The two pushed back their chairs and left.

James frowned, but turned to his companions. *What good would it do to speak to such comments?* And besides, he was tired. Six days out of the week Congress met from ten in the morning until evening, with a break at four in the afternoon, followed by committee meetings or other appointments. Even Sunday, following church, was usually spent catching up on paperwork. James had not rested in months.

A short, handsome person standing with the group caught his eye. His silver hair shone, combed back, and his dark eyes flashed as he addressed those about him. James recognized the quartermaster general, Thomas Mifflin. Mifflin had held the post of quartermaster general since last August. He had resigned from it in October, but Congress accepted his resignation in early November, asking that he continue in his post until they could choose another to replace him. James took a tankard of cider from the bar and joined the group.

"James, you know General T-t-thomas Mifflin, Board of War member?" Elbridge Gerry said.

"We have met," James said, shaking Thomas Mifflin's hand. "I trust you are well."

"Thank you for your sentiments. But have we a third for the Board of War?" Thomas Mifflin turned back to the group, speaking emphatically. "In fact, I believe we should have five members." Those present nodded agreement.

"We can bring the motion up soon. S-s-such business cannot wait," Elbridge said.

"Adjutant General Timothy Pickering has agreed to be on the board. Adding more members should be a priority." Thomas Mifflin's eyes darted about, as if to secure his listeners' agreement to his proposal. He continued, "In fact, I would like to recommend the former Commissary General Joseph Trumbull for his knowledge of supplies and materials, Richard Peters, the old board's secretary, and General Horatio Gates as the other board members. I appreciate your support."

The delegates around him nodded approval. *Surely General Gates's knowledge and abilities would suit the position well,* James thought.

"I fear the inaction of the army, now idle while the British strengthen their hand in Philadelphia, has caused the loss of Fort Mifflin and soon Fort Mercer," General Mifflin continued, with a slight sneer.

"We can commend the efforts of Commodore Hazelwood and Colonel Greene commanding gunboats and galleys to keep British ships from reaching Philadelphia. But the general in charge of the army," here General Mifflin lowered his voice significantly, "disdained to strengthen Fort Mifflin and Fort Mercer, so they are vulnerable."

"We must prevent the British from s-s-supplying Philadelphia," Elbridge agreed, his tone sour.

"Your observations are significant," James said, meeting General Thomas Mifflin's gaze solemnly. "We commend the heroism of those defending the forts. I fear I must excuse myself, gentlemen." He swallowed the last of his drink, bowed, and turned.

As he was leaving, Richard Henry Lee stopped him by the door. "You will remember that today I moved to recall Silas Deane. We thought we had fully concluded that decision in August, but it was tabled. Now we have the approval to write, as the Committee of Foreign Affairs, to inform the commissioner of his recall."

"Silas Deane has caused problems with his indiscriminate promises to French officers. Yes, we should compose a letter to him soon."

He stepped out into the street. The sky was clear, and the stars spread a spangled view. A layer of snow covered the kitchen garden behind the Golden Plough Tavern.

Reaching his residence, he sat down to the dinner his landlady had saved for him, his head ringing with worries and concerns. The beef stew tasted surprisingly flavorful—one of the best meals he had eaten in the rustic, pine-boarded *stube*. He finished his meal in silence, then climbed the stairs and entered his room, propping his door open to permit the warmer air in the hall to circulate. Wearing his coat, his hands icy, he took out his writing materials and set to work on a letter to Joseph

Whipple, the brother of his friend William Whipple, whose lottery tickets had been stolen from him.

Joseph had sent to James the numbers of William's missing tickets. General William Whipple was on assignment with his regiment. With care, he explained to Joseph that he had sent the list of ticket numbers to Baltimore to be published as a warning that a pickpocket might try to sell them. That was the least he could do to try to prevent an unfortunate purchase.

His conversation with those at the tavern and General Mifflin came back to him. It was regretful that Forts Mifflin and Mercer had been taken. *What was the main army doing, if not attending to such needs?* "As long as the war continues," he wrote, "three times more men will be lost in the main army by marching and countermarching over hills and through rivers than in battles." In frustration, he added, "I should deceive you greatly if I led you to look for anything favorable from the main army." *A sour statement, but pretty much my sentiments.*

He concluded the letter, then folded, addressed, and sealed it. *We are left to feed and clothe an army throughout the inaction of a long winter.*

He felt justified in his sense of disgust. *But we must persevere, despite the obstacles. Things do look bleak right now, but the war wears on. We can but do our best.*

November 28, 1777, Friday

James found his senses awakened as the aroma of baked bread filled the *stube*. He poured himself a steaming cup of tea and placed a slice of fresh bread on his plate and nodded good morning to Reverend John Witherspoon, already piling his plate with food. A heavy, energetic man, Reverend Witherspoon kept up with many of his duties for Princeton College as well as for Congress.

The night before, he had been up past midnight writing a letter to General Horatio Gates. He had urged the general to come to York to head up the Board of War, as Congress had voted yesterday. He shared his concerns with the general that the Fabian tactics of the commander required many new recruits, while the naval departments fell into disgrace.

After breakfast, he wrapped his coat and scarf on tightly and stepped out, leaving Reverend Witherspoon to finish his meal. Drifts of snow obscured the forms of fences and paths.

The courthouse door swung open and the young caretaker cheerfully waved him in, his shovel in hand from clearing the steps. "Come in, come in. The fire is going."

James shook off his coat and took a seat near Richard Henry Lee, seated near the stove reading a gazette. He opened his satchel to prepare for the day.

"I wrote to General Gates yesterday evening," James said to Richard Henry, holding up a folded page. "I encouraged him to accept the position of president on the Board of War, to which Congress invited him yesterday. If it were not for the defeat of Burgoyne, we would be in a very disagreeable position. We need all the capable leadership we can summon."

"Brigadier General Thomas Conway made it clear his choice for president of the Board of War was General Gates."

"General Thomas Conway." James half closed his eyes in thought. "I remember when the *Amphitrite* brought the first group of French officers here, those recruited by Du Coudray. Thomas Conway's name headed the list of the officers. An Irishman, with the French military.

"And since May, apparently he has been successful as a brigadier general. However, in late September Congress received a letter from Conway, complaining that General William Alexander, Lord Stirling, had placed Baron de Kalb above him in rank. He was outraged because Silas Deane had assured him that de Kalb would never be placed above him. In France, Thomas Conway outranked Baron de Kalb. The man can carp.

"And consider the story that Colonel Wilkinson said he heard on his slow journey here to deliver the news of Saratoga to Congress. Apparently, Wilkinson learned from an aide to his superior, General William Alexander, that General Gates said he had received a letter from Thomas Conway in which Conway criticized the commander-in-chief as a 'weak general.'"

"Such will do Conway no good in the sphere of generals he must work with," Richard Henry observed blandly. "I have heard something of the sort myself. But until we know more, we should not be too sure that he really meant to disparage the commander. Complaints from officers can only cause unpleasant consequences to our country and its cause."

"True."

"On the other hand, Thomas Mifflin has made it clear he thinks Gates's knowledge and authority to be necessary to effect changes in the army." Richard Henry Lee wrapped his black silk handkerchief smoothly about his damaged hand. "I myself need a rest. I am looking forward to returning to Virginia in the near future. I must address my health."

"You will be sorely missed. And John Adams will not be in attendance in Congress for some time, as he will likely accept the position in France for which he has been nominated."

The door swung open and Henry Laurens entered, followed by several delegates. Taking his seat, the president looked about the room, his long face firm, his expression confident.

"Gentlemen, we must work together for the good of our country to provide necessities for the army in this bloody and expensive war. We agreed to require taxes in the amount of five million dollars during the year 1778, to be paid quarterly from the states in equitable proportions, rather than just proceeding on credit. We must remind them of this responsibility. Also, I recommend we send a committee to consult with General Washington regarding the best means to carry on a winter's campaign."

"President Laurens, I nominate Robert Morris, Elbridge Gerry, and Joseph Jones for the committee to confer with General Washington in his camp," Richard Henry Lee said, standing.

"All agreed? So chosen," Henry Laurens said.

"A matter of great importance now requires our attention," the president said solemnly. "We are recalling Commissioner Silas Deane. As we choose his replacement, keep in mind that our commissioners should be able to negotiate a treaty of alliance with France. And they should be firm in their commitment to our country."

"On November 21, we nominated commissioners to the court of France. I now call for a vote."

After the votes were counted, to no one's surprise, John Adams was elected commissioner. Elbridge Gerry leaned over to James and said quietly, "I told him before he set out for Braintree. Modestly, he responded that he was not certain he was deserving of the honor."

James nodded. "We will write to him our congratulations later. He will be quite adept in that capacity, once he learns some French."

"To assist the commissioners at the court of France, I submit we appoint William Carmichael, merchant in France, to be their secretary," President Laurens added. "Are there other reports?"

Elbridge Gerry stood. "The committee on p-p-provisions for the army reports that fresh food should be issued to p-p-prisoners in the east, while s-s-salt provisions should be reserved for the army of the United States in the next campaign. The expense of preparing salt provisions r-r-renders them worth securing for the army's use.

"Very good," President Laurens said. "There being no objections, Congress so resolves."

James looked about at the tired group as the hours went by. *We are the country's sole power for peace and war, to paraphrase the Articles of the Confederation.*

Hours later, he opened the door of his room and stepped in. It was cold. He propped his door open, then with his coat on prepared to write to John Adams.

> *Elbridge Gerry would have penned a letter, but he begs you to excuse him as he must leave in the morning to travel to the camp of the army along with Robert Morris and Mr. Jones. Their committee of three will have a confidential conference with the general. In fact, I hope they will realize that nothing good will come of the army retiring to winter quarters.*

What benefit is an army in retirement? he wondered.

> *Some of the recent troops have been arriving extremely well attired. They must be wearing the clothing shipped on the* Amphitrite, *never delivered to the army until now.*
>
> *I encourage you to accept the commission that has been voted today for you. Your great sacrifices of private happiness led Congress to hope you will accept. Though you do not yet know the language, you are well suited to the business. Confidentially, Doctor Franklin's age alarms us. I urge you to study the language while on the ship's passage. A French gentleman should be able to assist you. Though I am hopeful of your acceptance, I imagine your dear amiable Partner may dislike my recommendation for you to travel farther from her than Baltimore or York Town.*

He folded and addressed the packet, then placed it on the stack of papers for the courier in the morning. He wrapped a muffler about his neck and crawled under the covers, shivering for some time before his bed finally warmed and he slept.

Chapter 12

Valley Forge

December 1, 1777, Monday

Richard Henry Lee looked at James quizzically. "Are you able to join me? We need to inform the commissioners of the reasons for the return of the French officers who arrived under Monsieur Du Coudray."

James yawned and pushed back his papers. The day had been long and tedious, much of it spent on matters of pay, the auditor general William Govett's soft voice reviewing disbursements for purchases with such patience and steadiness that he had caught himself falling asleep. He shook off his tedium.

"Certainly, my dear fellow. We can compose a letter at our office. I doubt that Thomas Paine will be present to assist us in writing."

"Thomas Paine does well enough when he is here, making copies and filing papers. But he is often gone, and even when he is here one has the sense he is not—not truly focused on our work."

The sun had set; the sky was a deep blue velvet, the early dark of winter. A brisk wind rattled the windows. Around them, the delegates picked up their papers. Those present, a small group of no more than about fifteen, were somber, subdued. *Perhaps I am not the only one who finds long business matters tiresome. Though important. It is all important.*

"I am most pleased we will not be allowing Burgoyne's army to sail from Rhode Island this fall," James observed.

Richard Henry nodded agreement. "General Howe's request to have the prisoners ship from Rhode Island would enable the British to return their troops to England in time to have them rejoin their forces here in the spring. We need not be in the business of resupplying General Howe's troops."

"If indeed we do permit those troops to leave at all. True, it is a burden to feed and house them, but why would we send nearly six thousand men back to England when they will only come back to confront us? It is war."

"I am sure we will return to the question before long."

118

"In addition to the letter regarding the French officers' return, we should write to the commissioners explaining the progress of the war and General Washington's current situation. We can inform them of the completion of the Confederation and our progress with taxation." James stood, but sat back down as sudden comprehension dawned.

With enthusiasm, he continued. "We really have much to be pleased about. This year the enemy began with two armies. Now one is beaten and has been forced to lay down its arms. Forts Ticonderoga and Independence on Lake Champlain have been surrendered to us, and while they are destroyed, they can no longer serve as defense.

"I would add that we had a near victory at Germantown; General Howe is fortunate the weather, as well as the unseasoned nature of our young troops, saved his day, when he might have lost all. Philadelphia cost Howe at least four thousand troops."

Richard Henry held up the fingers of his right hand, ticking off more positives. "And for our forces, General Washington has now eighteen thousand troops positioned fourteen miles from Philadelphia."

"We must convey some of this good news. We have not heard from the commissioners since the 25th of May, though they likely have written us several times—messages lost to us. And we need to request a loan of two million in sterling. We could then withdraw some of the paper we have printed from circulation to put us right until we have taxes flowing in."

James leaned back in his chair, his hands clasped behind his head. "If war broke out in Europe it would be to our benefit. It would force Britain's navy to deal with those of France and Spain and open commerce with our allies that is currently denied to us. We have products, such as tobacco, naval stores, rice, and indigo, desired by countries in Europe, yet the superior fleet of the enemy renders their shipment nearly impossible. Further, we contracted with the Farmers General of France to send them four hundred hogsheads of tobacco some time ago and have not been able to do so."

Richard Henry Lee nodded. "Overall, we have many positive circumstances to communicate to our commissioners."

Both stood and reached for their coats.

"I find it interesting that the Marquis de la Fayette is cut of such different cloth than Du Coudray," the Virginian said, tying his woolen muffler about his neck. "General Washington, who is clearly impressed with Lafayette, requested Congress permit his appointment to the command of a division in the Continental Army. Congress is quite willing to honor that request, particularly as General Greene just reported that in the Jerseys the Marquis happened upon a picket of the enemy, killed twenty, took twenty, and wounded many others with no losses. Lafayette seems delighted with the militia and General Greene remarks the Marquis seems determined to risk danger. His bravery sets an example for all."

"He is a valuable officer," James agreed, thinking of the young French noble's love of liberty and devotion to the American cause.

"Shall we?" He stood.

"At your service," Richard Henry Lee responded.

It should not take us long to write the letter, James thought, pulling his scarf tightly around his neck. *We have been through the substance.*

December 8, 1777, Monday

"To conclude the matter of recalling the commissioner, the Committee for Foreign Affairs will write to the Honorable Silas Deane and direct him to return to America at his first opportunity and travel straightway to Congress."

"Thank you, Mr. President. The committee will be happy to oblige," James said. He almost turned to Richard Henry Lee, usually sitting at his elbow, but then recalled the affable Virginian was no longer in attendance. He had departed two days ago on leave, his silk-wrapped hand waving farewell from his carriage as it pulled out on the icy rutted roads. *I am the committee, so I will write that letter myself, thank you.*

"We have received a letter from our committee at camp." President Laurens picked up a packet.

The room grew quiet.

"General Washington shared his officers' sentiments about mounting an attack and choosing a place to quarter the troops during the winter. The delegates were discussing with the general whether a winter's campaign would be advisable when they were interrupted by the approach of what seemed to be the entire of General Howe's army, now posted opposite the right wing of the American army. The committee expects an attack, but none has occurred as of yet."

The listeners drew in their breath.

"There was skirmishing between the militia and the enemy the day before. One officer was wounded, another officer and a couple of privates killed. At the same time about fifteen British and Hessians were taken prisoner. Because of these events and the impending engagement likely to take place, the committee has postponed further discussions."

"The committee is pleased to inform Congress that the army is much stronger than it has been. They pray God grant our forces resolution and spirit. I might add we can look forward to the committee's recommendations about improving discontent among the officers."

"We should hear before long regarding the engagement, if there is one," Francis Dana said, speaking for the group.

James fetched the small warmer box from his room and carried it down to the kitchen. He had discovered the iron container under his bed. When he realized it would hold coals to heat his room, he wondered how long it would have taken Mrs. Hendricks to inquire whether he would like to use it. Reaching the kitchen, he held it out without a word to the old servant, who sat with his feet on the hearth smoking his pipe.

Reluctantly, the old fellow got up, filled the box with coals from the fire, and handed the iron container to James, a scowl on his face.

"Thank you," James said, taking the smoking box by its wooden handle.

"Yah, *gut*," the servant said mournfully, returning to his seat.

In his chilly room, the warming box gave off just enough heat for James's teeth to quit chattering. He decided to wear his heavy jacket as well as his woolen muffler. The iron box he placed beside his table on a piece of slate. It gave off the smell of burning pine, a pleasant odor.

James picked up his quill and sharpened the end with his pen knife. *Lately, clerks in Congress are as scarce as hen's teeth, so I must shoulder the burden. First order, write to Silas Deane. Then to John Adams.*

He refilled his ink bottle and lit more candles. *My eyes are weary, and no wonder. Reading and writing, day in and day out.* Outside, the dark night sky was clear and peaceful, the stars bright. A cloud scudded over the moon.

> *December 8, 1777*
> *Sir,*
>
> *By accident I find myself called upon singly to execute the duty of the Committee for Foreign Affairs in communicating to you an order of Congress of this day respecting your return to America. The order stands in need of no comment from the committee to elucidate it, and being drawn in terms complimentary to your abilities of serving these United States upon your arrival here, I take pleasure in conveying it, being, Sir, Yours.*
>
> *James Lovell*

He signed the letter with a flourish. *There. I have spread a small plaster over a great sore. It will be Congress's pleasure to question Mr. Deane, at length, and meanwhile we have the steady John Adams in Paris.*

It was well past midnight when he set down his pen. The night watchman had passed his window some time ago, his cry of "All's well" swallowed up in the frosty air. He folded the letter and enclosures to John Adams into a packet and then stacked it with the letter to Silas Deane. He rubbed his red-rimmed eyes and blew out the candle.

December 16, 1777, Tuesday

"General Gates may be here by Christmas, mark my words." Thomas Conway, newly appointed inspector general, perched on a chair to the rear of the York courthouse, his dark, hawk-like eyes fixed on his listeners, his head held high in an arrogant pose. To his right, Francis Lightfoot Lee, member of the Board of War for Congress, listened intently.

"And General Gates plans to stay here this winter, I understand," Francis Lightfoot said to Thomas Conway.

"He is indeed. He will take the home adjoining the Golden Plough Tavern. Meanwhile, I am working on a plan for training the troops that I intend to submit to the commander-in-chief." Thomas Conway's smile was smug, his eyes darting from President Henry Laurens to the delegates seated near him.

Only three days ago, Congress had unanimously voted Thomas Conway inspector general, even though he had recently submitted his resignation. *Probably testing the waters as to his popularity, though it appears he has his supporters. At least it appears General Howe has withdrawn his troops, so besides the enemy without we can now contemplate the enemy within.* James smiled to himself uneasily.

He turned to Francis Dana. Recently arrived in York, Francis Dana, delegate from Massachusetts, was an acquaintance from Harvard.

"President Laurens told us last week that he had received a letter from General Gates, sharing that General Washington had written to him. An unknown person had sent Washington extracts from Thomas Conway's letters criticizing the commander. General Gates was careful to explain that he did not know who would have sent the statements to Washington. He wished to have Congress informed of the matter to better be able to apprehend whoever had done it. I believe he used the word 'punish.'"

Francis Dana nodded. "I think we have known about this unfortunate libel since November. Colonel Wilkinson let slip the information that Thomas Conway had sent General Gates a letter judging Washington harshly. The wording, if I have it right, alluded to a 'weak general and bad counselors.'"

"We heard the story," James said with a shrug. "Criticism should not hurt anyone, but in these times, should there be division among the officers, it could be disastrous. Further, if the enemy caught wind of it, it would be quite harmful.

"I can imagine that if Washington feels threatened, as he may well, he will ride it out. I am sure we all want the same: the success of our army." James looked up to see three cloaked and booted figures entering the courthouse.

"The committee has returned from camp," James observed. "We can look forward to a report."

President Laurens stood. The servant dropped a load of wood by the stove with an awkward crash and muttered an apology.

"Good morning, gentlemen. Among other business, we must provide time for Colonel Rawlins to speak with us regarding the information he has of treatment of our prisoners at the hands of the enemy. And we have our camp committee, returned." He turned to Robert Morris, Elbridge Gerry, and Joseph Jones, now seated. "May we hear the report?"

Robert Morris strode to the front. Speaking for the group, he said, "After the threat of conflict with General Howe's forces dissipated and the enemy retreated to Philadelphia, we reviewed the recommendations of the officers. We concluded with General Washington that the troops must be put into winter quarters, the most proper that can be located.

"An attack on the enemy's lines would be too hazardous at this time. If our forces were to approach Philadelphia over the frozen Schuylkill River, it would allow the enemy full view of our movements and permit them to employ a line of redoubts about the city."

"Our troops want for necessary clothing and b-b-blankets. Also, the officers s-s-suffer from uneasiness and indifference," Elbridge said, rising from his seat.

"A winter's camp would allow for training, reinforcements, and preparation for spring, when, with renewed health and vigor, the army would be set for a campaign," Robert Morris continued. Joseph Jones nodded agreement. "The army should occupy a post that would offer clear sight of advance of the enemy, access for supplies, wood, water, and forage, and comfortable quarters for officers and soldiers.

"The general is considering the recommendations of Brigadier General Duportail, chief engineer for the army. Duportail advocates establishing a winter camp near Wilmington, close to Philadelphia, so that when the Schuylkill freezes, we could attack—a situation that will keep them respectful of us. He also notes that encampment will deprive General Howe from roaming and foraging into the country, eliminating a source of provisions for his army. Howe will be prevented from extending his control of the region, depriving him of opportunities to recruit and add to his forces. And we would be close enough to strike, should we choose."

Robert Morris placed the committee's report before the president.

President Laurens cleared his throat and stood. "Thank you, gentlemen. I suggest we allow this report to rest while we consider all it suggests. I also request that Congress meet daily until one o'clock in the afternoon, recess until three o'clock, and then resume meeting.

"And, I would have you remember that in two days, on December 18, we observe the day of thanksgiving proclaimed for our good fortune in success on the battlefield as well as in surmounting our difficulties. The states are all informed and will celebrate the day as they each determine. Services will be held that morning. We will convene in the afternoon. Until tomorrow, gentlemen."

December 25, 1777, Thursday

Christmas came and went with such swiftness that James was astonished. The delegates took a day off from meeting. Most attended services at Christ Lutheran church, then returned to their lodgings to rest.

James had received a lengthy letter from Mary the week before, assuring him of his children's well-being and inquiring if he could send her a payment for winter clothing, buttons, and thread. He sent his family his good wishes along with a slightly larger amount of money, though he knew it would not be enough. Thinking longingly of his family, he put in a note to each of his children.

Mrs. Hendricks spread a fine dinner for the occasion: roast goose, whipped potatoes, raspberry tart, and mince pie. Her lips pursed, she ladled gravy in silence, perhaps worried about the state of her larder. Reverend Witherspoon, returned recently from a leave of absence, enjoyed his meal with evident gusto. He related stories of his imprisonment at a Scottish castle after the Jacobite victory; a terrible time, according to him. James listened with sympathy, saying little of his own trials, then made his way to his room as soon as he finished eating, collapsing when his head hit the pillow.

Rising in the dark of early winter, he found himself refreshed and energetic. The memories of prison guards' violent curses and moldy bread for days on end had fled. *At least for now, God willing, I can rest in peace.* He fastened on his heavy coat, met Reverend Witherspoon in the hall, apparently on the same errand as he, and together they strode through the snowy streets to the Golden Plough Tavern. A wreath of holly and red berries festooned the outer door of the tavern. The square room, smelling of freshly split wood and spices, was crowded with townspeople, congressmen, and officers. The tavern keeper, a jovial, heavy fellow with a thick German accent, ladled cups of steaming cider to his guests from a large bowl. Sugared biscuits glittered on a plate like sand dollars at the seaside.

A group of delegates stood near the jamb with President Henry Laurens. James joined them, his hands cradling a cup of the spiced cider.

"I was so indisposed I could not set my feet to the floor for days. Having the strength not only to get out of bed but also to cross the street is a great improvement." Henry Laurens nodded seriously, his face pale.

"We are glad you are on the mend," Reverend Witherspoon said. "Your work is invaluable, be assured."

"I have heard from my son John recently, lieutenant colonel and aide de camp for General Washington. I am relieved to say he is recovering from the wound he suffered at Germantown—a musket ball through his shoulder. He reports the army has not yet fixed upon the precise location for their encampment. The site must be defensible and allow a bridge over the Schuylkill for protection. Once they have chosen a situation, they will construct huts. Meanwhile, they have no tents, so sheltering in the snow must be terrible." Henry Laurens's voice was scratchy and raw.

"The heights that run from the r-r-river there may prove to be an excellent location," Elbridge Gerry said. "Those great hills extend for miles into the c-c-country."

"We should hear before long what Washington decides. The army is hardly in condition to withstand winter weather without permanent housing."

"The officers are demanding half pay when they leave the s-s-service and pensions for their widows, considerations General Washington s-s-supports. These benefits may improve their resolve, if we can see our way to it."

"I can only imagine how hard this time must be for our troops. They lack tents, their shoes are broken, their clothing is tattered. And what have they for food? We have no commissary general at this time, Colonel Pickering having resigned. General Washington writes he is reluctant to force nearby farmers and villagers to relinquish their food supplies, though that would be acceptable under military law," Reverend Witherspoon said.

"Yet, as Washington commands the territory of his army, should he not obtain supplies from the villages nearby?" James said. He didn't wish to seem impatient with the general, but surely that was the obvious answer to the needs of the army.

"Congress has resolved exactly that, as we must remind him," President Laurens agreed.

Just then the door opened, letting in a gust of snow. General Horatio Gates entered, stamping his feet. Homely in appearance, his thinning gray hair cut short, he shook off his cloak. His hazel eyes, while short-sighted, missed nothing. The delegates present greeted him with a round of applause and three cheers. General Gates bowed and gave the group his warm, fleeting smile.

He turned to James nearby and grasped his hand. "It is good to see you," he said.

"We will be pleased to have the pleasure of your company, General," James said.

"Our paths will cross before long, I am confident." He shook hands with those thronging about him, then left with the innkeeper to arrange for his lodgings at the adjoining house.

James turned to see Mrs. Clymer near the door with a friend. Holding a black fur muff, she and her companion were laughing at some private joke.

"Good evening and season's greetings," James said to her. "You are brave to step out in this weather."

"My friends the Eichelbergers invited me to this gathering," Ann Clymer said. "Martin Eichelberger, the tavern keeper, built the Golden Plough over thirty years ago and still runs it. I brought them some sugar biscuits for the holiday." She gestured to the nearby silver tray.

"These are yours, then. Allow me to offer you one." James held out the tray.

"Thank you. It is good to see you," she said, withdrawing her hands from her muff. "I hear we will not have our friend John Adams with us for some time."

"Indeed not. However, he goes to France to improve our relations, a task I am confident he is well prepared for."

"I hope his voyage is peaceful."

"My respects of the season," James said with a bow. He turned to the door of the crowded, busy tavern. *Enough holiday cheer. I have work to do.*

Wrapping his muffler about his neck, he caught a glimpse through the kitchen of the dining area of the house now occupied by General Gates, the table set with fine blue and white china, candles twinkling, a glistening plum pudding resplendent on a platter. *Very well. Gates can live there in style. It will give him time and opportunity to confer with the Board of War.* He was surprised that Thomas Conway, newly appointed inspector general of the army, had not been present in the tavern. He and Gates seemed to be in agreement on many topics.

He stepped out to the dark of winter as others entered the crowded room. *York offers few choices in establishments. Yet we are safe and our work goes on. If only we had a letter from the commissioners. We have heard nothing from them since the 26th of May. It is difficult to piece together the attitude of foreign courts with so little communication.*

December 31, 1777, Wednesday

The last day of the year. An eventful time, the days passing from hope to calamity and back to hope. Even now, it seemed to James that their endeavors hung by a thread, the difficulties so outrageous that only by the most persistent of efforts could success even faintly be envisioned.

At least now the army's winter encampment had a name: Valley Forge. Some eighteen miles northwest of Philadelphia, the camp's situation had all the benefits suggested to General Washington by chief engineer Duportail. Twelve thousand soldiers, accompanied by some four hundred women, cooks, washerwomen, and nurses, and their children, were beginning to build huts. That many people would make a sizeable city, one of the largest in the United States.

All morning Congress had been dealing with business matters, payments and disbursements, tedious and tiring.

At one in the afternoon, the group took its recess. James found the apple and bread he had pocketed at breakfast. The room quieted, some working, others leaving for the warmth of a tavern.

Yesterday, late at night, he had written to John Adams. He had confided in his friend the greatest risk that he knew existed: that the army would be disbanded before long, as the commissary and quartermaster's departments were in shambles. He wished his friend Joseph Trumbull, capable and creative, would again resume the commissary general's position.

This afternoon, he knew, Congress would take up the problem of clothing manufacturers charging exorbitant prices rather than those agreed upon for clothing desperately needed by freezing soldiers. *Scoundrels.*

Elbridge Gerry pulled up a chair next to James and placed his feet on the stool near the fire. "Are you as chilled as I?" he asked.

"At least as chilled," James responded. Last night he had worn gloves in his room to complete his writing. The courthouse was warmer than his room, but even so, a bitter chill lingered.

"We heard from Dumas, the intelligence source in Holland, that a story of Samuel and John Adams that was heard at the Hague goes that one or the other of them were born and married abroad but left wife and children to make a fortune in America. Dumas requests of us a short narrative of the honorable characters of Samuel and John Adams so he may inform the public of their virtue."

"That is r-r-ridiculous," Elbridge said, in disbelief.

"Enemies seek to blacken good names through calumny," James said with a sigh.

"I am sorry to hear it, but not s-s-surprised. And had you been at camp with us, you would have even less hope than you d-d-do. The sights we saw did not lend themselves to c-c-confidence in the army's situation. Men with torn shirts, no j-j-jackets, bloodied feet, sleeping in the s-s-snow with no tents. They are brave and hopeful, yet their physical situation is p-p-pitiable. The sooner they are able to settle and hut, the b-b-better."

"The new inspector general can send all the regulations he likes to Washington, yet men who are ill equipped to survive winter weather and undernourished will do poorly in training. Thomas Conway said that once the instructions for maneuvers and camp duty are printed, the same that are practiced by the four major military powers in Europe, they will guide all the officers of the army. But regulations can do no good in these conditions." James rubbed his hands ruefully. "I am sorry. My ill temper is getting the best of me."

"I am of a like mind," Elbridge said, taking out his notes.

The young servant pushed his way in the door carrying a load of firewood.

James finished his quick meal, took a swig of cold water from his tankard, and set out his writing paper and pen. He turned to his friend.

"I must write to General Washington," he said. "The task of keeping the *Journals* safe in our haste to leave Philadelphia fell to me. It is time I request our worthy commander-in-chief to dispatch appropriate personnel to retrieve them."

"No doubt. It would be imperative to s-s-safeguard the record of C-c-congress. Why was it your responsibility?"

"Others served with me on the committee for assembling and printing the *Journals*, but when we evacuated, I was the only one there." James rubbed his temple with some anxiety. "I have been reluctant to write to General Washington about the *Journals* until now, as his time has been wholly occupied with other matters. But now that they are settling into winter quarters, he may be able to consider the matter."

"Where are the *J-j-journals*?"

"The *Journals* from 1775 and 1776, along with the type sets used by the first printer, William Bradford, should be buried at the farm of John Roberts, ten miles outside of Philadelphia."

"How c-c-came they to be there?"

"When I returned to Philadelphia, following our first sally into the country, one of my purposes was to care for the *Journals*. But at the time of our evacuation, there was almost no one around to assist in moving the *Journals*. I found the paper supplier, Frederick Bicking, who recommended his neighbor, an honest Quaker, who could bury them at his farm outside of the city."

"His honesty would be vitally important. The *J-j-journals* are not only necessary as a record of our proceedings, but would be d-d-dreadful ammunition should they fall into the hands of the enemy."

"I will write General Washington today. He should find an officer familiar with the area who could lead soldiers to dig them up."

"If the type sets used for the f-f-first printings of the *Journals* are recovered, the next printings of the *Journals* could be matched to the earlier ones. There is now a p-p-printing press in York."

"Yes, William Hall and David Sellars have moved their press from Philadelphia and set it up in the home of Major John Clark. The first paper to be printed in York came out a little over a week ago. No longer will we have to send to Lancaster for printing, as we did for the supply of Continental money printed this fall and the Articles of the Confederation. The general should be able to send soldiers to dig up the *Journals* and the buried type sets. They should find these safe at the farm of John Roberts, outside of Philadelphia."

"Very g-g-good," Elbridge responded, picking up his pen again to attend to his work.

James shrugged off thoughts of harm to the valuable *Journals* and composed himself to write the letter. Once the *Journals* were returned to Congress, he could rest easy that his duty was done.

**"Valley Forge, 1777. Gen. Washington and Lafayette visiting
the suffering part of the army."**
Library of Congress Prints & Photographs

Chapter 13

Reason and Clarity Should Rule

January 1, 1778, Wednesday

"General Washington reports that since the resignation of Quartermaster General Thomas Mifflin in December, vital supplies, such as shoes, beef, and flour, have been extremely slow in coming. He suggests Colonel Hay for the position, who is experienced as deputy quartermaster general. The commander-in-chief reminds us that field equipment, carriages, and horses are desperately needed by spring."

President Laurens set down the letter and looked around the room, his face tense and strained. There was a prolonged silence. *Why is it that General Washington does not appoint his own officers? Of course. Congress, the civilian government, must exercise authority over the military, so selecting officers is clearly Congress's duty.*

No one spoke. President Laurens sighed and continued. "We will take up the appointment of a quartermaster general at another time. I beg you to consider whom you would recommend." *The first day of the new year is a revisiting of the problems of the old.*

Back at his lodging James took his iron box to the kitchen and held it out while the servant filled it with coals, doling them out with his tongs as if they were nuggets of gold. He carried the box up the narrow stairs. In his icy room, the heat from the small container was invaluable. At his table, he prepared to write to John Adams. He rubbed his cold hands briskly, then pulled on his gloves before picking up his pen.

General John Burgoyne had written to General Heath, in charge of the prisoners from Saratoga held in camps outside of Boston. Burgoyne had demanded his army sail before spring. Congress assigned a committee to recommend a response to Burgoyne. John Adams would recognize that reason and clarity should rule in that situation as in others. His lawyerly tendencies would rise.

Jesting, but in some respects serious, he suggested in his letter that perhaps Congress should apply to the firm of Grotius, Puffendorf, and Vattel, or Da, Du, and Dy, lawyers, to find common sense. He chuckled at his joke, then expressed his

130

concern that a month of winter had already passed, General Howe would be ready for battles in the spring, and the states should fulfill their quotas. He concluded his letter by extending his sincere compliments to John Adams and his lady. *It will be hard for Abigail to accept that John will be on his way to France, perhaps even leaving when this letter arrives, but we have dire need of him in that quarter. She must manage her affairs without him.*

January 12, 1778, Monday

In the sunlit courthouse, James opened a letter, breaking the red sealing wax. "It was in the packet from General Washington," the clerk said.

The letter was in the handwriting of John Laurens, aide to General Washington. He read it, then turned to Elbridge.

"I have just received word from the general that the *Journals* have been recovered from their burial place on John Robert's farm. He states Colonel Hartley's regiment will deliver them to us here."

"Excellent news," Elbridge responded. "And were the t-t-type sets discovered?"

"They were not. The officer General Washington sent to the farm outside of Philadelphia reported that perhaps they were buried in a slightly different place."

"At least the *Journals* are being returned."

"Yes. I rejoice that they will be back before long." James folded the letter and placed it in his satchel.

Before he could say more, President Laurens called the meeting to order. He glanced about. *There are so few here. Maybe eighteen?*

That evening, James took out from his satchel the recent letter to him from Benjamin Franklin. He unfolded it in his room, then laid it out flat. The eminent doctor stated he had received James's letter to him in which he described his method of writing in cipher as well as the one about the difficulties caused by Silas Deane's recommendation of French officers. Dr. Franklin thanked him for the method of secret writing but said nothing more on the subject. *At any rate, he has the cipher to use if he wishes, though he did not agree to use it.*

In response to James's concerns about the French officers, Benjamin Franklin said he regretted the number of officers but stated the commissioners also had turned a great many away. "You can have no conception of the arts and interest made use of to recommend and engage us to recommend very indifferent persons." Dr. Franklin wrote a bit of verse to indicate the many applicants the commissioners turned away compared to those they sent.

Poets lose half the praise they would have got,
Were it but known what they discretely blot.

He enclosed some military papers from the Baron von Steuben, a Prussian officer who had traveled to America, and suggested they might be useful. *Very well. We will see what Baron von Steuben has to offer. I will reply to Dr. Franklin when I find time. Our numbers are so few at present that I must serve on several committees.*

January 19, 1778, Monday

"The worm is indeed in the harvest," James said in a whisper to Elbridge Gerry.

Solemn of face, President Laurens read the complaint of nine generals. Their grievance was the indignity and disgrace they felt when Brigadier General Thomas Conway was appointed above them as inspector general. The generals stated they did not doubt they would receive the relief of Congress. They described Conway to be an officer they had commanded in the field offering no merit that would entitle him to such a station.

Henry Laurens's face fell when he opened a similar letter from General Nathanael Greene.

"General John Sullivan has also written to General Washington stating he feels the same dishonor. I would gladly undergo another month of gout if it would alleviate this strife."

"What to do—there's the rub," Reverend John Witherspoon said. "I suggest we let the matter lie on the table while we consider it."

In a brief recess, James turned to Elbridge. "In December, we learned that Thomas Conway caused offense by his words about a certain great man. And now he causes more?

"A week ago, we read Washington's letter to President Laurens, obliquely referencing the dishonorable charges about him that Thomas Conway made in his letter to General Gates. Washington said little in that letter but turned the matter over to us, along with his response to Gates, charging us to send his letter to General Gates. Thus, he put the whole matter in the open."

"As is best. Shall we adjourn to the tavern for a c-c-cup of cider?"

"Decidedly," James said. He checked his pocketbook and, casting caution to the wind, put on his coat.

The two stepped out into the winter thaw.

As they approached the Golden Plough, James remembered the proposal that Congress recently considered of officers receiving half-pay in retirement. He stopped in the street, aggravated. "The half-pay measure for the officers that we are deliberating is far too similar to the practice in Europe. Are we not in a young country where work is easily gotten?"

Elbridge's slender face grew taut. "We must accept that half-pay for a l-l-limited time and pensions for the widows of officers who lose their lives in the service are necessary s-s-steps for making commissions valuable, so that an officer may recognize his self-interest and accept the rigors of his duty without complaint."

"Do you think so? I can only say that some who have been in this war from its beginning, such as Samuel Adams, have not forgotten that at its start the war was patriotic."

"Indeed, it is and was, but if we expect military officers to be s-s-subordinate to the civil authority vested in Congress, they must have a sense of p-p-personal satisfaction." Elbridge faced his friend, his tone straightforward.

"I have just returned from a s-s-session in camp talking with General Washington and officers. Believe me, there are r-r-reasons to reward excellent officers. Those in command will have their authority strengthened so as to promote discipline, essential to an army. S-s-some can argue that our country is yet young, and such a system may not be practicable. Others may say that true patriotism does not need assurances of rewards. I say that such measures are r-r-required." Elbridge turned towards the tavern.

"Congress supports Washington in all ways," James said, slowing his steps. "He is the commander-in-chief, though he acts at times as if he lacks authority. Last month's resolve, reminding him of his right to take supplies, was meant to rap him over the knuckles, as one might chastise a demi-god."

"Strong language for a g-g-general who needs our help, I think." Elbridge glanced at James, his face anxious.

James bit back his words. He could not say his real frustration, that Washington had lost two major battles this fall, Brandywine and Germantown, while General Gates had won a significant victory at Saratoga. *Was there not a disparity?* Yet Congress supported General Washington, and he was not about to argue that confidence.

"We must s-s-stand behind him," Elbridge said. "And we do."

"And we will be sending a Prussian general to him, Baron von Steuben, bearing a recommendation from Benjamin Franklin. He promises to have a great understanding of military training, and he served on the staff of Frederick the Great." James felt optimism returning.

Elbridge reached for the stout door of the tavern and held it open. James nodded thanks as he entered. *In the long run, we may need to provide payment to our officers when their service is finished. Perhaps I should listen more closely to the opinions of others. Mine can change.*

He suddenly woke from a deep sleep, sweating, his teeth chattering with cold, his head on fire. He sat up, his bedroom icy. Again, he was in prison, that cell where alone he had battled fever, illness, starvation, the British guards' taunts and insults ringing in his ears. His stomach felt nauseous, his hands clammy. He swung his legs out of bed and reached for the glass of water nearby. His heart pumping, he gradually regained his calm, evened his breath. The coals in his warmer box had nearly expired. His breath hung foggy in the crystal cold air. He opened his door wide, wrapped his muffler around his shoulders, laid his coat over the blankets, and got back into bed, his breath gradually quieting again. *These days mirror the state of the country*, he thought, as he felt the terror dissipate. *We are cold, frozen in place, our plans on hold, our breathing tortured. Will our plans materialize, hope spring to life? We do not know.*

January 26, 1778, Monday

Flakes of snow spiraled down from lowering gray skies as the delegates approached the York Courthouse. President Henry Laurens opened the door for James with a wan smile, but the wind tore it loose from his fingers. It banged shut before James could grasp the handle.

"Not a harbinger of today's events, I hope," James said gamely, stamping his snowy feet.

"Not in the least. Good morning," Henry Laurens said distractedly.

The delegates gathered, fewer than twenty in number. The iron stove simmered with heat, but the corners of the room remained cold and drafty. Piles of coats and mufflers filled vacant seats. The caretaker lit candles during the day, the sun hidden behind heavy clouds.

The new Board of War suggested four days ago that Congress approve sending a force into Canada, an "irruption," they termed it. Congress would provide money and appoint officers. The goal would be to free the Canadians from the English and turn the country, vast and wintry at this time of year, over to the French. Thomas Mifflin, recently resigned from his position as quartermaster general, recommended the invasion, his black eyes snapping, his language brisk. Thomas Conway, inspector general, stood by, silent and brooding. General Horatio Gates listened closely from his place near Conway.

Not since Benedict Arnold had tried assaulting Quebec two years ago, turning back with a bullet in the leg and a disease-ridden force to struggle through the forests to Lake Champlain, had anyone tried to take Canada, though months ago Washington had himself suggested it. Congress approved the mission.

The following day, the Board of War requested officers for the expedition. They proposed the Marquis de Lafayette be given command, assisted by Major General Thomas Conway and Brigadier General John Stark. James noticed that the Board of

War failed to indicate that they had discussed the matter with General Washington at all. *Very likely they have not. And no wonder, considering who is on the Board of War. General Gates, Thomas Conway, and Thomas Mifflin: all have expressed their disapproval of General Washington at some time.* Congress agreed to appoint the requested officers.

Before the work of the day began, James filled his tankard with water from the pitcher at the front of the room. As he passed President Laurens, he heard the president say quietly to Secretary Thomson, "I heard from Lafayette. He strongly opposes the appointment of General Conway as his second in command for the expedition. He says Conway has spoken of his friend Washington in abusive terms and causes dissension and strife."

President Laurens lowered his voice and stopped speaking as James poured water. He paused near the president's table. Had he put the president on the spot by what he overheard?

Henry Laurens looked up at James, a mixture of discomfort and relief on his face. "Mr. Lovell, we should not be surprised, should we, that Lafayette supports General Washington. We received word earlier this month from the general himself that he was aware of the critical words written by Thomas Conway regarding him."

"Lafayette and General Washington agree on most affairs," James said. "And Washington's desire to keep matters open between him and Congress is admirable. Honesty can only improve our affairs." He nodded to the president, then returned to his seat. *Somehow, we have cleared the air.* Charles Thomson silently took his seat, his face expressionless.

The president called the meeting to order, his cultured, refined voice bearing no hint of emotion or conflict.

The Treasury Committee offered warrants and payment requests. Towards noon, Eliphalet Dyer of Connecticut entered the room, stopped at the president's seat, and handed him a sealed manuscript. "I found this on the steps outside, sir," he said.

Henry Laurens opened the pages and examined them. He began reading out loud, as was his custom, but stopped after a few words: "That if the army is not...." he said no more, but in a few minutes his normally calm face turned red and he stuffed the pages into his pocket.

He turned back to the delegates to see every one of them staring at him in curiosity. "It has no signature. Such an anonymous production is best left to the fireplace." He shuffled some pages in front of him, clearly annoyed, and returned to the day's business.

James found himself wondering. *An anonymous note? Could it be someone had the affront to criticize Washington openly?* He hoped not. Such underhanded methods would do no good, if indeed that was the substance of the message. He resolved not to let the matter trouble him.

January 28, 1778, Wednesday

The clatter of hooves on the cobblestone street startled James as he reached the York Courthouse. A party of horsemen, headed by none other than the Marquis de Lafayette, halted in the street. Swinging down from his gray horse with ease and grace, Lafayette handed the reins to a rider and proceeded up the walk to the courthouse. James watched as the slim, dignified French general, only twenty years old, his head high, approached, his pace brisk and energetic. He wore the uniform of an American officer, but James knew him to be one of the richest men in France. Yet he appeared at ease as part of General Washington's Grand Army, the general's confidante.

James bowed briefly as Lafayette reached the door. He opened it courteously for the young general. A glimmer of recognition flickered in Lafayette's face.

"It is good to see you, my friend Mr. Lovell," the Marquis said.

"And you as well. Welcome to Congress."

"I come to meet with the Board of War. I understand they have a suggestion for me."

"The Board of War meets at the law office of James Smith, on the west side of South George Street. I believe you will find them there." James motioned towards the street. With perfect composure, Lafayette swung his cloak over his shoulder, turned, and left.

"So, Lafayette must be here to take up his orders," he said to Elbridge Gerry, entering the courthouse.

"Apparently so," Elbridge said, taking his seat near James. "Such a command would c-c-constitute a great challenge. There is nothing easy about traveling in the winter, nor would undertaking an attack on a Canadian city be a s-s-simple matter. Young Lafayette would require a deal of c-c-confidence in himself and in his mission in order to undertake the mission."

"He has confidence in himself, that I grant you. We will see what he thinks of the proposal."

"I wonder how the camp c-c-committee is doing at Valley Forge."

"They have much to do, but they should have ample time to help with the restructure of the army."

Henry Laurens called the meeting to order. *Once more into the breach. Is that from Henry V? Henry V, who prevailed at the Battle of Agincourt despite odds. We contend with forces beyond our knowledge or control, but we give it our best. We have only this winter to reform the army and prepare to meet Howe. Are we up to the challenge?*

Chapter 14

A Toast to the Commander-in-Chief

February 2, 1778, Monday

It was only by chance that James overheard a story of telling consequences. He left his lodgings early. Holding his hat down tight against the wind, he made his way along the icy street to the York Courthouse. Inside, the ten-plate stove was blessedly hot, crackling with energy. Lit candles filled the air with the scent of beeswax.

A few delegates were already seated, talking and reading their notes. President Henry Laurens, a well-dressed Southern planter, was visiting with Francis Lightfoot Lee of Virginia. James could just hear their words as he settled in his seat.

"Lafayette told me of this occurrence a couple of nights ago," President Laurens said, his voice low. "General Gates hosted the Board of War and other friends at his house. Lafayette was invited as well, to discuss the plans for the intrusion to Canada. Gates told him he must not wait for all the supplies, but hasten to Albany and await developments there. However, the Marquis said to the General that he had no intention of going without first making clear the specific orders." Henry Laurens cleared his throat and glanced about. The room was quiet, those present busy with their work. He glanced at James, recognized he was listening, and nodded in his direction, but did not stop his quiet conversation.

Apparently, he trusts me. James set his pen down and turned to listen.

"Following the meal, General Gates offered toasts to the members of the Board of War, then to Lafayette. But before any drank to the toasts, Lafayette stood and said he would only drink if the toast were given to General Washington as well. The group fell silent and he saw their faces redden. Clearly, his recognition of Gates's glaring omission of a toast to the commander-in-chief had struck a note. General Gates, visibly flustered, said that of course, yes, let us drink to General Washington. Following that, all then drank to his health."

Francis Lightfoot leaned in even closer to the President.

"Lafayette then stated he would not undertake to lead the intrusion with Thomas Conway as his second, but he would accept the post if Major General McDougal were his second. If McDougal were not able to serve, then he required the Baron de Kalb." Henry Laurens sat back, his hands folded on his lap. "General Gates saw that he must acquiesce to Lafayette's demands, so he agreed to everything. Today we take up the matter in Congress."

"I would say that is remarkable, the young Marquis standing up to the Board of War," Francis Lightfoot said approvingly. "I would add we are all indebted to him. General Gates played the fool setting up that intrusion without first discussing the matter with General Washington. He is the commander-in-chief. Undercutting his authority in any way will lead to no good. The expedition itself, that is another matter. Lafayette has as good a chance as any to see to its success—in midwinter never a certain thing. We will see what will become of it."

James shook his head. *General Gates has overstepped his bounds. Lafayette had every right to speak to him as he did.* He wondered how General Gates would act today. He glanced back at President Laurens, who looked at him pointedly and shrugged. *"Best someone knows of this," I imagine he thinks.*

The door opened, and a number of delegates entered, followed by General Lafayette. Smiling, handsome in his Continental uniform of dark blue trimmed with red, Lafayette greeted Henry Laurens with a slight bow and shook his hand. President Laurens motioned to a seat nearby. The members of the Board of War followed, General Gates among them, and took seats at the rear of the room.

In the morning, Congress approved all of Lafayette's requests and funding for the intrusion into Canada. General Gates sat silent and tight-lipped, eyeing the proceedings in a wary manner.

As Congress took up business matters, the Board of War left the room to resume their work at their office on South George Street. Lafayette remained sitting, looking quietly amused.

"I have before me a motion for Congress to consider choosing a quartermaster general," the president continued. "General Washington has written with an urgent request for us to consider appointing Colonel Hay, who served successfully as deputy quartermaster general. The officer appointed will be responsible to create a new arrangement of that department, as well as attend to the needs of the army for tents, camp equipment, and transportation." President Laurens looked up from his notes. "Are we ready for a vote?"

"Should we not wait until the camp committee finishes its work of restructuring the army?" someone said.

The room was quiet. "Very well, then let us proceed to vote."

To James's dismay, the seventeen delegates present voted down the motion by a narrow margin. *Had not General Washington made it clear that he urgently needed a quartermaster general?*

He missed Francis Dana, now chairing the committee at camp. *How long will the camp committee be gone? Probably weeks. The task of restructuring the army is monumental. If it goes well, the military would benefit. Meanwhile, short of members as we are, we struggle on.*

February 5, 1778, Thursday

Seated in his chair at the front of the room, Henry Laurens beckoned to James as he entered the courthouse in the early morning.

"You might like to know," the president said, "I received an unexpected visitor early in the morning two days ago, the day after Congress approved the intrusion into Canada."

"Oh?" James asked. "And who was your visitor?"

"General Gates came by my residence. From what he said, I had the impression he wondered how I had reacted to the disclosure of his plans for the intrusion of Canada. I made it clear that my friendship with General Washington has never been stronger. I support our commander-in-chief, I realize he has the best plans for our country, and I believe no one else can direct our military with the assurance he has." Henry Laurens glanced at James, his expression determined.

"I understand and thank you for telling me. I do agree with you. What did General Gates say?"

"He said he too supported General Washington. He said little beyond that, but left me with a sense of his assurance that Washington was in charge."

"As he is," James said. "General Gates will serve as the fine officer he is, though General Washington is the commander. Thank you for sharing with me your encounter. I appreciate your confidence."

The door swung open and a tall figure in a long black coat entered, a great gray dog on his heels, followed by two assistants. Gray-haired, his dark eyes swept the room as one used to command. He removed his black military hat adorned with a white plume and approached President Laurens.

Speaking in German, the officer introduced himself. President Laurens glanced over at James. James stood and approached the officer. *Perhaps the stranger knew French?*

"*Votre nom, Monsieur?*" James asked.

"*Ah oui, vous parlez Français. C'est bien. Je m'appelle le Baron Von Steuben.*"

"I am pleased to meet you, Baron Von Steuben." Henry Laurens stood and shook hands with the dignified officer.

"Je voudrais vous présenter mon secrétaire, Monsieur Pierre Etienne Du Ponceau." The baron's secretary Du Ponceau stepped forward and bowed as the baron presented him.

"Et voici mon aid-de-camp, Louis de Pontière," Baron Von Steuben said, motioning to the younger aide-de-camp, who likewise acknowledged the introduction with a brief bow.

"We are delighted to have you. Welcome to Congress."

James brought the group over to his table and found chairs for them. "Where have you come from?"

"De Boston. Nous avons passé un moment merveilleux."

"So, they treated you well in Boston. Glad to hear it," James said. He found himself eyeing the great tall gray dog with curiosity.

"Il est mon lévrier Italien, Azor." The baron patted the head of the large animal, who turned his golden eyes on him in affection. *"Il va avec moi partout."*

"So, your Italian grayhound Azor goes with you everywhere," James said, partly for the benefit of Elbridge and the other delegates staring at the unusual visitor and his large dog. "He is quite unique." He patted the tall dog gingerly, surprised that Azor sat to receive more stroking.

In French, James assured the baron that Congress was glad to have him present and would no doubt enjoy visiting with him in the coming days. Baron Von Steuben stated that if the delegates approved, he would be off to Valley Forge to offer his services to the general before long.

"Have you a place to stay?" James asked.

"Oui, nous restons au le Golden Plough." The baron motioned in the direction of the tavern.

"Very good. I will no doubt see you at a later time," James said.

By now the delegates had assembled. The atmosphere in the courthouse was tense, somber. Funding, always a problem, lurked in the background of all Congress did like a shaggy beast in a haunted forest.

"We have a guest to introduce—the Baron Von Steuben," James said, standing. The Baron bowed, impressive in height and dignity. "Baron Von Steuben comes to us with papers from Benjamin Franklin. His expertise is military training. And this is his secretary, Monsieur Pierre Etienne Du Ponceau, and his aide, Louis de Pontière." The baron's assistants stood and bowed.

"The baron understands that we can pay him nothing, does he not?" Benjamin Harrison of Virginia said for the Board of War, his eyes riveted on the striking figure.

"Et je ne demanderai aucon paiement," the baron said, shaking his head enthusiastically. *"Seulement après la guerre, selon mon service."* His aide-de-camp, young Louis de Pontière, smiled.

"He does," James said. "He agrees he will be paid only after the war, depending on how he has performed. He will be on his way to join Washington's camp before long. When the roads clear, mind you," he added. No one laughed.

Given the storm that raged outside, it was a great relief to all present to have the Golden Plough bring over pans of hot soup and warm bread in the afternoon. Several suffering from a cold or a cough, the delegates remained in the York Courthouse while the irrepressible young caretaker loaded wood into the stove. Someone put a kettle on the top and before long there was a pot of hot tea. The Baron Von Steuben and his companions shared stories of their arrival in Portsmouth in December.

"You were almost arrested because you wore red clothing, like the British uniforms?" James asked incredulously.

The baron laughed and pointed to his current uniform, a suitable dark blue. "*Nouveau*," he said, flashing his teeth in a smile.

"I am glad you received a new uniform and were treated well in Boston," James said, hearing the story of how the baron and his associates were wined and dined there. "Your training—you believe it will help the army?"

"*Mais oui, j'ai été assistant de Frédric le Grand et j'ai appris toutes les techniques d'entraînement militaire et de guerre.*"

"You learned in a special class as aide of Frederick the Great of Prussia all the techniques of military training. Very good," James said. Those listening gave the Baron Von Steuben their full attention.

"*Entraînement, exercises, discipline. Très important, Sainte Mère de Dieu.*" The baron spit fervently into his cup. James raised his eyebrows at the unusual use of an epithet for emphasis, but merely nodded. *The camp will no doubt benefit from the baron's discipline, and possibly from his enthusiasm as well.*

February 18, 1778, Wednesday

In the evening, seated at General Roberdeau's formal table, James helped himself to sliced ham.

"Our committee at c-c-camp seems busy," Elbridge remarked. "Work goes on with the construction of rows of huts on the high g-g-ground at Valley Forge, despite the extreme conditions. Each hut will house t-t-twelve men and will have its own fireplace. The huts are well protected by redoubts and earth works to the s-s-south, the Schuylkill River to the north."

Across from James, Baron Von Steuben turned and dangled a ham bone in front of his greyhound. "Azor," he said softly. The huge dog bit into the bone and lay down, crunching contentedly.

"Tell me, have you had a chance to visit with de Francey?" General Roberdeau asked, passing the platter of vegetables.

James nodded. "Yes, today. Beaumarchais's secretary represents him as self-proclaimed defender of the ideals of liberty and the American cause. It was the Count de Vergennes's suggestion that Beaumarchais create the covert operation Roderigue Hortalez and Company to buy surplus arms and supplies in France and ship them to America. He hired De Francey as his assistant because he speaks fluent English.

"Beaumarchais gathered and sent to us a million livres from the French Farmers General, for which we promised to pay hogsheads of tobacco and other produce. He followed that with shiploads of goods for the army on the *Mercury*, then the *Amphitrite*, and then six more ships."

"Even the brilliant fighting at Saratoga could not have been accomplished without the weapons," General Roberdeau observed, helping himself to a pastry. "Hundreds of cannon, thousands of arms, clothing, cloth—the list is amazing."

"De Francey, young and energetic, has been in the country since the beginning of December," James said.

"But why did de Francey come to Congress?"

"Beaumarchais is troubled, as he has received none of the agricultural products promised him, specifically, tobacco, indigo, and rice. The Committee of Secret Correspondence, replaced by the Committee for Foreign Affairs, never informed Congress of Silas Deane's contract with Beaumarchais, so it was some time before Congress was aware of the debt.

"And another fact has just come to light. Our diplomat Arthur Lee, upset that Beaumarchais had negotiated with Silas Deane rather than him, wrote his brother, Richard Henry Lee, stating that there was no payment expected for the shipments. This information contradicts de Francey's words and has confused the committee." James eyed those present with a significant glance. "Beaumarchais wants to know why he has received none of the promised shipments in payment. De Francey has not of yet had time in Congress to explain his visit."

"What did de Francey have to say about the French attitude towards us?" Henry Laurens asked.

"Only by America's valiantly striving against Britain would France be convinced that open assistance could be possible. Yet being naturally desirous of gain, King Louis will 'lend us the *sine qua non* to provide bait for carrying on this shark fishery.' In other words, France will loan us money to carry on the war. For now."

"This seems to reflect France's actions. We can only hope that country's commitment to us deepens to a greater support of the war." General Roberdeau turned to Baron Von Steuben.

"Baron, I understand you are off to camp tomorrow."

"*Mais ouis, je suis apprové,*" the baron answered, glancing at James's face to be sure he had understood the question correctly.

"We hope your journey to camp tomorrow is fortuitous," James said.

"We thank you for your service and wish you the best," General Roberdeau said. "For myself, within a couple of months, as the weather permits, I plan to investigate the possibility of a vein of lead in Sinking Valley, a hundred miles to the west of here. A lead smelter there would greatly benefit the war effort."

"We wish you the best of fortune in this venture," Henry Laurens said. "And thank you for this evening."

"We may have another opportunity to gather before long." The general stood to bid his guests farewell.

The time was well spent, James thought, as he stepped out into the frosty air.

Chapter 15

The French Will Support Us

March 21, 1778, Saturday

oday we called off the intrusion to Canada. James mounted the stairs to his room. Lafayette had returned in anger when he reached Albany and found supplies, troops, and provisions lacking. Furious, he had called the expedition "madness and treachery."

James took out his ink and paper and sharpened his quill to write to Abigail Adams. He wished to support her, especially now that her husband was gone. This would be his third letter to her. He was beginning to think of her as a correspondent. *A friend, perhaps. She must miss John greatly*, he thought.

He thanked her for the letter she had sent from a merchant in France and explained that it had interested Congress.

If they won, he said, it likely would not be due to their efforts, but to the humiliating mistakes of the enemy and the favor of Providence, undeserved. In closing, he referred her to the parable of the beam and the mote, acknowledging his imperfections but asking her to accept him anyway. He signed the letter her humble, affectionate servant.

March 23, 1778, Monday

The sun was low in the sky, the night wind rising, when James stepped out of the York Courthouse. Across the street a group of travelers had pulled up at the stable, their horses mud spattered and impatient. Amongst them he saw a familiar face.

"Francis!"

Francis Dana's face lit with recognition. "I will be at the Golden Plough. Please meet me there."

In the crowded tavern, soldiers, townspeople, and congressmen elbowed one another, jostling and talking in boisterous tones. James and Elbridge looked about for their colleague, back from meetings at camp.

"Did you know Francis Dana and I once shared a room? At Harvard, towards the end of my time there."

Francis, his face flushed, entered the Golden Plough. "It is good to see you," he said with a smile, shaking hands with his friends.

"Have you finished your work at camp?" James asked.

"I must return for a couple of weeks, perhaps until April. The work is not finished. But what a time it has been." He shook his head.

"Bring the C-c-congressman a cider," Elbridge hailed the barmaid. She smiled and handed Francis a tankard.

"I have had an experience worth relating. We were wise to send a delegation to camp. General Washington's plans to improve recruitment, reorganize regiments, and retain officers through a pension following the war should yield an effective fighting force by spring."

"Excellent," James said. "How do the troops appear?"

"Cheerful and stalwart, for the most part. Disease has claimed many, perhaps a thousand. Supplies have begun to improve, but are still precarious. Generals Nathanael Greene, quartermaster, and Anthony Wayne search the countryside for livestock, horses and cattle, sheep, and hogs."

"And Baron Von Steuben?" James asked. "How is he doing?"

"Baron Von Steuben is accepted by the men. At first, they were not sure. But he makes an impressive figure, with his formidable appearance, military attire, and huge pistols tucked in his belt. Washington appointed him temporary inspector general. Von Steuben talked with the officers and men, inspected their huts and weapons. He saw that discipline was lacking, so he set to work to write drills for the army to coordinate all their movements."

"That must be quite a t-t-task. I believe each regiment is accustomed to different drills, depending on which s-s-state they are from."

"Exactly. Yet it was essential to align them. Von Steuben does not speak English. He writes drills in German, then his secretary Duponceau translates them to French, and Washington's aides John Laurens and Alexander Hamilton write them in English. The brigade inspectors make copies of the drills, lesson by lesson, in the orderly book for each brigade and regiment. Then copies from the orderly book go to each company and officer. The baron uses a unique system to train the regiments. First, he chose one hundred and twenty men from different units to be the commander-in-chief's personal guard unit, then he trained that unit. The guard unit then demonstrates the new lesson for the others, after which they practice it."

"And is it working?" James asked.

"Absolutely. The men are eager to learn and acquire the movements in rapid order. It helps that the baron swears in colorful German or French. The men listen and sometimes laugh at his language. He also is training them in the use of the bayonet, which is not fully utilized by our forces."

Francis took a long drink from his tankard and held it up for more as the barmaid passed by. "Do you have some food?" he asked. Soon a steaming plate of *schnitz un knepp*, ham bits with apples and dumplings, stood before him. Francis rolled his eyes and took a bite. "Not bad," he assured the others.

"I must tell you of an amazing event that I experienced, one that changed my way of thinking about General Washington, indeed of the whole war." Francis looked up from his plate.

Elbridge's sharp eyes opened wide.

"R-r-really. Do tell us."

"Our camp committee has been living and working at Moore Hall, about three miles from the stone house where General Washington lives. When we first arrived, Washington gave us a long statement of his goals for the army, many pages in length. It impressed us with its clarity and vision, and clearly showed us Washington's respect for us as the civilian authority. Some of the ideas we have sent to Congress came from this document, though we altered them as we saw fit. Washington spent a day with us from time to time. So did his aides, John Laurens and Alexander Hamilton.

"The men's huts are laid out in a line on the high ground, behind which are entrenchments. In front is the low land. Beyond that lies Philadelphia. On the other side of the huts, the land slopes down to an open space where the men drill and practice. At the far side of the open field, the Schuylkill River offers protection from the north. A bridge over the Schuylkill allows access to the farms on the north. There is a kind of market set up there, so the army can buy produce from the farmers nearby.

"Washington's headquarters is the two-story stone house near the river. Martha Washington, who stayed with her husband this winter, helps organize his household, assists with correspondence, and even puts on plays for entertainment. She offered us a delicious meal when we visited there.

"One day, Washington invited me to dinner, as I am chairman of our committee. We talked for hours." Francis took another bite of his *schnitz un knepp*.

"It was clear that General Washington was most concerned about the condition of the army. In particular, he had suffered the resignation of officers lately—over fifty from a single division. Offering pensions to officers would enlist their personal interest in fulfilling their roles, he explained. Patriotism alone will not cause men to stay.

"Finally, it was late at night, too late for me to go back to Moore Hall. I accepted General Washington's invitation to stay the night. I began to make myself comfortable in the bedroom upstairs. But I could not sleep. I decided to get up and take some air. Outside in the darkness, snow on the ground, I saw another figure standing not far off. It was the general. I spoke to him and he responded, 'Mr. Dana, Congress does not trust me. I cannot go on thus.'

"Almost without thinking, I answered, 'I trust you, General. And Congress, at least most of it, trusts you.'"

"Of course, we do," Elbridge said. "We just have our p-p-part to play."

"The authority of the country," James said quietly, "does trust those to whom extraordinary powers are given. If questions have been asked, that does not mean trust is lacking. Indeed, Washington has our confidence."

"I can see that conferring with General Washington will result in a stronger force for our service, and in that I take hope and pleasure. I return in a few days to camp, but in May my farm requires my attention." Francis finished his plate and wiped his mouth. "I must now bid you good evening."

"And we as well," Elbridge said, standing.

"Thank you for your confidence," James said. "Your insight gives me much to think about."

"It is my conclusion that our army is in good hands—those of someone we should trust and support. Good night, gentlemen. I will see you in the morning." Francis shook the hands of each of his colleagues and left.

"And good night to you, friend Gerry," James said.

Back at his lodging, James devoured the meal that Mrs. Hendricks had set out for him. He filled his iron box and resolved to write to General Washington about some matters of interest to the general. The visit with Francis Dana had impressed him greatly. Though he had his flaws, the commander-in-chief was trustworthy. James's own questions about him meant only that he sought the best for the country.

April 1, 1778, Wednesday

As James left the York Courthouse in the late afternoon, he could see the Saturday market just down the street. Villagers and farmers crowded open stalls in the long building, examining cheese, potatoes, and sausages, as well as barrels, baskets, yarn, and household items. York depended on the market, held two days each week.

He stopped to examine wooden toy horses. *The Count Pulaski, general of the Continental Army's cavalry, might approve,* he mused, and so would his boys. But he must set unnecessary items aside.

"Hello, James."

James looked around, his gray-green eyes narrowed. Across the market he recognized John Thaxter, Abigail Adams's cousin. Thaxter flashed him a warm smile.

"I received letters from Master John and John Quincy, written before they were to embark," he said with enthusiasm, as James approached.

"And your work goes well with the secretary's office?"

"As well as can be expected," the young man answered. "The employment will pay the bills. And I heard from Abigail. In her letter she said she was most troubled at John's leaving. She said that only the belief that his particular abilities might be useful to his country kept her from grief."

"I understand."

"Abigail is an unusual person." John Thaxter leaned against the stall, thinking of his cousin. "I have come to know her in my years living with the family, studying with John and tutoring John Quincy. In her letter she says that she finds it most perplexing that women do not receive the same education as men do, only instruction in writing and arithmetic. To her, women's part in society is as important as that of men, especially when their influence in families is considered.

"She asked me to give you her regards. I am to tell you she will appreciate all the news you can send to her which you can share with a woman. She also says you should know she has a 'large share of Grandmother Eve's curiosity' and has had a 'very indulgent partner' but now must claim knowledge from others."

James laughed. He appreciated the quality of curiosity in Abigail. It made her easier to relate to, someone he felt he could get to know.

"I trust John and his son will have a safe journey, though the Atlantic in winter is nothing to be trifled with. We should hear from them before long. I will be writing to Abigail Adams soon, so I appreciate your conveying the messages," James said.

He bid good-bye to John Thaxter.

Abigail had just written him about a rumor that had greatly distressed her, a story she had read in the *Boston Gazette* that Benjamin Franklin was attacked in his bed by an assassin sent from Lord Stormont, the British Secretary of State. According to the article, Doctor Franklin had survived only because the knife struck a rib. Now he lingered in his bed.

Of course, this story was a complete work of fiction. James knew this because the sources with which he was in contact had said nothing about it. Yet it would upset Abigail, fearful that the next victim of British treachery might be her dear husband.

In his room, he took out Abigail Adams's recent letter and read it again. *She signs her name Portia.* A nickname given her by John Adams, Portia was the heroine of Shakespeare's *Merchant of Venice*, intelligent, witty, holding high standards for her chosen partner. *The name suits Abigail well.*

He began his letter with care, thinking of the dark-haired, busy Abigail pouring over every word of news she could get of her absent husband.

April 1, 1778
Dear Ma'am,

I tell you that the report of the assassination of Doctor Franklin is false, and I say this not merely to give your anxious mind relief. You say the Boston Gazette published the infamous story of December 12, that a letter from Bordeaux mentioned the illustrious Dr. Franklin was stabbed in his bedchamber at the instructions of Lord Stormont.

We have just received a packet from our agent at Martinique in the Caribbean, Mr. Bingham. Mr. Bingham associates with many who would be sure to know if the eminent Dr. Franklin had suffered any harm, and he mentioned nothing. Further, the Connecticut Gazette stated the Doctor was well at the end of December.

Don't think harshly of me if I say your fears for your husband's safety have given me delight, since I know you to be constant in your love for him. I have plenty of compassion for the afflicted, as my friends know, but if you think your expressions of pain will only cause me to pity you, know that they will far more likely cause me to admire you than to have compassion.

I may rejoice at knowing your unhappiness, since it proves the source of your love. As to our friend Mr. Gerry, he takes unique in knowing your heart is not at ease, since he disdains the married state, though he instantly denied that. I can only surmise he means soon to take a partner and find the truest path to earthly pleasure
May you remain on that path until you enter Paradise.

James Lovell

He signed his name with a flourish and prepared the letter for the express.

Readying for bed, James shifted his shoulder uncomfortably as a pain shot down his back, fiery and sharp. He felt as though he had been stabbed with a knife. *But it is only from writing, quilldriving. Repetitive movements, day in, day out. We suffer wounds in this war,* he thought, bending over with difficulty and removing his boots. *Abigail feels the loss of her Friend, as I indeed miss Mary and my family, and my endless tasks cause me pain. May we see better days ahead.*

April 22, 1778, Wednesday

"I declare these United States will accept no overtures of peace from the British without a full withdrawal of their forces and acknowledgement of our independence." Robert Morris's deep voice rang out in the Zion German Reformed Church of York as the delegates honored Congress's proclamation for fasting and prayer.

Bright sunshine streamed in through the high windows. Dressed in a black frock coat with white collar, calm yet passionate, the heavy-set Robert Morris demonstrated the group's commitment.

Only a few days ago we heard wonderful news, James reflected, *almost too good to believe.* Letters from Paris reported the commissioners and the French ministry had engaged in conferences. The French sent couriers to Vienna, Lisbon, and Portugal to gauge support. When they returned, France would acknowledge the independence of America. He had written Abigail Adams to tell her of the tidings.

A week ago, at Monsieur de Francey's urging, Congress resolved that the commissioners prepare to pay M. Beaumarchais for the merchandise and materials of war he had channeled to the United States. *I will have to write the commissioners,* James reminded himself.

"The English know the French support us," Robert Morris said firmly.

The delegates stood and burst into applause, loud and sustained.

"Soon, we will respond to a secret British publication declaring parliament's right to impose taxes within the United States and to deal with disorders."

James glanced about. The delegates frowned. Someone behind him said contemptuously, "Disorders, indeed."

"We are about to have a valuable alliance with a trusted nation, yet the British still think they can claim our control. I declare they cannot. I ask your prayers, gentlemen, and diligence as we move forward to hold what is ours." Robert Morris's powerful bass voice echoed in the quiet church.

In the afternoon, Congress met. James knew the group, now energized, would consider responses to the enemy's statement. Now they had a margin of hope.

Chapter 16

An Alliance!

May 2, 1778, Saturday

At the Corner Tavern, a rustic place less familiar to James than the Golden Plough, Richard Henry Lee raised his tankard of cider to James. "I am all ears."

"It is good to have you back," James said. "A few days ago, we accepted the contentious Thomas Conway's resignation as major general, the vote being nearly unanimous. He had a way of putting a fly in the ointment."

"What might he do now?" Richard Henry Lee asked.

"I am sure I do not know, but his sly tongue has caused enough confusion as it is. And as inspector general he did next to nothing.

"It has been a long and taxing winter. General Gates, removed from his position on the Board of War last month, has taken up his assignment at Fishkill, where he will have control of all the forts on the Hudson for the northern department. He will do well in whatever capacity he is assigned."

Richard Henry Lee nodded, noncommittal. "And the machinations of the enemy continue," he said, motioning with his silk wrapped hand for another tankard of cider. *He is somewhat theatrical.* "I hear General Washington's intelligence recently discovered a secret paper declaring parliament had the right to impose taxes on the United States."

"Ah, that. We printed it in our papers to broadcast British deceit."

"Yes," Richard Henry Lee said, placing a few coins on the table.

"Were you aware that the royal printer in New York, James Rivington, listed in his *Royal Gazette* in March a pamphlet of letters previously published in London, the *Letters from General Washington to several of his friends in the year 1776?*"

"I had heard something of it. The gist of the letters was to present Washington as lacking in confidence to the American cause and so mislead the public."

"But the truth will prevail."

Both nodded. James finished his drink when a loud clanging resounded. The incessant pealing continued, a deep, vibrant tone.

"It must be the bell at the courthouse," James said, setting his tankard down.

Hastening to the door, they could see a crowd had gathered at the courthouse.

"We had best investigate," Richard Henry Lee said.

At the courthouse, the two joined the throng. The bell in its cupola continued its wild clanging.

From the top of the steps, President Henry Laurens proclaimed loudly, "France has agreed to an alliance! Congress is called to a special session."

The delegates entered the courthouse in a buzz of excitement. Outside, the crowd milled about, awaiting further news.

The door shut, President Laurens gestured to a pale, road-worn traveler as the assemblage hushed. "Gentlemen, this is Simeon Deane, brother to commissioner Silas Deane."

Simeon Deane bowed slightly to the delegates. His voice firm, he said, "I first arrived from France at Casco Bay, Falmouth, on April 16, on the *Sensible*. From there I made my way to Boston and then to York. I bring dispatches from the commissioners in Paris and signed copies of the treaty."

President Laurens held up a large sheaf of papers. "From the commissioners, we have the Treaty of Commerce and Alliance, concluded between the king of France and the United States of America, on the 6th of February."

The delegates stood, shouting "Huzza," stamping their feet, and clapping. James felt his heart racing. *It is almost too good to be true.*

"And we have letters. James Lovell, one for you from Benjamin Franklin and one for the Committee for Foreign Affairs." President Laurens handed two packets to James. "We will read over the Treaty for the first time. And I expect you will join with me in thanking God for his heavenly grace that we have reached this moment."

"Hear, hear!" the delegates responded, breaking into applause again. James felt a ticking inside, conflicting joy and anxiety. *Anxiety because of all that must go right, not because of the treaty,* he reminded himself.

President Laurens picked up the Treaty and began to read, translating what he could. "'Louis, by the grace of God, king of France and Navarre, to all who shall see these presents, greeting.'"

May 15, 1778, Friday

Earlier in the day, Robert Morris's surprising return to Congress broke the tie on the vote for half-pay for officers, turning it to the affirmative. It helped also that Gouverneur Morris's suggestion of half-pay for seven years after the cessation of conflict swayed several. *I am one of the few who maintained my vote of "Nay." Gouverneur*

Morris, a lively businessman from New York, seems to have much in common with Robert Morris, even their names, though they are not related.

The evening sky had turned a dusky purple. James prepared to write one more letter before he left the courtroom, this to Benjamin Franklin.

At length, he had received a letter from Dr. Franklin, written over a year ago, dated December 21, 1777. Benjamin Franklin explained why Silas Deane had promised commissions to so many French officers. He said it was difficult for the commissioners to resist the pleas of powerful men who might stop the flow of supplies from France if their service in America were refused.

As the doctor put it, "You can have no conception how we are still besieged and worried on this head, our time cut to pieces by personal applications besides those contained in dozens of letters by every post, which are so generally refused, that scarce one in a hundred obtains from us a simple recommendation to civilities."

The doctor went on to say that Silas Deane had ceased recommending so many French officers to Congress and was acting in every way as a loyal and effective agent.

James remembered that a letter had just come from Arthur Lee, Congress's other agent in France, stating a different opinion of Silas Deane. *Dr. Lee charges Deane with speculation, keeping poor records, and over-billing Congress. To what extent those accusations may be true, I have no way of knowing. Benjamin Franklin certainly has said nothing of them. My only concern is the recall of Deane so that we may learn the truth.*

James rubbed his head. He would answer Benjamin Franklin's letter as an individual, rather than jointly with Richard Henry Lee. For certain, he need not involve Thomas Paine. He appreciated Paine's style and substance, but the secretary to the Committee for Foreign Affairs had proven undependable.

Congress has taken great trouble to avoid creating enemies of officers whose services were not needed. And we require explanation from Silas Deane as to what we owe to Beaumarchais and Roderigue Hortalez. A month ago, we resolved the commissioners pay Roderigue Hortalez any money owed. Once Deane has satisfied Congress's questions, he may return to a commission in Holland, as far as I am concerned.

His thoughts in order, he composed the letter. He informed Benjamin Franklin that he could not possibly realize the many threats and accusations made against Congress because of the numerous disappointed foreign officers that Silas Deane had encouraged to come to offer their service. And he explained Silas Deane's recall was wanted to clarify matters, particularly what Congress owed to M. Beaumarchais. He signed the letter with a flourish and sealed it for the dispatch.

June 8, 1778, Monday

"Will we really leave York and return to Philadelphia?" James closed his eyes, then opened them wide. "The spacious floors of the Pennsylvania State House." He yawned. It was early; the robins chirped outside the York Courthouse.

"We have reports that the British are readying t-t-transports to leave from Staten Island," Elbridge said. "General Henry Clinton has arrived in Philadelphia to replace Howe, who has r-r-resigned. Could he be taking his troops and returning to New York?"

"I would like to believe they are leaving." James poured himself a cup of water. "Yesterday, we heard that Silas Deane has arrived in America. So before long, we should have accurate information about our account with Roderigue Hortalez and Company. *Le Fier Roderigue*, a fifty-gun ship owned by Beaumarchais, arrived at the James River at the end of May. She brings the most valuable cargo we have yet received: enough cloth for fifteen thousand men, four thousand suits of clothing, soldiers' blankets, military stores, the entire worth five million livres."

"This is wonderful news. And answers from S-s-silas Deane will no doubt help to clear up any mystery."

The York Courtroom buzzed with activity while the delegates prepared for the day. James set aside his concerns and the room quieted as President Laurens took his seat.

"Gentlemen, today we take up the report on the letter from Commissary General Jeremiah Wadsworth. Since a number of vessels have been captured bearing provisions for our armies, we must consider an embargo to prohibit exporting supplies, including wheat, flour, rye, corn, rice, beef, pork, and other food from the United States. Conserving produce for our army should be our first priority. Chairman of the committee, please proceed."

James regarded Henry Laurens, admiring his patience. Not for the first time, he thought of the difficulty of administering their present crisis with the issues and personalities involved. *In truth, though the road to end the war might be long, we have survived a difficult, harrowing winter and have emerged in a much better position. The army's winter retirement turned out to be for the best, despite my earlier misgivings, gaining discipline through improved training. Now we have achieved an alliance with a powerful ally. The time in York has been well spent.*

James set Abigail's letter down. *Did I cause offense? What was her state of mind when she read my letter? Do I not think of her as one of the strongest women I know, one worthy of admiration?*

He read through the pages again, noted the even, neat handwriting, betraying no hint of the emotional distress that the words implied. *Apparently saying kind things to her only causes her to bristle.*

The only way to answer her letter would be straight, direct. He reread what he had written.

June 13, 1778

York

Friendly though unjust Portia!

Do you want me only to write about the news as in the gazettes, suffering, deceit, and cruelty from Britain, patience, fortitude, and humanity from America, and say nothing of my opinion of you as a lovely suffering wife and mother? Apparently, I must, or you will call me a flatterer. Following many months in prison and now working closely with a small group of men, plodding politicians at that, I did not think myself able to write in such a style as to provoke one who might capably polish our manners to label me an adulator. Now that I have called you unjust, I shall not comment on any of the remaining parts of your letter, but shall continue to admire you in secret.

The information you sent me about the capture of the Boston cannot be good, as other gazettes do not mention it. I do not wish to offer you false hope, for I have enough regard for you to be confident you could bear bad news. Nor is this flattery, for I will gladly send you whatever knowledge I should receive about my worthy friend, he who is your dearest, whether it is good or bad. And I will continue to hold you in high esteem, though you may now and then call me names or misinterpret the honest sentiments of your most humble servant.

James Lovell

It is true that we both are concerned for John, though I believe we will hear of his safe arrival before long. His ship is most likely all right. She need not fear for misplacement of my affections. At least Mary, though she misses my presence, need not fear for my safety. He folded the letter, addressed it, placed it in his satchel for the post.

June 20, 1778, Saturday

The York Courtroom was quiet as a library in the early morning. The smells of mint and honeysuckle drifted in from the garden. Secretary Thomson bustled about, arranging papers for the day, John Thaxter at his side. The courthouse servant hummed "Yankee Doodle" as he swept the floor. Richard Henry Lee hunched in his seat near his brother, Francis Lightfoot Lee, their voices low.

We may be leaving York before long, James thought, taking his notes out of his satchel. *The fifteen thousand British troops have evacuated Philadelphia and are marching east under General Clinton and General Cornwallis, while our forces entered the city a few days ago. Our army presses on their heels. And a French fleet under Admiral Count d'Estaing has nearly reached the American coast.*

Richard Henry Lee approached James. "This afternoon, I recommend the Committee for Foreign Affairs meets at our office to write the commissioners. I have a suggestion for us to consider."

"A suggestion?" James said, motioning to a nearby chair.

Richard Henry Lee seated himself, his fine aquiline features composed and serious. "I suggest the committee adopt a common cipher for all its correspondence."

"I have thought of something similar. In fact, I have written to Benjamin Franklin sending him directions for a cipher, but that worthy gentleman has not given me his thoughts on the matter."

"The cipher I suggest," Richard Henry Lee said, with some urgency, "was sent to me by my brother Arthur, with a copy of *Entick's New Spelling Dictionary* and directions for cipher using the book. He and I, along with our brother William, use the cipher when we write. In our system the cipher number is the page in Arabic numbers followed by the column, either *a* or *b*, then the place of the word in the column given in Roman numbers. I find that by writing the most sensitive words in the cipher, I am able to speedily write pages with my meaning obscured."

"I agree that adopting a cipher would be ideal for diplomatic correspondence. But getting everyone to agree to use the same system is difficult."

"A problem worth returning to. Perhaps in time we will find a solution." Richard Henry Lee stood. "I will see you this afternoon at our office."

"Agreed." James nodded.

He turned to President Laurens as the Congress came to order.

June 27, 1778, Saturday

"The proclamation of Major General Arnold, military governor of Philadelphia, reveals his impatience with disruptions in the city." James looked up from the boxes of diplomatic correspondence he was packing in the law office. Congress was adjourned, the delegates dismissed to travel to Philadelphia. If possible, they would meet at the Pennsylvania State House on Thursday, July 2.

"I hear Arnold still limps, his wounded leg from Saratoga not allowing him to walk." Richard Henry Lee tugged another box of letters onto the wheelbarrow. Once at the York Courthouse, it would be loaded on a military cart.

"That may be why General Washington assigned him to the position of military governor rather than to a field command." James pulled a stack of letters from a shelf and placed them in a box.

"All the states but Maryland, Delaware, and Jersey have agreed to the Articles."

"We may yet be able to sign the engrossed parchment ratification of the Articles. That would be an accomplishment."

"The heat is nearly suffocating." Richard Henry Lee sighed heavily. He opened the door of their small, crowded room. The late afternoon sun poured in. "But I must leave you for another meeting."

"By all means. I can finish this." James wiped his forehead with his sleeve.

And tomorrow we leave for Philadelphia. The old bay nag that the stable sold to me will have to do. Fortunately, I can travel with friends.

Chapter 17

Return to Philadelphia

July 1, 1778, Wednesday

To his surprise, James found himself relaxing as he rode through towns and countryside on the road to Philadelphia. His saddle chaffed, and the heat was nearly suffocating, but each day he relaxed in the jolting of his horse's steps and felt the weariness of months of paperwork slipping off his shoulders. He rode with Francis Dana and Dr. Samuel Holten, recently arrived from Massachusetts. The countryside was in full bloom, people out in fields and gardens. Innkeepers received them cordially. When the heat grew oppressive, the congressmen took their coffee sitting under shady trees.

Seeking to avoid the road through Lancaster, where inns would be crowded with those leaving York, the group crossed the Susquehanna, rode south through Pennsylvania, then to Delaware, staying first in Newark and then in Wilmington. At Chester in Pennsylvania, not far from Philadelphia, they stayed at a pleasant rooming house offering first-rate cider. Here, the welcome news reached them that Washington's troops had successfully held their own at the Battle of Monmouth Courthouse, a one-day engagement pitting well-trained British troops hard on the road to New York against the Continentals pursuing them. As Francis Dana remarked to James, while not quite a victory, the American army's stand showed determination and capability, in spite of the overwhelming heat that claimed a number of lives. It was said Washington led the charge with courage.

A few miles from the Schuylkill River, the bitter smell of charred wood hung in the air like a curse. James realized his view of the river was unchecked by the groves of trees which had before the British occupation blocked the sight of the flowing current. Now, open fields lay before them, cattle and sheep gone, seized by the enemy or moved by their owners. Fences lay broken, chimneys stood naked and alone in the wrecks of burned houses, signs of malice in the enemy's retreat.

Reaching Philadelphia, James saw homes bare of trees and orchards, hacked down for firewood. Debris was everywhere. At an elegant brick home, an owner watched in dismay as servants carted out heaps of refuse.

"How are you?" Samuel Holten asked the homeowner.

"The dirty scum used my house as a stable," the man said angrily. "They cut a hole in my dining room floor to shovel manure down. It will be long before it is back to rights."

"How terrible." Dr. Holten tipped his hat and the delegates rode on. They passed other homes, public buildings, workers carting or burning trash.

Yet some structures stood apparently whole and unhurt.

At the Pennsylvania State House, the tall doors stood open. The group dismounted and entered in apprehension. The stench hit them like a wall of filth. An officer met them.

"You don't want to come in," he said, shaking his head. He gestured towards the meeting room where polished floors and comfortable chairs once stood. "They used it as a prison. Human waste—it is everywhere. Upstairs, they housed sick and wounded Americans, a sort of hospital, but gave them no care. We find that the prisoners were so hungry they tried to eat the leather seats on chairs. They even scraped wood from paneling to boil. Many died here. In time, the State House will be restored to its shape. But for now, I understand you will be meeting elsewhere. College Hall, nearby, is said to be clean."

The delegates left shaken and quiet, the dirt and refuse speaking to the abuse those kept there had suffered.

Francis Dana shivered, freeing himself from the specter. "There is a large house that may have rooms to let, on Second Street," he offered.

"I could inquire," James said.

"I have made another arrangement already," Dr. Samuel Holten said. "I will contact you later." He turned towards Walnut Street.

Francis led the way to Second Street. Not far from the City Tavern, he stopped at a large, older brick home. At least three stories tall, its wooden trim was bare of paint, the front fence broken. A weathervane at the top stood crooked. They dismounted and rapped with the brass knocker on the front door.

A tall, thin woman swung the door open. Bright hazel eyes examined the delegates; tufts of brown hair escaped from a white cap. "What can I do for you?" Her voice was low, musical.

"I am inquiring after rooms for rent." Francis introduced himself and James.

"Do come in, please." She held the door open, her wide smile showing uneven teeth. "I am Miss Dalley, and this is my sister, Mrs. Clarke." She motioned to a round figure in a cushioned chair in the parlor. "We have rooms for rent, do we not, Agnes?"

"We certainly do." Mrs. Clarke regarded them over her spectacles. She set down her needlework and took out an account book.

After a discussion of the price of accommodations and warning that supper would be served promptly at seven, James and Francis Dana followed Miss Dalley upstairs. A narrow corridor led past several rooms.

"This will be your room." Miss Dalley pointed to a room in the middle of the hall, furnished with a table, wardrobe, bed, and fireplace. Through the window, he could see tall elms shading the garden.

"This will do," James said.

"Samuel Adams will be here soon. Would you have a room for him as well? And for Elbridge Gerry and Henry Marchant?" Francis Dana asked.

"Oh yes, we do. We have been hoping you would return, and as far as we are able, all is in readiness." Miss Dalley's brown eyes opened wide in excitement.

July 7, 1778, Tuesday

Once settled in at Mrs. Clarke and Miss Dalley's home, James daily walked the short distance to Philadelphia College Hall, a sturdy brick building that had escaped ransacking by the British. There he gathered with other congressmen. On July 7, Congress at length had sufficient representation to hold a meeting.

Secretary Thomson and his staff bustled about, arranging papers. John Thaxter waved a greeting when he saw James.

James turned to Elbridge, sitting nearby. "Just a few days ago, I wrote to Abigail Adams to congratulate her on what must be her husband's safe arrival in France. In a Boston gazette, I found an innocent entry reporting his arrival in France, so simply stated it is likely to be true."

Elbridge nodded, relieved. "We can rejoice at that. His s-s-safety is vital."

"I also assured her she need not fear an advance to the north from the devastated British army now arriving at Sandy Hook."

"True. At Monmouth Courthouse, their loss was profound. Since the enemy abandoned Philadelphia, their f-f-forces have dwindled by some three thousand killed, wounded, or deserted."

"As you may know, the Count d'Estaing with a fleet of French ships is approaching our waters. The new French minister to the United States, Conrad Alexandre Gérard, is with him, as well as Silas Deane."

"We will need to p-p-prepare a welcome for Minister Gérard."

"He will be our first official minister from another country."

"Did you hear that Thomas Conway challenged General Cadwallader to a duel?" Francis Dana said, taking his seat.

"I heard something, though I am unclear of the details."

"Thomas Conway is still in Philadelphia. Apparently, Conway made a disrespectful comment about General Cadwallader, who is a staunch supporter of General Washington. General Cadwallader challenged him to a duel. They met on the commons and Cadwallader, drawing the first fire, shot Conway through the side of the face."

"We know Thomas Conway to have an unguarded t-t-tongue. It seems it has at length gotten him into trouble."

President Laurens looked about the room. "Ten states are represented," he observed, ticking off the members present. "Gentlemen, we may proceed. Congress is in session."

The delegates took out their notes. Secretary Thomson and John Thaxter bustled about the front of the room, arranging mail. *It feels almost as if nothing has changed since York, and yet it has. The British have abandoned their conquest of Philadelphia. A French fleet is on the horizon, bringing with it what might be an early and great success. And soon we will welcome our first minister from France.*

In the afternoon, the president motioned to Secretary Thomson. "The letters from General Washington, please."

Taking the letters, Henry Laurens glanced at one, then looked up. "We have news of one event that places an individual in much disgrace. Our army had great success at Monmouth Courthouse. But General Charles Lee dishonored himself by directly defying Washington's order to attack the enemy's rear. The day was saved by Lord Stirling, General Nathanael Greene, General Anthony Wayne, and their valiant troops. Washington has placed General Charles Lee under arrest, pending a court martial and Congress's decision."

Henry Laurens set down the pages and wiped his forehead. Heat simmered in the room, the doors and windows of College Hall shut tight against listeners.

"Most peculiar," Samuel Adams said. "But Lee's conduct has been suspicious in the past. This time, there is no escaping examination of his behavior."

"We can congratulate General Washington and the army on their performance," Francis Dana said, his voice cheerful.

James agreed, joining in with the applause. "The lessons learned at Valley Forge have served them well."

July 9, 1778, Thursday

He took Abigail's recent letter out of the drawer of the table in his room and smoothed the ivory paper. *She is the manager of her family's farm and children,* he reminded himself. *My wife too is the sole caretaker of our family. But Mary is less anxious about me than Abigail about John.* He read it again.

> *Braintree, June 30, 1778*
> *Dear Sir,*
>
> *I have often written to you expressing my fears, so I owe you a letter stating my happiness. Your warm heart will realize the joy I felt today when I received letters from my dear friend telling me of his safety and health. In early April he arrived at Bordeaux and reached Paris on April 8, though I cannot imagine the narrow escapes he passed through. The first letters he wrote me were lost when the vessel carrying them was taken. I cannot conceive the dangers he was in, but I know the Boston that carried John across the sea encountered a violent storm and was struck by lightning, splitting the mast down nearly to the powder room. He wrote me nothing of political events, distrusting their safe delivery.*
>
> *I thank you for your letter of June 13, though I contest your calling me "unjust." Yet the inner strength you have shown when you endured painful captivity and suffering makes me think I can trouble you with my own apprehensions, especially now that the calm anchor of my life has departed. I hope to take on some of the courage and virtue that you have displayed, by writing to you and sharing my fears.*
>
> *Yet fortunately my anxieties have proven without base, so in future I shall attempt to suppress them. I am much indebted to you for your sympathetic efforts to lighten my worries, and your polite expressions to one who is much obliged.*
>
> *Portia*

He set the letter down, pleased that she wrote about her happiness in learning of John's safety, pleased also that she felt she could write to him to share her worries. *If we cannot care for our friends, what are we?*

July 14, 1778, Tuesday

"We heard that the French fleet under Vice Admiral Count d'Estaing arrived at the mouth of the Delaware River," James said, pouring himself cider from the pottery jug. Through the window at Miss Dalley and Mrs. Clarke's dining room, he could see the flourishing garden, thick with vegetables and flowers.

Portraits of family members hung about the room. On a table stood a china platter and tureen, chipped but serviceable.

"Corn soufflé," Miss Dalley announced, setting a dish down. She folded her tall, angular body into a chair at the end of the table.

Mrs. Clarke nodded politely from the other end of the table.

"The arrival of the French fleet is good news," Henry Marchant said.

"It is indeed," James said. "Silas Deane and Monsieur Gérard arrived on the Count d'Estaing's flagship, the *Languedoc*. It carries twelve hundred men, over ninety guns, and more than a hundred carriage guns. In total, with the Count d'Estaing are four thousand soldiers, twelve ships of the line, and four frigates.

"The count left Minister Gérard and Silas Deane at the entrance to the Delaware River on Friday and is headed to New York. He outguns the entire British fleet. If he meets the British in battle, he should prevail." James's eyes lit up at the thought.

"We have s-s-specific directions from Silas Deane to greet Monsieur Gérard with the d-d-dignity befitting an official representative of the French government. Gérard's official title is minister plenipotentiary," Elbridge said.

"The Board of War has arranged for a ceremony to honor the minister's arrival in the city. We emulate the ritual observed in European nations, yet ours is a republic, not a monarchy. We tread a fine line between respect for a foreign dignitary and aping trappings of authority," Henry said.

"Is it so important?" Miss Dalley asked. She pushed back a brown curl escaping her white cap. "At the riverfront I saw the barge carrying Congress's welcoming group to Monsieur Gérard's ship. The oarsmen were decked out in splendid suits of crimson, embellished with silver. The volley of gunfire from the military when the barge reached the French ship was deafening."

"Indeed, it is important. A fine c-c-carriage took the minister to Benedict Arnold's residence on High S-s-street, where he will be lodged until a more permanent house can be arranged." Elbridge finished his meal and pushed his plate back.

"We look forward to questioning Silas Deane," Henry said thoughtfully. "Arnold, by the way, is under suspicion for being too lenient with the Tories, and possibly working illegal business deals with merchants in the city."

The group broke up following the meal. James took the stairs at the end of the hall to his room. *And there is a fireplace. I should not be cold this winter. Though I have no extra funds for a new shirt or mending, at least I have a decent room.*

Chapter 18

The Count d'Estaing's Fleet
Leaves Rhode Island

August 6, 1778, Thursday

What James thought might be the mumps kept him down for nearly a week in late July. His jaw swelled; he ran a fever; he could not eat. He stayed in his room, where he attempted to keep up with paperwork and letter writing. When he could no longer read, he took to his bed, curtains drawn against the light. Miss Dalley brought him tea, water, and soup, and shut his door with a glance of sympathy.

After several days, his health improved and he returned to Congress early in the morning, now meeting at the Pennsylvania State House. The doorkeeper Andrew McNair, standing at the handsome double doors, greeted James with a smile to match his hefty size. "It is good to see you well, sir. My family and I had to leave, nasty time, but we're back."

James looked about the Assembly Room. *Not long ago, men died here, imprisoned with wounds and illness, left in pitiable condition to starve to death.* He shivered. The handsome building had suffered in the British occupation, but now gleaming floors replaced the filth that had strewn them, and fresh green curtains blocked the sunlight. The spicy scent of pine shavings filled the air, as artisans had spent weeks repairing nicks and gouges in the carved woodwork. The walls, newly washed and painted, shone. The only trace of the disaster was the carpenter installing a new bar at the rear of the room.

Samuel Adams, dignified in a new suit with satin lapels, stood at the front of the spacious room, making final preparations for the ceremony that Congress would hold later in the day to welcome Minister Gérard. He gazed at the mahogany armchair at the front of the room where President Laurens would sit for the ceremony.

164

"Our formal introduction for French Minister Gérard will establish respect for Congress," he said to James. "Those in Philadelphia have not benefitted from the example set by the British during the occupation, with their gambling, horse racing, and frivolous amusements. Our republic should not ape the splendor of the British court but exemplify plain and simple manners."

"Frivolity such as the *Meschianza*," James said. Both were silent, thinking of the elaborate festivities General Howe hosted to celebrate his leave-taking. Organized by Major John André, the head of British intelligence, the event featured a mock medieval tournament, fireworks, dancing, and lavish refreshments.

"And at the same time, we are concerned that Congress present a reception worthy of the standing of the United States among the nations of the world," James added. "We have been reminded, these last days, by our delegates from Virginia and South Carolina who have lived in London and seen the pomp and ceremony of the British court, that official recognition of sovereignty requires a dignity and splendor not usual to our proceedings."

"We have consulted treatises on international law, especially *Le Droit des Gens, The Law of Nations*, sent to us by Dumas at the Hague. And we determined a compromise with those among us who would prefer the pomp of a European court." Samuel gazed at the finely polished mahogany armchair centered on the two-foot-tall platform with resignation.

"Not quite a throne," James admitted. "But enough to satisfy our southern delegates, and yet reflect the plain manners of a republic."

"We walk a fine line," Samuel said, shaking his head in wonder. "I cannot imagine what it would be to sit on the throne of a monarch, as Benjamin Rush claims to have done, nor do I wish to. Our republic must reflect the simple manners of our people, while at the same time command respect. Monsieur Conrad Alexandre Gérard senses the importance of these things. He refused to attend the ceremony until he had reviewed the draft of the proceedings. He requires formality, but even he felt too much would not suit us as a country. And we are a republic. We require that Minister Gérard bow not only to President Laurens, but to the members of Congress, expressing our belief that power resides with the people."

"The French Minister has good sense. I wish you and Richard Henry Lee a fine day as you carry out your duties. Our president, in his modesty, abstained from voting when the question was put as to where his chair should be placed. Surely President Laurens's humility speaks to our nature as a republic."

As he took his seat, James glanced again at the mahogany chair, standing in splendid isolation. *Henry Laurens might only be a figurehead, but the moment the president stands to accept Gérard, the power of the country is embodied in him, if only symbolically.* The thought was compelling.

Delegates trickled in. A hum of excitement filled the State House chamber.

Before long, President Henry Laurens entered the room and called the meeting to order. "Richard Henry Lee and Samuel Adams are excused to accompany Minister Gérard to the Pennsylvania State House. The peace officers and their escort are assembled at the door, with the coach."

Richard Henry Lee and Samuel Adams departed. James caught a glimpse of the fine black coach and six matched white horses.

"Our preparations are in order for the reception of Monsieur Gerard," the president said with a nod to the waiting delegates. The strains of violins and rattle of drums echoed from upstairs. Known as the Long Gallery and used only for special occasions, the room spanned the length of the State House.

The muttering of a crowd outside grew. The doors to the State House opened and a couple hundred officers, dignitaries, and wealthy citizens of Philadelphia poured in. They crowded the rear of the meeting room, filled the area behind the bar, and then quieted as they gazed about the chamber with expectation. One of the conditions of the southern delegates, James knew, was to have the ceremony of reception held in an open manner. Never before had a meeting of Congress been open to the public.

With a shrug of resignation, Henry Laurens strolled to the mahogany chair on its platform and took his seat there. A hush came over the waiting assemblage.

Before long, the sounds of drum rolls, regular and cadenced, told of the official arrival of Monsieur Gérard. Richard Henry Lee and Samuel Adams entered the open doors of the State House. Accompanying them was the tall, imposing French minister, regally attired in handsome maroon brocade, followed by a young man in a blue silk coat. Monsieur Gérard's sharp eyes quickly took in the room, scanning everyone present. He walked sedately to his chair, centrally placed and facing that of the president, and seated himself, gazing at President Laurens with an air of anticipation.

Richard Henry Lee announced, his voice carrying in the quiet chamber, "This stranger is the Minister Plenipotentiary from His Most Christian Majesty." All stood—President Laurens, Minister Gérard, the members of Congress—and bowed to one another.

When all had taken their seats, Samuel Adams said loudly, "His secretary has a letter for the president of Congress."

The young man in the blue silk coat bowed to the president and handed him a letter. President Laurens broke the wax seal and read aloud in French the letter from Louis XVI, the King of France.

James had no difficulty understanding the letter. Glancing about, he saw that the delegates were waiting patiently. He knew a translation would be available before long.

Louis assured his friends and allies of his affection for the United States, shown by the treaties between the two countries. He stated he had nominated Monsieur Gérard to live with them as minister plenipotentiary, empowered to negotiate with their commissioners. Louis trusted Gérard would communicate his assurances of friendship. He closed by asking God to keep his friends and allies in his holy keeping. The letter was signed on the 28th of March, 1778, at Versailles.

Monsieur Gérard then stood and offered a speech in French. Few understood his words, but the sentiments were clear to all. President Laurens replied with his own address. All then stood. Gérard bowed again to the president and the members of Congress. President Laurens returned the gesture, and Gérard left the Assembly Room, attended by Richard Henry Lee and Samuel Adams, his secretary trailing behind. *Next, we will have the banquet festivities. The Long Gallery upstairs is laden, the orchestra tuned up. We have turned a corner. The reception for the first official envoy from an ally to the United States is underway.*

August 28, 1778, Friday

"We have before us, gentlemen, letters of the greatest import, sent to me by General Washington, regarding the French fleet under Count d'Estaing." President Laurens cleared his throat and looked about the delegates with a grave expression. "The French fleet had to abandon the attempt to engage the British ships at New York. The harbor at Sandy Hook proved too shallow; the huge French ships would strike bottom in navigating it."

He held up a letter from General Washington, glancing at it from time to time as he reviewed the latest information from the commander-in-chief in camp at White Plains, New York.

"Leaving New York, the Count d'Estaing sailed north to Rhode Island. Since July, we have had a force of ten thousand there, under the Marquis de Lafayette, General Nathanael Greene, and my son, Colonel John Laurens. The troops were to coordinate with the French and drive out the British, who have controlled Newport for the last year and a half."

The stage is set for a confrontation. James glanced at the delegates. The room was silent, all listening with rapt attention.

"But just over a week after arriving, the Count d'Estaing received word that the British fleet was approaching Rhode Island. He took his ships out to sea to battle with them." Henry Laurens paused and wiped his forehead with a handkerchief.

"The French ships pursued the British, but the wind blew up into a fierce gale. The storm took out all the masts on the count's flagship, the *Languedoc*, just as the enemy approached. Cannonballs struck the *Languedoc* before the enemy retreated. The Count d'Estaing took his ship back to Newport a week after it left, crippled, and informed the Americans that he was leaving Rhode Island for Boston."

The delegates gave a collected sigh of frustration at this event.

"General Greene and the Marquis visited the *Languedoc* in port, trying to convince the count to engage the British, as they had planned. But d'Estaing refused. They assured him a combined assault would take only forty-eight hours, but they could not persuade him."

A number of delegates grumbled. James frowned. They were so close to retaking Newport.

"Now we know there was another factor determining the count's decision to abandon recapture of Newport. According to General Greene and Lafayette, the captains of the French fleet are upset that they must serve under Count d'Estaing. He is a land officer. They are united to prevent him from doing anything that might bring him credit. The count is helpless, despite French promises of relief, because of the defiance of his own unwilling officers."

"What a waste of time and effort," Samuel Adams said.

"General Washington writes now that we could attack Newport, or even retreat. But using all his resources, knowledge from deserters, and intelligence, he cannot determine what the British plan will be."

He stopped and set down the letters. A silence fell over the group, each considering the dilemma facing the Americans in Rhode Island.

"I respect the choices of our generals," Samuel Adams said, standing, "and believe we can leave the military situation in their hands.

"Are we in agreement?"

"Aye, yes," those present responded.

"Let the record so state. I will write to General Washington to inform him," Henry Laurens said.

"*Le Vaisseau le Languedoc.*" Ozanne, Pierre, 1778–1779.
Library of Congress Prints and Photographs

The carved wooden sign of the Indian King displayed the image of a profiled Native, feathers straight, sternly greeting visitors to the tavern. James followed Elbridge Gerry and Richard Henry Lee inside. Well-to-do citizens clustered in groups, sipped rum punch, nibbled on pastries. They glanced at the members of Congress, then resumed their conversations. *A drink would be good for my health, despite the state of my pocketbook*, James thought.

"Silas Deane has now spoken in Congress three times," Richard Henry said, taking a seat at a table.

James waved to a passing waiter, who took their orders. "The first time Silas Deane attended, he stated he wished to settle his accounts. He provided a partial listing of funds he said the commissioners owed him, but said he left his vouchers in France. He brought letters from Dr. Franklin and Monsieur de Beaumarchais attesting to his excellent service."

Elbridge's sharp eyes swept the crowded tavern before he spoke. Seeing no one interested in their conversation, he relaxed. "Benjamin Franklin's letter indicated that he thought enemies of the agent had misrepresented Deane's d-d-dealings. By 'enemies,' he implied your brothers, Arthur and William, c-c-commercial agent for Congress." He glanced apologetically at Richard Henry.

Richard Henry stiffened visibly, picked up his glass of Madeira, and choked back words along with the wine, a frown growing on his face.

Elbridge continued. "When we questioned him as to his expenditures, Dean became d-d-defensive. He said he did not have answers at p-p-present. And he protested he was being provoked into c-c-condemning himself. When a motion was made that his report be given in writing, he left abruptly."

"I think he has been compliant," James said, setting down his tankard of cider after a long swallow. He pictured the slight, gray-haired merchant from Connecticut, face pale, cheeks flushed. "Any animosity Arthur Lee may have held towards Silas Deane surely did not cause Deane's recall."

"I think there is more to this story. It is clear to me that Silas Deane has engaged in underhanded and reprehensible behavior. That is also is my brother Arthur's opinion." Richard Henry's voice held an edge of bitterness.

"Congress is not finished questioning him." *There is no need for Richard Henry to feel defensive regarding his attitude towards Silas Deane.* "It is highly suspicious that he has no paperwork to substantiate what he says. Without proof, we cannot separate business dealings from which he profited from those he brokered to benefit the country."

"I agree," Elbridge said. "He may c-c-cool his heels while we consider other matters. At present, we can neither pay him nor t-t-trust him to return as commissioner."

"There certainly is no inclination to return him to France," James said. He drained his tankard. "Gentlemen, thank you for your company."

Richard Henry pursed his lips but remained silent. Together, the three left the tavern, the evening stars brilliant and the streets quiet.

Chapter 19

A Rift Among the Commissioners

September 1, 1778, Tuesday

The first letter's neat writing was blotted, like luminous clouds on a summer day. It and its companion had arrived yesterday. This evening, after working on documents for the Committee for Foreign Affairs, he found time to read Abigail's letters. The evening was warm and moist, promising rain later.

> Braintree, 24 June 1778
> Dear Sir,
>
> I do not know whether I should answer your letter of April 1, for indeed, Sir, I begin to think of you as a very dangerous man. A corrupt statesman once said that every man had his price. I think of Sir Robert Walpole, who gained friends through flattery. Speaking truth might have been better, but he judged others by his own corrupt disposition and I do the same when I state that I am unworthy of the words offering me praise, and I must call Mr. Lovell an ingenious and well-spoken flatterer, whose praise is not wholly due to a weakness in human nature, for a desire to appear worthy of esteem by those of great virtue and ability shows proof of a wish to imitate and nurture a good heart.
>
> The recent wonderful news from the court of France in some way compensates for the anxiety I felt from it before, and I now may look forward to the pleasure it must give my Friend upon his arrival to find his country so well supported, and a prospect opening for its future glory and welfare. But you are kind to advise me to confine my imagination to a future happy day. Oh, Sir, you have shown me a reason for being which is

my food by day and my rest by night, shedding a ray of light upon the gloomy hours, days, and months as they pass.

The letters that you mention in yours of March 21, written to my partner, arrived and were delivered to me, and according to his directions I opened them all and read them with the pleasure which your writing must always give your correspondence. However, the plan of friendship will reach you before this letter. But it was not for this we have endured hunger, cold, nakedness, the sword, and pestilence, but rather for the laws, the rights, the generous plan of power delivered down from age to age, by our renowned forefathers.

Excuse the length of this letter. I nearly tossed it in the fire, but considering how long it took me to write it, and the cost of the paper, and my curiosity to know what was in Mr. Deane's packages, this being the most convenient way to ask for that information, I let it come with the signature of

Portia

James grinned, realizing his flattery had not prevented her response. *She is unduly sensitive. But if I can make her Friend's absence less burdensome for her, I will. It is hard for us to part with those we love for long periods of time.*

The other letter was shorter.

Braintree, 19 August, 1778
My dear Sir,

I just received your letter of August the 6th. How sorry I am that I have not before this told you that as the Scotch song says, "I had banished all my grief, for I was sure the news was true and I was sure he's well." Indeed, Sir, I have been so absorbed by my own happiness, selfish, to be sure, that I scarcely thought of sharing it. But I owe you a debt of gratitude, who, despite the many public cares which must take all your hours, have frequently given up sleep for the kind purpose of giving comfort and easing the fears and anxieties of this friend, who owes you much. No more proof was required to convince me that the good sense, kindness, and thoughtfulness of Mr. Lovell could be unchanged by any business or employment in which he could be engaged—and he may be assured, if it gives him any satisfaction, that the marvelous talent he has in showing these virtues will ever cause women to remain fond of him in a particular manner.

Portia

He read again the reference to the Scottish song. *Mary would appreciate that. Her Scottish father often shared stories and songs from his homeland. Yes, I wrote to Abigail in August. But I would never wait for an answer before I shared with her the news of her beloved John's safe arrival. Such news must be on its way, post-haste.* In the margin he read a brief note requesting him to ship her some flour, if possible.

The watch called the hour of midnight, a lonely, harsh voice. *We have had a long week,* he thought, remembering yesterday's debate. Congress had at length resolved to encourage those drafted into the militia who chose to enlist for three years, or until the war's end, with a bounty of twenty dollars. *More brave lads may join the service,* he thought, blowing out his candle.

September 18, 1778, Friday

"Sir, I have additional information regarding the actions of Silas Deane and the agent William Carmichael." Richard Henry Lee stood, his dark eyebrows furrowed in anxiety, his arms crossed, black silk-wrapped hand on top. James shifted in his chair. *When would Congress ever be satisfied with its knowledge of the actions of the merchant from Connecticut?*

"Please proceed," President Laurens said, looking up calmly from his notes.

"This relates to William Carmichael's employment in bearing messages for Benjamin Franklin and Silas Deane and to his acting as secretary for them. Carmichael was quite familiar with their business pursuits. I have information that Mr. Carmichael charged Mr. Deane with misapplication of the public money," Richard Henry said impatiently.

"Very good, Mr. Lee, but you will provide that information in writing." President Laurens spoke in crisp, brief syllables. *It is getting late, and Richard Henry's temper seems to be getting the best of him.*

"Now we will hear a report from the committee appointed to consider the commissioners' letters."

The committee's report revealed Arthur Lee's displeasure that Benjamin Franklin and Silas Deane had sent their dispatches by way of Mr. Carmichael without first consulting him. According to Arthur Lee, the other commissioners had previously agreed with him to have Mr. Stevenson, another agent, take the dispatches, but instead they chose to employ Mr. Carmichael. However, they had not informed Arthur Lee about the change. In harsh language, Arthur Lee had expressed his bitterness and sense of betrayal at the other commissioners' lack of confidence in him.

"We will take that statement into advisement," President Laurens said. "Richard Lee, have you now a written report?"

"I do." Richard Henry Lee stood and held up a paper. "Mr. Carmichael said in Nantes that Mr. Deane had used public money for his own purposes. Mr. Carmichael also said an open rupture had occurred between Arthur Lee and the other commissioners at Passy. Benjamin Franklin and Silas Deane decided to conduct business without consulting Arthur Lee. Furthermore, Mr. Carmichael has no doubt that the decision was made based on Mr. Deane's insinuations. Mr. Carmichael said he would disclose these more fully when he arrived in America, and he recently has." He stopped speaking, lowered his paper, and glared balefully at the president.

"As Mr. Carmichael is now here, I suggest Congress hear from him in person," Samuel Adams said abruptly. "I have always found Arthur Lee to be an honorable person, so if Mr. Carmichael can enlighten us as to why Mr. Deane and Dr. Franklin are at odds with him, it would be beneficial."

Richard Henry sat down, his clenched jaw and folded arms showing his effort to hold his emotions in check. *Arthur Lee is his brother, after all.*

"Very well. Congress will request Mr. Carmichael appear for questioning," Henry Laurens concluded. "We are dismissed."

It is best, James thought, picking up his papers and preparing to leave the Pennsylvania State House, *that we hear directly from Mr. Carmichael. And, there are members of Congress who find ways to profit from the war effort. If Silas Deane has done so, he is not alone. In any case, when it comes to commissioners, we already have thrown in our weight with Dr. Franklin. He is minister plenipotentiary to France, America's sole representative, appointed just four days ago. And if we gain an alliance with Spain and open trade with Holland, as we hope, we had better choose someone other than Arthur Lee for commissioner to those countries. It appears Arthur Lee rankles the eminent Dr. Franklin. Perhaps Arthur Lee is just a trifle difficult to get along with. There is a rift approaching.*

James returned to his room, tired and preoccupied. He had not heard from Mary that week. Unusual, as she was generally as regular as clockwork. Her customary news involved the children, their health, and food shortages. Her letters often frustrated him, as he could do little about the problems they so painstakingly depicted. Still, they were an assurance she was managing.

He mounted the narrow stairs wearily and pushed open his door. General Horatio Gates was on his mind. He felt the general's talents were underutilized.

Further, he was concerned about the news that General Gates had been challenged to a second duel by his former aide, General James Wilkinson, early in September at Harrison, NY.

James took out paper, lit a candle, and wrote to Horatio Gates that he was too valuable to be wasted in a duel.

He blew out the candle, then made ready for bed.

In the still early morning hours, he woke in a sweat. Flies, flies were everywhere under him, around him, buzzing horridly, stinging. The air was hot, sultry, close. He could scarcely breathe. He threw off his covers and sat up, his shoulders tight and painful, his head throbbing. He had been lying on rough straw in a jail cell, the echo of a gunshot resounding in a hall outside, clanging and resounding like an iron bell, the shriek of a dying soul pulsing through his body. He clutched his aching head with both hands and breathed deeply, waited until his heart stopped pounding. *What now? I must be working too hard. And I fear for my family, and the progress of the war.*

He took deep breaths until his head cleared. *What else?* There was the matter of Silas Deane, hanging over Congress like a malignant boil. The merchant from Connecticut's actions had created a deep division.

James hated it that discord and distrust were developing among the members of Congress, some at the least condoning Silas Deane's actions, others suspicious and critical. The split was long and deep, he saw, causing a fracture where before there had been none. *And when those from such different backgrounds and interests labor together, day in and day out, differences are bound to arise.*

He lay back down, his heart rate slowing, determined to do his best to promote harmony. *I must not allow this conflict to discourage me. As I wrote to my friend General Horatio Gates tonight, I always make the best of every mishap.*

September 19, 1778, Saturday

Somewhat to the delegates' astonishment, as the day drew to a close, President Laurens stood, a sheaf of papers in his hand. His voice raised in urgency, he declared he had a matter to present as a delegate, not as the president of Congress. The congressmen, taken aback, agreed. Henry Laurens had waited on the edge of his chair for over two hours, visibly upset, until the business of the day had reached its conclusion.

As a delegate, Henry could present personal information that would be inappropriate coming from the president. *He will have something momentous to say, judging by his behavior.*

The president faced the assembled congressmen and paused before he spoke, as if to collect his words. "Ralph Izard is as fine a gentleman as we have ever chosen for a diplomatic mission." His words spilled out harsh and rapid as if a dam had broken and waters rushed forth. "His letters to me reveal an unfortunate, contemptible lack of consideration in the treatment he has been given by the two senior commissioners at the court in France, Dr. Benjamin Franklin and Silas Deane."

Around the room rose a sigh of recognition of the characters involved. Everyone had opinions about Benjamin Franklin. His morality was likely not in question. Nor his principles. He was dedicated to America, to freedom. But his methods? James realized that even for those most enamored with the famous scientist for his abilities and talents, his actions seemed at times peculiar. And his age was always a factor. He simply sees things differently. According to rumor, he was beloved at court, particularly by the ladies. The French found him fascinating, endlessly treating him to parties and galas. Was he perfect? No, probably no one thought of him as perfect.

Silas Deane was another matter. Ralph Izard's testimony against Silas Deane could influence Congress as the group deliberated the commissioner's record. James listened keenly as Henry Laurens spoke. His voice sharp, he shared several private letters from Ralph Izard, a fellow delegate from South Carolina, now in Paris after Tuscany's refusal of him as commissioner.

"Ralph Izard confided in me that from the first time he arrived at the court, he sensed a great split among the commissioners. Dr. Franklin and Silas Deane constantly sided against Arthur Lee. He found such conduct unjustifiable. In particular, he described Mr. Deane's behavior as unreasonably haughty and offensive. This high-handed behavior he could not understand.

"He found that the commissioners shared no news with him, not even that of the glorious win at Saratoga, nor did they report to him when a ship would be leaving for America so he could safely send dispatches. He confronted Benjamin Franklin with his concerns. The doctor apologized and said he would change his behavior, but in fact he did not change at all."

A murmur of disbelief and sympathy swept through the listeners.

His voice impassioned, Henry Laurens continued. "In two letters, Ralph Izard stated that to his certain knowledge, his dispatches to Congress were opened by Silas Deane. According to Ralph Izard, Mr. Deane is not a proper person at all to be employed by Congress." He stopped, his forehead dripping with sweat. The congressmen around him were silent, each lost in thought. Henry Laurens wiped his face with his handkerchief and handed the letters to Charles Thomson.

The secretary set the letters down. "Gentlemen, I suggest we let these lie on the table. We are adjourned."

October 15, 1778, Wednesday

For three days, William Carmichael, the secret agent appointed by Congress as assistant to Silas Deane, appeared at the Pennsylvania State House, summoned to offer information about Silas Deane's activities. Sophisticated, schooled at the University of Edinburgh, William Carmichael appeared at ease. His fine suit of gray silk was impeccable, his expression alert.

After hours of questioning, the gist of William Carmichael's response was that he had offered to assist Silas Deane in such matters as copying letters and translating conversations. But Carmichael stated he paid little attention to the purchases Silas Deane made, as he wished no responsibility for them.

William Carmichael's responses were acceptable, but they failed to clear suspicions of Silas Deane's misappropriation of public funds. In fact, they further implicated Silas Deane. At one point, William Carmichael stated Silas Deane used public money received from Monsieur Beaumarchais to purchase vessels for the interest of private citizens, including his own.

James was inclined to agree that there had been no reason yet offered for Congress to absolve Deane from further responsibility. Until more information surfaced, Congress's first commissioner would have to wait. Meanwhile, William Carmichael's testimony merely made understanding of Silas Deane's financial transactions more difficult.

October 21, 1778, Wednesday

After a week in bed suffering a fever, James felt able to return to Congress.

"How has it been?" he asked Elbridge Gerry at breakfast. Miss Dalley sallied into the dining room, a tray of steaming rolls in her floury hands. A fire glowed in the hearth; fresh split pine scented the air.

He eyed Miss Dalley with new respect. "Thank you for your kind attentions to me while I was ill," he said.

"It was nothing," Miss Dalley said, pushing back brown curls under her cap, leaving a streak of flour on her forehead. "Warm broth—it was the least I could do. You are most welcome." She curtsied, her tall figure bending awkwardly.

Elbridge picked up a fresh roll, and then reached for the pot of jam. "A few days ago, we received a letter from the C-c-count d'Estaing. We resolved to thank him officially, stating we held the highest opinion of his zeal. We noted his s-s-spirited and brave offer to join in the command against Rhode Island."

He glanced in his nearly empty teacup.

"Reading your tea leaves?" James said mildly.

"One might say," his colleague responded with a smile. "Though d'Estaing was not able to complete the c-c-command he first began, still, it is better to thank him for what he intended than to bewail what he did not accomplish."

"Thus, reading your tea leaves correctly."

"Congress also passed a resolution giving the Marquis de Lafayette l-l-leave to return for a visit to France, and authorized President Laurens to write the Marquis a letter of thanks for his zeal, c-c-courage, and many services to the United States."

"Appropriate. He manages to be a source of hope and inspiration to many."

"We also will have the minister plenipotentiary at the c-c-court of Versailles create an elegant sword to be presented to the Marquis with the thanks of the United States. And we wrote a letter of thanks to the French king for his part in s-s-supporting our liberty and independence."

"Excellent," James said. He imagined the gray-haired, plainly dressed Dr. Franklin handing a shining silver sword to the Marquis. "We need to keep our friends' good will alive and flourishing."

"Most c-c-certainly."

"It is nearly time we leave for the State House." James pushed back his plate. "I was able to do little in the days I was ill. The fever had to run its course. But I did write to Jonathan Trumbull, senior, the governor of Connecticut. Poor fellow—his son Joseph, my friend, passed away from an illness, and he requested my help to settle his son's accounts. Joseph was so good to my family. He was the best commissary general Washington will ever have."

He paused, then looked out the tall windows at the trees behind the house, flaming orange and red.

"I have sent John Adams at least fourteen or fifteen letters but have heard nothing."

"With the Marquis de Lafayette traveling to Paris, it would be a g-g-good opportunity to send a l-l-letter. But you have just recovered from an illness. Grab your c-c-coat and hat, my dear fellow. It is unseasonably windy and r-r-rainy outdoors."

Chapter 20

The Newspaper War Heats Up

December 7, 1778, Monday

"What did you think of Deane's d-d-defense?" Elbridge Gerry asked James. The warm fire crackled before their table at Clark's Inn.

"I think he should not have published it," James said, taking a drink from his tankard. "Since the Pennsylvania Packet came out Saturday, we are beset ith criticisms. The fine people of Philadelphia ask, rightly, why Congress's business is put into the public eye."

Elbridge Gerry nodded.

"Congress is entitled to ask its commissioners questions about their use of public money. If Arthur Lee's charges rub Silas Deane the wrong way, our former commissioner should have responded to them in Congress, not in the Pennsylvania Packet."

"I agree." Elbridge took a bite of his pork cutlet. "He need not feel so defensive. Silas Deane has his s-s-supporters in Congress. He is not alone in profiting from supplying the c-c-country, if indeed he did."

"The worst of it is, as Deane questions Congress's methods, he causes division and distrust. His appeal to the people, 'To the Free and Virtuous Citizens of the United States,' merely makes more enemies for us, of which we have ample." James bit into his roll gloomily.

"Congress has many more c-c-concerns keeping us busy than the finances of Silas Deane, important though those are."

"And Deane's accusations against Arthur Lee, one of our long-serving commissioners, have created a partisan atmosphere, one of doubt and distrust in our decisions. The waters are muddied, there is no mistaking it," James said gloomily. "Shall we return?"

"Mr. Lovell, I have something for you," Secretary Charles Thomson said. He held up a small black book. James came over to the secretary, passing by William Carmichael. William Carmichael had entered Congress as a delegate from Maryland the previous month. *Is it my imagination that he cast a glance of recognition on the volume?*

"What have we here?" he said, taking the book and examining it.

"I have had possession of this article since early September. It was given to me by Robert Morris. It contains notes that relate to the business of the Committee for Foreign Affairs."

James read the title. "*Entick's New Spelling Dictionary.* Of course. I am familiar with it—and with some of its purposes." He remembered Richard Henry Lee telling him he communicated with his brothers using a cipher derived from the dictionary.

"Dr. Arthur Lee sent it to Paris, to be delivered to America. Last spring, the book reached Congress. It was given to Robert Morris, to his puzzlement. Robert Morris turned the dictionary over to me in September. I discovered concealed within it a portion of a letter from Arthur Lee suggesting treasonous behavior on the part of Joseph Reed, president of the Executive Council of Pennsylvania. As it is from an American commissioner whose disagreements with another are now well known, I give it to you."

"Its repository with the Committee for Foreign Affairs is rightly placed," Charles Thomson said, with a slight bow.

Curious, James took the book, turned to the back, and saw a folded paper tucked in the lining of the cover, barely visible against the spine. Joseph Reed was a prominent lawyer in Philadelphia and delegate to Congress. Reed was popular and, as far as James knew, honest. Arthur Lee's charge seemed to him a little far-fetched.

"I will take note of the contents. Thank you," he said, returning to his seat. William Carmichael caught James's eye and motioned to him.

"I see you have the *Entick's New Spelling Dictionary,*" William Carmichael said, as James stopped near his seat. "When I traveled to America in the spring of 1776, bringing with me letters from the American commissioners to Congress, I brought what I think was that volume to Robert Morris. I did not know its purpose."

"It contained a letter, secreted in the flyleaf, from Arthur Lee to the Committee of Secret Correspondence." James opened the black book and pointed to the small slit that showed the folded page.

"Then it has reached its destination. Good day," William Carmichael said, turning to his seat.

"The same, I am sure," James said. William Carmichael appeared unscathed by his testimony to Congress earlier. In fact, he appeared to be pleased to be part of the group.

Seated, James opened the spelling dictionary. He extracted the page, unfolded it, and began reading. The letter described the value of tobacco to France, which Arthur Lee indicated was more than Americans realized. And it did indeed caution the Committee of Secret Correspondence about Joseph Reed, though part of the page was torn off.

James placed the spelling dictionary in his satchel. Later, he would copy the letter into a blank page or two at the rear of the book and add a statement explaining how and when he received it. Keeping records was important, he knew. He took out his notes and prepared for the session of Congress.

The afternoon swam in a sea of business matters. Warrants from the treasury took up a great deal of time. *It seems that every other moment in Congress is consumed with finances. We cannot move without the consideration of loans, taxes, the depreciation of our currency.*

At some point he looked up to see John Jay's eyes on him.

John Jay had just arrived as a delegate from New York. Straight as an arrow, with a prominent nose and penetrating eyes, he had served in Congress in the past and was the chief justice of the New York Supreme Court. James remembered that just a few years ago John Jay had been supportive of independence, even before Henry Laurens was himself convinced. *He will make a good member of Congress.*

Towards the end of the session, President Laurens stood, his usually calm face agitated and upset. "I have just received two letters from Ralph Izard. I place them before you, knowing you wish to have all correspondence from the commissioners be open. And we have a visitor who wishes your attention, though his presence is unbidden," he added, his voice filled with scorn. He motioned to the door, where the slight figure of Silas Deane could be seen, pacing back and forth, as he glanced at the stolid doorkeeper who barred his way.

A clerk handed a note to the president, who glanced at it, then tossed it to the floor in anger.

"Why should Congress give up its time, consumed as it is with matters of national urgency, when Mr. Deane chooses to air his grievances in public, rather than to provide clarity about his affairs in Europe?" The president's tone rose in bitterness. He glanced about the Assembly Room, waiting for a response from the delegates. None came. There were frowns, some shifting uneasily in their seats.

"I suggest Mr. Deane provide his report regarding his affairs in Europe to Congress in writing, and if he must speak with us, he may return at six o'clock tomorrow," Henry Laurens said, forcing calm to his voice.

"Hear, hear," voices said.

"So resolved," President Laurens confirmed.

That evening in his room, James took out the little black spelling dictionary given him by Secretary Thomson. Outside, frost and ice gripped much of Philadelphia. Rain had frozen everywhere, coating trees, walkways, streets. Despite the small fireplace in his room, a woolen jacket felt good. From its place in the back flyleaf, he withdrew the folded letter from Arthur Lee and laid it out flat.

Taking out a quill and ink, he copied the letter onto blank pages at the back of the book. At the bottom, he found in Arthur Lee's spidery handwriting an explanation of the purpose of the book: its use as a cipher. The cipher was one that Lee had planned to use in writing to the Committee of Secret Correspondence.

> *This book is better than the last I sent you. It is to decipher what I write to you and what I write by. This is done by putting the page where the word is to be found and the letter of the alphabet corresponding in order with the word. As there are more words in a page than the letters of the alphabet, the letter must be doubled or trebled to answer that, as thus: to express the troops, you write 369, k. k381vv; ing, ed, s, etc., must be added when necessary, and distinguished by making no comma between them and the figures, thus: for betrayed, put 33ed. The letters I use are these: a b c d e f g h i j k l m n o p q r s t u v w x y z, which are twenty-six. I cannot use this until I know it is safe. You can write to Mrs. Lee, on Tower Hill, in a woman's hand; if you have both books, say the children are well; if the first only, the eldest child is well; if this, the youngest child is well. They will let this pass.*

Quite a system, James thought. *It would rely on each of the correspondents having the same edition of the dictionary, but it would work. And apparently there are two volumes to the spelling dictionary. I like my own keyword system better because those using it can fashion a unique table for reference in creating ciphers. Maybe I should contact John Adams and inform him of my keyword cipher. Surely, he would find it useful in sending messages. Just because I have not heard from Benjamin Franklin regarding the cipher I sent to him does not mean he is not using it. Perhaps he is.*

And what keyword would I suggest John Adams use? He thought a moment. *What word would both he and I be likely to recognize?* He envisioned the dinner they had enjoyed in Braintree the night before they had set out for Congress: the candlelight shining on Abigail's dark, smoothly arranged hair, the succulent roast, the paintings on the walls. It was at her brother-in-law's house, the home of Richard Cranch. *That will be it: I will ask John Adams to remember the family name of the home at which we enjoyed a meal together before setting out for Baltimore. Cranch.* He set aside his writing materials and yawned. A good day, after all.

December 10, 1778, Thursday

James broke the silence as he and others at Miss Dalley and Mrs. Clarke's boarding place warmed themselves by the fire in the parlor. "Francis Lightfoot Lee's letter to the public, criticizing Silas Deane's statement in the *Pennsylvania Packet* and defending Congress, has created a stir. His words were reasoned and considerate. He suggested people suspend judgment regarding Silas Deane's public, inflammatory statement, until the real friends of independence, those trusted to secure the public good, should ascertain the situation with facts. Of course, at the same time he upheld the honor of his brother Arthur." He set the gazette down.

"Our new president, Mr. John Jay, will find himself plentifully occupied with s-s-such matters," Elbridge Gerry said.

"I found myself amazed when Henry Laurens resigned yesterday. He said he resigned because he was unable to prevent the disarray that occasioned Silas Deane's address in the paper. Deane's publication has excited anxiety in the minds of the people."

Elbridge nodded. "Mr. Laurens will continue as delegate from S-s-south Carolina. And, no doubt, Mr. John Jay was aided in his election to the presidency t-t-today by his relative ignorance of matters pertaining to S-s-silas Deane, having just arrived in Congress three days previous."

"Therefore, it will be our duty to assist him in any way we can." Samuel Adams glanced up from his gazette.

"I must retire to my room to work. I wish you each a pleasant evening." James stood and placed the paper he had been reading on the side table.

"And I the same," Samuel Adams said. The evening broke up.

December 15, 1778, Tuesday

Thomas Paine had stirred up a hornet's nest. A letter he wrote criticizing Silas Deane was published by Mr. Dunlap in the *Pennsylvania Packet* on December 15. The pseudonym "Common Sense" did nothing to conceal the identity of the author.

"He should never have spoken out as he did," Henry Laurens fumed during a break in the day. "It begins to look as though Congress's business shall be aired publicly. He criticizes us for choosing Silas Deane as ambassador, calling his charges against the Lees 'coarse and vehement.' He says his intention was to prevent the enemy from drawing unjust conclusions and to protect the honor of Congress. But the result of his letter was the opposite." He slapped the newspaper down before him in irritation.

"Being tried in the court of public opinion is a miserable experience. I find that Paine is far more interested in pursuing his own views than in attending to the clerical needs of the Foreign Affairs Committee," James said.

"His writings are influential, his appeal great. I would hope that the negative sentiment he fostered towards Congress will evaporate."

December 24, 1778, Thursday

Silas Deane began his report to Congress on December 22 and continued the following day. Congress then put him on hold and on Christmas Eve formally welcomed General Washington. The general, tall of stature, imposing in bearing, greeted the delegates solemnly, shaking hands with the disciplined, calm manner of one used to making multitudes of decisions. Washington said little, but looked about him with a thoughtful, even critical gaze. James, shaking hands with him, felt once again a bulwark of strength that held firm, despite disappointments and difficulties.

Elbridge Gerry turned to James when they returned to their seats. "I understand he came to Philadelphia with the intention of discussing s-s-strategy for the campaign."

"Martha will be with him, no doubt."

"Even so. They are s-s-staying at the residence of Henry Laurens, on Chestnut S-s-street. We are invited to dinner there."

Congress chose a committee representing a cross-section of the states to meet with General Washington: two New York delegates, a Virginian, one from Connecticut, and one from South Carolina. *A good distribution, reflecting the British occupation of Rhode Island and New York.* James hoped the discussion would prove fruitful.

December 31, 1778, Thursday

After the day of thanksgiving had been celebrated on the last day of the year, the gray-haired commissioner and former commercial agent was called to present his final report. Silas Deane spoke with a fire in his eyes, as if daring those listening to contradict him. At the conclusion of his report, it was apparent to the delegates that Arthur Lee's accusations of Silas Deane's mismanagement of funds were incorrect. However, his explanation was still unsatisfactory. Congress dismissed him, informing Deane that he should remain available for further questioning and that his request to return to France would not be honored. The Connecticut merchant's impatience was palpable as he stormed out of the chamber.

Has he not given us all he has? James wondered. *Then too, once the public's appetite for reading about the dissension amongst Congress has been wetted, it will be insatiable. And perhaps the newspaper war has only just begun.*

Chapter 21

Can You Tell Me of Mr. Adams?

January 5, 1779, Tuesday

James opened the paper to see yet another letter from Thomas Paine. Paine's first letter in the *Pennsylvania Packet*, signed "Common Sense," had appeared a few days ago. Now he read Paine's continued disclosure that America, now France's ally, had benefitted before the alliance by an early and generous friendship. It stated that the supplies Mr. Deane prided himself on delivering from France were promised before the agent ever arrived there: arms, ammunition, supplies, and officers shipped on the *Amphitrite*.

"Early it was," he exploded to Elbridge Gerry at breakfast, "but secret it was as well. He says he has found papers that show the supplies sent to America before the French alliance were gifts. And his signature 'Common Sense' tells everyone who wrote the letters. His position as secretary for the Committee for Foreign Affairs is well known also. Poor foolish Paine, what has he gotten us into?"

James went to Congress that day expecting to hear some contest of Paine's *faux pas,* and he was not disappointed.

Minister Gérard bristled with indignation. "I must make it clear that all the supplies furnished to the United States—merchandise, cannons, or military goods— were sold to Monsieur Beaumarchais by the French department of artillery, he paid for them, and he is a creditor of the United States.

"There must be no question that the military goods were purchased, not gifts, prior to our alliance. I have spoken with Mr. Paine myself, and find him unrelenting in his exposition of what must only be a disaster to our relationship. I expect that Congress will control his behavior."

Angry, Monsieur Gérard took his seat. The rest of the day, tension simmered in the Assembly Room.

Our secretary, bold and useful as his writings have been to promote our cause and inspire soldiers and civilians alike, has overstepped his sphere of knowledge and written what he had no right to state, James thought, as he gathered his correspondence when Congress adjourned. *We must mend fences ere the damage is done. And have we not enough difficulties to attend to?*

Taxes, for one, he mused. *Today we resolved to raise $15 million for the year, allocating quotas equitably among the states, excepting Georgia for the present.*

And affairs in the south do not go well. At the end of December, Savannah fell to the British, the three thousand enemy soldiers sent from New York being more than a match for the American units under Major General Robert Howe. Those Americans not captured retreated to South Carolina. And we are mired in fiscal difficulties and now must deal with the meddling of an impetuous secretary who has exposed to the public Congress's work in foreign policy.

He wound his woolen muffler about his neck, jammed his hat on his head, and stepped out into falling snow.

January 14, 1779, Thursday

"Thomas Paine resigned from his position as secretary to the Committee for Foreign Affairs. At the same time, he suggested that Congress would not give him a hearing, prompting our apology. He has stirred up enough controversy that his leaving can only make me smile." James glanced at the stack of correspondence before him with a sigh. "And we stated to Minister Gérard that we disavow the letters to which Paine refers, that Congress is convinced the supplies sent by the three ships were not gifts, and that prior to our alliance His Most Christian majesty did not provide any supplies whatsoever to America. Our disapproval of the writings recently published is clear."

"So," Elbridge said, "we c-c-confirm our alliance by stating what we know not to be true."

"That is the gist of it," James said grimly. "We do what we must."

January 19, 1779, Tuesday

In his room, window curtains drawn against bitterly cold air, James smoothed out the ivory pages of Abigail's recent letter. *She is concerned for her husband. Think of all those parted from their families, the men in uniform, the sailors on their ships, the prisoners moaning in jails, not to mention delegates at their posts, and do what you can to ease one person's suffering.* His head ached from long hours poring over documents and listening to Henry Laurens explaining charges against Robert Morris, whom a newspaper article had accused of using his own company to ship goods for the army, but who contended he had merely used his firm's name to expedite the shipping. He picked up Abigail's letter.

> *January 4, 1779*
> *Dear Sir,*

May I be permitted to call your attention from the important and weighty matters of state to answer a question of interest to me. From information I just found, there is a new arrangement of the commissioners, Dr. Franklin being appointed minister plenipotentiary for France, Mr. Lee for Spain. My question is, where is my Friend to be placed? I would certainly hope not at a greater distance than he is at present. The public service may require a move; to that service he is devoted, and so must attend it where ever it is required, whilst I must endeavor to act the part allotted to my sex—patience and submission—a lesson I ought to be well versed in since I have been so often called to employ it.

I wish to know if any vessels have arrived at the south from France by which you have received letters from my Friend. This day marks 10 months since he left his home. During this entire time, I have heard from him only 5 times, the last letter dated August 27, nearly four months ago. This is a painful situation and my patience is sometimes nearly exhausted. I should complain more except I am conscious I am writing to a gentleman who lives in continual mortification and self-denial, having already been absent from his family nearly two years, though the frequent exchange of letters must greatly lessen the pains of absence.

Am I entitled to the journals of Congress? If you think so, I should be much obliged to you if you would convey them to me. I would like the answer to another question, what shall we do with our currency? I fear it will be a Herculean labor to pull it out of its present pitiful condition. If the embargo should cease this month, Mr. Lovell will not be unmindful of his assured friend and humble servant,

Portia

He set the letter down and prepared his quill to respond.

Jan. 19, 1779

Yes, lovely Portia, you have written to one who lives in continual mortification and self-denial, who therefore can and does sympathize with you in your distress.

I am pleased when you mention my disinterested support of the public good, for I know you speak from an awareness to which the herd of worldlings are complete strangers. They would stare at your opinion, and ask, seriously, "What fortune does he sacrifice?"

I fear not from you the suggestion of vanity when I say I hope my example may strengthen your patience. I will strengthen my own by looking up to your dearest friend, whom even the worldling will admit displays a striking example.

You say it is near 11 months since he left Braintree. I find I am relieved by that stretch of time from an anxiety founded on my consideration of your dear sex that Mr. A's rigid patriotism had overcome. He used, in that spirit, to contemplate with pleasure a circumstance in you, similar to Mrs. L's aggravation in my absence from home. In spite of his past rebukes to me, I will take pleasure in your escape from worry.

You may be assured, dear Lady, that not a line for you has arrived here, nor anything relating to the public from your husband's hand, or I should have communicated both to you quickly.

Personally, I have not had a single line of answer from him, though my calendar proves I have written 16 or 18 times.

I am sorry you do not see all the papers from this quarter. The vanity of a recent representative will work its own destruction. The Lees are men of morality as well as science, and the advantage of speaking of them behind their backs will not turn out so great as was first hoped by the Innuendo-Man, so R. H. Lee quaintly calls Mr. D.

She will know I mean Silas Deane, he thought. He dipped his pen in the ink and continued.

As to our money, until we get a foreign loan, we can only patch and patch.

As for Mr. Thaxter, he has never written me a single line or sent me a verbal message about where I will find my saddle-bags which I lent to him.

> *"Past 12 o'clock and a rainy morning," says the watchman under my window. Taking his hint and quitting, for the present, my conversation with virtue, sense, or beauty, shall I not find, on my pillow, a rest sweet as that of a cradled infant? Or, if fancy will maintain her control jointly with Morpheus, shall I not realize the slumbers of the Arcadians, and, in that, know myself your affectionate friend.*
>
> *James Lovell*

He set the letter in the stack of correspondence to post the next day. Matters both urgent and pressing tumbled through his mind. *We will, I hope, soon petition the Count d'Estaing to send a fleet to assist us at Savannah. But why have I not heard from Dr. Franklin? I must inquire whether there is any reason for his lack of correspondence.*

February 15, 1779, Monday

"Our commander-in-chief and his wife Martha must be back at c-c-camp by now," Elbridge Gerry said. He stepped with difficulty through the drifted snow.

"So many bountiful dinners they attended in the month they were here. I myself was invited to several. One would have thought Philadelphia society would never tire of hosting the Washingtons."

"Money matters seem t-t-turned upside down," Elbridge said. "Continental c-c-currency is worth perhaps one-eighth of its face value. Have you heard about the horse that c-c-cost twenty thousand dollars?"

"I can well believe it." James tugged his tricorn hat down against a gust of wind. "General Washington must think often of the soldiers, subsisting on meager provisions in the hills at Morristown. The grand entertainments he attended here do not always suit him, I think. At dinners, I saw him cast his eye with dislike at the repasts."

They trudged on in silence, approaching the Pennsylvania State House.

Elbridge spoke first. "The British have gained ground in S-s-south Carolina and Georgia. And they have held Savannah since the end of D-d-december."

"I wrote to Benjamin Franklin at the end of last month, expressing our hope that the Count d'Estaing assist us with a detachment of his fleet. And I just wrote to General Benjamin Lincoln, now commander in the south, expressing my sympathy that he lacks provisions for his troops."

That night, after a long day, he collapsed in bed. Thoughts tossed him from one side to the other as he restlessly sought slumber. His hungry family, his frayed shirts, his exhaustion from writing and attending meetings, and endless committee work all clamored for attention. At length he fell asleep.

He woke with a start to the sound of an iron door clanging, laughter malevolent and cruel, the rattle of a chain. He sat up, drenched with sweat despite the frigid air in his room, and looked about him, then realized the life-like sound had occurred in a dream. Yet the sense of being locked away was so real he decided he must sit and breathe deeply for some minutes before his head cleared.

He thought over the evening. He had enjoyed a pleasant enough meal with his colleagues. But his rent had been raised, from £60 to £200, and worries over food shortages for the army and his family filled him with apprehension.

Perhaps it was those concerns that had flooded his heart with fear. *Fortunately*, he concluded, *it has been some time since I suffered such a nighttime trepidation.* He composed himself as best he could, listening to the wind sighing.

February 16, 1779, Tuesday

"Joseph Reed complains of misdemeanors in the administration of Major General Arnold while he was military governor of Philadelphia. General Arnold will be suspended from command in the army of the United States while inquiry is made into his public conduct." General Whipple handed a packet to James, who sat up in his bed, his hair disheveled. The general eyed his friend with concern.

"I am sorry I had to stay home today, but really my health required it. To be sure, I was not idle." He sighed and motioned his visitor to a chair. The snug room had just enough space for an additional chair. The New Hampshire delegate looked about with some trepidation at the fireplace, the wardrobe, the rumpled bed, and lastly at James himself, untidily attired in his robe. Apparently deciding he would be safe if he stayed a few minutes, General Whipple sat down, then tugged off his heavy coat. James noticed the naval officer edged a few inches away from him.

"We also resolved that the commander-in-chief put Major General Arnold to a court martial and required the council of Philadelphia to supply evidence of General Arnold's wrongdoing."

"Benedict Arnold aspires to the land and lifestyle coveted by his fiancé, Peggy Shippen," William said. "Her father, the wealthy Judge Shippen, also wants to see his daughter housed in the manner to which she has become accustomed."

"The fact that Judge Shippen leans towards Loyalists does not seem to deter General Arnold. When he became military governor of Philadelphia, he bought up stores that should have gone to the army and then sold them dearly, thus making what could be considered illegal profits. His leg may not be healed from his wound and he may walk with a limp, but his injury has not slowed him down."

"Scruples are not what endeared Miss Shippen to General Arnold. We will see what the committee uncovers."

"I will join you tomorrow," James said. "Thank you for your kindness in stopping by. The work is for now somewhat under control, to my relief."

"Good night, then." General Whipple stood, pulled his heavy coat on.

"Until tomorrow."

Chapter 22

The Debt Owing to M. Beaumarchais

March 29, 1779, Monday

The Baron Von Steuben, flanked by his tall Italian greyhound Azor, his yellow eyes watching every movement, waited in the rear of the Assembly Room. His personal secretary Peter Stephen Du Ponceau stood to his side. James nodded in friendly fashion to the baron, formal in his Continental uniform. Baron Von Steuben raised his gloved hand in greeting.

After some preliminary business, President John Jay stood. "We owe thanks to Inspector General Baron Von Steuben for his organization of drills providing discipline to our troops. His book *Regulation for the Order and Discipline of the Troops of the United States* contains drills and practices to ensure a standard, coordinated method of maneuvers for the whole army. It is our pleasure to recommend the printing of the regulations for the troops."

The delegates stood, offering a round of applause. Major General Von Steuben bowed.

"So ordered."

"A good business," Elbridge Gerry said to James, as the clapping subsided.

"Most beneficial."

"We will now turn to the business of the defense of our southern states," President John Jay said, with his customary directness. James sighed and settled into the task.

March 30, 1779, Tuesday

He picked up Abigail's letter. The carefully written pages had arrived a few days ago, but he had scarcely glanced at them. Now he read her words with pleasure.

> *Braintree*
>
> *February–March 1779*
>
> *Since I last wrote I have been relieved from much anxiety by*
> *the arrival of the Mifflin, bringing a large packet of letters*

192

written on various dates, one dated as late as December 2nd. In reply to some pathetic complaints, my Friend assures me he has written three letters where he received one, and that he has full as much reason to complain of his friends as they have of him. From Mr. Samuel Adams he has received only one short card, from Mr. Gerry not a syllable, from Mr. Lovell only two or three very short letters.

My heart recoils with indignation when I see generous plans of freedom sapped and undermined by guileful arts and machinations of self-love, ambition, and avarice. Whether the late indiscreet appeal to the public may be considered in this light, time will determine, but an open and avowed enemy to America could not have fixed upon a more successful method of raising jealousy among the people or of sowing the seeds of discord in their minds.

I ask if you are at liberty to tell me the important news which is said to have arrived from Spain, which is good, very good, and so good that nobody must know it. Various are the conjectures concerning it.

Mr. Thaxter acknowledges your reproof just, and kisses the rod, makes his excuses I suppose in the enclosed letter. I will seek one in the benevolent friendship of Mr. Lovell for the freedom I take in scribbling to him. I love everyone who manifests a regard or shows an attachment to my absent Friend, and will indulgently allow for the overflowing of a heart softened by absence, pained by a separation from what it holds most dear on earth. A similarity of circumstances will always lead to sympathy and is a further inducement to subscribe myself your friend and servant,

Portia

He unfolded the enclosed note and scanned it, noting the polite and brief contents, then set it aside. *I may get my saddlebags back after all, if Thaxter finds a way to send them.*

He turned to his committee work.

April 30, 1779, Friday

The Delaware River flowed quietly, a light wind fluttering red and blue flags on ships, sailors working ropes or moving cargo.

"I think it is the warmest, most pleasant day we have had yet," James observed to Elbridge Gerry.

"The intelligence we received today about Arthur Lee makes it c-c-clear we have no option but to consider removing him from his p-p-position as commissioner."

James sat beside his friend at a bench by the river. "The Count de Vergennes told Minister Gérard he does not trust Dr. Lee, and in fact said he fears him. And, as Minister Gérard is the plenipotentiary so revered his 'lickspittle does not fall to the ground,'" he said with sarcasm, "we may have no choice but to fall into his position regarding Arthur Lee."

"Apparently." The lawyer's shrewd eyes swept the river.

"Our debates over the past months have reached this point. It is imperative we have a commissioner in whom we have confidence."

Elbridge glanced at James, shrugged, and then abruptly changed the topic. "Walking out is g-g-good for the soul." He looked over the wide, gently rippling current.

"On a day such as today, yes."

The two were silent for a few minutes, breathing the fresh, cool air.

James picked up a small flat stone nearby and, without thinking, threw it with a sidearm motion, sending it skipping lightly over the waves into the distance before it sank.

"I wish that the coming months would pass as quickly as that stone skipping over the water. My sons and I would throw stones like that at home from time to time." A feeling of longing for his family overcame him. For a moment, tears filled his eyes.

"I am sure your country appreciates your s-s-sacrifice. Shall we?" The street lamps glowed lemon yellow in their glass globes.

"At once, my friend."

June 5, 1779, Saturday

"I see that General Daniel Roberdeau and the panels appointed at the town's meeting have begun a process to improve prices in the market," he said to Elbridge Gerry.

Elbridge nodded his head and ran a hand over his silver-gray hair. "They have s-s-set new prices, especially for f-f-foods." Footsteps echoed on the brick floor as the delegates gathered.

"If the cost of whiskey and rum falls, I will be amazed, but they may have success with rice, coffee, or salt."

"They plan to charge Robert Morris with misconduct for his b-b-business practices."

"Robert Morris may be guilty on some counts, but he is not alone in reaping profits off of our current circumstances, not at all."

"And the problems in western New York grow, where s-s-settlers contend with attacks from the Iroquois and their Loyalist supporters. But Major General John Sullivan's expedition will l-l-leave later this month to move against them."

"At least three times last year, the Iroquois attacked defenseless settlers—one so terrible it was termed a massacre."

"Of the s-s-six Iroquois tribes, the Oneida alone have an agreeable attitude."

"Treaties and talking have not solved the problem, so Major General John Sullivan heads a large force of Continentals, at least three thousand, to deal with the Iroquois."

President John Jay sat at his table looking over papers. *He is no Henry Laurens. Henry would be up past midnight writing, taking care of business, if needed. John Jay is sometimes late to send out needed correspondence, but then he has a pretty wife here to keep him company. Not that I am always as timely with my writing as I would like to be, but I do make prodigious efforts.*

"It appears we are ready to start proceedings." James turned to listen to the president.

"Let us hear from the committee who considered the recent memorial of Monsieur de Francey, agent of Monsieur Beaumarchais," John Jay said, glancing towards Henry Laurens.

"We conferred with Monsieur de Francey and now have invoices of cargoes shipped from France by Monsieur de Beaumarchais, on the *Amphitrite*, the *Seine*, the *Mercure*, the *Amelie*, the *Therese*, the *Mere Bobie*, the *Marie Catherine,* and the *Flamand,* with interest. Cargoes consisted of goods advanced to Silas Deane, including arms and armaments. The total is over four and a half million livres, nearly £200,000 sterling."

The delegates sucked in their breath at the huge figure.

"The Committee for Foreign Affairs should write to the commissioners at the court of France and request they send a report of their proceedings in Monsieur Beaumarchais's accounts, as was ordered on April 13, 1778." Henry Laurens glanced at James.

He nodded in response. *I can do that. As I did last April. Or perhaps May. We were counting on Silas Deane to explain the amounts owed by Beaumarchais. Unfortunately, Deane was no help.*

July 19, 1779, Monday

"It is the season for complaints, I fear," James said to Elbridge Gerry. The slender lawyer pushed his half-eaten bowl of cold squash soup aside, wrinkled his nose, and looked at James.

"Shall we take ourselves elsewhere for something more s-s-substantial?"

"Most definitely," James said, standing. "'Squash' and 'soup' and 'cold' should never be used in the same sentence."

In the hall they encountered Miss Dalley. "I hope you gentlemen found the meal to be agreeable," she said. "Cook wanted to try out the recipe, and…."

"It was interesting," Elbridge Gerry said, noncommittal. "We have an engagement elsewhere, as it happens."

"Very well, then," she began.

James cut her off abruptly. "Good evening." He followed Elbridge Gerry out of the room.

Walking towards the town, the evening sultry, James said, "She has moved me up to the third floor, where there is no fireplace. This on top of raising the rent recently."

"In the name of 'fairness,' she told us she drew the names of those who must move to make r-r-room for two more lodgers. I hardly think it was a fair decision."

"For now, I fear I must make the best of it." James shrugged.

"Shall we go to Tun T-t-tavern on Water Street? It serves fine beer, and a good steak as well."

"Much to my liking." *I can stand myself to a meal, though it will pinch my pocket.*

"Speaking of complaints," he added, as their strides lengthened, "I would call Arthur Lee's vindication of his actions yet another. He responded point by point to Silas Deane and Benjamin Franklin's lack of trust in him."

Elbridge nodded. "Thomas Burke, that southern Irishman, was right to move that Arthur Lee's statement, along with the letters and vouchers he enclosed, be s-s-sealed up until Congress is prepared to consider it."

"It is another source of vexation that the war is going badly in the south. General Benjamin Lee wrote to us he is mortified by his losses."

"It is not his fault that he lacks adequate f-f-forces."

"Recently Fairfield and New Haven in Connecticut were horribly ravaged by the British."

"General Tryon lead his troops on an expedition up the Connecticut River and then overland to New Haven Bay, savagely d-d-destroying everything in their way. The Marine Committee plans to retaliate by burning and destroying B-b-british towns in Great Britain and the West Indies."

The three-story Tun Tavern hummed with gatherings of sailors and soldiers. James and Elbridge took their tankards of beer up the stairs to a quiet room.

"We did get some welcome news today. General Washington wrote that General Anthony Wayne did well at Stony Point in his assault on the British-held garrison there."

"Stony Point is particularly important, as it is there that King's F-f-ferry permits the c-c-crossing of the Hudson River."

James paused for a drink of his beer. "And we still debate the fisheries," he said, wiping his mouth with the back of his hand.

"It is an essential part of our p-p-peace preparations. New Englanders depend on c-c-cod and haddock in the waters off of North America. Any t-t-treaty must include those rights."

"At least the king of France approves of our having just one commissioner there. The king will no doubt be pleased we have requested paintings of him and Queen Marie Antoinette for our chambers, in honor of the birth of their little princess."

"I am sure the paintings will be grand. Displaying them will p-p-please the French as much as it will annoy the British, when we s-s-settle the peace."

A serving girl, rosy with heat and exertion, appeared with their plates of steak. "Will this be all, gentlemen?"

"Quite enough, thank you." James cut a piece of the tender, sizzling meat.

"Cold squash s-s-soup, indeed. This is more like it."

At his lodgings, he trudged up the two flights of stairs to his new room. It was plain and simply furnished. To his relief, one wall was set against the brick expanse of a central chimney. *The chimney will make the winter bearable. But the narrow window was but three hand breadths in width, permitting little air flow. This means both the summer and the winter will be warm. Ah, me.* The small table was adequate, though plain, and he set his things on it, forced the window as wide open as it would go, and settled down to read his letters.

He opened one from Mary. She reported that the garden was doing well at home, its care entrusted to the older children. Shortages in flour and basic supplies were apparent at market, but the family could already gather carrots, new potatoes, and lettuce. Mary hoped for a bountiful harvest. James prepared his quill and responded, sending her his hopes for a good growing season as well as the usual funds. He knew how his family depended on him.

A letter had arrived from Abigail Adams. *She must be responding to mine, written in early June.*

June 18 – 26, 1779

> *Do you love the natural sentiments of the heart? Take*
> *these, then, as they flow from the pen of Portia. After taking*
> *a ride this afternoon, I stopped at my brother-in-law Cranch's,*

when one of his family came to my carriage and told me a gentleman from Boston had left a large packet for me in the house. My heart leapt for joy—I asked him to deliver it immediately to me. The bulk of the packet insured it a clasp to my bosom. My spirit jumped for joy. It was dark; I could not see the handwriting but was in no doubt where it had come from. It was a dozen miles to my house, which seemed like an age to travel. I jumped out of the carriage, and called for a light before I got to the house, but when I held the packet up to the light, I saw Mr. Lovell's handwriting. Oh, I thought, the letters must have arrived at Philadelphia, and he, ever a good friend, had sent them to me. I broke the seal, and the dear delusion vanished like a vision. An involuntary tear (it could not be helped) found its way down my cheek, and for the first time I did not feel the pleasure which had always before accompanied a letter from Mr. Lovell.

It has been six months without a single line from my Friend. Having my expectations so raised and then so damped must excuse me for the impolite reception to my much-valued correspondent. He may in future have my leave to make use of whatever expressions he pleases to prove my benevolence is as strong as my power, since I have from acquaintance with him discovered the talent for which I once censured him comes naturally to him, and that far from being a lazy servant he demonstrated that talent ten times over. Nor would I rob him of the pleasure he takes in that too pleasing art, since it must be acknowledged that he is accomplished and proficient in it.

I will not disclaim the label of "amiable," since it is a quality which if I do not already possess I would wish to obtain even to the value of her whose price was far above rubies.

I imagine I should close this letter with no further addition lest you should discover that I am not in a very good humor. But not until I have assured you that I am with sentiments of esteem your friend and humble servant,

Portia

He lit a candle and prepared to answer her letter.

July 19, 1779

> *Your favor of June 18/26 is this hour come to hand.*
>
> *"Do I love the natural sentiments of the heart? Yes, AMIABLE correspondent, I truly love them; and your little story was far, very far from non-natural. You were betrayed, it seems, by a combination of circumstances such as a tender sensibility and the dusk of the evening, to make a pressure to your lovely palpitating bosom which soon after cost you a crying spell. If I do not forestall you by making a remark here myself, I shall expect that in your next letter you will turn my false wit upon me, and you will tell me that your misfortune had very natural consequences. But I hope you have by this time realized more substantial pleasures than the receipt of a packet from my esteemed friend. I have written to you lately to express my opinion of his return. A letter from Windship implies you are soon to be happy.*
>
> *Everything that wears the appearance of injury to him may be resolved into the dilatoriness which springs from the nature and constitution of a certain assembly here.*
>
> *Promise me that you will be upon your guard against tremors at the sight of writing upon large packets not in the handwriting you wish most to see, and I will put up a set of journals for your Mr. A. that you may read all the weaknesses of some who are called great men.*
>
> *Your obliged friend and humble servant,*
>
> *James Lovell*

She will enjoy reading the Journals, *and in them find all our flaws, but also our strength.*

Chapter 23

"A Wild Part to My Brain"

August 6, 1779, Friday

"It is unfortunate that the Americans' hold on the garrison at Stony Point was short-lived," James said, stifling a yawn. "Three days after General Anthony Wayne captured the fort, General Washington ordered it evacuated, as the Americans' force was not sufficient to keep it."

"True," Elbridge Gerry answered. "But before leaving, we destroyed everything and c-c-captured supplies and equipment. Not a bad piece of work."

The State House was quiet during the afternoon recess. Flies batted against closed windows. Heat swirled in the brilliant sunshine that seeped between the green curtains.

James loosened his shirt collar and reached for a pitcher of water, then withdrew long, folded pages from the stack before him. "I just received a letter from Benjamin Franklin, written over a year ago. He refers to letters that I sent to him from the Committee for Foreign Affairs. He says he never saw those letters."

"Loss of our d-d-dispatches is likely more common than we can know."

"Benjamin Franklin went on at great length about the difficulties of having multiple commissioners at the court. He states Arthur Lee is very angry, as he was not consulted in drafting the treaty with France. Dr. Franklin complains the expense of maintaining four commissioners is great. In comparison, he notes that the British have only one, Lord Stormont."

"Our minister plenipotentiary c-c-clearly has made up his mind that working with Arthur Lee will b-b-be out of the question."

"On the other hand, Arthur Lee reminds us that the other commissioners were directed to consult him on matters such as drafting the treaty. Yet they refuse to do so."

James picked up the letter. "Dr. Franklin makes it clear that at court their every statement is heard, and if what the commissioners say is at all dissimilar, it causes doubt in the minds of their listeners. According to him, the difficulties of consulting several commissioners on every matter and the time spent resolving the debates that arise make accomplishing business tedious and time consuming. And, since the three assigned there do not live in the same house, meeting itself is a problem. He says even their servants quarrel, taking their masters' part. He wishes we would separate them."

"Most interesting. What else d-d-does he say?"

"His other news is that the Spanish galleons have at length arrived. He expects a treaty to be concluded with Spain before long. Yet this letter was written a year ago, and there is no treaty yet."

"We have excused S-s-silas Deane from his attendance in Congress. He may return to Europe and s-s-settle his accounts."

"We will give him final payment, to be sure, but we will not accede to his ridiculous request to pay him for his time to return to Europe and settle his affairs."

"An outrageous s-s-suggestion, I agree."

James caught Elbridge's eye and nodded his thanks. *What are our colleagues for, if not to support us as we move forward?* He set the matter aside. The afternoon session was beginning.

August 27, 1779, Friday

An evening committee meeting finished, James wearily climbed the two flights of stairs to his room.

In keeping with his strategy to retain control of the Hudson River, a week ago General Washington had ordered a surprise attack on the British post at Paulus Hook, as its position at the mouth of the Hudson River was strategically important. Major Henry Lee, dubbed "Light-Horse Harry," had led a successful bayonet charge, gaining control of the post and taking one hundred and fifty prisoners. *I can be proud of my son James Jr., one of his adjutants.*

Control of the Hudson River corridor, including West Point, will keep New England from being cut off and offer movement for General Washington's Continental armies. I have just sent to the general the latest intelligence from Europe. Louis XVI has awarded Lafayette his own regiment of dragoons to accompany him to America. Also, the Count de la Luzerne will replace Minister Gérard, who requested a recall due to his health.

In his room, James found himself nearly dizzy with heat and fatigue. He took a drink of the tepid water on his nightstand and sat down. *What should I do next?*

A week ago, Congress received a letter from John Adams, home in Braintree on a visit.

Now he took up his pen to write to Abigail Adams. *Why do I write to her? Well, she is my friend, as surely now that her husband is home as she was when she pined and longed after him.*

August 27, 1779

Talking about friendship and other classes of affection would, just now, be but an insipid business between you and me. I mean all the insipidity for your side of the question; for on mine it would be of a worse kind. I am as certain, as I am that I am now spoiling paper, that I could not get through any one branch of the topic without a sort of envy in my bosom, a passion as mean as it is troublesome. I am not apt to be plagued with it; but, somehow or other, under the influence of contingencies, relating to you and me and a friend of both, which have happened since the 3rd of this month, my brains, I mean the wild part of them, are so affected that it would take me a hundred struggles to get a clean shot of envy if I once begin that talk above mentioned.

Now I bar your ever telling me that you did not know I had a wild part to my brain. Why, there is scarcely a parson in twenty parishes that has not more or less of it. Nay, consult the Journals which I send you, and you will be convinced that the wiseacres in Chestnut Street, Philadelphia, are furnished with the same variety of the qualities of the cerebellum. And if all the members of Congress have a wild part to their brain, for mercy's sake, tell me who can be without it. I hope no one will be so malicious to my system as to whisper to Portia, "But what is all this stuff about the brain? It was your bosom that the suspicion arose about?" Oh, I recollect it. But, my monitor, I have caught you astray. Even Portia thus is sometimes wild. How could you ask me such a question? You whose bosom has so often lately throbbed and even ached at only hearing that a vessel did or did not sail, at only reading the superscription of a packet a little larger than usual; nay, at only thinking at midnight when you neither heard nor saw anything? Do remember me to the person to whom you give the Journals. The Porter says the post is going.

James Lovell

September 21, 1779, Tuesday

James stood and steadied himself with his hand on the chair until the room ceased spinning and his head cleared. He rubbed his eyes. A catnap before the evening dinner—that was all he had promised himself. The sun sat low on the horizon; a strong breeze rattled the window. He had been so sick, at the end of August, for days, unable to do more than stay in his room, write letters, fall back into bed, that even now the weakness lingered. He had lost weight; the glimpse he had seen of himself in the parlor mirror showed hollow cheeks, gray streaks in his brown hair. For thirty-three months he had labored. Now he somehow had to regain the strength to persist and pick up the work again.

His return to Congress he credited to the rhubarb treatment. Perhaps the use of tartar emetic had helped, though the purge was nearly as bad as the illness. In a letter to John Adams in Braintree, he reported he was "engaged in a severe wrestling match with a chap who had successfully laid many on their backs lately," one known in France as *trépas*, but here as the grim reaper. He smiled sardonically.

James pulled on his worn black jacket and wrapped a silk scarf about his neck to hide the frayed collar. He tied his hair back and wiped his shoes clean. *Next month I will turn forty-two*, he mused. *I shouldn't feel like an old man, bent and feeble. Nor will I*, he determined, straightening himself up and leaving his room, shutting the door behind him with a firm motion.

Chapter 24

Military Governor Benedict Arnold

October 6, 1779, Wednesday

John Adams had only been in Braintree a few days before he left for Boston to help write a new Massachusetts Constitution. *I imagine Abigail is bereft. And now he must go overseas again. He will be minister to negotiate a peace with Britain, when that time comes.*

In James's last letter from John Adams, the commissioner had thanked him for his kind attentions to Portia, but said his rogueries were so bewitching that he would hesitate to trust him any nearer than Philadelphia and Braintree.

Reading those words, James laughed. *I merely try to liven her dull days from time to time.*

A commotion sounded outside the meeting room at the Pennsylvania State House. He started from his reverie, then glanced at Elbridge Gerry. At the rear the double doors stood open. Several people, including the sergeant-at-arms and a burly policeman, were struggling to hold back the military governor of Philadelphia. General Benedict Arnold could be seen pushing to break through the group. Arnold leaned heavily on a cane with one hand and waved a paper with the other.

"You would treat me like an imposter? And I the governor of the city? I deserve the protection of Congress, not their disdain."

He beat the floor with his cane and glared at the sergeant-at-arms.

"Most sorry, your excellency, but those are the Congress's orders. No one comes in without an invitation."

"Bah. Give them that, then." The general thrust the paper into the sergeant-at-arms' hands, turned, and stamped away in fury.

James turned to Elbridge Gerry. "His intrusion might relate to the riot."

"Just three b-b-blocks away, at the b-b-brick house at Third and Walnut."

He picked up the nearby gazette and scanned the headlines. "Nothing here about it. Daniel Roberdeau and city leaders have tried for months to control the rising prices. But since the British left, merchants have struggled to keep goods in stock, and those they have are expensive. The people blame Benedict Arnold, given his role in the city."

"Regardless of what General Arnold's complaint is, I doubt very much Congress has any appetite for taking it up. It will be a matter for the court martial." James looked up to see newly elected President Samuel Huntington standing to convene the session. The double doors in the back slammed shut, and Andrew McNair took his post at the door.

October 16, 1779, Saturday

"Major General John Sullivan's report was difficult to read." Dinner at the congressmen's lodgings was nearly finished. The horrific account came back to James, bringing a pang of regret. "Writing from Chemung, in the lakes region in western New York, Sullivan described the destruction of numbers of Cayuga villages, including fields and orchards, and the killing or capture of Cayuga and Mohawks. The Oneida assisted him."

"That should end their attacks on s-s-settlers in the area. I heard a s-s-sad tale that the general pushed his t-t-troops and horses so hard that the horses succumbed to weakness or s-s-starvation and he had to shoot them all." Elbridge Gerry shivered.

"Killing Indians, burning villages, shooting horses—not easy tasks." The vision of a mother and children fleeing a burning village, their corn and fruit orchards in flames, the shrieks of the dying echoing in their ears, crossed his mind, but he shook it off.

"And at another time, perhaps avoidable. But now, we cannot fight an additional enemy." Dr. Samuel Holten glanced at his companions, who silently nodded their agreement.

November 17, 1779, Wednesday

Congress held a formal audience to officially welcome the new French minister, the Chevalier de La Luzerne. A nobleman of impeccable credentials, elegant in black silk, Luzerne bowed as he was introduced. From his chair facing President Samuel Huntington, he delivered a message to Congress confirming King Louis's affection towards his friends and allies.

James shook the chevalier's hand following the ceremony, introducing himself in French. Luzerne's eyes opened wide, warm with pleasure. The tall chevalier's silver medals heightened his commanding presence, while his curled hair glistened with white powder.

"*Je suis ravi de vous rencontrer. Ce sera un honneur de travailler avec vous, M. Lovell, pour le bien de votre merveilleux pays,*" the chevalier said, his voice cultured, refined.

"It will be a pleasure to work with you as well, M. Chevalier de La Luzerne," James confirmed in French.

Congress then took up matters of finance. The state of inflation was such that currency amounted to somewhere around one-fortieth of its face value. The serious attitudes of all present told the tale of the severity of the nation's money problems.

"We must r-r-request $95 million from the s-s-states in taxes. By next year we may have to increase that to $180 million. The s-s-states should also retire $6 million each year of Continental currency to attempt to staunch the tide of inflation. And we must p-p-print no more paper money." Elbridge, his usual pale, thin face flustered and red, spoke in clipped accents, betraying his anxiety. *If we can even collect the taxes,* James thought. Elbridge and the members of the committee sat down heavily, as if the weight of all those taxes were on their shoulders.

December 22, 1779, Wednesday

Pulling the window curtains tight across frost-whorled panes, James unfolded the paper with the familiar handwriting. He had written Abigail a couple of times in November, short notes to accompany the weekly *Journals* that he knew she read. She passed the *Journals* to John, forwarding them to the Navy Board at Boston. In his notes he had been careful to address her in formal manner as "Dear Ma'am," not the informal "Portia." *This loss of her husband, after missing him so for a year, must be truly painful,* he thought. *I had better let her wounds have some time to heal. No teasing for now.* He held the paper out to the light.

> *Braintree*
> *November 18, 1779*
>
> *In a letter from my dear absent Friend, written on board the frigate the day before he sailed, he informed me that the evening before he had received a letter from his much-esteemed friend Mr. Lovell, in which he complained that "Portia did not write to him." Could Portia have given a greater proof of the high value she placed upon his friendship and correspondence, she would not have withheld her hand. But can Mr. Lovell so soon forget that he had prohibited her from writing by prescribing conditions to her that he knew she could not practice?*
>
> *He must have stripped himself of the sensitivity that vibrates with every thought of his mind and every beat of his heart to suppose she could.*
>
> *"Give sorrow vent. The grief that cannot speak*
> *Whispers the o'er fraught heart and bids it break."*
> *Fame, wealth, and honor, what are you compared to love?*

Do not lecture me, sir, the world thinks differently, I know. You should not call for my pen unless you are determined to forgive my weakness. Two sons have left with their father, the oldest but twelve years old. Mr. Thaxter too, who has lived with our family for nearly six years and was like a brother to me in kindness and friendship, is another of the absent family members, while one daughter and a little son are my only companions.

Your former kindness and attention lead me to rely upon your future friendship, which, not withstanding my former prohibitions, I hope is not forfeited by the present sentiments of

Portia

James recognized the lines she quoted. *From* Macbeth, he thought. *When Malcolm consoles Macduff for the loss of his family. She is truly bereft.*

Though it was late, he wrote a brief response. He folded the letter and tucked it away. Then he remembered he had not sent her the *Journals. Ah, me,* he sighed. *Tomorrow.*

Chapter 25

A Cipher for Dr. Franklin

February 23, 1780, Wednesday

"He still is not here, is he," George Partridge said, as he took a seat by James in the meeting room.

"No. Elbridge feels strongly that his privilege as a member of the State House and a representative of his state has been denied. In truth, he has a point. Others have called for Yeas and Nays on questions of order, as he pointed out to President Samuel Huntington in two letters, and they were given the vote requested. But when he called for the same thing, he was denied the vote, so he feels he is defending a fundamental principle of the union."

"So, he chooses not to attend until he is heard. I suppose it is important. If we allowed a rule to be ignored at times, and not at others, it would be no rule at all."

"Meanwhile, we are down one representative from Massachusetts."

"And we are down one general. General Charles Lee at his court-martial was charged with disobeying orders at Monmouth, conducting a shameful retreat, and showing disrespect towards the commander-in-chief. We rightly voted that his services would no longer be required in the army of the United States."

Samuel Huntington stood to convene the day's session.

The trial of Major General Benedict Arnold, postponed for six months, took place in Morristown, where General Washington and his troops were spending the winter. Benedict Arnold mounted a vigorous defense of his actions in Philadelphia and was acquitted of all but one of the charges against him. He received a reprimand from General Washington.

James thought of General Washington and the army in the Watchung Mountains. They had camped there three years before, following their victories at Trenton and Princeton. The mountains protected them from the enemy some thirty miles away in New York. According to reports, the army spent the days confined to their huts, suffering with scarcely enough food.

Preparing his pen, he wrote to the commander-in-chief.

> *I wish you to be persuaded that I will not omit giving you any information in my power from time to time which I can judge may lead either to your ease in the formation of military plans, or to your relief from anxieties about supplies expected from Europe.*

He referred to a recent conquest of John Paul Jones in the North Sea.

> *The stories of the display of our 13 stripes in Holland may be pleasing to many, but I have proof that our decisions conform to Dutch politics, a more solid benefit than the indulgence of the proud affections of our rising Navy.*

General Washington should know that the Dutch will likely support us. And he will appreciate that last reference. In the North Sea, John Paul Jones's ship the *Bonhomme Richard*, bearing a flag of thirteen red, white, and blue stripes that the Dutch called fondly the John Paul Jones Flag, engaged in battle with the British *Serapis*. The *Serapis* sustained heavy damage, and the *Bonhomme Richard* as well. His ship burning and sinking, Jones refused to strike his colors. When the captain of the *Serapis* surrendered, realizing the *Bonhomme Richard* could not be saved, Jones took command of the *Serapis* and sailed to the island of Texel in Holland.

> *And, as exciting as that event may be to readers of gazettes and naval captains, I hope that before long the Dutch will give us tangible aid, perhaps even a great loan. They are not adverse to tipping the balance to favor France and the United States, and Henry Laurens is on his way to the Netherlands.*
>
> *I am, with much esteem, your Excellency's most humble servant,*
>
> *James Lovell*

"Combat memorable entre le Pearson et Paul Jones."
Library of Congress Prints and Photographs

February 24, 1780, Thursday

"To Be Sunk in Case of Danger" he wrote prominently on the packet.

James had spent the past hour or more writing to Benjamin Franklin, the moon outside obscured by thick clouds. He, or the Committee for Foreign Affairs, one and the same, had just received a letter dated September 30th from the minister plenipotentiary, the first from Dr. Franklin since last summer. Two letters in nearly a year. Clearly other dispatches must be at the bottom of the sea, or in enemy hands.

Dr. Franklin said he should be able to obtain most of Congress's requests for supplies. But he warned it would cost the court a great sum. He admonished the Committee of Commerce to tell merchants not to embarrass him with bills. Franklin insisted he acted with frugality and said he spent all of the allowance Congress gave him in paying accounts.

James penned a brief response. He hinted at a new plan Congress was devising: departments instead of committees. These would be run by citizens, not members of Congress. Departments might prove more effective than committees, since attendance in Congress was sporadic.

At the end of his letter, he prepared for an important page. Gripping his quill securely, he labored over his handwriting. The Chevalier de La Luzerne had advised him that he and his correspondents should write in cipher in these dangerous times. James determined to follow the chevalier's advice, a course of action he himself felt to be imperative and which he had already put into motion. He now reminded the minister plenipotentiary that he had sent him a sample cipher, based on an alphabet square. Perhaps the use of a cipher key would be more convenient to the doctor. He would send him a written sample using a cipher key to again encourage Dr. Franklin to send sensitive diplomatic correspondence in cipher.

On a clean sheet of paper, he ruled four columns to the left, then neatly wrote the numbers 1 to 27 in the far left-hand column. *I will use the letters COR for the key. They could be the first letters of "correspondence," for example.* In the next column over, beginning with *C*, he wrote the alphabet followed by an ampersand for "and," then started the alphabet again after the ampersand. In the next column over he did the same thing, starting with the letter *O*, and the fourth column over he began with *R*, completing it the same way.

1	c	o	r	1
2	d	p	s	2
3	e	q	t	3
4	f	r	u	4
5	g	s	v	5
6	h	t	w	6
7	i	u	x	7
8	j	v	y	8
9	k	w	z	9
10	l	x	&	1
11	m	y	a	2
12	n	z	b	3
13	o	&	c	4
14	p	a	d	5
15	q	b	e	6
16	r	c	f	7
17	s	d	g	8
18	t	e	h	9
19	u	f	i	1
20	v	g	j	2
21	w	h	k	3
22	x	i	l	4
23	y	j	m	5
24	z	k	n	6
25	&	l	o	7
26	a	m	p	8
27	b	n	q	9

"Benjamin Franklin's COR Cipher."
James Lovell to Benjamin Franklin, February 24, 1780.
American Philosophical Society

In a short explanation, he wrote, "Let the alphabet be regularly squared. Agree upon any number of the perpendicular columns, which you may change as often as you please, referring to any number of letters in any epistle known to have been received, as for instance, suppose, the three first letters of the 8th, 12th, word of mine of such and such a date. Should this come safely, you need only mark the reply with one of the figures of the transpositions above to determine what is the key."

He surveyed his work, confident it would enable Dr. Franklin to write with his cipher. He closed the letter, keeping the warning "To Be Sunk in Case of Danger" clearly visible, and addressed it.

The hour of midnight had come and gone. As he piled his blankets over him, he reflected with gratitude that these days sleep came easily. Violent dreams or anxieties had not troubled him in some time. *Perhaps I am just too tired to worry. In any case, I am grateful.* James fell asleep thinking of Mary, his home, and her delicious turkey stuffing.

April 17, 1780, Monday

Dr. Holten looked up at James. "Good morning to you. You have on a fine new pair of breeches."

James ran his hand down the smooth brown leather. "They are likely to be the only pair I will have made for some time." He was not about to admit it, but the leather breeches that he had ordered from Lancaster had nearly bankrupted him. The leather had cost $130, and he had paid $200 to have them made.

"And you and I now are the sole representatives for Massachusetts. Two days ago, Elbridge Gerry responded in the negative to Philip Schuyler and Robert R. Livingston's suggestion that he return. He refuses to compromise on his stance that he was denied the privileges of a member of Congress when he was denied the vote for Yea or Nay on a question of order. He sent a message that he would no longer 'take up the time of the House' on the subject. Firm and unyielding he is. We will miss his contribution to our work."

"And we will miss George Partridge, gone home to family."

James frowned. "Elbridge Gerry has been part of this Congress for the past four years. He contributed to the supply chain for the army as far back as Lexington and Concord. I fear that we do not find men of the same determined, patriotic zeal as were here in the first part of my delegation. We are too used to this war. We are not alarmed; we do not prepare for the councils of our enemy."

With difficulty, he set his thoughts aside to prepare for the session.

Chapter 26

The Keyword—Cranch

May 4, 1780, Thursday

Voices echoed from the Assembly Room, sharp and strident, rising and falling in debate. In the Assembly library, James took a seat by a window in the bright afternoon light. It was imperative he write to Dr. Benjamin Franklin. Was the minister plenipotentiary using the cipher James had sent him in February? He should include some phrases written in the cipher to test him. Minister La Luzerne's words had been direct, to the point, and moreover accurate, the gist of them being that diplomats must employ ciphers in their correspondence.

I had best explain that this letter will be brief, since the Massachusetts delegation has only two members, he thought, dipping his pen in the ink. *The sensitive words I will write in cipher.*

> *Our Affairs at the Southward are to be judged of by the Gazettes. We 11. 14. 8. 12. 1. 3. 27. 13. 11. 17. 6. We have a very good Prospect that the late War between 3. 6. 18. 23. 3. 4. 13. 6. 14. 24. 18. 13. 16. 26. 4. 23. 3. 4 is the last that will spring up between those Tribes. They have convinced each other by every Skirmish that they ought to be in perpetual Amity on the Ground of reciprocal Benefits.*

If he uses COR for the key, as I described to him in my letter of February, he should be able to make out the words "may not boast" in the first sentence, and "the merchant & farmer" in the second.

Lovell, May 4th 1780

Hon'd Sir,

64

I cannot write with official authority nor have I time to enlarge ... upon our public affairs owing to the particular Circumstances of the mass. delegation which forces me to attend in Congress and the Vessel will probably sail before our adjournment this afternoon. I refer you to the Journals & Gazettes together with Mr Robert Mease's Conversation It is not necessary that I should recommend this Gentleman to your Civilities; your Knowledge of his Family, and his present Care to forward Pacquets to you, both secure for him your Attentions.

We have had no Letter from you since one of Sep. 30th read Feb. 23d. nor have we at any Time rec'd a Copy of the Instrument annulling the 11th & 12th articles the publication of which Articles in our News papers make some public Proceed' here necessary in regard to the annullment it was some time in Novr. 78 as appears by the Copies of some Letters delivered by Mrs Adams the originals of which did not come to hand.

Our Affairs at the Southward are to

be judged of by the Gazettes. We 11.14.8.12.1.3.27
13.11.17.6 We have a very good prospect that the
late War between 36.18.23.3.4, 13.6.14 24.18.13.
16.26.4.23,3.4 is the last that will spring up
between those Tribes. They have convinced
each other, by every Skirmish that they
ought to be in perpetual Amity on the
Ground of reciprocal Benefits.

I do not feel easy till I have
my Pacquets on Board. If I have
Time, I will again write to you by
the same opportunity more largely.

Be assured of my greatest Respect
for your Character and my sincerest
Wishes for Cyour Prosperity being, Sir,
Your Friend and
most humble Servant
James Lovell

"James Lovell to Benjamin Franklin, May 4, 1780."
American Philosophical Society

He completed the letter, assuring Dr. Franklin of his continued wishes for his
health and safety. Then he took out more paper. He had just time enough to write
to John Adams and inform him of the cipher.

May 4, 1780
Dear Sir,

The bearer, Mr. Mease, is brother to the late Clothier General and is closely connected with an Irish gentleman here for whom I have great regard as a zealous republican and friend to America.

I chiefly rely on them and his conversation to what ought to be the task of the Committee for Foreign Affairs if that committee was not a mere shadow without a quorum or secretary or clerk. I send regularly to Mrs. Adams the newspapers and Journals for you that she may not be without some information of that kind herself during your absence.

If you receive anything from me in ciphers, it will be using the same mode as that which I have communicated to Dr. Franklin and which will serve great numbers with equal safety. It is the alphabet squared as on the other side and the key letters are the first two of the surname of the family where you and I spent the evening together before we set out from your house on our way to Baltimore.

Your affectionate humble servant,

James Lovell

The surname of the family where we dined before leaving Braintree was Cranch, as John Adams surely should recall, he being Richard Cranch's brother-in-law. So, the key he should use is CR. On the back of the page, he wrote the numbers 1 to 27 in a perpendicular column, and next to each the alphabet, then the ampersand, making 27 in all. He began the following two columns, the second column beginning with *b*, the third beginning with *c*, and left it to John Adams to complete the square.

Then he added directions.

Make use of any of the perpendicular columns according to your key letters. You may reply to me by the use of any new ones. For instance, you may refer to the 2nd, 3rd, 4th, etc., letters of a word, the 1st, 2nd, 3rd, 4th, etc., in a paragraph of any one of your letters of such and such a date known to have been received by me, or you may say "reverse the letters you have chosen," or "add one more to those you have used,"

*or by any such direction you may give me the key of your
answer.*

I will give you a sample as follows.

He wrote some sentences from the report that John Adams would have received from Congress, offering to pay for books for John Quincy Adams but not for his education. In brackets he wrote a few of the words in cipher, using the key *CR*. He concluded his letter with advice to his friend.

*You ought to use ciphers in your public letters but you
should communicate your key to Mr. Thompson to serve in
my absence.*

He folded the letter, put away his pen and ink, and slipped back into the Assembly Room.

May 4 1780

Dear Sir

The Bearer Mr Mease is Brother to the late Cloathier General and is intimately connected with an Irish Gentleman here for whom I have great Regard as a zealous Republican & Friend to America It is more on account of that Connection with my Friend than of any personal acquaintance that I have been led to introduce Mr Mease to your Civilities. His Care of sundry Packets for you would indeed alone have been sufficient to merit your attention I chiefly rely on them and his Conversation to what ought to be the Task of the Committee of foreign affairs if that Comm was not a mere Shadow without a Quorum or Secretary

or Clerk. I send regularly to Mrs
Adams the News Papers & Journals for
you that she may not be without
some Information of that kind herself
during your Absence. She sends them
to the Navy Board, doubtless with the
addition of Something still more
agreable to you individually considered.

This Testimony of my affectionate
Remembrance of You will reach
your Hand at all Events as I mean
it to be useful to Mr. Mease whatever may be his Lot as to a Safe
Passage. If you receive any
thing from me in Cyphers it will
be upon the Same Mode as that which
I have communicated to Doctr Franklin
and which will serve great Numbers
with equal Safety It is the Alphabet
squared as on the other Side and the
key Letters are the two first of the
Surname of the Family where you and
I spent the Evening together before we

set out from your House on our
Way to Baltimore

your affectionate humble
Servant
James Lovell

Hon. Mr Adams

all your Letters from Spain came safely
Give my Love to your Family, to Mr Dana
in particular & tell him I imagine all
his came safely too though no Body at
Philada. knows any thing about them.

1 a b   a
2 b c   d
3 c d   e
4 d e   f
5 e
6 f
7 g
8 h
9 i
10 k
11 k
12 l
13 m
14 n
15 o
16 p
17 q
18 r
19 s
20 t
21 u
22 v
23 w
24 x
25 y
26 z
27 &

make use of any of the perpendicular
columns according to yr Key Letters.
— you may reply to me by the use
of any new ones. For Instance you
may refer to the 2 3 4 & ca Letters
of a Word in a Paragraph of any one
of your Letters of such a date known
to have been recd by me, or you
may say "reverse the Letters you
have chosen" or "add one more
to those you have used", or
by any such like Direction you
may give me the Key of your
Answer.

I will give you a Specimen as follows

"Letter from James Lovell to John Adams Using CR Key."
James Lovell to John Adams, 4 May 1780.
Massachusetts Historical Society

May 7, 1780, Sunday

Miss Dalley appeared at the door to the dining room.

"You have a guest," she said. Just behind her stood a tall young man with dark hair, a smoothed-back cowlick, and eager green eyes.

"What—Jemmy?"

"Father! It is such a pleasure to see you." Young James, whom the family had always called Jemmy, approached his father for an embrace. His clothing dusty, Jemmy, the oldest of his children at home, looked as though he had been on the road for days.

"I can hardly believe it is you. It has been two and a half years since I saw you, and look at how you have grown!"

Nearly as tall as James himself, gangly, a wide grin on his face, Jemmy appeared as pleased as James had ever seen him. *He must be eighteen.*

"Mother sent me with news." Jemmy glanced at the other delegates seated nearby, who had stopped eating to watch the reunion.

"You must join us," Miss Dalley said. She pulled a plate from the sideboard. "Here, please help yourself to dinner."

Jemmy sat down in haste, then spooned up some of the chicken and spaetzle.

"It has been hours since I ate. Nathaniel Peabody at Headquarters gave me some money, but it did not last long."

"How did you travel?" James asked.

"I left Boston following the post. I borrowed our neighbor's horse. I must see to him before long. The post riders let me accompany them, knowing you were my father. They came to Headquarters, where I met up with Nathaniel Peabody. Very helpful he was. Then I left with directions to come to Philadelphia. It has been quite a journey. I never knew I could ride so far." His words tumbled out in breathless excitement. He picked up his fork and began the meal.

James nodded. "It is quite a journey. But why did you come? Your mother wrote nothing of your visit."

"She decided to send me instead of writing. We have sickness at home. Joseph, William, Mary, Thomas, all the little ones are sick, can scarcely keep down liquids, much less food. Everyone but Johnny. And Mother is ill, nearly too ill to care for the others." Jemmy's face turned serious. "She wonders if you could come home for a spell," he said, mumbling around the food.

"Of course she does." James scratched his head. The thought both seemed alluring and impossible. "But you must understand that I am so needed here, I cannot leave just now. Is there no one who can help her?"

"Dr. Gardner has sent around one of his servants daily, and Mrs. Wilson from church has made us some meals."

"You know I must attend Congress tomorrow. How long can you stay?"

"A few days, then I should return."

"I am sure I could find time to show you around Philadelphia in the evenings. You may at least see the Pennsylvania State House, where Congress meets."

"He may stay here, I am sure." Miss Dalley regarded Jemmy with a kind smile.

"Thank you. But the longer he stays, the less help he can give his mother, so his visit must be short. But tell me, how are the others?"

"Mary helps Mother with the little ones a great deal. George, the baby, is now four. You can imagine him following Charles around. Charles is sometimes patient with George and sometimes not."

"Are they learning their letters and reading?"

Jemmy shrugged. "Sometimes. William and Thomas argue, though, when Mother tells them to read. They would prefer to play ball or marbles. But they are too sick now to do much."

James shook his head. His family needed him, that was clear. But so did his country. *Hard though it is, I must put my country first*, he thought.

"You are a good lad to come to see me. It will be such a pleasure to have you here and show you around. I will take you to City Tavern to dine."

Jemmy's eyes grew round at the thought. "I would like that."

"When you return, we will send with you some mail, as you would be a reliable carrier. You wouldn't mind that, would you?"

"No. I would be glad to help."

With a flourish of satisfaction, Miss Dalley scooped up the last piece of pie and passed it to Jemmy. He nodded his thanks and finished it in a few bites. James patted his son on the back. *How he has grown, how I would enjoy going straight home with him to see the family.*

May 17, 1780, Wednesday

"We have not yet heard whether Charlestown fell to the enemy. General Sir Henry Clinton's siege was still in effect when we heard last, so the city likely remains in our hands." Dr. Samuel Holten, his face apprehensive, looked up at James.

James set down his satchel of papers. It had been hard to say farewell to Jemmy. Their time in Philadelphia had been an unforeseen pleasure; they walked around the city and enjoyed a meal of roast squab at the City Tavern. *He practically ate the bones.* Jemmy visited the Pennsylvania State House, though not during a session, his expression reverent. Now he was gone, riding again in the company of the post. *It is best he returns to help his mother. I surely hope the family will recover soon.*

"True. We do not know how General Lincoln, the American fleet, and the few French ships are faring."

"It was hard enough to lose Savannah last fall. But the Count d'Estaing's attempt to assault the garrison failed and he retreated to the West Indies."

"In New York, the enemy is throwing up new works at the narrows. The militia form lines from the east to the north river outside of the redoubts, and they exercise constantly. There is movement underfoot." Samuel Holten's usually tranquil face appeared uneasy, distraught.

"This campaign will test us. Today we hear from the committee at Headquarters. John Mathews has arrived to deliver their report," James said quietly to his colleague.

President Huntington tapped his gavel.

"The Chevalier de La Luzerne would have us informed of some sensitive information. Any day, a great armament of naval and land forces from France will arrive to act alongside our forces. We will convey this information to our generals, especially General Benjamin Lincoln, now under siege in Charlestown.

"I ask that you keep this information private, for now," President Huntington said. A buzz of comments swept among those present.

"Mr. John Mathews?"

John Mathews of Charlestown, South Carolina, slender, alert, his hair gray and curled, came to the front of the meeting room. All eyes turned to him.

"Your committee at Headquarters is impressed with the most strenuous need to prepare the army," he said, his voice crisp with anxiety. "According to dispatches recently provided by the Marquis de La Fayette, just returned from France, we will supply provisions for the sizeable force the French are sending. A small committee should be given power to draw forth the resources of the country.

"Nearly dictatorial powers will allow them to supply whatever our military force and that of our ally need: carpenters, teamsters, waggoneers, horses, carriages, builders, and provisions for the army."

Mathews paused. "I might add that the regiments are at present totally unfit to take the field."

"Dreadful," James said under his breath.

"Thank you and the committee for your work," Samuel Huntington said. He bowed to the delegate from South Carolina, who returned to his seat, his footsteps ringing purposefully.

Throughout the day, the thought of the army, in need of clothing, food, and essentials, weighed on James's mind, while French ships loaded with men, armaments, supplies sailed towards them.

Chapter 27

Losses in the South

July 14, 1780, Friday

In the middle of the morning, a clerk placed letters before James. One bore the delicate, even script of Abigail. He had written to her in mid-June, sending her news of the calamitous loss of Charlestown. It was still hard for him to believe that General Lincoln had surrendered his Continentals. But now that General Gates had been sent south to assume command, he felt sure the situation would turn around.

He opened the letter and read the familiar handwriting.

> _June 13, 1780_
>
> _Dear Sir,_
>
> _Your repeated favors merit my acknowledgment that with so many correspondents you should think so often of Portia. At the same time, a sigh mingles with my gratitude, that a heart so kindly disposed towards others whose life and work are devoted to public service should feel anxious for the situation of those dearest to him, and that he cannot even have the consolation of visiting those dear connections without great difficulties._
>
> _But I quit a subject which always gives me pain to reflect upon, and I thank you for your alphabetical cipher, though I believe I shall never make use of it. I hate a cipher of any kind and have been so much more used to dealing with realities with those I love, that I should do poorly with modes and figures. Besides, my Friend is not adept at understanding ciphers and hates to be puzzled for a meaning. If Mr. L_____l will not call me "saucy," I will tell him that he has not any need to make use of them himself since he commonly writes so_

225

much in the enigmatical way that nobody but his particular correspondents will ever find out his meaning.

Believe me, whatever some interested sordid wretches may say or write, the people have confidence in Congress. May I ask for your continued favors, they amuse me in my retirement. I live secluded from the exciting world and have not been more than

four miles from home for these 6 months. I do not mourn that as a loss. The society of a few select friends and my correspondents give me more solid satisfaction than dissipations for which I am not disposed. I feel so interested in the fate of my country that she does not feel a misfortune in which I do not participate. You will not wonder, Sir, that I am anxious to know her situation from one so capable and disposed to give information to his assured friend and humble servant,

Portia

She finds me enigmatical? Very well, if it amuses her to think so.

July 26, 1780, Wednesday

"It was good to hear that the French fleet sailed into the harbor at Newport." James wiped his forehead as he walked. The warm air was thick with the scent of flowers and summer growth.

"Their presence is invaluable," Dr. Samuel Holten agreed. "Did you notice that a few days ago Major General Benedict Arnold paid us a visit? He handed a letter to Secretary Thomson, then waited behind the bar in the gallery until his request was granted. He asked for $25,000 in return for his recommitment to serve in the army." Dr. Holten glanced at James.

"I do remember. He left rapidly, looking triumphant. He still limps."

"He said he would get his orders at Morristown. I heard him say he had a great interest in commanding West Point."

"West Point? That fort on the Hudson is of vast strategic importance. The decision would be up to General Washington."

"Today we heard that several frigates will be placed under the direction of General Washington to cooperate with the French fleet at Newport."

"I hope that by this time next month we shall hear good news from our combined army and navy."

"Here's home, for now." Samuel Holten opened the white gate.

August 9, 1780, Wednesday

"Please come in, my dear fellow." Henry Laurens held out his hand to James. In the doorway of the City Tavern, James pulled off his wet coat. Merchants, delegates, and citizens crowded the tavern. Men in silks and women in gowns bantered over candlelit tables, raised glasses, laughed uproariously.

The two settled in a secluded corner in the rear of the establishment.

"It was good of you to summon me," James said.

"I will be leaving Philadelphia soon. My voyage to procure a loan from the Dutch has been delayed for myriad reasons. But I sail with Captain Pickles on Congress's packet, the *Mercury*, likely within the week."

"Excellent. And until you arrive, John Adams is commissioned to attend in Holland. If he is unable to do so, Francis Dana will serve. You are well?"

Henry Laurens frowned. "I am concerned for my son John, who is in this city on parole following his capture by the British in South Carolina. He is confined to Pennsylvania."

"I understand. My oldest son serves with Major Henry Light-Horse Lee's battalion. His safety is always on my mind. Perhaps an exchange can be arranged for John."

"General Washington has already made that request."

A waiter boasting enormous sideburns stopped by them and set down two tankards of amber beer.

"It has been a long while since my appointment in October to travel to the Hague. I hope to arrive there safely." Henry Laurens took a drink.

"And you will be minister to negotiate a treaty of amity and commerce with the Netherlands. And your estate?"

"It suffered great damage; buildings and crops burned." Henry Laurens shrugged his shoulders, as if to express his feelings of helplessness. "But my family is safe. A few of my slaves have run off, though the majority of them are loyal to me. Our army is recruiting slaves. And some will join the British. You know, I do not like the institution of slavery. I did not invent it. One day I will free my slaves," he said, apologetically.

"It is abominable," James said. "But the south must be saved. The recruits now raised in Virginia are ordered to join the southern army under the command of Major General Gates."

"We are reaching a critical moment."

James finished his cider, the cool liquid refreshing his spirits. "Have you packed the paper I gave you?"

"It is safe in my trunk," Henry Laurens answered. "Unofficial though it may be, the treaty proposal prepared by Mynheer VanBerkel and William Lee may prove to be acceptable by the Dutch."

"Very good. That is the least I can give you." James looked at the former president with concern and some admiration. Despite his personal difficulties, Henry was willing to undertake this mission on behalf of the Congress.

The waiter bowed and cleared their glasses as the southern planter handed him some coins.

"You needn't have paid for me," James said, in protest.

"Never you worry. We will both come out of this all right. Shall we?"

James led the way to the door. The sun was setting, the late summer twilight luminous, raindrops sparkling on grass and trees. "Have a care, Mr. Laurens. I trust your journey will be safe."

August 31, 1780, Thursday

President Samuel Huntington entered the Assembly Room, his face ashen, tense. The delegates stopped talking. A silence fell over the room. *The calm before the storm,* James thought.

"I have grave news for us," Samuel Huntington said. "The letter," he said. Secretary Thomson picked up a paper and handed it to the President without a word.

The president began reading, his voice even.

> *In the deepest distress and anxiety of mind, I am obliged*
> *to acquaint your excellency with the defeat of the troops under*
> *my command. I arrived with the Maryland line, the artillery,*
> *and the North Carolina militia, on the 13th of this month*
> *thirteen miles from Camden; and took up a position there,*
> *and was the next day joined by General Stevens with seven*
> *hundred militia from Virginia.*

It is General Gates. He took a deep breath. *The worst possible news. Oh, maybe not the worst,* he corrected himself. President Huntington continued, his voice somber and determined.

> *At daylight the enemy attacked and drove in our light*
> *party in front, when I ordered the left to advance and attack*
> *the enemy; but to my astonishment, the left wing and North*
> *Carolina militia gave way. General Caswell and myself,*
> *assisted by a number of officers, did all in our power to rally*

the broken troops, but to no purpose, for the enemy coming round the left flank of the Maryland division completed the rout of the whole militia, who left the Continentals to oppose the enemy's whole force.

"General Gates writes to us from Hillsborough, North Carolina," Samuel Huntington said, looking up at the group. "Bear in mind that is 180 miles from Camden, so the general covered a respectable distance with great speed."

"The militia do not fight with bayonets, but the British do," General Artemas Ward called out.

"You could be right, General. That could be the reason they broke and ran. These militia are not trained to use the bayonet as are the Continentals," Philip Schuyler answered from the other side of the room.

"Thank you, General," Artemas Ward answered.

"His letter gives particulars of the battle. We do not know yet the numbers of the dead and wounded. But we can see that General Gates is no longer in control in the south. It appears General Lord Cornwallis, serving under General Clinton, has taken the upper hand."

In a stir of conversation, the delegates discussed the unsettling news.

Chapter 28

A Traitor in Our Midst

September 11, 1780, Monday

In the sitting room at Miss Dalley's, James found a seat in a cushioned chair. He needed a moment of rest before retiring to write letters.

"How are you feeling?" General Artemas Ward asked from across the room.

"As well as can be expected," James said. It was still amazing to him that he served with the venerable general, leader in the French and Indian wars, commander at Bunker Hill.

The new roomers entered, a trio of merchants. Miss Dalley had apologized for their behavior, but James thought her apology highly insufficient. Their loud, boisterous behavior and rude jokes were insufferable. Yesterday, the one who affected a powdered wig, dirty and untended, had slouched into the dining room. In a drawl, he asked, "Did you catch a glimpse of that lass?"

"No, but my silver dollars say I will," the heavy one had responded, reaching into his pocket and jingling his coins as he took a seat. "Damned if I won't!"

All three then burst into guffaws, the skinny one with the filthy clothing nearly choking, his face turning red.

"Ah, but look, we have congressmen in our midst," powdered wig sneered. "Must not talk of such doings. After all, we are only joking." He glanced snidely at James.

James looked at him directly. "I am sure you are. General Ward, would you care for a stroll?"

"As good a time as any," Artemas Ward said, standing.

Laughter and cursing floated out the window as James and Artemas Ward stepped out the front door.

"How long will they stay?" James asked rhetorically. "We have tried to board with the wife of Colonel Pickering. Yet now, Colonel Pickering has need of his rooms for other family members."

"Samuel Adams is also disappointed that we cannot move," Artemas Ward said. He looked regretfully across the city towards the river.

"I put up with the extra flight of stairs at Miss Daley's until these scoundrels showed up. Their noise, cursing, rudeness, make staying here miserable."

"Remember, rooms are scarce. We must make the best of it," the general said with stoic composure.

A few steps later, James recalled, "The loss of Baron de Kalb at Camden, that brave general from France who loved liberty, is one we must mourn."

Artemas Ward nodded mutely, his footsteps keeping pace with those of James.

"It is a pity that the French fleet is boxed in within Narragansett Bay. It is ironic that we have some five thousand French soldiers and dozens of ships ready to help us, yet they cannot aid us in the south. General Washington writes he requires light horse for North and South Carolina, as well as supplies. Bread, meat, forage, horses, and wagons are needed. Most of all, men."

"In less than four months our army will be reduced to one half its current size." General Artemas Ward looked up at the sky, his eyes scanning the flight of a hawk soaring overhead.

They turned down the street lining the river, passed ships bobbing at anchor. A few sailors lounged at the wharfs. The setting sun cast a peach glow through a haze of clouds.

Artemas Ward drew back his shoulders, then took a deep breath. "Does it not do you good to be outside, breathing fresh air?"

They strolled back to their lodgings in companionable silence.

James broke it first. "My family has suffered greatly, of late. My wife, my only daughter, and my oldest son were in bed last I heard. My wife was bled twice on the same day. They even appealed to John Hancock, whose silence was their only answer."

"You and many others are sacrificing to our cause," Artemas Ward said thoughtfully. "Our part here is important."

James grinned good-naturedly. "You are right, my dear fellow. We dare to persist."

September 30, 1780, Saturday

"Gentlemen, I have the duty to share with you a letter containing news that we could never have imagined. It is from the commander-in-chief."

Samuel Huntington cleared his throat and looked about the room expectantly. The delegates shifted in their seats, set aside their work, waited. The session had just opened. James noticed Mr. Huntington's tense stance, his anxious demeanor.

"Received today, important communication from General Washington."

26 September 1780

Robinson's House in the Highlands
Sir,

I have the honor to inform Congress that I went to West Point to survey the post and visit with Major General Arnold, whom I had appointed in command of the garrison. I did not find him there, so returned to his Headquarters, but he was still absent. I received a packet from Lt. Colonel Jamison, who had captured a John Anderson who wanted to go to New York, along with papers in the handwriting of General Arnold. The prisoner claimed to be in reality Major John André, Adjutant General of the British army. This circumstance caused my suspicions, and I realized that Arnold had acted in a most agitated manner when he received a letter shortly before he left. I concluded he knew that André had been captured, so I tried to apprehend Arnold, but he had already escaped in a barge where he went to the ship of war Vulture, lying below Stoney Point. He wrote to me after he arrived on board, a copy of which is enclosed.

I have taken measures to secure West Point, and I hope to interview André tomorrow.

The party of a few militia who took Major André acted with integrity and virtue. They were offered a large sum of money for his release, which they turned down. Their country should thank them and they should be rewarded.

I enclose a copy of Arnold's letter written when on the Vulture.

I have the honor to be your Excellency's most humble and obedient servant,

Go. Washington

A hush fell over the room. Each glanced at the other, trying to distill this horrific information. General Arnold, a traitor. The last James saw him, he was blustering, limping, pleased to get the money he had requested from Congress, apparently determined to return to duty. And he had wanted the command of West Point, which he had gotten. But a traitor?

James turned to General Artemas Ward, seated nearby. His voice hushed, he said, "At least they have Major John André in custody. Let us hope he remains there and that they get the truth from him."

"He is head of the British intelligence, you know."

James nodded. The handsome, aristocratic André had planned the extravagant *Meschianza* party to honor General Howe's retreat from Philadelphia and had befriended Peggy Shippen and her sisters.

President Huntington was speaking. "You may be sure I will provide any further news I receive from General Washington. Meanwhile, we have the report on the hospital department to consider."

As the delegates turned to other business, the thought that one of their own, so highly placed and well-regarded by the commander-in-chief that he had been given the responsibility for West Point, the key to control of the Hudson River, hung over all. *This day is indeed dark, but we have just averted the danger,* James thought, with a shiver of apprehension.

October 12, 1780, Thursday

Wind whipped the trees, stripping them of their red and gold leaves. James clamped his hat down firmly. Rain beat down, sending sheets of water coursing through the streets. At the State House, he nodded his thanks to the doorkeeper.

"How are you feeling?" General Artemas Ward asked as he approached.

"Better, thanks to the use of tartar emetic, *sal merseille*, and warm baths." James pulled his sodden coat off. "Our household servant has been throwing me nasty looks ever since our landlady dispatched him to haul tubs of hot water up two flights of stairs for my particular use."

Samuel Huntington entered, an anxious look on his usually calm features. He went straight to Secretary Charles Thomson. The two conferred a moment, then Secretary Thomson handed the president a stack of papers. Samuel Huntington cast his eyes over the room.

"If you please, gentlemen, we have rather an important matter to consider today." The room quieted.

I wonder if we will finally hear what happened to Major André, or news of that traitorous scoundrel Benedict Arnold.

"Allow me to review General Washington's message to General Nathanael Greene. General Greene was given charge of the Board who heard Adjutant General Major André's case. Major André came within the American lines to meet with Arnold in an assumed character. He was apprehended in disguise and carried a false pass with a feigned name. Sensitive papers were found concealed on him."

The delegates drew sharp breaths. A few spoke out. "Then we know the results of the deliberations?"

"We do." President Huntington drew himself up to his full height, dignified and authoritative. *He looks the judge he was.*

"General Washington sent to me a copy of the proceedings of a Board of Officers in the case of Major André, adjutant general to the British army. Major André was executed due to the findings of the Board, on Monday, the 2nd of October, at twelve o'clock, at our former camp at Tappan." Those listening sucked in their breath at the news.

"He acted with great frankness throughout the proceedings until his execution. Though his wish was to be shot, General Washington states that according to the practice of war, when one assumes a disguise to pass through enemy lines, such a request cannot be granted. Major André was hung.

"The general adds that the circumstances of Major André's capture, his trial, the major's own words testifying that he had received the greatest attention from every person in whose charge he was placed, and his execution, all show that the proceedings against him were not guided by passion or resentment.

"Finally, I would add that the fact that General Washington did not meet at all with Major André, instead trusting in the decision of his officers, speaks to the fair treatment Major André received.

"Major General Greene has been named commander at West Point for now." President Huntington set his papers down and took a deep breath.

The delegates were silent for a moment, comprehending the depth of the treachery that General Arnold had committed. West Point, the American garrison guarding the Hudson, the passage leading from north to south, would have been a prize awarding the British considerable advantage in the next campaign. And it had been so narrowly saved. A buzz of excitement broke out, exclamations of disbelief, amazement, relief.

"Was there ever a chance that we could capture Benedict Arnold?" one or two asked.

"Apparently it was close. Before General Washington knew of his treachery, he was even at Arnold's door, intending to eat breakfast with him. Arnold, however, managed to escape."

The discussion went on for most of the day, every detail reviewed and noted. At the end of the day, Congress resolved to give the letters and their enclosures to the Committee of Intelligence.

October 22, 1780, Sunday

At the morning service at Christ Church, not far away on 2nd Street, James alternately paid attention—listening with half an ear to the steady rhythm of the preacher's words—and dozed, repeatedly catching himself and starting awake. Looking about at the tall white walls, the morning sun shining through glass windows, he thought he saw Mrs. Clymer across the pews.

As he was leaving, he caught a glimpse of her silver piled hair. In a few steps he reached her side.

"James," she said, holding out her gloved hand, her smile genuine and warm. "How nice to see you."

"Indeed, a pleasure."

"How are you?"

"My lodgings have lately proven difficult. I reside on a third floor, and we have some fellow boarders whose presence is most unsavory."

"I am sorry to hear that. As it happens, I have two extra rooms in my home that I have been thinking about putting to good use. I have taken in lodgers in the past. A couple of lodgers would help me greatly to make ends meet. I have one room you could have, and one other, if you know of anyone who requires it. I must have tenants of good character with references, of course. You certainly have those." She cocked her head, her black feathered hat tilted to one side, appraising him steadily.

"What a fine suggestion," James said. He felt a glimmer of hope. "I will be glad to come take a look at the room this Saturday."

"You would be most welcome to do so." Mrs. Clymer clapped her gloved hands, her beads jingling under her white lace shawl. "You know where my home is?"

"Indeed, I do." James bowed. He remembered the white clapboard house on Walnut Street, not far from the Pennsylvania State House. "Elbridge Gerry and I took tea with you there."

"When you see Elbridge Gerry, tell him I will take that salt mackerel he promised, and I will drink to his health when I have it," she said, good-naturedly.

"I will let him know. He has returned to his home in Boston."

October 28, 1780, Saturday

On Saturday, Ann Clymer welcomed James at her home. "Do come in. Your room should be in order. Then perhaps we could take some refreshment."

James followed her in, her coil of silver hair gleaming in the long oval mirror at the entryway. She opened the first door past the parlor to reveal a white painted room with a braided rug, the ceiling edged with carved cornices. The fireplace caught his eye and he nodded approval. A tall window looked out onto a garden bordered by apple trees.

"Will this suit you?"

"Yes, indeed." He ran a hand over the polished surface of the walnut table and glanced at the ornate wardrobe. "What payment do you require?"

"We will work that out. I am sure my charge will be similar to any other boarding situation in Philadelphia. I want you to come home to that long-suffering wife of yours." Ann Clymer laughed, then stepped back. "You may from time to time be surprised by the voices of my three grandchildren playing here, but I hope that does not annoy you."

"Not in the least," James said. "Besides, I am so busy, I rarely have time to relax at my lodgings."

"Two meals each day will be provided, though if you are not going to dine here, I would appreciate knowing that. And I have one more room, if you know of anyone who might need accommodations."

"My friend General Artemas Ward is interested. You will hear from him."

James approached Miss Dalley that evening to give her the news of his move.

"Have you written that nice Elbridge Gerry lately?" she asked, before he could say anything.

"I have and I will."

"I have a suggestion to make a little money, not so much speculation as wise apprehension of the situation, if you know what I mean." She nearly winked at him. "Perhaps Elbridge Gerry would be interested."

"I will be sure to let him know." He looked at her curiously. "As difficult as times are, surely we should take advantage of whatever we can that would help supply our needs. Done honestly, of course."

"Of course." She nodded.

"And now I must let you know of my plans to move."

Miss Dalley soured, but seemed to forgive him. *She is a businesswoman, after all.*

October 29, 1780, Sunday

He moved on Sunday, helped by a hand cart and Artemas Ward, who inspected the other room at Mrs. Clymer's and made arrangements to take up residence there, his granite-hard face softened at the prospect.

On his first evening at Mrs. Clymer's, wrapped in his dressing gown, grateful for the small fire that warmed the room, James spread a sheet of paper on his table and prepared to write to Dr. Samuel Holten.

He thanked the doctor for his kind visit to his wife Mary, now in better health.

He remembered the news of the startling victory they had just received. In early October, at Kings Mountain, North Carolina, Patriot militiamen had surprised and attacked Loyalists, inflicting heavy casualties and forcing their retreat. Cornwallis had marched in flight to South Carolina. "Perhaps North Carolina is safe for now," he added.

But his eyes burned. He set his pen down and rubbed them. *A damp cloth might help*, he thought. Picking up his pen, he concluded his letter by confiding that he had lost his spectacles and had been writing for three days and nights. *Is it my eyes or my head that hurts?* He picked up a cloth, dipped it in his basin, and laid the cool material on his eyes as he stretched his legs out in front of the warm fireplace, content with his surroundings.

Chapter 29

Reconciled to Ciphers

November 3, 1780, Friday

He turned the paper riddled with notes, letters, and numbers. *Cipher, you will yield to me.* He began again listing possible letters that might correspond with the numbers 1 through 27, based on guesses for the ciphered words. *All twenty-six letters must be used, as well as an ampersand.*

That afternoon Secretary Charles Thomson had approached him, a packet in hand. "General Greene sends you these intercepted letters to be deciphered."

James took the packet. "I will give it my best." On the outside, the general had written his name in his generous, flowing handwriting. Major General Greene had been named commander of the southern department just days ago, a post fraught with difficulty following the defeats at Camden and Charlestown.

He had been working on the task since supper. Sleet clattered against the windowpanes. There were two letters in the packet, written from General Cornwallis at Charlestown to British officers and bearing his signature. One was to General Nisbet Balfour, the other to James Wemyss. The letters were dated October 7, 1780, the day of the recent Patriot victory at Kings Mountain. He picked up the letter to General Balfour. A single sheet, it was in General Cornwallis's elegant handwriting; the capital *C*s and *D*s swirled, an intricate angle on the capital *B*s.

> *Dear Balfour,*   *Charlestown, Oct. 7, 1780*
>   *I yesterday received yours of the 27th and the contents of*
> *the letter are unpleasant. I have ordered Wemyss....*

There followed a dozen or so lines of ciphered writing, interspersed with a few words, followed by the balance of the letter, consisting of a paragraph.

He puzzled over the writing for some time, trying one solution after another. Eventually he discovered the cipher to be a combination of two different sorts. A book cipher, or code, referred to specific words found in a dictionary, probably an edition of *Entick's Spelling Dictionary* agreed upon by the parties. The book cipher relied on a sequence, often of three numbers. For example, 6.1.14 would indicate a word to be found on page 6, column 1, line 14 of the dictionary. The correspondent, having the same edition of the book, would be able to locate the word. These were noted with a capital *B*. The other was an alphabet cipher, matching the numbers 1 to 24 with letters distributed in a random manner, the letters *i* and *j* assigned to the same number, the letter *z* omitted. Cornwallis had denoted use of that cipher with a capital *F.*

He looked over his efforts. A few places were still unclear, but he had a result. He read it over skeptically.

> *Dear Balfour,*　　　　　　　　*Charlestown, Oct. 7, 1780*
>
> *I yesterday received yours of the 27th and the contents of the letter are unpleasant. I have ordered Wemyss.... and join me at Cres. Creek. He will send you a copy of my letter.*
>
> *I can only beg that you will find all the quantity of (recruits, most likely) for provincials of any color. I am uneasy about Ferguson going into Tryon County.*
>
> *I fear his getting into a scrape and have ordered him to pay the colonists.*
>
> *I must leave it to your discretion in great measure to direct the execution of the last proclamation, but I would have it begin immediately with all fugitives and Continental officers unless you see particular cause against it: In any instance where this is the case you may depend upon my approving of your reasons. And I am much out of contact with militia. I have written to Cruger that Cunningham's Corps may go on. I would still have cavalry either a part of it or separate as you or Cruger think most likely to succeed. Cunningham's time for completing his Corps must be prolonged.*
>
> *I am, dear Balfour, most sincerely yours,　Cornwallis*

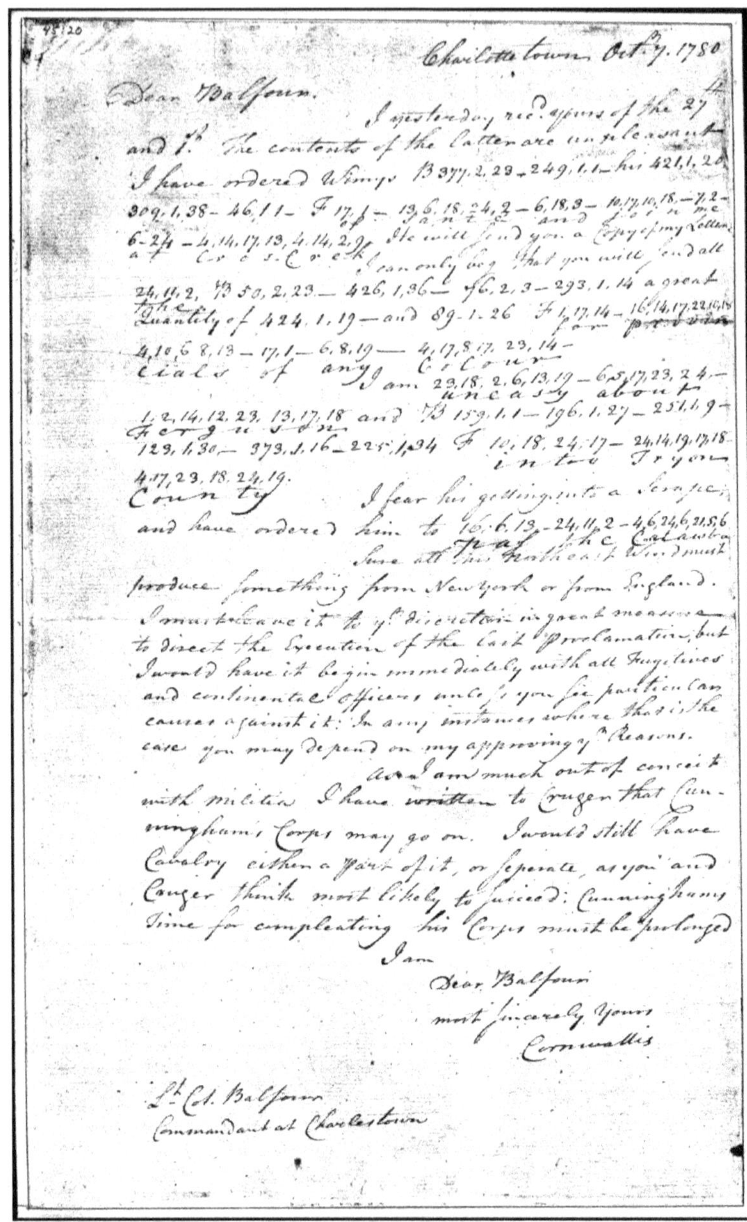

"Intercepted Letter, General Cornwallis to General Balfour."
Cornwallis to Balfour, October 7, 1780. Nathanael Greene Papers.
William L. Clements Library, The University of Michigan

James set down the page. *Major Ferguson was the surrendering British officer at the Battle of Kings Mountain, North Carolina. The victory cheered the southern American militia. No wonder Cornwallis feared Ferguson's "getting into a scrape." And perhaps General Greene will find it useful to know that Cunningham, no doubt a loyalist, was creating a corps of those like himself. The general's message makes sense.* James sighed, folded the results, and put the letter and his work in his satchel. He knew more now about the British cipher, at least that which General Cornwallis used. The battle over, it might have also been Nathanael Greene's intention to understand more about British cipher. If so, that purpose had been met.

He worked through Cornwallis's letter to James Wemyss, finding the cipher used to be consistent with that in the letter to Balfour. Then he summarized his findings in a page to General Nathanael Greene. *If Cornwallis continues with his cipher, the general may be able to decipher future interceptions.*

By this time, the midnight watch's harsh voice long since had called the hour of midnight. The rain had ceased.

Coughing, he opened the little bottle of camphor on his nightstand and inhaled the sharp, biting odor. His breathing cleared, he prepared for bed.

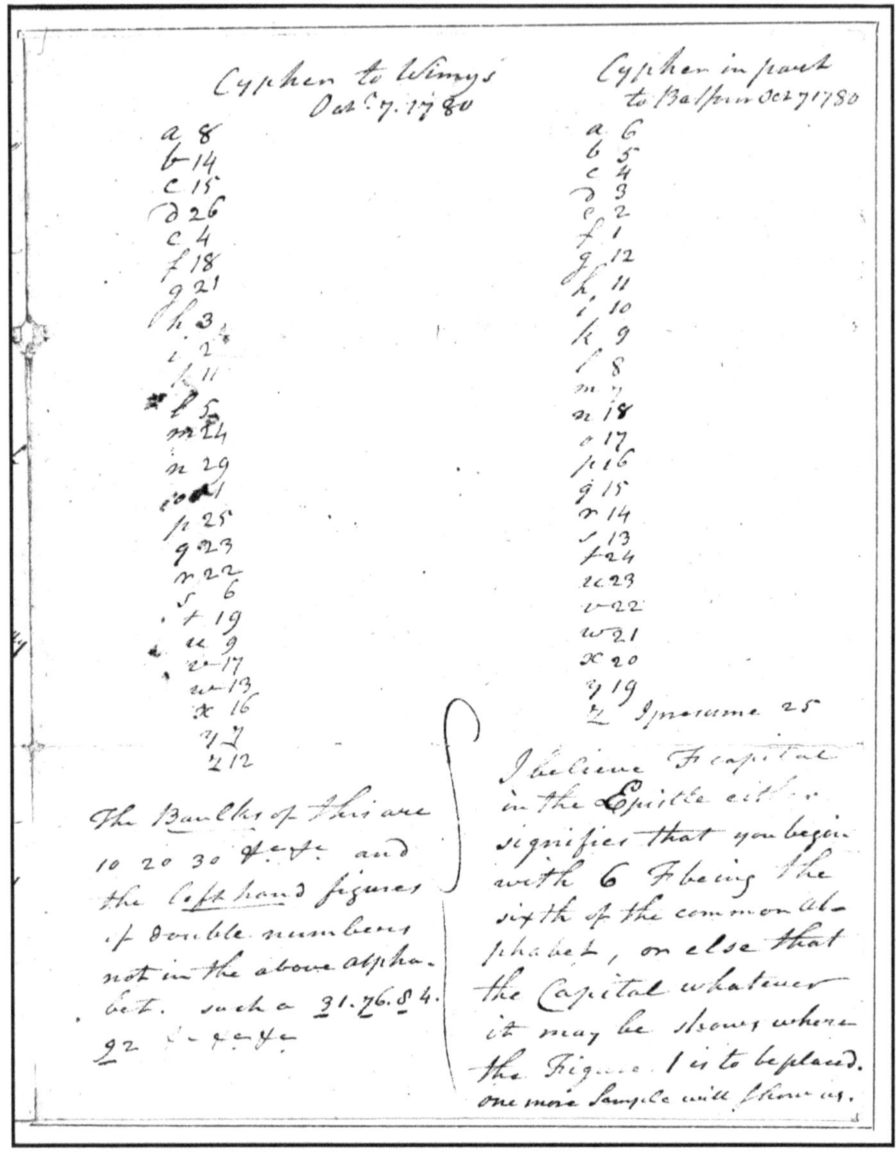

"Explanation of British Cipher, Cornwallis to Wemyss and Balfour."
James Lovell to Nathanael Greene, November 3, 1780.
Nathanael Greene Papers.
William L. Clements Library, The University of Michigan

November 4, 1780, Saturday

On Saturday, James handed the decoded letters with the original to a clerk standing near the president's seat. "Be sure the secretary receives this." The young man took the packet and bowed. James returned to his seat, passing Secretary Thomson, his fingers flying as he sorted papers. The secretary glanced up at him and nodded a greeting.

In mid-morning, William Palfrey was chosen by vote to be Congress's first consul to France. *Educated at the Boston Latin School, my father's pupil.* Palfrey had worked as a merchant with John Hancock and demonstrated remarkable ability with business, catching General Washington's eye early on. He had served as paymaster general for the army since 1776. In France, Palfrey would work with the minister plenipotentiary to assist in developing the interests of the United States in France. Competent and polite, William Palfrey accepted the appointment with a bow.

In a long, intense session, the delegates approved a levy to the states of a tax equal in value to six million silver dollars. Payment would be in barrels of beef, pork, West Indian rum, salt, and for those states producing them, flour or Indian meal.

That night he prepared an alphabet key for William Palfrey to take, giving him the keyword *UNT.*

For himself, he wrote out a page listing the alphabets assigned to Congress's agents overseas. John Adams's alphabets were headed with the key *CR,* the first letters of his brother-in-law's family name, Cranch. Henry Laurens was *YO,* William Palfrey was *UNT,* John Jay was *BY,* and Benjamin Franklin was *COR.*

This will help me as much as them. Now I have all those keys in one place. It can be difficult to keep track of whose alphabet is whose. Remembering the keyword, though: that is key.

**"Substitution Tables for James Lovell's Polyalphabetic Cipher System,
Keywords: John Adams—CR; Henry Laurens—YO; Benjamin Franklin—
COR; William Palfrey—UNT; John Jay—BY."**
PCC, Fold3: M247, r72, i59, p. 144

December 14, 1780, Thursday

James stamped his snow-covered boots as he entered the three-story gabled brick mansion known as the Slate Roof House. Pennsylvania founder William Penn had rented the home around the turn of the century. Now the mansion was home to several delegates.

Samuel Adams held out his hand. "Welcome to the Slate Roof House, my headquarters."

"Thank you for inviting me." James followed tall, stoop-shouldered Samuel to the dining room.

A delicious smell of split pine, roast chicken, and bayberry candles filled the air. He sank gratefully into a chair near his host.

"This evening we dine alone," Samuel said. He passed a platter of roast chicken and potatoes to James.

"We have achieved progress on several fronts," Samuel said, cutting his chicken. "I am grateful that at length Arthur Lee is reassured his recall was not to cast blame on him but necessary to end differences among the commissioners in Europe."

"It is well he knows his service was appreciated."

"I believe he plans to return to Virginia."

The two ate in companionable silence.

James pushed his empty plate back with a sigh. A black serving girl entered and picked up the empty plates. "Would you care for tea?"

"Yes, please, Sally."

The two settled themselves in easy chairs by the hearth. "Some of the latest gazettes," Samuel said, handing a couple to James.

James spread out the pages of a paper. "James Rivington's New York *Royal Gazette*. I wonder what the Tories think is news."

He scanned the fine print.

"John Laurens should be on his way to the court of France soon," Samuel said. "As special envoy, he should be well-placed to obtain the funds and supplies we so critically need."

"He is the right one for the undertaking," James said.

The maid brought tea and poured them each a cup from a silver teapot.

"John Laurens can be extremely persuasive, and he does not lack in persistence. We must have a loan and supplies to ready the army. His abilities may prove crucial."

A headline suddenly caught James's attention. "Oh, no," he gasped. "It is my letter." There, printed prominently, was his letter of three weeks ago to Elbridge Gerry. "They have been intercepting mail again."

"What did the letter contain?" Samuel set down the paper he was holding.

"Elbridge wrote to me that John Hancock, the first governor of Massachusetts under the new state constitution, was 'popular beyond all description.' I suggested one should remember the 32nd of Exodus, how the people worshipped a golden calf, a metaphor for the adulation of political leaders." He laughed, then turned a wry face towards Samuel Adams. "I suppose there will be offense taken at that, though none was intended."

"Offense is indeed a possibility. But I am of your opinion." Samuel shrugged.

"I must admit, unlike others, I could say, 'We have had a mild winter, thanks to God,' without adding 'and General Washington.'"

"I will be surprised if you do not hear from other parties regarding the golden calf allusion. What else did you say?"

"I wrote down the resolution giving General Washington full powers to raise and equip an army."

"Probably nothing the British did not already know. What else?"

"Elbridge had written me, 'Is it not time to pay a visit to Mass,' so I answered, 'Does my wife look as if she wanted a toothless gray-headed sciatic husband near her? I am more benefit to her at a distance than in σ.' I wrote the Greek letter for 'conjunction' here, thinking it quite sufficient." He added, "It was clear to me that 'Mass' meant 'Massachusetts,' not the papish service."

"Sufficient your reference no doubt was, though it may raise eyebrows." Samuel smiled, one of his own eyebrows lifted. "But yes, to me, the reference to 'Mass' is quite clear. People will understand what they want to understand, however."

"And, Mr. Gerry and I have had a kind of running joke about his offer to gift Mrs. Clymer with some salt mackerel. I wrote, 'I shall call on Nanny Cl____r tomorrow and talk of the mackerel.' Again, I see no issue with that. But Rivington's comment suggests we are referring to a secret assignment."

"Dear, dear. I am sure you did not imply that."

James ruffled the pages, annoyed. "Some days I do not see Mrs. Clymer, hence my suggestion that I would call on her. No harm done in the remainder of the letter."

He set the paper down, then finished his tea in one swallow.

"Thank you for the meal and the visit. I had best return to my lodgings. I owe John Adams a letter, using the cipher I sent him in May."

"Have a good evening." Samuel stood and shook hands with James. *John Adams's cousin,* James reminded himself. *Distant cousin, I understand, but cousin nonetheless.*

January 2, 1781, Tuesday

"Henry Laurens is now a captive in the Tower of London. The British cruiser *Vestal* cut short his voyage to the United Provinces in September. He is most unfortunate to have the distinction of being the only American to be held in that terrible place." Artemas Ward glanced solemnly at James.

"That news is most disquieting. I find it difficult to think of Henry Laurens under lock and key, perhaps ill. Being held in the forbidding Tower of London is a dire punishment, one reserved for British enemies of state," James said. He shuddered at the thought.

"And we read that the British discovered in Henry Laurens's trunk the unofficial treaty that I gave him last August. It is just a draft and has no legal authority. Yet they used it as a pretext to declare war with the Dutch."

James set his teacup down. Lucy, the shy young servant, arrived to clear the table, then left with a curtsy.

Artemas Ward stood up. "I must bid you good evening, sir. I have work to do."

"As do I. Until tomorrow."

Down the hall, past the painting of Mr. Clymer glowering from an oval frame, James found his room warm, a fire crackling.

Surely John Adams has learned about Henry Laurens's captivity by now. And he will need the cipher I sent to him last May. I must let him know of the mutiny of the Pennsylvania Line on New Year's Day. One artillery and ten infantry regiments had threatened to leave the army. Their dispute was over lack of pay, clothing, provisions, and terms of enlistment. They had signed on for three years or the duration of the war, but they had served three years with no pay, nothing but their signing bounty of $20. But they did refuse the rewards that British agents offered. In fact, they turned those spies over to the army. *They are disgruntled, not traitorous.*

He wrote to John Adams, informing him that he now had the power to negotiate a treaty and loan in the United Provinces. He explained that Colonel John Laurens was on his way to France, seeking a loan from the court. In cipher, he laboriously wrote out phrases in numbers:

> *I can only say that we are { bankrupt with a mutinous army*
> *} The latter owing very much to the { delay of clothing }.*

Jan.^{ry} 2^d. 1780 [1781]

Dear Sir

your Favor of Sepr 20th reached me at Christmas. I inclose you a Resolve but am not able to give you a Copy of what I officially wrote to cover it by Col. Palfrey and by Way of Boston. you will oblige me by returning a Copy of that Letter which ought to appear on the Books of the Com.^{tee} for for. affairs those Books being soon I hope to be placed in some regularly established Office.

Col. Laurens being on his Way to France via Boston will be able if he sees you to communicate more in one Evening than I could in many Sheets. I can only say that we are 27. 11. 12 2b. 16. 4. 14. 3. 21. 19. 18. 18. 26. 23. 19. 3. 7. 24 13. 19. 2w 26. 1. 11. 8. the latter owing very much to the 2. 15. 10. 11. 23. 25. 4. 13. 10. 25. 26. 3. 6. 19 12. 17. I hope you will remark that so long ago, as Oct 26. 1779 the Powers you now have were voted to M. Laurens, and would have been earlier, but from fear of embarrassing those whose Friendship we wished for,

you will hear from y.r Family immediately
I presume by Col. J Laurens.

affectionately yours

[James Lovell]

Mr about.
Jany. 2. 1781
Col. John Laurens

"James Lovell to John Adams, 2 January 1781."
Massachusetts Historical Society

January 30, 1781, Tuesday

That evening, he opened the letter from Abigail that had arrived that afternoon.

> *Braintree,*
> *January 3, 1781*
>
> *Your favor of December 19 was delivered to me today. I will hasten my thanks to you for it, and for your confidential communications. I cannot, however, comprehend your letter to my best Friend for want of the promised key. I am more reconciled to ambiguity and ciphers than formerly, and not a little thankful that the robberies have been committed now rather than twelve months ago.*
>
> *You judged rightly when you thought you should communicate happiness by telling me of the honorable testimony of Congress about my absent Friend. My little vessel passenger sails, pursues the triumph, and takes on the storm. Nor will it be considered presumptuous if I graft my love, immortal, on his fame. The first pleasure arises from the deserving and the next from the approving voice of his country.*
>
> *I wish you not to mention the possibility of my having lost a letter by the robbery of the mail to Mr. Adams. It will make him still more reserved and cautious. He is enough so now to freeze a person.*
>
> *You will greatly oblige me by a continuation of your favors to your—I will not scruple to say—affectionate*
>
> *Portia*

I will send her some of the recent letters I have received from her Friend. She will find the alphabets enclosed, and the reference to the Cranch family, the first two letters of which are the key to her cipher, was given to her in the last letter. All should be well.

Chapter 30

The United States in Congress Assembled

February 20, 1781, Tuesday

John Paul Jones had arrived in Philadelphia to receive Congress's recognition for his bravery. The naval commodore had received the cross of military merit from the king of France. He brought with him letters and packages from John to Abigail.

James sent Abigail the letters and a small package by way of a friend who was riding home. The other packages posed a more difficult problem. He must find a wagon.

Today, Congress was dispatching ten thousand troops south to Georgia. The Board of War would purchase clothing, muskets, tents, blankets, and other supplies.

On the way home, James remembered that Miss Dalley had sent word the other day asking him to stop by her house. A private matter, the note read. *Very well, I will see what she has on her mind.*

She opened the door to her home, nearly tripping in her eagerness to invite him in.

"Dear Mr. Lovell, thank you so much for stopping by. May I take your coat? Shall we go into the parlor?"

"I have a few minutes, so, yes." James followed her into the small room, cold, the fire nearly dead. He heard the chatter of voices from the dining area. *So, she has plenty of boarders.* "I cannot stay. What can I do for you?"

Miss Dalley almost stammered in her anxiety. "You know how difficult money matters are just now. I must do what I can to keep my sister and me afloat."

James nodded. "Financial security can be precarious."

"Could you reach out to that nice Elbridge Gerry back in Boston and ask him to arrange an exchange of paper money for specie? Bills of exchange that would pay in gold or silver would be the best investment." She plucked at her curly brown hair, her voice anxious. "I have a letter for him here. And in this package," she said, holding out a brown paper wrapped bundle, her voice dropping conspiratorially, "I have $3,000 in paper money. Would you see that this reaches him?"

"I will do what I can to get it to him safely." He thought over the riders he knew that might be heading to Boston as he tucked the package into his satchel.

"I do so thank you!" Miss Dalley exclaimed. She nearly threw her arms about him. James saw her sudden rush forward and checked himself as she took a quick step back.

With a smile, he said, "I will let you know what Elbridge Gerry's response is. Perhaps he will be able to help you with your finances. Who knows? He may even be able to help me. Good night, Miss Dalley."

"Good night, I am sure. I look forward to receiving a response from Mr. Gerry," she gushed.

He tipped his hat and left the room.

February 27, 1781, Tuesday

His room stood in a state of clutter. Two wooden poles, suspended between a chair and his table, held an assortment of clothing and cloth goods. The wardrobe doors were draped with linens and cambric. An open area under the window was spread with ornate fans, lady's gloves, their original color faded to a variety of hues, and men's handkerchiefs. Behind the door were stacked the remains of crumpled, rotting packing cases.

He surveyed the situation and sighed. *Abigail must be told. A good thing I decided to open her three packages.* A parcel he had sent to Elbridge Gerry was also partly rotted. When he opened the one addressed to Colonel Peabody and found it damaged, he realized he should open Abigail's packages. The condition of Abigail's three bundles shocked him. *This is either a terrible problem in transportation or the most negligent packing I have ever seen.*

He wrote to Abigail, explaining that the boxes John sent to her were cracked, poorly packed, and smoked with warm, damp fermentation. But he assured her the articles that he had laid out would probably be all right, once thoroughly dried and repacked. Presents to Abigail and other family members from John, they bore the marks of a merchant at L'Orient.

A shiny glint caught his eye as he surveyed the various articles and he gazed at the fine French fan in admiration. Dipping his pen in the inkbottle, he continued the letter.

> *I must particularly acquaint Miss that, though the fans*
> *stuck together a great deal, they are now by no means ruined.*
> *They would have been lost if they had dried in that position.*

> *One of them is the prettiest of the shining kind that I have yet seen. The green mold is next-to-entirely removed from the gauzes, among which the gloves were placed for their safety.*
>
> *The fate of the South is balancing between Cornwallis and Greene; and of the middle states—War between the Commanders near Gardner's Island. I never have yet been so agitated by present moments since the war began. God be better to us than our deserts!*
>
> *Your very humble servant,   James Lovell*

James looked about the crowded, disarrayed area. *These articles will dry and be gone before I know it. What we do for our friends.*

March 5, 1781, Monday

Only three days previously, Congress had convened for the first time as the United States in Congress Assembled. New York had ceded its western land claims, and finally Maryland ratified the Articles of the Confederation. President Samuel Huntington listened intently as Secretary Thomson read aloud the Articles of the Confederation. Article III especially seemed to speak to James: "The said states hereby severally enter into a firm league of friendship with each other, for their common defense, the security of their liberties, and their mutual and general welfare…."

It had been a long road since Congress had completed the Articles in York in the spring of 1778, he realized. Samuel Adams remarked it had been an even longer road since they were first proposed in June of 1776. But their ratification by all thirteen states was quite an achievement.

March 27, 1781, Tuesday

"The Chesapeake has seen action," Artemas Ward observed, in his straightforward, calm way. "But fog prevented the glorious conclusion that we sought. General Washington requested the French fleet leave their base at Newport, Rhode Island, and join the Marquis de Lafayette's army to meet General Benedict Arnold in Virginia."

"Though the French fired on the British multiple times, inflicting significant damage, when the fog rolled in, the French could not prevent reinforcements to Arnold. Now the British are in control of the Chesapeake."

The first stars winked in the azure sky. James relaxed as the two stood by the river, feeling the fresh wind on his face. Down in Virginia, a momentous naval battle had occurred. The French ships had tried to carry out the commander-in-chief's objective, but the weather was against them.

It seemed like ages since he had stood here, remembering what it was to feel carefree when he skipped stones with his sons. *And like a stone, we should skip over the hard events.*

"Shall we return?" he asked, standing up.

"As good a time as any," Artemas Ward said with a sigh.

March 31, 1781, Saturday

A letter arrived from General Nathanael Greene giving news of his brave encounter with the British under Cornwallis at Guilford Courthouse. After a heated conflict of about two hours, the enemy gained the field and four pieces of artillery, then forced Greene's troops to retreat. The Carolina militia fled, but the Virginia militia fought back, though grilled by incessant fire. Eventually, they too retreated. General Greene concluded by saying that Cornwallis lost six hundred men, while the Americans' loss was about three hundred. He congratulated the Virginians on their brave action, though he regretted the loss of men and valuable officers. He requested General Washington send beef to the army, as there was little food in the exhausted country around the conflict.

"Maybe Cornwallis will think twice about persisting in his attempts to take the Carolinas," General Artemas Ward said.

The fire in James's room crackled and snapped, sending bright sparks whirling up the chimney. Ann Clymer had taken ill. On the few occasions James had seen her during the last couple of weeks, she had coughed and waved him on, cheerfully refusing to speak with him.

It occurred to him with a sigh of relief that he no longer suffered from the violent dreams he had endured for years. Now when he slept, it was a solid, quiet slumber, nearly devoid of dreams. *I think I am so exhausted that all I can do is sleep. Those dreams were terrible—if indeed they were dreams, so lifelike they felt. Perhaps I am not doing so badly. I put one foot after the other, taking each day as it comes.*

Chapter 31

Close Call to Disaster

April 10, 1781, Tuesday

"Would you accompany me to take some refreshment? There are matters I would be privileged to discuss with you." Robert Morris, his blue eyes glinting, approached James at the Pennsylvania State House. Near him stood Gouverneur Morris, no longer a delegate, but frequent business associate of Robert Morris.

"I will be happy to do that," James said. *What could Robert Morris, widely thought to be the candidate for Superintendent of Finance, want to discuss with me?*

"We will find a comfortable place to talk at City Tavern, I am sure."

"Excellent." They set out in the soft evening air of early spring, horses trotting by on the streets. Gouvernor Morris, taller than Robert Morris and leaner, limped slightly, his wooden leg clicking on stones. James remembered hearing of the carriage accident that had taken the New York senator's leg.

At City Tavern, they were shown to a secluded place in a corner. The maid brought tankards of cider and James, thirsty, took a long drink, while Robert Morris ordered plates of roast beef.

James set his tankard down and waited in patience. *What could the financier want from me?*

Robert Morris cleared his throat. "I have a duty, one for someone who is good with figures, absolutely honest, and utterly committed to the success of our country."

Gouverneur Morris nodded agreement with Robert Morris's words. "The person must be incorruptible, impervious to the charm of ill-gotten money."

James regarded the heavy-set Robert Morris steadily, his fine suit of gray wool, his tailored shirt of crisp white linen, all speaking of wealth and success. As a merchant he was unparalleled, buying and selling and accumulating personal funds even as he made deals that assisted the army. He waited for Robert Morris's next statement.

"You have those qualities and would be suited for this duty."

"What would it be?" James asked, curious.

"In Boston, we need a Continental tax receiver—one who would collect the taxes that belong to the nation, then turn those over to us. As you know, there are funds that too often line private pockets which should be made available to Congress."

"It would mean relocating to Boston," James said. A prickle of apprehension ran up his spine.

"It could mean that. It also means you could work both as a delegate and as the Continental tax receiver. Of course, you would have to travel frequently."

James looked down into his half-empty tankard. The prospect of leaving his work at Congress, just now, when the situation was so precarious, the enemy advancing in the south, his contacts in foreign affairs precious—he could not imagine doing so.

A waiter set down plates of sliced roast beef and pickled beets and refilled their tankards.

"I am afraid I could not undertake such an assignment at this time," he said after a pause, his voice reluctant.

"We understand," Robert Morris said, his voice tinged with regret. "Maybe later the opportunity will be more suitable."

"Perhaps," James said. Having made up his mind, he felt confident that his decision was right, though his heart tugged to think of being home with his family.

"You are kind to think of me," he said, taking a bite of the beef. "I appreciate your consideration."

"Of course. You have your current position to fill, one which is invaluable, to be sure."

Gouverneur Morris began to talk of business matters—orders to fill for the army—and James ate quietly, listening. He still had work to do that evening. Robert Morris's proposal posed a tantalizing opportunity, but not one that he could undertake, at least not at this time.

"Thank you for your offer," James said, finishing his meal. "We need good, incorruptible public servants to assist us with our finances. I hope you find the right person for the situation." He stood and shook Robert Morris's hand.

April 18, 1781, Wednesday

Congress has done everything in its power to support the war, James realized, as the lengthy report went on.

The committee detailed all the attempts to shore up the country's treasury by taxation, letters, bills of credit, and quotas, as well as endeavors to support the military by offering pension plans. Their conclusion stated the debts from abroad now totaled six million dollars, with annual interest of three hundred and sixty thousand dollars. For the credit and honor of the United States, they recommended a fund be provided to defray the interest and pay the principal. Meanwhile, the ministers abroad required support.

"This report should be circulated to all the states." James Duane set the thick pages down on Secretary Thomson's table, his face clouded with worry.

James writhed inwardly as the information was read. It was all true, all horribly impossible to handle in any other way. Had they made mistakes? Not in the whole. It was simply the situation that had to be managed. They had dealt with it as best they could. The fault belonged equally to everyone and no one.

He felt his heart sinking as the account was delivered, unemotionally, blandly, yet filled with implications for the young country. A sinking ship came to mind, but he pushed the image away. What would happen was certain. They would survive and carry on, but in what manner was nearly unimaginable. Still, upholding honor and truth was important. Congress would follow the report's recommendations.

That night he wrote a short note to Dr. Samuel Holten. He had little news to give. He felt grim and despondent, his state of mind an echo of recent events.

> *Cornwallis has retreated quite out of Greene's reach.*
> *The time of the Virginia militia being expired, our army is*
> *weak. There were the greatest marks of distress left by the*
> *British. Their dead were buried by our people. You were in*
> *Congress at an easy, happy period of business, though you*
> *did not know it, nor did I then guess it.*
> *Yours affectionately,   J.L.*

April 24, 1781, Tuesday

James left the Pennsylvania State House in the driving rain, his hat pulled down tight. Water flowed in streams down the muddy street as carts splashed by. At the corner of Chestnut and 6th Streets, he stopped just as he nearly collided with an elderly gentleman who was turning to enter the walkway to a house.

"Most sorry," the old fellow said. Bright blue eyes looked anxiously from under a round hat, a long white beard hung down under a scarf. James had never seen him before.

"Good evening." He tipped his soggy hat.

The stranger spoke anxiously. "Could I trouble you to give me directions to a shop on Market Street? The sign displays a book. I have an acquaintance living there."

James thought quickly. "The book shop would be farther down, I think between High Street and 2nd."

"Thank you. Much obliged." The old man turned into his walkway.

At his lodging, he shut the door with a bang. He pulled off his wet coat, then set it and his hat by the fire to dry. After a brief meal he took up his writing. As a congressman, he was often in a position to help others. He had just received information that would be of assistance to two citizens. He composed the letters, feeling the responsibility that came with his position.

A knock sounded on his door.

"A message for you, sir," the balding servant said. He handed James a folded note.

"Thank you," James said. He held it out to the light. Written in a hasty scrawl, the note seemed to be from a tailor to whom he owed the final payment on a new shirt. It read: "I must request the payment from you, immediately. Circumstances demand it. Thank you."

Where can I get cash? I have none here. He remembered the printer whose friendship he had made when he had arranged for the printing of the *Journals*. The printer had said that should he require a small loan, he could ask. *This might be the time.*

He put on his hat and coat, still damp, wrapped a scarf about his neck, and stepped out into the storm. He turned towards the printer's shop on Market Street.

The image of a bookshop crossed his mind. *Wait—did I direct the stranger to the wrong place? The store with the image of a book is actually the printer's shop. I have indeed misdirected the stranger.*

He turned abruptly and crossed the street to return to the elderly gentleman's house. He would find him and accompany him to the correct place. A cart dashed by, sending up a spray of water. He shielded his face from the splash, then, his hat flopping in the rain, continued. Ahead was an alley he had crossed before. He headed into the dark, narrow space.

In confusion and pain, he awoke, his back and side wrenched in agony, rain pouring down on him. He was lying in a dark pit in a sea of mud, shaking with cold. How long had he been there? Hours, was his guess. He tried to raise a leg and groaned at the spike of pain that rushed through his body. The effort was nearly too much, and he bit his lip while misery washed over him. The walls of the pit were earthen, rain-soaked. Above, he could see the faint outline of the entrance against the black of night, maybe ten feet overhead. He couldn't get out even if he could stand.

Flat on his back, he started to shout. "Help," he called out, weakly, then stronger, as fear and desperation took over. "Help, help me!"

Over and over, he called. He raised his arms and found to his relief that they worked. But he could not stand, his right leg putting him in extreme distress when he tried to move. He could only lie still, helpless, in the cold water, shouting until his voice turned hoarse.

At length, he thought he heard a faint response. He willed himself to listen, searching the black square of sky above him.

"Hello—someone there?" came the distant voice.

Now James could make out an anxious face hanging over the edge of the pit. Light from a lamp illuminated the muddy earthen walls. In it he saw the anxious face of the night watchman.

"I have fallen down. I cannot get up," James called back.

"Just wait, sir. I will find someone." To his distress, the night watchman disappeared, and he was left alone again. He shivered violently and tried to lift his right leg, despite the deep, throbbing pain. *Have I broken it?* To his relief, he found he could lift it a few inches. *No, it may just be sprained, or fractured.*

He waited in suspense, feeling the rain drop on his face. Finally, after what seemed like an hour, a loud voice called down, "Here we be, sir. We are sending down a rope ladder, but you must grab it."

"I will do my best," James said, his voice cracking.

The last rung of a rope ladder stopped not far above him. He grabbed it with both hands and heaved himself upward with all his strength, hoping his wet hands would not slip. "Pull," he called to the men above, "and I will try to stand."

The ladder jerked upwards, rubbing against the muddy walls of the pit. James held on and managed to get his feet under him, though his whole body recoiled at movement.

"Wait," he called. "I am going to try to put my foot on it." He gingerly set his left foot on the ladder's lower rung, then by sheer will placed his right foot there as well.

"When you are on, we will pull you up. Got it?" the men above him asked.

"I am ready," James answered.

They hoisted him up, his face and chest awkwardly bumping over the muddy wall, his legs and back aching.

Finally, sprawled on the ground above, James gasped and wiped mud from his face.

"Here, I will help you to your home. Where would that be?" one of the men who had come to his rescue said, in a kind voice.

"On Walnut Street, near the corner of 7th," he muttered. "I thank you."

Strong arms gripped him and he managed to make his feet move. Supported by his rescuer, he set out in the direction of Ann Clymer's house.

"What did I fall into?" he asked, turning towards the sturdy workman.

"There was a store there, an old, rundown thing, but they took it out. You fell into the cellar," he said, almost apologetically.

James shuddered.

Lucy opened the door, gasping in disbelief. "Here, use this, Mr. Lovell," she said, handing James a stout cane. "It was Mr. Clymer's."

Leaning on the cane, James turned to the workman.

"I owe you more than I can pay. Thank you for coming to my aid."

"I am glad to help. You are safe at home now, thanks be to God."

"Indeed," James answered fervently.

In his room, he shrugged off his muddy clothing. Wrapped in his robe, he shivered under a blanket by his fire, sipped the cup of tea that the worried Lucy brought. *I don't think I require a doctor. I will see what tomorrow brings.* Grateful his fall had not been worse, he crawled into bed, still shaking.

April 30, 1781, Monday

It would be two weeks before James could attend Congress. His bruises covered much of his back and legs, turning from black to a hideous purple and green. His legs, while not broken or fractured, did not permit him to walk. Apparently, the tendons were strained, particularly those of his right leg. Samuel Adams visited, looked with sympathy and disbelief at his bruises, and assured him his absence would cause no problems. Mrs. Clymer clucked and muttered over his condition, opening his door just enough to shake her head and ask after his health. She made sure Lucy brought him tea, broth, and toast, while the balding servant kept the fire well supplied. Artemas Ward stopped by his room to inform him about proceedings in Congress.

Whether the stranger he had encountered on that cold, rainy night ever found the place he was looking for, he never knew. He managed to send funds to his tailor, accepting a loan from Artemas Ward. The weather improved, and before long, trees sprouted leaves outside his window, and birds sang. He found himself thinking of his home, the close call to disaster stirring up emotions he had long suppressed. Yes, his duties were important, but so were his home, his family. He wrote Mary nearly every day, sent money to her by way of Elbridge Gerry, and enclosed letters to his children.

Chapter 32

They Must Confess They

Cannot Conquer Us

May 8, 1781, Tuesday

In a few days he was able to sit up. Walking, however, was a struggle. General Gates came to see him. In a brief conversation, his lips pursed with disapproval, Horatio Gates explained that without a Court of Inquiry, his name and actions at Camden could not be cleared. Congress could urge that Court of Inquiry.

James could say little, but he encouraged the general to persist. As they said good-bye, he felt confident that his friend might yet play a valuable part in the war.

He wrote to Elbridge Gerry, sharing with him his fears about the fluctuating state of currency and his sorrow that William Palfrey's ship was sunk while he was on his way to serve as consul in France.

Tomorrow, I may try to go to the State House, he thought, sealing the letter.

May 28, 1781, Monday

"Good morning, Mr. Lovell." Robert Morris greeted him with a smile. "And how is your health?"

"Better, I assure you. I am fortunate that nothing was broken in my fall."

"It is good you have returned. We need you, these days," Robert Morris said.

Robert Morris's proposal for a national bank had been favorably reviewed, the better to make short-term loans to Congress and payments on the national debt.

"Good morning," General Artemas Ward said in his gravelly voice, handing James the gazettes.

"Money—aye, there is the rub," James said, opening a paper.

"And representation." General Ward looked about the room, far from crowded, with only twenty-four delegates present. "Perhaps before long George Partridge and Samuel Osgood will join us."

261

"General Cornwallis has returned south to Hillsborough, North Carolina. He is sending raids into the Virginia countryside."

"But Lafayette is responding to those attacks, though he commands about half the number of troops that Cornwallis does."

They ceased their conversation as President Samuel Huntington initiated the session. James could not help but admire the president's white linen shirt and fine wine-colored woolen jacket. Without thinking, he tugged at his own patched coat sleeves.

"We have a letter from General Washington," Samuel Huntington said. "The French troops at Newport under the Count de Rochambeau will march to join the commander-in-chief on the North River to form an operation against New York. The general thinks an attack against New York preferable to sending the men south, owing to the difficulty and expense of traveling by sea and the effects of a long march by land in the heat of summer.

"And a report from the committee who met with the Chevalier de la Luzerne."

James glanced at the Chevalier de la Luzerne, who sat, as he usually did, in the middle of the delegates, listening to the proceedings closely.

Daniel Carroll, a plantation owner from Maryland, stood to read the committee's report. "The Chevalier de la Luzerne received a letter from His Most Christian majesty, who recognizes the distressed state of the finances of the United States. The king determines to aid our defense as far as he is able. He states his sincere affection for the United States.

"As proof of his affection, the king has resolved to set aside six million livres to purchase clothing, arms, and ammunition. He also permits Dr. Franklin to borrow four million more this year. The king intends to enable the United States to act with vigor."

The delegates responded with applause.

Daniel Carroll cleared his throat. "The Chevalier de la Luzerne has stated the necessity for Mr. Adams in any negotiations with Britain to act according to the directions from the Count de Vergennes, or whomever negotiates in the name of the king. Mr. Adams must remain constantly in connection with French negotiators."

James's eyebrows went up. The Chevalier de la Luzerne tapped a manicured nail on the arm of his chair in silent approval of the committee's report.

"Finally, the French minister would have us remember that the surest way to obtain the security of the United States is to compel the English to confess they are not able to conquer them. It is most important to carry on the war with the utmost vigor."

Daniel Carroll handed his report to Secretary Thomson and bowed to the president and the French minister. The Chevalier de la Luzerne nodded his appreciation and dusted his hands together lightly, as if the matter were already concluded.

It sounds as if the French want to keep John Adams on a tight leash. That may not be received so well.

May 29, 1781, Tuesday

A couple of weeks ago James had informed Abigail of his fall in a short note. Now he opened the letter he had just received, which enclosed a copy of one she had written on March 17.

He read it with a growing sense of alarm.

> *Braintree, 10 May, 1781*
>
> *Upon opening your favor of April 17, my heart beat a double stroke when I found that the letter that I supposed had reached you was the one captured. The letter, which I would not have sent to any hand but yours, was in reply to two of yours and contained some restrictions on the conduct of a friend. I enclose a copy.*
>
> *I cannot open my lips in defense of a friend whose character I would wish to justify, nor will I keep it a secret from him that his long absence from his family has caused pain to his friends. I have but a very small personal acquaintance with the Lady who is nearest to him, whom I esteem and with whom I commiserate. Those who know her better speak highly of her. I have as little personal acquaintance with the gentleman connected with her, but it has so happened that I have stood in need of his services, and he has exhibited a diligence and friendship in the discharge of them that has bound me to him in the bond of friendship. Add to this, he is the particular friend and correspondent of him who is dearest to me and for whose sake alone I should esteem him, but it would mortify me not a little to find I had mistaken a character, and in the room of a philosopher a man of the world had appeared.*

He sighed and scratched his head. *She misunderstands me*, he thought. *My service has kept me here, but it is a matter of duty. How could that cause pain?*

Enclosed he found a copy of the letter she had sent him in March, which she assumed had been stolen. In it she advised him against using terms of endearment to address her.

> *...consider certain names addressed to a Lady—we will suppose her for argument's sake amiable, agreeable, and his friend. I found by trying that those epithets would only be bearable. If they were carried a syllable beyond, to lovely, to charming, they touched too delicately the finely tuned instrument and produced a discord where harmony alone should subsist.*
>
> *I had many things in mind to say to you in the political way when I took up my pen, but will defer them for the subject of another letter or until you tell me that you have received this in that spirit of friendship with which it flowed from the pen of*
>
> *Portia*

He set it down with a frown. *She need not fear for my wife's affections, though she expresses concerns for her. And she proclaims restrictions. There should be nothing in my speech that would require restrictions. I must admit, I have been chastised.*

He glanced through the letter again, focusing on the last line. *At least she writes in the spirit of friendship. She thinks I should go home for a visit.* He glanced around his room, the familiar piles of papers, the worn clothing hung in the wardrobe. *I should like nothing better, when the time is right.* He let his thoughts fly back to his wife, his children, their home. Flustered, he took out paper to respond.

> *May 29, 1781*
>
> *Yesterday's post brought me your letters. I have a Friend to whom I communicate most unreservedly all the occurrences which tend to govern my pleasures and my pains; your letters will of course be submitted to that view. You say "You have a very small personal acquaintance with the Lady whom you esteem and commiserate—you have as little personal acquaintance with the gentleman connected with her." Had you greater with both, you could not fail to think more highly of the former, and not so well or so ill of the latter as you seem at present to think, if I, who am perfectly intimate with them, may conclude from your recent letters.*

> *Glory or shame, great in degree of either kind, depends upon the behavior of the Americans in the coming six months.*
>
> *And now, away with you, products of an honest pen! Come to my aid, ye products of insincerity! It is not the candid, but the sentimental to whom I send you.*
>
> *"I have the honor to be with the most perfect consideration your excellency's most obedient & devoted humble servant."*
>
> *James Lovell*
>
> *PS By way of Nota Bene, "excellency" in English is of both genders.*

And as generals, and congressmen, and statesmen, and businessmen so style themselves, so must I, he thought, finishing his close with a flourish of his pen. *If she would have it so.*

June 5, 1781, Tuesday

Elbridge Gerry's letter to him of May 20, printed in Rivington's *New York Royal Gazette*, caused him to cringe. The letter discussed currency speculations with Miss Dalley. *While speculation is perfectly acceptable, it is not the kind of information I wish to have printed.*

It was high time he sent Elbridge Gerry directions to use a cipher. The keyword would be the first three letters of the maiden name of the wife of the gentleman whose money he had sent to Elbridge for the lottery. He began by directing Elbridge to number a column 1 to 27, for the twenty-six letters of the alphabet and the ampersand. Beside it, Elbridge should place two other columns of letters. The first of these should begin with the second letter and the second should begin with the third letter of the key. Elbridge then should look alternately at these columns for the letters of the words in a cyphered message and write the letters accordingly.

Enciphering critical words, he warned Elbridge that the Count de Vergennes influenced the Chevalier de la Luzerne. La Luzerne in turn softened up diners at elaborate meals on the social calendar of many in Philadelphia. *Sycophants or worse,* he muttered unhappily. The French administration in America calculated to put Franklin, Jay, and now Adams into a position of the strictest agreement with the Count de Vergennes. The result would change the nature of the commission and instructions given to John Adams.

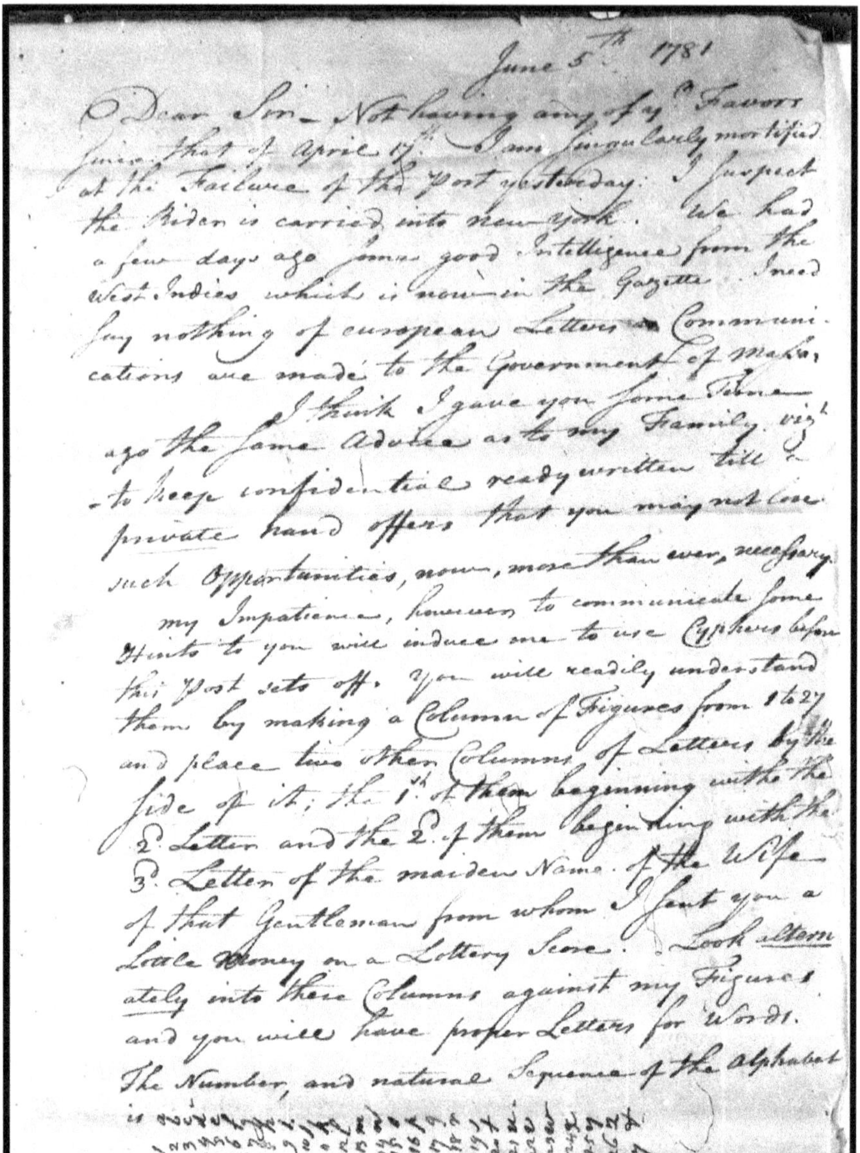

June 5th 1781

Dear Son— Not having any of yr Favors
since that of April 17th I am singularly mortified
at the Failure of the Post yesterday. I suspect
the Rider is carried into New-York. We had
a few days ago some good intelligence from the
West-Indies which is now in the Gazette. I need
say nothing of european Letters & Communications are made to the Government of Mass.

I think I gave you some time
ago the same Advice as to my Family, vizt
to keep confidential ready written till a
private hand offers that you may not lose
such Opportunities, now, more than ever, necessary.

my Impatience, however, to communicate some
Hints to you will induce me to use Cyphers before
this Post sets off. You will readily understand
them by making a Column of Figures from 1 to 27
and place two other Columns of Letters by the
side of it; the 1st of them beginning with the
2d Letter and the 2d of them beginning with the
3d Letter of the maiden Name of the Wife
of that Gentleman from whom I sent you a
Little Money on a Lottery Score. Look alternately into these Columns against my Figures
and you will have proper Letters for Words.
The Number, and natural Sequence of the Alphabet
is [cipher table in shorthand]

I retained yr 2 Bills with yr Whip & Linnen.

I still continue lame, tho but slightly
the Family is well and some of it not a little
uneasy tho Fear that you are not so in Health.
aff. yr J L

There appears to be a desire in the vexed 27.18.18.18 14.20.1.27.10.1.18.15, the obedient if not designing 19.14.26.5.27.5.5.16.4.24.6.5.1.10, in america and the too many soft sycophantic or worse principled 17.5.27.1.4.15.6.4.18.14.18 to accomplish a total Change in the Nature both of the 26.1.9.26.5.5. 15.22.11.27, 23.22.10.5.16.4.17, 16.16.22.11.27.15.1.2.23, 24.17.24.26.15, by 6.24.16.7.22.10.20.2.4.24.27.7.25. 5.27, and 6.14.24.13 by making almost the whole Business subservient to the 27.22.15.16.14.18.16. 22.11.27.24.4.21.8.11.22.26.18.11.19.16.9.11, with the strictest Injunction to 14.26.16.11.4.27.25.6.4. 6.4.1.9.14.26.5.27.5.5.16.18.14.

June 13th Noon

I have this moment yr. Letter of May 20 printed by Buington as Mr. Gerrish's. I suppose that some Folks who were angried at the former Discovery will endeavor to make Harm out of these Transactions between you & me. As Accident has brought the matter to their Know-ledge they will chuse to conceive it to be what I wished to have concealed. I am quite indifferent

I have more Reasons than you hinted for believing old Delegates will be put aside. Plausible Arguments may be drawn from the Confederation. But tho' Connecticut acted upon it in regard to Mr. Sherman, she has now again sent him. — Genl. Ward might have been ac-comodated with hard Cash by yr. Treasurer, if he had been a Worshipper. He has been forced to put off his Paper at 4.

I will be more particular as to the figured Business by Genl. Ward some time this Week — yours affly

Honble Mr Gerry.

June 15, 1781, Friday

Dining with Samuel Osgood and George Partridge at Miss Dalley's, James said, "We authorized the minister plenipotentiary at the court of Versailles to exchange General Burgoyne for Henry Laurens. The British should be happy to agree to that."

"Henry Laurens should be released before long," Samuel Osgood said. A former aide to Artemas Ward, he replaced General Ward, who had departed for home.

"Next week we shall elect a secretary for the new Department of Foreign Affairs. I look forward to this election. I will be able to place the papers I have cared for in the hands of another person. Being secretary for a committee which sometimes exists but much more frequently consists of one person alone has its challenges."

His fellow delegates looked at James curiously, and with some sympathy. "You have been here how long?" Samuel Osgood asked.

"About four and a half years. I have not been home in that time." James shifted uncomfortably in his chair. "My children and wife miss me and write to say so. But the time will come for me to return home, I am convinced." He remembered Abigail's advice that he should go home for a visit. *She is right, though I cannot do so yet.*

A knock sounded on the door.

"Please come in," Samuel Osgood called.

Miss Dalley put her head in the doorway. "Cake, anyone?"

June 16, 1781, Saturday

The following day, James settled at his chair. His bruises had turned from purple to yellow. Now he could nearly walk without a cane.

He needed to write to Abigail. She must understand the circumstances of his fall. Much to his dismay, he had heard that rumors had reached Boston that he had been drunk and fallen down a stairwell. People will talk, he knew, but such talk made him cringe.

With care, he relayed his actions of that night. As a friend, she mattered to him. He laid bare his self-reproach for at least one expression he had used in his letter to Elbridge Gerry of last November, reported in the Loyalist press. Finally, the reasons why he remained in Philadelphia, rather than return home as she had suggested—these also must be explained.

How could she censure me for using words such as lovely, charming, and the like in her praise, when her virtuous behavior excites no other such words?

He set the letter in his satchel. *At least for now, I have set her right on several accounts.*

June 21, 1781, Thursday

In the Assembly library, warm and smelling of books and dust, he prepared to write to John Adams to explain the recent addition of negotiators. Using cipher for significant words, he explained that new negotiators were added at the request of France. He could not refrain from making a kind of joke, a stab at America's prominent position in determining a peace with world powers, but was careful to put sensitive words in cipher. "You would be made very happy by such an event being grounded on a desire to alleviate the distress of a great {discretion but blush, blush} America...." *We are not so great, yet,* he thought, *but we have every hope we will become so.*

John Adams said he did not understand my cipher. I sent him directions over a year ago. Perhaps he did not understand which keyword to use. I asked him to remember the name of the family with whom we dined in New England. I should have said in Braintree so he would remember the name Cranch.

Writing out the directions for the cipher again, he listed an alphabet alongside the numbers 1 to 27, adding the numbers 28 through 30 to be used as markers or baulks at the beginning, end, or within words.

> *Make two columns of letters under the rule of sequence laid down here. Begin your first column with the first letter and your second column with the second letter of the family name formerly referred to. Go on to & then follow a b &c. &c. &c. Look alternately into the columns, and so find what my figures represent, and vice versa to write yourself.*
>
> *28, 29, 30. To be used as Baulks in the Beginning and End or within your words.*

The afternoon session had begun by the time James finished his task. He folded up the letter, bundled up his writing tools, and hastened back to the Assembly Room, his leg aching once more.

[21 June 1781] <u>XLII</u> 88

Sir

France appears to be most perfectly
satisfied with the 14.1.3.2.3.24.18.23.3.14.17.18
18.25.16.2. 23.15.18.26.15.17.2.3.2 19.2 for an Arrangement final of the most 11.25.2.15.16.11.18
15.18.15.16.23.17.30.28. 26.26.4.12.21.10.19.12.20.26
8.6.22.26.4.16.15.12.13.3.10.8.15.4.16.3.1.17.25.12
11.16.15.26.14.2.15.2.3.13.8.13.4. You would be
made very happy by such an Event being found
on a desire to alleviate the Distress of a great
2.19.17.13.16.15.18.19.13.24.27 4.18.12.10.4.17.18.27
22.19.2.6. America 13.13.24.17.4.10.3 25.4
10.3.7.23.26.3.3.22 23.13.13.24.13.19.1.7.24.3.5.3
1.23.3.6.19.12.17.21.19.18.18 The Ministers of his
most Christian Majesty the Independence
of the United States according to the Tenor
of our Alliance 9.15.14.3.17.25.10.15.19.22.18.19
11.11.18.4.11. I might have mentioned a Circumstance not very material in the present Turn of Affairs 11.10.22.13.1.10.15.17.2
13.1 13.24.3 13.26.24.19.13 24.13.10.4.2.15.26.2
14.22.3.24.7.26.13. It is a Satisfaction to me
and others alike interested that your other
26.26.1.4.18.11.15.12.3.17.17.16.15.19.24.18.25.19
13.6.15.2. I hope therefore that we may
conclude our 18.26.14.2.25.1.21 17.11.4.15. I
presume you will be at very little Loss to
come at the Clue of this Labyrinth 9.1.26.
5.7.15.16.24.13.6 persuaded of the absolute Necessity
of the most cordial Intercourse between 6.19
11.10.23.25.19.2.18.1.13 24.5.22.23 26.16.3.2.17.18
2.16.13.1.13.1.2.15.16.2.13.16.18.18.26.3.9.19.12.14 an
Suppleness know not where to stop especially
when under the spur of 26.3.10 15.26.2.18.11.11.16
12.13.19.17. It is needless to turn Well-digger on
this Occasion the whole is at the Superficies — I
must officially convey to you some Papers. I shall
use this same Cypher. I suspect that you did

not before understand it from my not having said supped in <u>Braintree</u>. I guess I said New England ——

 The President has sent the Papers before referred to. I furnished the Instructions in a Cypher. If any Thing prevents your coming at the Purport Doct. Franklin can certainly decypher his. I was intended to send only one Sett by one Vessel, but I think that would have added Something to the List of Oddities in this Business.

 I do not despair of being able to write again by this Opportunity.

Dr Franklin came into the River day. Letters from Mr Dana are recd. April 3d. Of late is still Oct. 24. ——

Sincerely JL

June 21. 81 ——

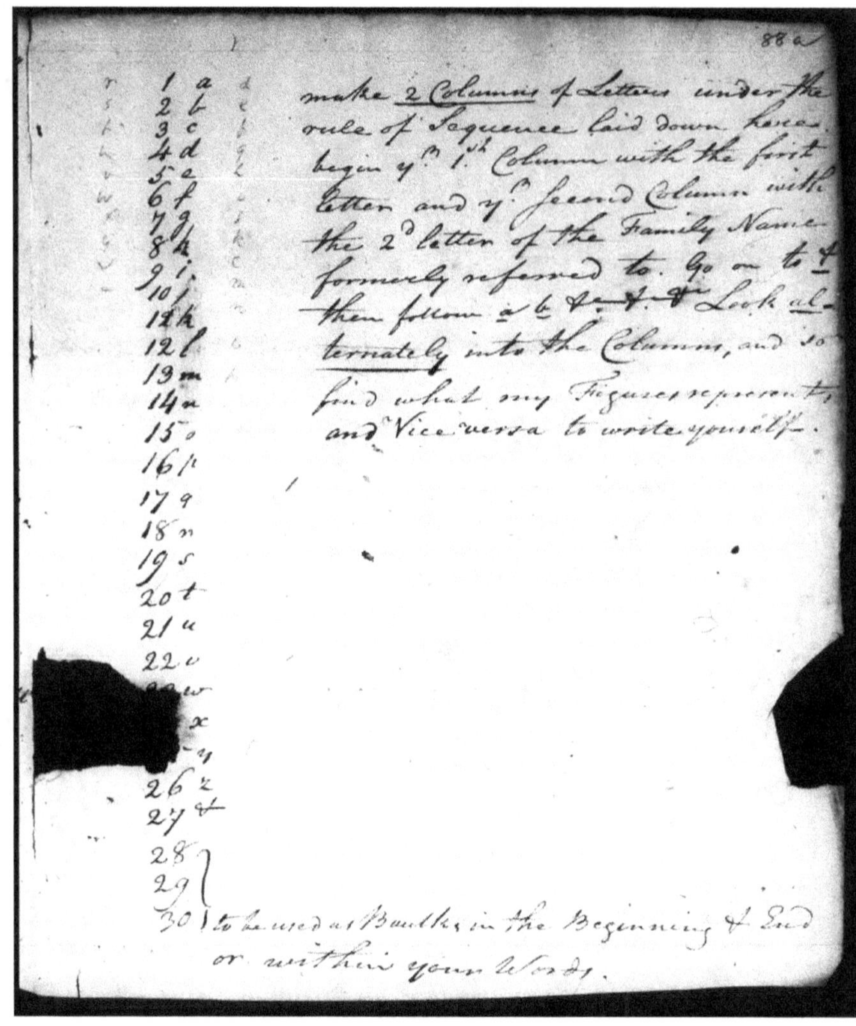

"James Lovell to John Adams, 21 June 1781."
Massachusetts Historical Society

Chapter 33

My Humble Desire to Serve You

July 13, 1781, Friday

The previous day, James had stayed in his room with a headache, drawing shut the heavy brocade curtains to block out the sun. The days had piled up like cascading tiles, each one weighty. The commemoration of independence, the fifth year, had come and gone. America was five years old, and the speeches, the military parade, the fireworks, did not reassure him, for she was not yet born.

Thomas McKean of Delaware was now president of Congress, Samuel Huntington having resigned due to ill health. Thomas McKean, who had served as a delegate on and off for four years, would be the fifth president James had served under.

He rested, appreciative of the broth and sliced strawberries that Mrs. Clymer brought him, and by nightfall some of his energy returned, his head cleared.

Today, returning to Congress, he felt the stirrings of health. The day went well, his strength equal to the hours of meetings, the pages of writing.

He had just received a letter from Abigail. Written on June 23rd, she included a conversation between herself and Cornelia, a friend whom he suspected might really be Mercy Otis Warren, a friend of hers who wrote poems and plays and supported independence. It was clear that through this more than likely fictitious conversation, Abigail could offer ideas she otherwise would not mention.

He needed to respond to these ideas, and also reassure her that no criticism of her dear Friend had been intended when his commission to negotiate a treaty of commerce and trade with Britain had been shared among five commissioners.

Following a late meal, he retired to his room. Pulling Abigail's letter from his satchel, he read again the familiar handwriting.

23 June 1781

And is there no medium, Sir, between terms which might be misconstrued, and the cold formal adieu of mere ceremony tagged with a title.

I will give you a specimen of a conversation that passed not long since between Portia and a Lady of her acquaintance for whom she entertains a high esteem as one of the best female characters in America, though Portia would fain believe she errs in judging of one character.

Cornelia: Have you seen the intercepted letter of your friend Lovell to Mr. Gerry?

Portia: No, Madam, but I have heard much of it, and some severe criticisms of it. I wish to see it.

Cornelia: I have read it, and can give you an account of it. It is enigmatical, as all his letters are, but there are some things in it which for decency's sake ought never to have been there. Were I his wife, they would make me miserable, but I believe he cares little for her.

Portia: Oh, Madam, do not judge so harshly. I have ever thought him to have a high value for her, he has never mentioned her but with respect and tenderness.

Cornelia: True, I am not acquainted with her, but I hear her well-spoken of by everybody, and believe her much too good for a man that can allow his pen such a license in writing of her, and can leave her three or four years together.

Portia: Pray, my dear madam, do not measure a gentleman's regard for his wife by the last reason given. Is it not misfortune enough to be separated from our best friends without the world's judging us, or them, for it? How would you wound me should you think thus of my own dear partner?

Cornelia: The case is different with him. It is one without much hazard or risk. But not the other, and I tell you, my friend, that this gentleman whom you think so favorably of, is in my opinion an urbane man of the world, and looks upon the whole sex as common prey or free plunder.

Portia: Oh, my dear Madam, I cannot think so. Were I once satisfied that such was his sentiments and character, I would instantly renounce all acquaintance with him. I must condemn the levity of his pen, but he cannot have a bad heart.

I never heard his conjugal character criticized—did you, Cornelia?

Cornelia: No, only as the world will naturally believe that a gentleman possessing domestic attachments would visit his family in the course of four years, when only three hundred miles distant.

Portia: Why, Madam, he may have reasons which he would not choose to manifest to the world.

Cornelia: Then let him be uniformly delicate and I will believe them.

Thus ended a conversation but not a conversion.

I hold you in duty bound to explain yourself. Not a vessel from Holland or a line from that quarter. My heart sickens at the recollection. Oh, for the wings of a dove that I might fly away. May America show herself equal to the call.

I hope you have recovered from your fall, if it was an honest one from your horse and not down a pair of dark stairs. I will not receive your sarcasm so have blotted it out, and in lieu of it "read Portia's affectionate friend," and in return bestow the sincere emanations of friendship which glow in the bosom of

Portia

He groaned. *How could she imagine me to be a profligate? And does she really think me to be capable of those things she insinuates? Others may question my reasoning, but Portia? No, she understands and believes in me. And the fall? She suggests some think it to have been a drunken stumble.*

He read again the conversation Abigail had written in her letter. *Cornelia, whether a real person or an imagined soul, attempts to convince Portia of my depraved character and poor decisions, yet Portia makes it clear that she trusts me enough to let me know there are those who doubt my principles and actions. However, she expects I will explain myself.*

I must describe the event so clearly that she understands the horrible accident that befell me when I toppled into that cellar. It nearly cost me my life. People will talk, but a friend will only believe the truth.

And she seems to think I should assume guilt for being apart from my wife. My absence is in the service of my country. Voluntary separation from those we love is a form of offering, as Abigail should well know, and absence of a partner in a physical sense must not create bitterness. Further, my family's sustenance depends on my position. And despite the stories bandied about by mean-

hearted individuals, who seek to disparage with no proof of misbehavior, my actions have been fully honorable.

He picked up the letter, read the close again, and felt a moment of relief. *At least now she understands the foolishness of a formal close, between friends. And whether Cornelia is a real person or not, she expresses Abigail's fears.* He reached for his pen.

> *Led astray by Cornelia's fancy, your mind had taken a "dark" turn, and you found dreadful things in an innocent phrase "on this subject."*

He explained to Abigail the hideous accident that nearly cost him the use of his legs and included Mary's words he had just received: "I think, however, you will be obliged to come and show yourself this fall."

> *My wife has never yet suggested I should come visit. Now I must go to see my family, since she bids me come. Yet I fear our finances if I leave. Still, whatever the difficulties are, when I think the time is right, I will return home.*

The star-studded sky shone through his window, luminous and peaceful, the apples ripened on the trees by the garden. The serene scene out his window was a great contrast to the ache and turmoil in his heart. There was so much he could not control, so much to be decided. At least he had explained himself to Abigail.

July 17, 1781, Tuesday

President Samuel Huntington read a letter from General Nathanael Greene on the taking of Fort Cornwallis. After a siege of a little more than two weeks, the defenses of Augusta fell. General Greene congratulated General Pickens and Lieutenant Colonel Henry Lee and their men on the fort's capitulation. The general stated in particular that Lee's Legion deserved the highest honor. James thought of his oldest son, James Jr., with Lieutenant Colonel Henry Lee's battalion of light dragoons. His heart swelled with pride.

At his lodging, he read Abigail's recent letter with some anxiety. He set it down, then stared out the window at the stalks of corn in the garden, thinking it through.

She says I am sometimes very saucy yet takes my correction patiently. Of course, she understands and supports me. We have much in common, as do I with her husband. And Abigail reminds me what this is about. I suffer misrepresentation, poverty, and abuse, to stand by my country, as does her husband.

And she still mistrusts Benjamin Franklin, whom she says is blackening the name of her Friend. Her anger in his defense is palpable. He thought over the correspondence he had maintained with Dr. Franklin and frowned. *Perhaps Dr. Franklin is not quite the monster she paints him, but he is wily and unpredictable.*

She offered to send a chaise so that Mary could come to visit her and stay with her brother Cranch. But Mary answered that she was indisposed. It was kind of Abigail to reach out to Mary. She assures me that she would love her.

Yet I must, in all honesty, respond to the suggestion that Mrs. L. visit her. I do not think it wise. Mary is innocent of the falsehoods that circle about me, the very ones from which Abigail would protect her. And she must remain innocent.

She should visit with Samuel Adams. He could clarify her questions, explain that it is the Count de Vergennes who insists on a joint commission of several ministers, rather than her husband on his own, to ensure that any negotiations are aligned with the French.

Abigail's friendliness towards Mary warmed his heart. Yet he must warn her not to persist in her kind efforts to visit with his wife. He picked up his pen.

August 10, 1781, Friday

At the end of July, Colonel George Morgan arrived with three Indian boys to ask Congress for funds for their tuition at Princetown College. The boys and their families camped in the sheds on the east side of the building, the feathered warriors observing the delegates come and go, their stares aloof but benign, their fires blazing nightly next to the State House.

Congress commended Major General Greene for the zeal, gallantry, and perseverance that he and his men displayed in the southern command. They had succeeded in retaking much of South Carolina and Georgia, except for British holdings on the coast. The British were no doubt disappointed that the Loyalist support they had envisioned in the south had been countered by strong militia support. Congress also recognized the bravery of Francis Marion, leader of backwoods fighters.

James wondered what had happened to the intercepted message he had deciphered for General Greene last year. He had turned it over to Charles Thomson, who pleaded no knowledge of mishap, but he had never received acknowledgment from General Greene of its receipt.

August came on hot. Sultry, heavy heat hung over the sessions of Congress in the Pennsylvania State House, its windows shut against spies, the green baize table coverings littered with papers and ink.

At times, hearing reports of British atrocities, hunger in the troops, lack of funding, James shivered despite the sweltering conditions, imagining the State House haunted by the tormented spirits of Americans who had suffered and died there, penned in and left to starve. He pulled himself back with an effort from such fears to rejoin Congress's efforts to maintain an effective fighting force.

To his relief, he heard from Abigail, their friendship renewed. In the evening, after writing to John Jay, he took out Abigail's latest letter and read it again.

July 14th, 1781

My dear Sir,

Your favor by General Ward was not delivered to me until today. The generous acknowledgement of having transgressed forbids any further recrimination even though I had more than the right of a friend. The serious part of your letter richly deserved far better treatment than you had ever yet met with.

I am gratified to have from your own hand arguments to rectify the ideas of some who I really believe to be your friends, but who, not knowing or fully considering the circumstances you mention, have been left to wonder at a conduct they could not account for. The affectionate regard you profess for a Lady whom I believe every way deserving of it entirely banishes from my mind the insinuations of Cornelia, and I should wish no pain be given to a Lady I must more and more esteem—and with whom I am determined to cultivate a more particular acquaintance. Possibly I may be able to render her some small services.

Will you balance accounts? And we will begin a new score upon the old stock of friendship.

You have not fulfilled one part of your promise which was to transmit to me some anecdotes respecting my Friend abroad. In the name of indignation can there be any thing more diabolical than what is put into my hands? False, insinuating, dissembling wretch—is it for this your gray head is spared— is this the language of courts? —is this the reward of an independent spirit, and patriotic virtue? This finished courtier has first practiced his arts upon the minister until he has instilled into his mind the most ungenerous prejudices—and having gained his point there, is now in the most specious manner crocodile-like whining over the prey he means to devour.

I ask not the support of my Friend because he is my Friend—I ask it no further than as you find he pursues the best good of his country.

She does not sign her letter, he thought, *nor is she over her outrage at Dr. Franklin's suggestions that we need a number of negotiators. She calls him a dissembling wretch, and more. But we have mended fences, I see, and our friendship can begin again.* He set the letter to one side, relieved.

I will respond to her. But I really do not know how I am to support my family, when I leave here. He rubbed his forehead in anguish for a moment. *And what indeed is Cornwallis doing at the mouth of the Chesapeake? Surely, he will be on his way to New York soon.*

August 23, 1781, Thursday

He glanced in concern at Abigail's packages, piled near his wardrobe. It occurred to him he could request a chest to be sent to Abigail when the Deputy Commissary General took a carriage to Boston.

He wrote Abigail a short note explaining his care of the articles.

I feared moths—have opened your goods—aired and shook the woolens. I discovered no other relief to your fears than that there are serge and buttons and twist for Mr. Wibert and some satinette or something like it for small cloths. I am recovered from a slight fever; have been abroad; and am again going to deliver this mark of my devo—no, no! Lov—worse and worse! my humble desire to serve you, —flat as dishwater! my respect, Madam, my affectionate esteem! Ma'am —

James Lovell

Laughing to himself over his little jest, he placed the letter with his papers for the post.

Chapter 34

French and Americans March to Yorktown

September 3, 1781, Monday

The shrilling of fifes and beating of drums reverberated across Philadelphia as the American army entered the city. "General Washington and General Rochambeau are in Philadelphia to conduct meetings," James said to George Partridge. The two stood on a street corner among the crowds. Twenty-five hundred troops filed by, their line extending nearly two miles long.

"I hear only a small part of the American army remains near New York to guard against British movements," George said.

"And there are more than twice as many French soldiers coming tomorrow. They have been waiting for the past year in Rhode Island, so they should be well prepared. Another three thousand or so are with the French Admiral Francois Count de Grasse and his fleet, expected from the West Indies."

"The plan, as I understand it, is for General Washington and the Count de Rochambeau to meet Lord Cornwallis at Yorktown, Virginia."

"Yes. They intend to block the British from receiving reinforcements at the York River, to the west of the Chesapeake Bay, near its mouth."

"I heard the Americans are anxious to be paid," George Partridge said, bumping into James as those near them jostled for a better view.

"And many lack uniforms or proper shoes. They cannot compare with the well-dressed, healthy French."

"There is a danger our troops may defy orders. They have been without pay for so long."

James nodded agreement. *Who knew how long our soldiers would continue to fight, months after they were last paid?* The problem was indeed critical.

Congress received Colonel John Laurens, just arrived from Boston after his successful mission to the French court. Bowing courteously, the young colonel presented letters from the king and Benjamin Franklin to President McKean. Applause echoed in the State House, the delegates appreciative of the king's promise of twenty million livres—six million as a gift, the remainder to be a loan given in clothing, armaments, and bills of exchange.

"It is said that when the Count de Vergennes did not immediately grant his request for aid, John Laurens went straight to the king. At an audience when he was expected merely to bow a greeting, he instead spoke directly to King Louis, courageously expressing our need. I am sure the king was taken aback, but he granted Colonel Laurens's request for aid," George Partridge said, during an interlude.

"John Laurens's boldness is fortunate for us."

George Partridge nodded. "And the ten million livre loan from the Dutch that he obtained will prove exceedingly helpful."

Would not Henry Laurens, locked up in the grim Tower of London, be proud of his son?

Secretary Charles Thomson handed a letter from General Washington to President McKean. In it, the general expressed concern about the vile treatment of American prisoners by the British. *The abuse of our troops in British prisons is a crime*, James thought, his stomach turning queasy.

The rhythmic beating of the drums approached, punctuated by piercing bugle horn calls. President Thomas McKean, who represented Delaware and whose parents had come to Pennsylvania from Ireland, as likeable a lawyer and statesman as James had met, set down the papers he was holding and glanced at the door, then towards the seated delegates.

"Time to see the parade." The doorkeeper opened the double doors wide. The delegates spilled out onto the steps facing Chestnut Street. Crowds of townspeople rimmed the street, curious and excited.

Near the steps James saw Colonel John Laurens. He would no doubt rejoin the army, now that his vital mission to France was completed. His black peaked hat was drawn low on his forehead against the sun; a gold-hilted sword glinted at his side.

A double column of mounted infantry rode into view, the horses brushed and shining, the American flag, red and white stripes with stars on a blue field, and the French flag, blue spangled with gold fleur-de-lis, leading the way. "The first division of the French army under the Count de Rochambeau," a mounted officer proclaimed. The members of Congress stood in wonder at the sight.

Lines of officers uniformed in white followed on foot. When the orderly, evenly spaced officers reached the State House, they turned and stood at attention, planting their colors at rest. Behind them marched cavalry, artillerymen, privates, filling the street as far as the members of Congress could see. Fifes and drums continued with a spirited tune. When the street was filled, in unison at a bugle call, the marching stopped, the officers in the front turned towards Congress, unsheathed their swords, then dropped their points to the ground in a royal salute. Behind them artillery fired, the sound echoing. The scorched smell of gunpowder drifted in the air. Bugles blew, flags waved, and the regiment turned in disciplined, even steps, passing in review, to the accompaniment of the ringing of church bells.

Moved, tears glittering in the eyes of some, the delegates took off their hats in a gesture of appreciation. President McKean offered a salute. From the rear at a command, the officers sheathed their swords and parted, making space for General Washington and the Count de Rochambeau to ride through, followed by their aides.

Mounted on huge horses, their full uniforms of white and blue splendid to see, the generals made a glorious sight. "Huzza, huzza," the delegates cried out spontaneously, as the crowd cheered.

General Washington tipped his hat, the Count de Rochambeau bowed slightly from his saddle. Without saying anything, the commanders turned into the lines of French soldiers and headed down the street.

"They are making for the commons to set up camp, no doubt," Samuel Osgood said, almost reverently.

The delegates turned back to the Assembly Room as the last of the regiment filed passed. After the thrilling sight, James let his breath out; he had been holding it in in suspense and excitement. The display elated and reassured him. Yet he could not help recognizing the marked difference between the two armies. The French strode with powdered hair, their spanking white gaiters fresh and new, while the Americans marched as the tired, though proud, force they were, their clothing bearing the effects of years of hard use.

"I understand General Washington has been busy deceiving the enemy," he said quietly to George as they returned to their seats. "In order to have General Clinton in New York believe he would attack there, he ordered large army camps to be built within sight of the city, as well as huge brick ovens for baking bread, to convince the British that his plan was to attack at New York. The French will never do without their own baked bread, so that was a sign that they would be arriving soon."

"Indeed," George said, his eyebrows raised.

"I would not put it past him, either, to have prepared false reports of a plan to attack Clinton, and be sure those fell into enemy hands."

"Very likely. Cornwallis's position at the coast at Yorktown could give us the upper hand. York lies on the peninsula created by the York and James Rivers."

James nodded. "Particularly if the Count de Grasse and his fleet arrive and prevent the British ships from evacuating Lord Cornwallis."

"General Washington and the Count de Rochambeau have marched south from Washington's headquarters. And Rochambeau's troops travelled even farther, hundreds of miles, from their base in Newport, Rhode Island, to meet up with Washington."

"And now all are on their way to Yorktown. They stopped by Philadelphia to pay respects to Congress. Now they will march to Head of Elk, then down to the coast. Admiral Francois Count de Grasse and his fleet may reach the mouth of the Chesapeake any day now. Perhaps they already have."

"However, we have information that British Admiral Hood with his thirteen sail of the line from the West Indies has reached New York, where eight ships joined him under Admiral Graves. The whole squadron is on the lookout for the Count de Grasse."

"And from Newport, Admiral de Barras sailed with his fleet, to join up with the Count de Grasse."

"The British and Admiral Hood may be just a hair's breadth from an ill meeting with the French fleet, or if we are fortunate, no meeting at all." George spoke solemnly and quietly.

"Are we ready, gentlemen?" President McKean said. Congress turned to their work, buoyed and exhilarated at the combined armies' presence in the city.

September 4, 1781, Tuesday

The remainder of the French troops passed through Philadelphia on the following day, once again exciting spectators and thrilling the members of Congress, who endeavored to work through the ringing of bells, the beating of drums, the piercing notes of bugles.

That night, James opened a letter from Abigail. Only a few days ago, he had written to John Adams, sending him his instructions to negotiate an alliance with the United Provinces of the Netherlands. Reading Abigail's letter, he found himself agreeing with her.

> *If ever America stood in need of wise heads and virtuous hearts, it is at this juncture. The ship wants skillful hands, your old sea men are chiefly retired, your hands are new and inexperienced. Scylla is on one side and Charybdis on the other—how will you steer between them? In avoiding the rocks, you are in danger of being swallowed up in the sands.*

She is right about our need for good leadership, he thought. *And she does not trust the French. But Abigail, we must trust them, with all but our most sacred trust, to gain our independence. That we stand committed to above all.*

His response to her was brief, the invigorating spectacle of the French army honoring Congress with the two commanders so hopeful that he could not take her fretting seriously.

> *September 4, 1781.*
>
> *I found Colonel Laurens had landed at Boston and had sent you a message of what satisfaction he could furnish relative to your dear partner and your children.*
>
> *We are, at this present writing, in high glee with our General in the city and the French troops encamped on the commons, and with the log book of a vessel this afternoon, putting the highest probability of complete success upon the present military movements. I want only my spectacles which are left at the State House to make me quite happy by enabling me to prosecute the pleasing task of correspondence with one of the ___est and ____est and ____est women. I am sure, Madam, there is nothing of flattery or improper affection in those half written epithets, though they partake of the superlative degree. I am equally sure that the spirit of misinterpretation of any one of your circle can find no malice there: It is impossible for a single heart in this city to feel malicious while the bells are so sweetly chiming—always, however, excepting the hearts of the Tories.*
>
> *James Lovell*

Folding Abigail's letter and setting it aside, he then wrote to Elbridge Gerry. To his relief, he had at length heard from his friend. Elbridge appeared to hold nothing against him for the publication of the intercepted letters and had offered a loan to him of $140. Chagrinned, he said he would accept the loan, as he had little choice. He described the joy that the arrival of the French troops brought Congress and the city, as well as the excellent report of Colonel Laurens. Finally, he hinted that naval movements had nearly completed their objective, though he refrained from further revelations out of caution.

September 10, 1781, Monday

Excitement still rolled through the city following the French troops' passage. Five thousand French with twenty-five hundred Americans made a sizeable force. Only one threat to success occurred, when Washington's troops refused to continue past Philadelphia until they had been paid. Fortunately, General Rochambeau, who was running low on money, received word that the Count de Grasse had succeeded in gathering up a fortune in Spanish gold in Havana before departing. With this to bolster his confidence, Rochambeau loaned General Washington half of his gold coins. Now paid, some for the first time in many months, the American troops marched on.

They planned to meet up with Lafayette and his men at Williamsburg, some four thousand troops, including Pennsylvania Continental Line troops under General Anthony Wayne and Virginia militia under General Baron Von Steuben. James only hoped the combined force would be equal to the British. Daily, Congress anticipated word from Washington of the army's success.

On September 6, President Thomas McKean, his wig newly curled, his black velvet jacket spotless, opened the session of Congress with a special dispatch from General Washington.

"The general announces the safe arrival of Admiral de Grasse in the Chesapeake with twenty-eight ships of the line," President McKean said. "He offers his warmest congratulations to the president on the happy event. As to his own arrival at Yorktown, he said that when he and the troops reach Head of Elk, if there are not sufficient boats for all the troops, stores, and baggage, he will send what he can by water and march the rest by land."

A general burst of comments came from the delegates. "Excellent news," someone called out.

President McKean nodded vigorously and turned to the matters at hand. Business as usual followed, yet hope for the army's movements prevailed, like a yeasty brew that could not be kept down. James felt excitement as he waited to hear of a positive turn to the momentous events unfolding.

"George Washington Visits the French Fleet."
Moran, Percy. *Naval History and Heritage Command*

September 18, 1781, Tuesday

James arrived just as the session was beginning and hastily made his way to his seat. The few delegates present sat grim and determined, aware of the importance of the day, the hour. The Virginia delegates appeared especially on edge.

President Thomas McKean, his face serious, reported recent intelligence. "Our army on the North River daily increases, large numbers of recruits arriving from eastern states, keeping the enemy in New York in check. The bulk of the army has marched south with the commander-in-chief. The enemy has sent a large detachment to New London in Connecticut. Mr. Benedict Arnold landed with about two hundred and fifty men and attacked the fort there. Our forces fought bravely, repulsed the enemy twice, but Arnold carried the day and put the majority of the garrison to the sword."

"The traitor," someone said energetically.

"Then Mr. Arnold set fire to New London and Groton, blazes which consumed most of those towns. He is now thought to have returned to New York."

President McKean took out a large handkerchief, wiped his eyes, and blew his nose loudly, recovered his composure, went on. "At New York, the enemy is preparing an embarkation of troops, likely to support their forces in the south. Should they decide to burn this city where we meet, we have a large body of militia from Pennsylvania and Jersey ready to oppose such an attempt.

"The enemy has a squadron of men of war under the command of Admiral Digby that has arrived on the coast from Britain. There are said to be between six and ten ships of the line. Digby may take command of the whole British fleet."

President McKean paused for a drink of water, then resumed his review. "Intercepted letters tell us that Sir Henry Clinton's conduct in New York has caused great discontent. He has been unable to raise men, though he offers bounties."

"Sir Henry Clinton quarrels with his subordinates and is far from congenial," someone said. Other voices echoed the comment. President McKean nodded agreement.

The delegates waited. Was this all for now?

"That, gentlemen, is the sum of our intelligence at this time. We may be sure to enlighten you further as reports come in." President McKean set down his notes and turned to Secretary Thomson for the next order of business.

September 20, 1781, Thursday

In the late afternoon, as James was preparing to leave the State House, Secretary Charles Thomson came up to him, a packet in hand.

"Sir, in the recent letter from General Greene, we find intelligence written in cipher. You being our decipherer extraordinaire, please apply your gifts to these missives. Then send the results to whom they may do the most good, most likely to General Greene."

"You may be assured I will do my best. Thank you."

"You will find a group of about thirty letters included, and then a few separate letters. According to General Greene's communication, General Francis Marion intercepted the group near Monck's Corner. Thank you for your work," Secretary Thomson said, bowing slightly.

He walked quickly through the evening light, wind whipping dried leaves about him. Reaching the house, he found Ann Clymer seated at the table, carving a roast, a small girl next to her. Ann set down her knife and adjusted her black shawl.

"James, this is Ann, my granddaughter." She looked fondly at the little girl, perhaps nine years old, a mass of yellow curls spilling from her white cap.

"Very pleased to meet you," James said. *She looks like my daughter Mary, when she was younger,* he thought. The girl smiled calmly back at him. "I fear I cannot stay to visit. Could you have a plate sent to my room?"

"That I could."

"Thank you. I shall retire." He nodded and retreated to his room.

Settled at his table, he examined the packet given him by Secretary Thomson. Major General Greene's letter to President Thomas McKean, dated August 25, included a collection of about thirty intercepted letters, many of them written in cipher. Gently, he laid them out on his table, pulled out additional paper for notes, and began his task.

His first observation was that three of the letters, the most recent, concerned British officers he knew to be in command in the south. The other documents were folded together and labeled with a cover sheet as "intercepted with others dated 7th of March 1781." These were undated, unsigned letters from correspondents in New York, Virginia, and Charlestown to officers in Colonel Alexander Stewart's army. They appeared to be ciphered with a similar key. He set these aside as being less important and placed the three most recent from British officers in front of him.

One was from Major J. H. Craig to General Cornwallis, written at Wilmington, dated July 23, 1781. Another was a letter from General Balfour to Cornwallis, dated March 1781. A third, from Balfour to Lieutenant Colonel Stewart, was written at Charlestown, dated August 12, 1781.

Major James Craig's recent assault on New Bern, burning ships and supplies, revealed him to be rash, glory seeking. The destruction was uncalled for, punitive. General Nisbet Balfour in similar manner had ordered the destruction of Charlestown, lest it be a center for Patriot shipping. Deciphering the keys used in their letters would be important for future intelligence.

He remembered the letters he had deciphered last November, from General Cornwallis to James Wemyss and Nisbet Balfour. His work had never reached General Greene, to his regret, having disappeared somewhere in the mass of papers that Secretary Thomson and his clerks handled. Probably not the fastidious secretary's fault, he knew. But from his point of view, it was understanding the cipher that mattered. The British changed their code, and for future interceptions, understanding those changes was vital.

The previous message from General Cornwallis to James Wemyss and Nisbet Balfour used a key with two different elements. One was a book cipher, or code, referring to specific words found in *Entick's Spelling Dictionary*. These were noted with a capital *B*. The other was an alphabet cipher. It matched the numbers 1 to 24 with letters distributed in a random manner, the letters *i* and *j* assigned to the same number, the letter *z* omitted. Use of this cipher was denoted with a capital *F*.

But how was this present cipher different? Because it undoubtedly was.

For the next couple of hours, he puzzled over the letters, using his understanding of British cipher from previous encounters. Gradually, he came to realize that while Balfour used the same cipher throughout, Craig alternated his cipher, using different keys for each of the three paragraphs. A couple hours later and he had a page neatly listing the key used by Balfour, then the three keys used by Craig. At the top of the page he wrote, "Balfour's Letter of August 12, 1781, to Lt. Col. Stewart is by only one arrangement of the same alphabet which is used in three by J.H. Craig, July 23, 1781, in his letter to Lord Cornwallis."

The keys themselves appeared to be assignments of letters to twenty-five numbers, the letters *i* and *j* both being assigned to the same number. In each key, the numbers used were 12-19, 22-39, and 31-39, differently arranged.

But neither Craig's letter nor Balfour's used Cornwallis's method of alternating a book cipher and an alphabet cipher.

It was late. His eyes swam, and he drank the cold tea left over from the supper that had been brought to his door by the timid Lucy. Revived, he continued.

It appeared to him that to confuse the reader, or to mark a new paragraph, a number of meaningless characters had been included within the letters. In a small space at the bottom of the page he wrote his findings.

> *As a variety of insignificant figures are interspersed;*
> *several of those are put in the beginning of the epistles; and*
> *among those is placed one of the essential elements; which,*
> *however, is only to show how to begin the arrangement of the*
> *numbers for use.*
>
> *The same thing is sometimes practiced for the different*
> *paragraphs of the same epistle. The insignificant figures are*
> *chiefly between the words though sometimes between syllables*
> *and particularly to divide what are termed the double letters.*

At the bottom of the page in small characters he wrote out a sample of ciphered words, using Balfour's code.

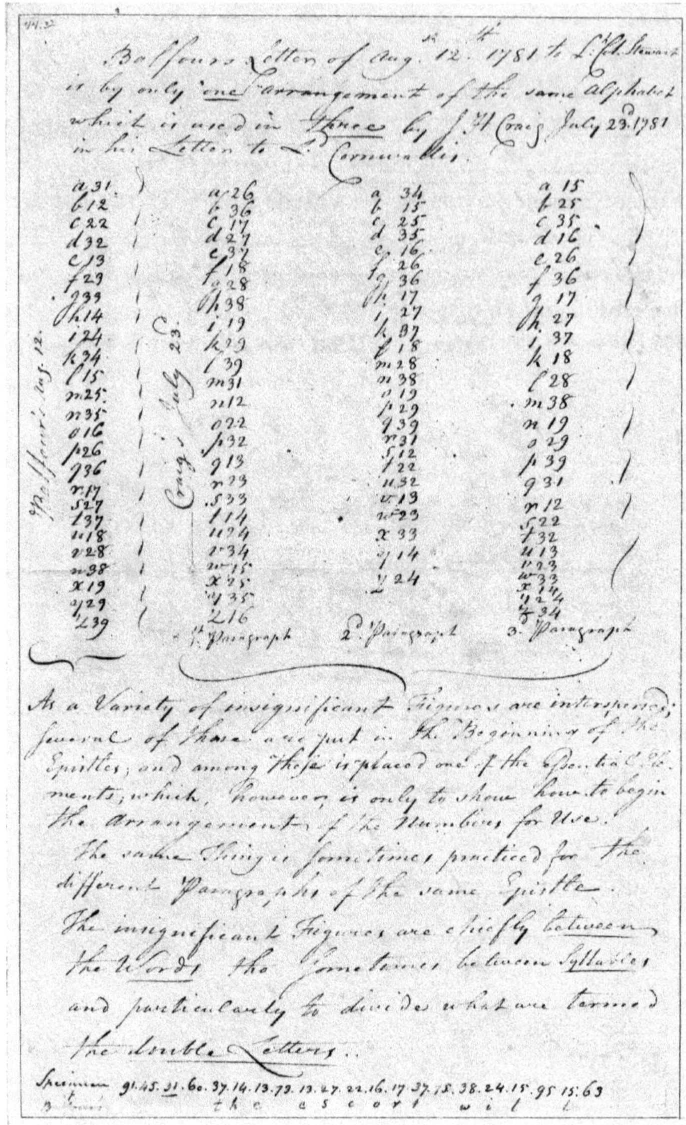

"James Lovell to Major General Nathanael Greene, September 21, 1781."
William Clements Library

He then picked up a few of the remaining intercepted letters, correspondence to officers, and looked through them. These were the letters General Greene had said were intercepted by General Francis Marion near Monck's Corner. They appeared to use the same key, a different one than those he had just worked out. He set to work. It was slow going, the task complex, the key indeed greatly different. And he was tired, though determined to persist. His frustration increased until some three hours later he realized he had figured out the key.

It being well past midnight, he determined to write a letter of explanation to General Greene in the morning. He rubbed his eyes and yawned, stood, and stretched. *We have not caught a big fish this time*, he thought, *but when we catch the little fish, it makes it easier for us to catch the big fish when we have the chance.* He smiled, folded the packet of letters together, and tucked it into his satchel.

September 21, 1781, Friday

He reached the Pennsylvania State House early. The grass sparkled from an early rain. Though tired from his late night's work, he felt better than he had feared he would. Few were at their seats, so he took out fresh paper and wrote a letter to General Nathanael Greene explaining his work deciphering the intercepted letters.

Philadelphia
September 21ˢᵗ, 1781
Sir,

You once sent some papers to Congress which no one about you could decipher. Should such be the case with some you have lately forwarded, I presume that the result of my pains, herein sent, will be useful to you. I took the papers out of Congress; and I do not think it necessary to let it be known here what my success has been in the attempt. For, it appears to me that the enemy makes only such changes in their cipher, when they meet with misfortunes. And therefore, if no talk of discovery is made by us here or by your family, you may be in chance to draw a benefit from this campaign in exchange for my last night's watching.

I am Sir, with much regard,
Your friend,

James Lovell

P.S. With greater pain than in the cases of Balfour's & Craig's epistles, I have also succeeded to find the key of the papers which are without date, signature, or intermixture of letters, said to be "intercepted with others dated 7th of March 1781." I do not suppose it now in use; however, I send it. JL

It occurred to him that his keys might prove of use to General Washington. He then wrote one more letter, this time to the commander-in-chief.

> *Philadelphia*
> *September 21ˢᵗ, 1781*
> *Sir,*
>
> *It is not improbable that the enemy have a plan of cyphering their letters which is pretty general among their chiefs; if so, Your Excellency will perhaps reap benefit from making your secretary take a copy of the keys and observations which I send to General Greene, through your care. With every wish for your success and glory, I am*
> *Your Excellency's Obliged and Humble Servant,*
> *James Lovell*

He folded the letter, addressed it to General Washington, and included the packet for General Greene along with the keys for General Washington to transmit to Greene, after his secretary made a copy of the keys for the general's use.

Secretary Thomson walked in, tall, punctual, precise. He set a stack of papers down on the president's table and turned to his own. James approached him.

"Please see that this packet is delivered," he said, holding out the packet.

Without a flicker of his eyes, Charles Thomson said graciously, "Yes, sir, I will. And I will be sure to let the secretary of the Chevalier de la Luzerne, the Marquis de Barbé-Marbois, know of your success. At General Greene's request he had a crack at deciphering the letters, but could not succeed. The Marquis will be pleased to know you did." He turned back to his work, no further words said. But James knew that the secretary knew that the work had been done, and done well.

In the afternoon, the committee who had reviewed the message from the minister plenipotentiary of France reported that they had met that day with the Chevalier de la Luzerne and learned of communications from the Count de Vergennes.

"When questions regarding negotiations for peace were submitted to the English ministry, the answer was that it would be in vain to think of peace, and that the dependence of her rebel subjects in America must be pre-established before any discussions," James Duane said. "From this, the Count de Vergennes concludes that Congress must be fully convinced that it is only by arms and the most vigorous exertions that our independence can be wrested from the court of London."

Someone responded quietly, "We knew that."

"The court of France feels that Congress now has great advantages as a confederation. They encourage us to use the resources of our country to give American patriotism new energy. The king entreats the United States to act boldly and energetically against the enemy."

A spatter of applause burst out on this thought.

"Finally, though we cannot expect more forces from France after this campaign, and we may not receive any further monetary aid, the king has made a gift of six million livres to the United States of money promised them."

James Duane concluded the report and returned to his seat.

President Thomas McKean stood. "Thank you, committee members. As I will write to our commander-in-chief this evening, it is our duty to make the most of the present opportunity. Should we carry the day in Yorktown, Virginia, and possibly in New York as well, the effect would be a triumph that would sway the minds of the courts in Europe, even expediting negotiation for peace."

"I will share with you that yesterday evening I received a private account of the two fleets, one under the Count de Barras, the other under the Count de Grasse. The fleets have now met near the mouth of the Chesapeake. There is no word that Admiral Digby has yet arrived from Britain, and it is said he has no more than six ships of the line. Lord Cornwallis will no doubt make a vigorous resistance, but the French fleet will be of great service to us."

Murmurs of approval sounded throughout the room. "Hear, hear," someone said.

"And, I have just received word that Admiral Graves returned within Sandy Hook yesterday. In a sea battle with the Count de Grasse, the *Terrible*, with seventy-four guns, was sunk, and five more ships were disabled by the Count de Grasse. In effect, the effort by Admiral Graves and his fleet to rescue Lord Cornwallis has been thwarted by the French fleet."

The delegates stood, elated, and applauded.

"Finally, it appears that, according to recent reports from France, we can expect the negotiation for peace will probably take place next winter."

The efforts of the American army to stand up to General Cornwallis at the port of Yorktown, coupled with a blockade by the French fleet in the harbor to keep British assistance at bay, might even yield the capitulation of thousands of British troops. The French king urges Americans to make a vigorous campaign. So we shall.

September 28, 1781, Thursday

Congress listened with rapt attention as General Washington's letter was read. American and French troops had just met the Marquis de Lafayette at Williamsburg.

The two French fleets had successfully engaged with the British squadron. The Count de Grasse, who chased the British fleet out to sea following the engagement, had returned to guard the entrance to the Chesapeake Bay.

Washington also stated that he lacked provisions for the combined force of over sixteen thousand troops.

In a recess, James was surprised when Richard Howly of Georgia came over to him. His face twisted in concern, Richard Howly held out a packet of papers. "I must apologize," he said. "These were in your keeping last year. I was given them to look over, as they concerned developments in the south. I thought I had returned them to Secretary Thomson, but I just discovered them this morning."

James took the packet and glanced inside. There were the missing letters he had deciphered last November, from General Cornwallis to James Wemyss and Nisbet Balfour, with their keys, intended for General Greene. "Thank you," he said, extending his hand to Richard Howly.

Richard Howly shook his hand sheepishly. Clearly, discovering the packet had been a great surprise to the Georgia delegate.

"Most gratified. You may count on my devotion," Richard Howly said, embarrassed. He returned to his seat with the air of one relieved of a huge burden.

The cipher is probably not in use anymore, but nevertheless may be useful for General Greene.

In the quiet Assembly library, he wrote to General Greene, explaining that intercepted letters he had deciphered last year had turned up.

That task finished, he then completed a cover letter to General Washington, noting the enclosed papers should be sent to Major General Greene, returned to the Assembly Room, and placed the packet before Secretary Charles Thomson.

"For General Washington. President McKean may be interested. Thank you."

The secretary acknowledged the message with no expression, but James thought he saw a wink in his calm eyes.

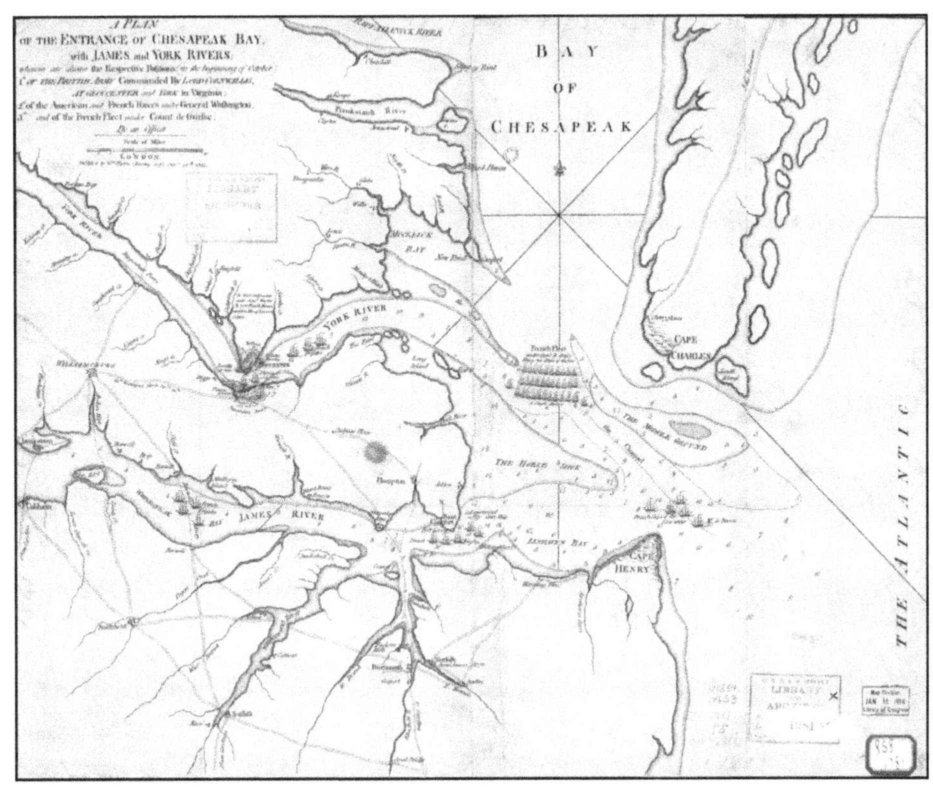

Faden, William. A Plan of the Entrance of Chesapeake Bay,
with James and York Rivers, ca 1845. The position of forces during
the 1781 Siege of Yorktown. *Library of Congress*

Chapter 35

Cornwallis's Message

October 9, 1781, Sunday

Congress eagerly awaited news of the combined armies. The bulk of the American and French forces were marching to the coast, a portion heading to boats at Head of Elk for a quick passage down the Chesapeake to Yorktown. General Washington and the Count de Rochambeau planned to pin the British at the coast with the thousands of American and French troops, while the French fleet would block British ships from coming to their aid. But Lord Cornwallis had been working for weeks, setting up defensive breastworks, ditches, and redoubts around Yorktown. These would enable the British to hold out for a considerable length of time.

Cornwallis owed his presence in Yorktown to General Clinton's orders. Now he was in the jaws of a vise. "Like squeezing a lemon," someone quipped.

On Saturday the 9th, James received a letter from Abigail. Following a committee meeting he held in Mrs. Clymer's parlor, he retreated to his room and spread the letter on his table.

> *September 26, 1781*
>
> *In truth, friend, thou art a Queer Being— laugh where I must, be candid where I can. Your pictures are Hogarths. I shall find you out by and by—I will not build upon other people's judgments. My philosopher (I like the name for my Friend exceedingly) used to say I was a physiognomist. I have tried not unsuccessfully to find out the heart of many by the countenance. I do not recollect that I ever had that opportunity with my correspondent; twice only in my life do I remember having seen him, and then my harp was so hung upon the willows that I cared not whose face was sweet or sour. Yet I do remember the traits of friendship and benevolence were so*

conspicuous that they demanded a return in kind, and something like compassion, pity, commiseration, call it by what name you please, I remember to have felt for the unjust sufferings of a worthy man. But I did not study the eye, that best index to the mind, to find out how much roguery there was in the heart, so here I have been these four years obtaining by piecemeal what I could have learned in half an hour.

Rejoice with me, for I have got a letter at last. My Dear Friend, well—that is a cordial to my heart. He longs to come home to his American dame—for all the French, Spanish, Dutch madams. That is flattering to my vanity—but he does not say so. I only find it out by his saying if he once gets back he will never leave me again. My dear Charles, sweet boy, has been sick of a fever, and no mother at hand to nurse and administer to the dear fondling. Thus do I run on because I know you take an interest in my happiness and because I know I can make you feel. I hate an unfeeling mortal. I rejoice to find you have recovered your health and spirits. Laugh and satirize as much as you please. I laugh with you to see what a figure your inventive genius makes in picking up terms— tis necessary to keep a watchful eye over you.

Now, to be a little serious, we are in great hopes and high expectations of good news from the south. May it be better than our deserts or our hopes will again be blasted, should an opportunity offer.

I did not misapply Cornelia for Portia. I knew it to be no fiction. There really existed the dialogue I related and nearly in the same words as I could recollect.

It was late. A chilly wind whipped the orange and red leaves on the trees; the moon was a thin sliver under high silver clouds. But it was not too late for him to respond.

She calls me friend, and so I am, but also a "Queer Being." Perhaps, but so is she, a Queer Being—she bristles at any comment that might be considered an insult to her Friend. He picked up his pen, finding the words flowed smoothly, his emotions soothed by the communication of friendship, cares, concerns.

Philadelphia
October 9, 1781.

Yesterday's post brought me your favor of September 26th. Your dear boy Charles should most certainly have had half of the bed of one of his father's devoted friends here, if the winds had so directed the ship's course in which he is a passenger, but I am told she is arrived at Falmouth in Casco Bay. I wish you a happy meeting with him.

In the first of Mr. A's letters which came by Newman he says about the Netherlands,

"This country is indeed in a melancholy situation—sunk in ease—devoted to the pursuits of gain—overshadowed on all sides by more powerful neighbors—unanimated by a love of military glory or any aspiring spirit—feeling little enthusiasm for the public—terrified at the loss of an old friend—and equally terrified at the prospect of being obliged to form connections with a new one—encumbered with a complicated & perplexed constitution—divided among themselves in interest and sentiment, they seem afraid of everything."

It is to be hoped that the events of this campaign will be such as to influence Holland & even Britain to do us justice. In Virginia, things are proceeding surely and faster than we had a right to expect.

Your attentions to Mrs. Lovell prejudice me so much in your favor that I can let you call me "queer" or anything else that hits your fancy, provided always that you do not call or even think me deceitful when I profess myself with affectionate Respect, Madam, your friend and humble servant,

JL

P.S. Perhaps after my profession of respect, it will be incongruous to hint that you also, Madam, are a "queer being." I verily believe you would be willing to hear anyone call your best Friend "old Darby," rather than to hear it said he appears lively as "Chesterfield."

You "did not misapply Cornelia for Portia." But, you did, most assuredly. "There was no fiction in the story." "The dialogue really existed as related." I supposed so; and therefore, all the little malicious things I have written were intended for Cornelia, and not for Portia.

October 12, 1781, Friday

Events at Yorktown occupied the delegates for much of the day. At noon, President Thomas McKean spoke with energy that belied his weary appearance, his eyes red with lack of sleep.

"The fleet of thirty-four transports that sailed from England under Admiral Digby has arrived at Sandy Hook. We hear that Admiral Graves may make a second attempt to relieve Lord Cornwallis. I will request that General Washington inform the Count de Grasse of the arrival of Admiral Digby."

"Not so many ships as to cause great concern, however," someone said cautiously.

"Probably not, yet any change could precipitate a movement that would be most unwelcome. Other information you will be pleased to know is that supplies are on their way for the army. Captain Gilland has arrived in the frigate *Charles-Town* to Casco Bay from France, bearing needed clothing and goods amounting to more than ten thousand pounds' worth. He also carries a million and a half livres. General Washington will be pleased to hear of his arrival."

"Hear, hear," some said.

"In addition, the general writes that he has the full support of General Rochambeau as they take positions about the enemy."

The president stood. "Gentlemen, you must excuse me at this time. Please carry on with your business while I have a private conversation in the Assembly library with a few of you." He turned to leave the room.

A clerk approached James's seat. "Sir, you are requested to meet with President McKean in the Assembly library."

"I will be there directly," he said. He glanced at George Partridge and Samuel Osgood, who waved him on.

In the library, fall sunshine splashed across the private space, James found President McKean seated near the fireplace, two others nearby.

"Thank you for coming," President McKean said. He motioned to his two companions. "Elias Boudinot and James Madison are part of a committee who reviewed the letters sent from General Nathanael Greene that you deciphered lately. I wanted them to hear the information I have to give you." The two delegates greeted James solemnly.

"We have intelligence that Sir Henry Clinton sent off three boats in the last week of September. They carried dispatches for Lord Cornwallis. One, the André, had a brass six pounder on her bow, eight blunderbusses, and twenty men carrying muskets. She sailed on the 26th. Another boat left on the 28th, the third on the 1st. We have taken captive the last two boats. One of the crew is a Tory who is willing to work with us. By giving a promise of pardon to the Tory, we learned that the dispatch he was carrying was hidden on the beach where he was taken, the fellow explaining earnestly that he had placed it under a rock for safekeeping."

James nodded.

"I have sent three capable officers to Little Egg Harbor to find the concealed message, taking with them the Tory who hid it. The remaining crew from the captured vessel is in custody, barred from speaking with any others. But the beach is so long and there are so many similar places on it that the officers have not yet found the message. However, we trust our informant, as he appears highly anxious to recover the dispatch and earn his pardon. The officers left on Sunday and I expect them tomorrow.

"Meanwhile, our fleet in the area is attempting to apprehend the first boat that sailed, the *André*; I have written to the presidents of Delaware and the Eastern Shore of Maryland for their assistance to locate her."

James sensed the importance of the weary president's words. "I imagine the dispatch to be written in cipher."

"Quite so. That is our suspicion. Once the dispatch is located, we will give it to you to work your magic."

"Not exactly magic, sir. Hours of labor. But, yes, I will be pleased to work on it. May I suggest, however, that once I have the message deciphered, I keep a copy for our use and the original be placed back in its former location on the beach. The British will be not be wise to the fact that their communication has been read and so should proceed with their plans. We can then use the intelligence for our benefit."

"That is an excellent suggestion," Elias Boudinot said.

"I agree," James Madison said. "Of course, it depends on the content of the message."

"Yes," President McKean said, "but in most cases, it is sound advice. Thank you, gentlemen. You may expect further contact from me should I receive the dispatch tomorrow."

James bowed and left the Assembly library. *Every element that could be brought to bear to give us an advantage must be pursued. Leave no stone unturned, and in this case may the right stone be overturned to divulge its cache.*

October 13, 1781, Saturday

James was again called to the Assembly library late in the afternoon.

President McKean sat alone, papers spread before him. His forehead was beaded with sweat even though the day was cool, deep blue sky and crisp orange leaves glowing through the tall window.

"I have the recovered dispatch for you, just delivered by the soldiers," he said, his voice low and urgent. "The compliant Tory is safely in solitary confinement." He held up a slim packet, soiled on the edges. "First, I have news to share with you. I have just finished writing to General Washington with a message from General Heath. Please, have a seat."

James took a chair and waited. President McKean's words came short and abrupt, his voice gravelly with fatigue. "Sir Henry Clinton is about to embark with four thousand of his best troops in a convoy of ships under Admiral Graves and Commander Digby, to include ten fire ships. Knowing their whole venture is at risk, they determine a desperate attack on the French fleet. If they can, they will relieve Cornwallis. They are expected to be prepared to sail in about six or seven days."

James drew in his breath but said nothing. He waited while the president searched through his papers. At length he retrieved a sheet of paper, then continued.

"An added piece of information is that General Heath reports receiving intelligence through a channel that has usually proven authentic. He states the Count de Grasse should be informed of this news, if at all possible. A deserter from the *Princessa*, Admiral Drake's ship, told him yesterday evening that when he left, troops were embarking at Staten Island. Furthermore, on his way to the ship, he met two scows full of horses and one loaded with three brass cannon, on their way to the fleet."

His eyebrows went up at this and he glanced at James meaningfully.

"It sounds like the British troops are leaving New York," James said.

The president nodded, then continued his explanation. "General Heath encloses a letter from an old correspondent. He states that the distresses of the Tories and Loyalists in New York, as well as those of the officers who serve under General Cornwallis, are hard to describe. This informant tells him this contest will be either the defense of General Cornwallis or his defeat, though he expects the latter, possibly even his capture. It is my understanding that General Clinton's own officers are frustrated with him—in a word, tired of waiting and enduring prolonged inaction, in poor living conditions, with little pay."

"I have heard something of the sort." James nodded. "General Clinton may intend to come to Lord Cornwallis's defense, but the outcome still depends on the advance of General Washington and the French on Cornwallis."

"Very true," Thomas McKean went on, his voice low but resolute. "And thus, the importance of this dispatch." He held up the soiled packet as a valuable trophy. "Every intelligence that will aid us in more knowledge of the enemy will be to our benefit."

"I understand," James said. "I will work on deciphering it immediately."

"Very good." The president handed James the grimy packet. "You may work here if you wish, or take it to your home if needed. Please let me know when you complete it."

"My experience with British cipher leads me to believe I will succeed. I will take it to my lodging to complete. I can work uninterrupted there and it will be secure from prying eyes."

"Very good."

James stood and tucked the packet into his inner jacket pocket. "Good day, sir."

"And good day to you." Thomas McKean extended his hand and shook James's own. Again, James felt the weariness of the president in his handshake. President McKean picked up his papers and James followed him out of the chamber, the president's steps slow and laborious.

Congress had adjourned. Andrew McNair opened the double doors for him. "Good night, sir," he said gently. "Have a pleasant evening."

"Could you have a plate made for me?" James asked Mrs. Clymer as he entered her dining room. She turned from the two ladies who had joined her for the meal.

"Of course," she said. "I will ask Lucy to bring it to you. But you must work?" she said, her tone anxious.

"Indeed. It will be a long evening. Should anyone arrive for me, please tell them I will see them tomorrow."

"That will be fine." Ann Clymer fingered her beads in some anxiety, then smiled at her friends. "The senator is very hard-working."

The ladies looked at James with admiration. "Bless you, sir," one said.

James bowed. "Thank you. Good evening." He turned and left. The enciphered letter seemed to burn inside his jacket like a brand. Anticipating the hours it would take to decipher it, he nevertheless felt eager to begin.

Lucy rapped on his door while he was arranging his paper, pen, and ink. She carried in a small tray with food and looked about apologetically. "Where would you like this, sir?"

"Here. I will take it. Thank you, Lucy." James took the tray and waited while she left. "Thank you for shutting the door," he said to her retreating footsteps as the door latch clicked.

He set the tray down, took some bites of the bean soup, then picked up the ciphered letter. Setting aside the covering paper, he spread the three pages out before him. They appeared to be in good condition despite the packet's stay under a rock in a harbor.

York Town Virginia.
8 Sept.ʳ 1781.

Sir

 I have made several attempts to inform your Excellency, that the French West India Fleet under Mons.ʳ de Grasse entered the Capes the 29ᵗʰ Ult.º I could not exactly learn their number, they report twenty five or twenty six Sail of the Line. One 74, & two of 64 & one frigate lay in the Mouth of this River. On the 6, the 74 & frigate turned down with a contrary Wind, & yesterday the two others followed. My Report dated last Evening from a Point below, which commands a view of the Capes & Bay, says that there were within the Capes only seven Ships, two of which were certainly Ships of the Line, & two Frigates. Firing was said to be heard off the Capes, the night of the 4ᵗʰ.

His Excellency
Sir Henry Clinton K.B.
&c.ª &c.ª &c.ª

486

Morning & Night of the 5.ᵗʰ, & Morning of
the 6.ᵗʰ

    The French Troops, landed
at James Town, are said to be three thousand
eight hundred, Washington is said to be
shortly expected, & his Troops are intended
to be brought by water from the head of
Elk under Protection of the French Ships,
the Marquis de La Fayette is at or
near Williamsburgh, & the French
Troops are expected there, but were not
arrived last night. 44, 32, 18, — 18, 16. 22, 26 —
14, 19, 13, 23. 16 — 14, 11, 13, 11, 6, 19, 7 — 4, 6, 18, 16, 7, 18, 7, 11 — 19, 5,
2, 11, 5, 11, 6, 3, 11 — 1, 29, 18, 8, 11, 7, 18, 25, 11, 6 — 18, 16, 7, 13, 19, 6, 29 —
9, 19, 16, 1, 7, 1, 19, 6.² 19, 12, 7, 19, 5. — 7, 29, 11, 7, 19, 14, 6. — 63, 32, 3 — c
23 — 3, 19, 9, 17, 26 — 36, 17, 7, 22, 23, 9, 1, 23, 3, 7, 5 — 3, 8, 8, 25, 24 —
7, 24, 5, 17, 14, 2, 8, 12 — 17, 29, 8, 25, 24 — 13, 6, 3, 11, 24 —
8, 25, 24, 3, 7, 19, 18 — 23, 12, 9, 17, 8 — 15, 24, 7, 18, 12, 23, 11, 22, 6,
18 — 13, 7, 17, 15, 23, 12, 23, 17, 9, 12 — 29, 17, 7 — 12, 23, 4, 26, 24,
22, 12, I will be very carefull of it.

    I have the honour to be,
with great respect,

    Sir

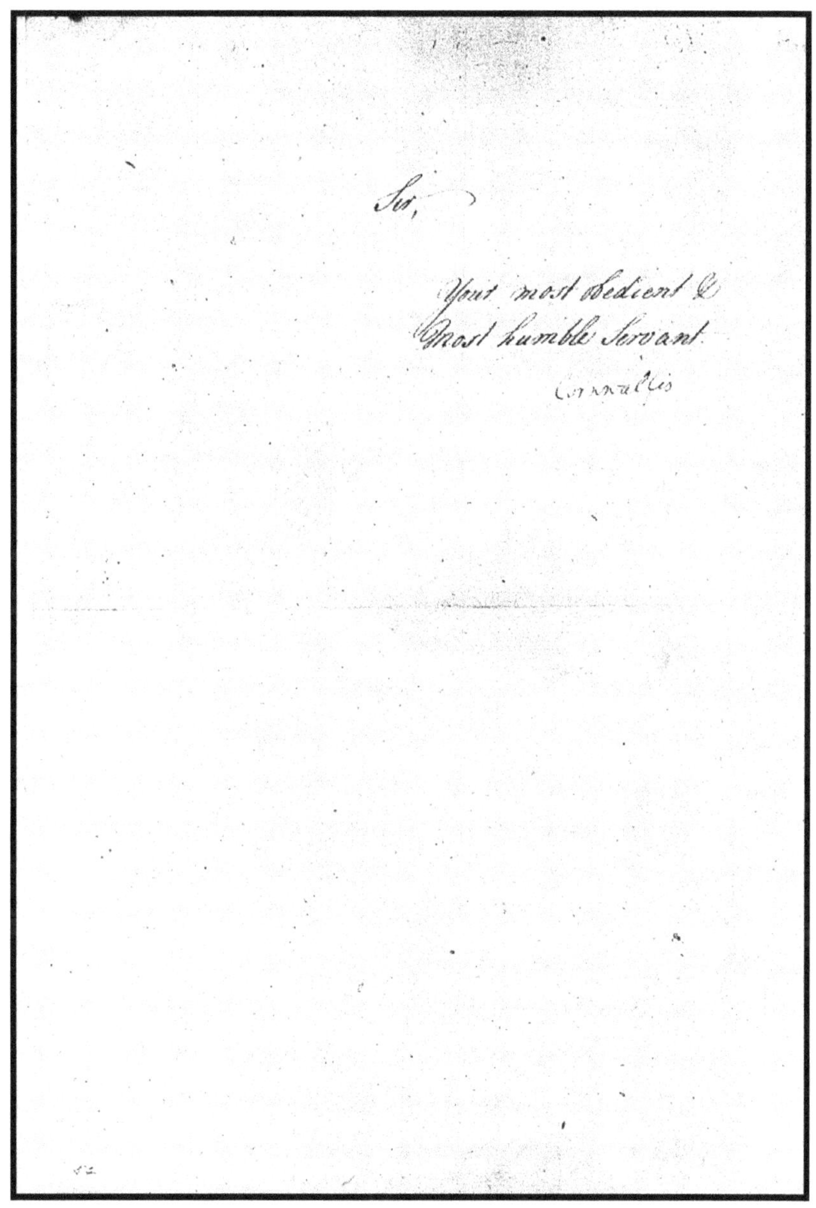

"Charles Cornwallis to Henry Clinton, September 8." George Washington Papers, Series 4, General Correspondence: September 8, 1781. *Manuscript/Mixed Material, Library of Congress*

The first page showed the message to be in the fluid, even writing of Lord Cornwallis. At the top was written "York Town Virginia," and the date "8 Sept. 1781." The letter was addressed to His Excellency Sir Henry Clinton, K.B., neatly written on the bottom left. K.B. stood for Knight Companion, a royal military order, he knew. James had no trouble reading the script on the first page, nor the second, until about halfway down on the second page: only numbers were given for about ten lines, separated by periods and occasional dashes. This was the enciphered portion of the communication. Then came the words "I will be very careful of it, with great respect," and the general's signature on the fourth page. He read the communication over, trying to figure out what was in the British general's mind.

York Town Virginia
8 Sept. 1781

Sir

I have made several attempts to inform your Excellency that the French West India Fleet under Mons de Grass entered the Capes the 29th Ult. I could not exactly learn their number, they report twenty five or twenty six sail of the line One 74 & two of 64 & one frigate lay in the mouth of this river. On the 6th, the 74 & frigate turned down with a contrary wind & yesterday the two others followed. My report dated last evening from a point below, which commands a view of the Capes & Bay, says that there were within the Capes only seven ships, two of which were certainly ships of the line & two frigates. Firing was said to be heard off the Capes the night of the 4th

His Excellency
Sir Henry Clinton, K.B.

Morning & night of the 5th & morning of the 6th
The French troops landed at James Town are said to be three thousand eight hundred. Washington is said to be shortly expected & his troops are intended to be brought by water from the head of Elk under protection of the French ships. The Marquis de La Fayette is at or near Williamsburgh & the French troops are expected there, but were not arrived last night.

The ciphered portion of the letter followed, numbers separated by periods, dashes interspersed in various places, then three lines of words:

I will be very carefull of it.
I have the honour to be, with great respect, Sir,
Your most obedient & most humble servant
Cornwallis

He remembered the various keys he had constructed from deciphering British correspondence. This transmission from Lord Cornwallis was missing the signal letters *B* and *F*, so was clearly different from the interception he had worked on a year ago, where General Cornwallis had used alternately a book cipher and an alphabet cipher.

Nor was the cipher the same as he had worked on a month ago, in September, from British officers Craig and Balfour. From time to time, numbers higher than 39 were given, such as 44 and 43. The message had no spaces indicating new words, so Cornwallis had omitted the spacing to make recognition of words by length more difficult. And he would not put it past the commander to use more than one cipher alphabet. But like the other British officers whose ciphers he had analyzed, it seemed Lord Cornwallis employed a simple substitution cipher, randomly assigning the letters of the alphabet to the numbers 1 through 29, but omitting the numbers 10 and 20.

He set to work and began the process of figuring out the arrangement of numbers.

By early morning he had the first sentence figured out. But then the cipher changed, and he had to start again. Yawning, he decided to get some sleep. He could think more clearly in the morning.

October 14, 1781, Sunday

The next day, James decided to work on the letter, rather than go to church. If he didn't decipher the message, a terrible consequence might follow. *Surely, the Almighty would understand that.*

At breakfast a knock sounded at the door. Lucy came to the table carrying an envelope in her hand.

"This just came for you," she said, handing it to James.

He pushed back his plate, excused himself, and, brimming with curiosity, took the letter to his room.

Seated, his door shut, he opened the slim packet. It was from General Washington, written on October 6th, addressed to him.

Head Quarters before York
6th Oct. 1781

Sir,

I am much obliged by the communication you have been pleased to make me in your favor of 21st ulto. My Secretary has taken a copy of the ciphers—and by help of one of the alphabets has been able to decipher one paragraph of a letter lately intercepted going from Lord Cornwallis to Sir Henry Clinton.

Your letter enclosed to General Greene will be forwarded by a good opportunity by which I expect to write tomorrow. I am sir,

G.W.

Excellent. Apparently, by using the cipher key from the British letters I worked on last month, his secretary was able to decipher at least part of an intercepted letter. I thought the key might come of use. Invigorated and inspired, he set to work again.

He had been right that after the first sentence of Lord Cornwallis's letter, the British general had changed his cipher. It was still an alphabet cipher, but a different one. He realized that the higher numbers used, such as 44 and 43, indicated a change from one to the other of the alphabet ciphers used.

He set to work to figure out the new cipher. But thoughts about General Washington kept intruding. Could General Washington, or his secretary, decipher a message written using the book cipher employed by the British? *The alphabet keys I have sent the general have helped him understand at least one captured message. But have I explained the book cipher adequately?* He could not remember having done so. What if the general came across a message written in the book cipher used by the British and had no means by which to decipher it?

He set aside his work on the message from Lord Cornwallis, placing books over the pages to keep them from sight, and pulled out paper. There were French Army officers posted near the State House, frequently coming and going, often taking messages from Congress. He could prevail on one of them to take a message to the general.

He wrote a note to the commander-in-chief briefly describing the book cipher used by the enemy, explaining that the *Entick's Spelling Dictionary* that the British used was the 1777 edition, published in London by Charles Dilley.

He concluded his message, threw on his coat, and left.

At the State House he found a number of French Army officers at their posts. One would be leaving for Yorktown that afternoon. He agreed to take his letter directly to General Washington.

He returned to his lodging and was back to his room in a quarter of an hour.

Invigorated by the brisk fall air and his walk, he felt ready to resume work. And he felt at peace, knowing General Washington would have the valuable information about the book code should he require it.

It was growing dark by the time he finished deciphering the message. He munched on biscuits and beef while reading over the words that had been written in cipher, considering their meaning.

> *As my works were not in a state of defence I have taken a strong position out of the town. I am now working hard at the redoubts of the place. The army is not very sickly. Provisions for six weeks.*

What can we, or rather, the generals, learn from this? The redoubts are in place, or at least well under way. That much our army has ascertained. "The army is not very sickly." *But sickly, to be sure, or Cornwallis wouldn't have mentioned it. They must have disease, possibly a lot of it. In the heat of the Virginia summer, that might be malaria, smallpox, or other fevers. Even the former slaves, who joined the British ranks given the promise of freedom, might be taken ill. And Cornwallis says they have adequate provisions for six weeks. That is not very long, to be sure. Yet it all depends on the assistance the British fleet may try to give them, and the efforts of the French under the Count de Grasse to prevent that assistance.*

All told, I think this message will make a number of factors clear to our generals. They must have it right away.

He copied out the whole message.

He looked again at the words he had deciphered. *It makes sense that Cornwallis follows the ciphered portion of the letter with "I will be very careful of it,"* he thought. *He means he will be careful of the remaining provisions.*

But his eyes opened wide when he realized the importance of these words. *Cornwallis had taken the time to indicate he should be careful of the provisions. That could mean the British army did not, in fact, have six weeks of provisions. They might have much less. Cornwallis might have wanted to hint about his difficulties to Sir Henry Clinton without actually spelling them out. The siege had been ongoing for nearly four weeks by now. The British might be running out of food.*

Further, Lord Cornwallis admitted his defensive works required work. That part of the message surely might conceal a request for help, at the least a statement of weakness.

Hastily, he took out more paper and wrote another letter to General George Washington, explaining his work to decipher Cornwallis's message. He also mentioned the letter he had just sent to him with the information about the book cipher. On another sheet he listed the alphabet cipher systems he had discovered in General Cornwallis's letter.

> *October 14th, 1781*
> *Evening*
>
> *I gave a letter for your Excellency this morning to some gentleman who is connected with the French Army. I now understand it will not reach you in eight days, but it will reach you doubtless then. It was merely to complete the account of the ciphers used by the enemy. I found, as I had before supposed, that they sometimes use* Entick's Dictionary *marking the Page, Column, and Word as 115.1.4. Tis the Edition of 1777 London by Charles Dilley.*
>
> *Since I wrote that letter, I have been happy in deciphering what the President of Congress sends by this opportunity. The use of the same cipher by all the British Commanders is now pretty fairly concluded. The enemy plays a grand stake. May the glory redound to the Allied Force under your Excellency's command. I am, sir,*
>
> *Your obliged humble servant,   James Lovell*

He folded up the original letter, placing it in its soiled cover sheet, then slipped into a separate envelope the deciphered letter, the key, and his letter to General Washington. He tucked both packets into his satchel, pulled on his coat, and set off on a brisk walk to the Pennsylvania State House. *Back under the rock for you,* he thought, holding the satchel with its precious contents close to him. His feet shuffled through fallen leaves, musty and moist.

He reached the Pennsylvania State House, relieved to see windows glowing with lit candles. A guard admitted him, and he found the library at the rear of the Assembly Room nearly empty. Thomas McKean sat alone at a table, papers spread out around him.

Visibly relieved, the president greeted James. "How did your efforts go?"

"As well as can be expected." James pulled out the packet. "I have copied the letter and the key to the cipher for you to send to General Washington, so this packet can be replaced, no one the wiser."

"Excellent. I will see that it is on its way soon. What did the letter say?"

James handed the president a copy of the deciphered letter with its key. "This is your copy."

Thomas McKean read the page, his brow furrowed. "What did you understand from this?"

"We have held the British in their position at York for perhaps four weeks now. No additional supplies have reached them. They are likely running out of food. General Cornwallis indicates they have six weeks' supply, but that might be an exaggeration. And that was four weeks ago. And he takes the opportunity to explain that he will be very careful of it, meaning the remaining supply of food. We must hold on, as if he does run out of food, he will be forced to capitulate. It appears to be a call for help, as Cornwallis states his defenses require work." James paused, then added, "He also mentions the army is not very sick. This implies that there is sickness among the British troops."

"Yes, we understand there is malaria. That is endemic to the coastal wetlands of Virginia, but Americans are generally not affected by it. The disease should not affect the French, as it takes quite a period of time for an individual to succumb. But the British? A different story. They have been in the vicinity for two months now."

His eyes lighting with expectation, the president said, "I will be sure the message gets to General Washington. I have sent him what I can glean from my intelligence. For one, we have reports that the British Admiral has twenty-nine ships of the line and a number of frigates, which have most likely headed for the Chesapeake yesterday, with five to six thousand land forces."

James drew in his breath but said nothing.

"Sir Henry Clinton was expected to sail on the 5th of this month. If he sailed before then, I would be quite surprised, and my friends who are faithful to me would know of it." Thomas McKean rubbed his forehead in exasperation and weariness. *What a tremendous burden he carries,* James thought. *But so do we all.*

"There are some seventeen thousand troops—Americans, including militia, and French—around Yorktown," James said. "The greater number by far, of course, are French. Though the British may send ships, the combined armies will make a strong stand. They have been firing on the enemy's defenses for days now."

President McKean nodded. "I will suggest to General Washington that he consider a unique opportunity. After Sir Henry Clinton sails, there will not be more than a thousand land forces remaining in New York. If an attack on that area were possible, it might be a great success."

"It is worth consideration. Regaining New York would be a remarkable triumph."

"Yes," the president said, seeming to sag against the effort such an onslaught would require. "In any case, it is up to the general, though my suggestion may not hurt." He brightened up. "Thank you for your help," he said.

"At any time that I can assist, please allow me," James said. He touched his hat and left.

October 24, 1781, Wednesday

A cool wind whipped dry leaves along the streets as Congress assembled at the Pennsylvania State House. A group of Continental Army officers and soldiers, booted, spurred, spattered with the dust of the road, arrived at the same time as did James. He stood back, watching as they dismounted, handed their horses to the doorkeeper, and entered the State House.

James followed them, noticing they did not enter the Assembly Room but stood outside in the hallway, talking with the secretary. At his seat, he leaned over towards George Partridge. "Someone is here, apparently from the army. I wonder what news they bring."

George Partridge, engrossed in his newspaper, set it down and looked about, his dark brows knitted in concern. "We should hear presently."

The president opened the session, glanced anxiously at the door. The visitors from the army remained in the outer hall, so he continued with business.

"Yesterday, when I gave my resignation to this position, you accepted it and decided to choose a replacement today. Do we have nominations for candidates to succeed me?" Thomas McKean spoke deliberately, his voice determined.

John Witherspoon stood. "I move we request Mr. McKean continue in his position as president until the first Monday in November, when a new Congress begins, according to the Articles of the Confederation. At that time, we can elect his successor."

All agreed when the motion was seconded. Thomas McKean bowed, a short, awkward motion, looking a little discomposed, James thought. "Very well, if that is your wish."

A knock sounded from the doors and the doorkeeper hurried to open them. James turned to George Partridge. In a low voice, he said, "It is too soon for terrible news. Yesterday, the president told us that the British fleet had not sailed from New York as of this Monday, and they were not likely to be fully ready until this Sunday, the 21st."

George Partridge nodded. "We have a few days yet."

The French minister, the Chevalier de la Luzerne, turned from his seat in the center of the delegates to gaze at the door, his eyes wide with curiosity.

The double doors opened to admit two Continental Army officers. The first, dignified, in full blue and buff uniform, his traveling cloak dusty, proceeded briskly to President McKean's seat. He held out his hand and firmly shook that of Thomas McKean, his expression calm and disciplined as one who had served in the army for years.

"I am Lieutenant Colonel Tench Tilghman, aide to the commander-in-chief. He has given me the honor of bringing glorious news to Congress." Colonel Tilghman held out a thick packet, offering a slight bow to the president.

"Greetings. You are most welcome." President McKean took the packet, opened it up, pulled out a letter.

The delegates, riveted, listened in silence. President McKean read the letter aloud, his voice choking from time to time.

> *Head Quarters near York*
> *19th Oct. 1781*
>
> *Sir,*
>
> *I have the honor to inform Congress that a reduction of the British Army under the command of Lord Cornwallis is most happily effected—The unremitting ardor which actuated every officer & soldier in the combined Army on this occasion has principally led to this important event, at an earlier period than my most sanguine hopes had induced me to expect.*
>
> *On the 17th of this month a letter was received from Lord Cornwallis proposing a meeting of Commissioners to consult on terms for the surrender of the posts of York & Gloucester. That correspondence was followed by the definitive capitulation, which was agreed to & signed on the 19th, a copy of which is also herewith transmitted—and which, I hope, will meet the approbation of Congress.*

General Washington went on to thank the Count de Rochambeau and his officers, as well as the engineers and artillery of both armies. He especially thanked the Count de Grasse for his support. He requested Congress honor his aide Colonel Tilghman who brought the news of the victory.

Congress and the Chevalier de la Luzerne stood and burst into applause, clapping, shouting "Huzza," and stamping the floor in excitement. The Chevalier de la Luzerne shook the hands of all those around him with great enthusiasm. James found his hand firmly enclosed in that of the Chevalier. "*Ah, mon ami, nous avons les meilleures et les plus merveilleuses nouvelles, n'est-ce pas?* Of a certainty, we can be proud of our united strength and hold high the joint effort of the United States and France."

"*Il s'agit en effet d'une heureuse announce.* We have looked for this news for a long time," James said. The French minister startled him by enveloping him in a huge embrace.

Parting from the Chevalier, James saw Colonel Tilghman watching the excitement calmly, a satisfied smile on his face.

When the ovation finally subsided, President Thomas McKean held up a larger packet. "These are the Terms of Capitulation," he said. "The contest has concluded and the Earl of Cornwallis, along with his army, is now captive."

"Hear, hear," someone called.

"I move that at two o'clock this afternoon Congress proceed to the Dutch Lutheran church to give our thanks to Almighty God for crowning the arms of the United States and France with success." John Witherspoon's voice rang with authority.

"Aye, aye."

"The Secretary of Foreign Affairs will communicate this intelligence to the Minister Plenipotentiary of France," the president said. James's ears pricked up at that. He looked about the Assembly Room for the new Secretary of Foreign Affairs, but Robert Livingston was not in sight.

The doorkeeper cautiously opened the door to a knock. The vice-president and members of the Pennsylvania Supreme Executive Council stood in the hall. "We would like to commend the members of Congress and the officers from the army bringing this exceptional news. May we enter?"

"Indeed. Please join us," President McKean said graciously.

However the Council had acquired the news, the group entered the Assembly Room, shaking hands, congratulating Congress on the joyous event. The burst of elation continued unabated for nearly an hour.

As the clapping subsided, James thought of the consequences of this surrender. Surely, at this point, those in Europe should realize that though the war was not over, it was nearly so. Eight thousand more British soldiers were now imprisoned. The British resolve must surely be fractured at this point, if not shattered.

The service at the Dutch Lutheran church, a sturdy brick structure at Fourth and Cherry, was packed. James squeezed into a rear pew alongside George Partridge and Samuel Osgood. The members of the Pennsylvania Council and their president found seats, and Philadelphia's citizens filled every available space. The Reverend Duffield, one of Congress's chaplains, gave the address, thanking the Great Disposer of all events for the smiles of His providence in the glorious success of the arms of the United States and her ally.

That evening, candles blazed in windows. The ships in the harbor displayed their colors. Fireworks would have been offered but were postponed due to rain. Such noise in the streets and shouts of joy Philadelphia had not seen or heard in a long while, perhaps never.

James walked briskly through rainy streets to the City Tavern. Inside, every room was packed with citizens celebrating alongside officers and soldiers. He saw Samuel Osgood and George Partridge seated in a corner and maneuvered through the crowded room to reach them.

"Have a seat. We were fortunate to get a table," Samuel Osgood said, pulling out a chair for him.

"We have much to celebrate," he said. "These months have been long and arduous."

James took a long, refreshing drink of cider.

"What do we know of the siege?" Samuel asked.

"It was attended with great good fortune, I know that," James said. "For one, General Clinton has been on the brink of coming to Lord Cornwallis's rescue for days, bringing five thousand troops from New York. He may have even departed from New York today. For another, we have had the blessing of Providence in the persistent efforts of the Count de Grasse and his fleet, who drove Admiral Graves away from the mouth of the Chesapeake and prevented their return with a blockade.

"In addition," James went on, his voice low, "the Count de Grasse is said to be needed in the West Indies and was determined to leave as soon as he was not required here. We are most favored that he did not leave and instead chose to maintain the blockade."

George Partridge and Samuel Osgood drew in their breaths at the thought. Samuel said, slowly, "We must celebrate our extreme happiness in the events as they have transpired."

"A toast," James said. He raised his cup with the others. "To the United States."

October 29, 1781, Monday

"We should hear more about the siege," James said, settling into his chair at the State House.

Samuel Osgood looked up from his gazette. "An officer who accompanied Lieutenant Colonel Tench Tilghman is here. He could tell us of the siege."

Samuel strode to the young officer sitting quietly near Secretary Thomson. After a few words were exchanged, he returned to his seat, followed by the officer.

"What can you tell us of the siege?" James asked.

"I am Lieutenant Colonel Tench Tilghman's assistant." Pride shone in the young officer's face. "When the combined armies reached Yorktown, we found the enemy had constructed ten redoubts as defenses, connected by trenches. We began digging our own trenches.

"General Washington ordered an artillery assault to take out British fire power. Our big guns shook the ground enough to rattle your teeth. Our heavy cannon knocked out most of the enemy's within two days.

"The general then ordered allied forces to dig a second parallel trench. The only problem was, in order for the troops to get close enough to the British to do any good, two of the enemy's redoubts had to be taken out. Colonel Alexander Hamilton volunteered to lead a squad to attack one, while the French advanced on the other. Washington ordered the use of bayonets, as they are faster than firepower. Both attacks were successful. Hamilton led his men on a nighttime charge, yelling war whoops. The sky lit up as bright as daylight with exploding shells. Their assault was over in ten minutes."

"Very brave of them," Samuel said, nodding emphatically. "I heard that Cornwallis, trapped, made one last desperate attempt to evacuate. He ordered his troops to cross the York River under cover of darkness in small boats. Unluckily for him, a storm blew up and prevented their efforts."

"And General Clinton did attempt a rescue, but he was too late."

"The British were running out of food, and many of their troops were terribly sick," James said.

"Yes, these were both factors in the surrender. On the 19th, after the terms had been settled on the 18th, Cornwallis's army, including quite a number of Hessians, marched out of Yorktown between mile long lines of Americans on one side and French on the other. Can you imagine how humiliated the British felt?"

Those listening nodded.

"Lord Cornwallis refused to be present at the surrender ceremony, pleading illness. He sent his second, Brigadier General Charles O'Hara. When General O'Hara attempted to hand over his sword to the Count de Rochambeau, the French general refused, gesturing to the commander-in-chief. But Washington gave the honor to General Benjamin Lincoln.

"The British laid down their arms. Now the American army is on their way to their camp on the Hudson River. The British will be moved to prison camps."

James said, "I understand that the Count de Grasse is wanted in the West Indies, so he is sailing south. His contribution to defeating the British was most timely."

"To my knowledge, that is correct," the officer said. "Now I must return to my place." He stood and bowed.

"Thank you for your report," James said.

The delegates were silent, reflecting on the marvelous good fortune of the victory. Privately, James congratulated himself on the successful deciphering of the message from Clinton to Cornwallis. Reading the message could have encouraged General Washington and the Count de Rochambeau to hold on and persist in their efforts, knowing the British were in dire straits, food and disease both serious considerations, reinforcements needed. Then too, the copy of the alphabet cipher he had sent to General Greene a month ago had assisted Washington's secretary to decipher another piece of intelligence, no doubt useful in planning and carrying out the campaign. All in all, he felt proud of the part he had played in the victory.

"The order of the day will likely be to extend our thanks to General Washington, the officers and army, the Count de Rochambeau, the French army, and the Count de Grasse," Samuel said, turning as the president approached.

"Undoubtedly. We also will remember the part played by General Nathanael Greene, who doggedly pursued Cornwallis until he had to retreat to Yorktown. And a tribute to Lieutenant Colonel Tench Tilghman, honored to bring us the terms of surrender," James said. He looked up as President Thomas McKean stood to open the session.

Chapter 36

The Firmness of Our Convictions

November 14, 1781, Wednesday

Entering the Pennsylvania State House, James pulled his dripping coat off and rubbed his hands together. The freshly cleaned hall smelled of pine smoke and beeswax.

Earlier in the month, President Thomas McKean had departed from his position. The delegates elected John Hanson of Maryland the first president under the Articles of the Confederation. President Hanson, a member of Congress since 1779, older than James, had been a staunch supporter of liberty in Maryland.

In the Assembly Room, the curtained windows revealed gray clouds and bare black trees bowing in the wind. The number of delegates had dwindled. It did not surprise James that the first motion of the day was for the president to write to the executives of the states, requesting attendance in Congress for all. "Only with full representation can we safely conduct the affairs of the United States," President John Hanson said.

"There are just nine states present today, with twenty delegates," George Partridge observed, his usually tranquil face displeased.

"It is cold enough that some have stayed in their lodgings, if they haven't left for warmer places," James said.

At a recess in the afternoon, Robert R. Livingston, the new Secretary of the Department of Foreign Affairs, approached him. Affable, thoughtful, Robert R. Livingston had a wealth of experience as a lawyer and statesman. James had already given him the cipher that he had provided to John Adams, Benjamin Franklin, and others.

"Would you have time for a brief conversation?" Robert Livingston asked.

"Certainly."

"Given the unpleasant weather, I will invite you to join me at Clark's Inn."

"Very good." *I can stretch my purse*, he thought.

318

Inside the dark, timbered establishment, an attendant bowed, then showed them to seats by a comfortable fire. A maid brought steaming cups of tea. James looked at Robert R. Livingston with apprehension. His own tenure as Secretary for the Committee for Foreign Affairs had ended, his labor of nearly five years intense, much of the time on his own. Now, while he wanted to help the new secretary, surely it was up to Robert R. Livingston to manage the duties of the office.

"I sense that John Adams is often unable to utilize the cipher you have provided him." Robert R. Livingston looked up from his plate with a hint of disparagement in his critical eye.

"I had wondered," James admitted. "I have sent him several letters regarding his position, Congress's directives, and intelligence in which I employed use of the cipher. He says little respecting those."

"It is a pity he is not utilizing your cipher. We must ensure he has access to one." Robert R. Livingston shook his head with dismay. "I wrote to him immediately following the news of the victory at Yorktown, introducing myself. I advised him to treat the friends of the United States, such as the United Provinces, with politeness."

"The advice should be well taken," James said. He bristled somewhat at Robert Livingston's words. *I would imagine John Adams capable of acting without causing offense.* He did not, however, voice his thoughts.

"Further, the United States must be respected abroad for our great resources and the value of our commerce. And, in opposition to the injustice and cruelty which characterize the English, John should present himself as compassionate and prudent."

"Knowing John Adams as I do, I would believe those qualities would accompany his overtures at all times," James said. "I will write to him and explain again the cipher. I will give you the letter so that you may enclose it within yours. In the meantime, thank you for speaking with me."

"Allow me to take the bill on this occasion," Robert R. Livingston said, standing and reaching for his coat.

"You are too kind," James said. He did not argue. The state of his finances did not permit his generosity when it came to dining out.

Following the glorious victory at Yorktown, Congress settled into a slump. A sense of complacency after the stunning defeat of Cornwallis combined with fatigue to create an atmosphere of weariness and discontent, as well as a lack of full representation in the group. James found his thoughts turning towards home. First, though, he had work to do.

A visit from the Washingtons was expected by the end of the month. Nothing could cheer Congress and Philadelphia as could a visit from the general and Mrs. Washington, he knew. And it was vital that Congress continue its work to maintain the army in full preparedness.

A couple days after his talk with Robert R. Livingston, on Friday, Congress considered a motion to send Washington and his full army to assist General Greene to drive the British out of South Carolina. The motion was voted down, the only states voting for it being South Carolina and Georgia. James thought the decision a prudent one. Meanwhile, General Rochambeau and his troops remained in Williamsburg.

November 26, 1781, Monday

As crowds filled the square at the State House, Congress adjourned to join the celebration of the arrival of the Washingtons.

James, George Partridge, and Samuel Osgood found viewing spots on the steps of the State House. In front of them and filling the square stood hundreds, smiling at the grand event. The Washingtons' coach approached, a handsome black affair with a matched gray team, and made its way around the State House, the crowds cheering and clapping. A band played stirring music as people elbowed one another for a sight of the general waving from his coach. Mrs. Washington beamed, the plume of feathers on her hat bobbing.

The coach turned towards Fifth Street.

"You should see the illumination that Charles Willson Peale, the artist, has painted at his house," George Partridge said, enthusiastically.

"It is really most artistic. At night the light from within causes the colors to glow. A ship with the name *Cornwallis* on its stern is seen to be departing. Portraits of General Washington and the Count de Rochambeau, crowned with laurels, are depicted with rays of glory and the words 'Shine Valiant Chiefs,' the entire composition encircled by stars and fleur-de-lis."

"I will have to see it."

November 28, 1781, Wednesday

Congress met on matters of business in the morning, but their attention was diverted by the expectation of the afternoon's event. At one o'clock, they hosted the official reception for General Washington.

The general entered from the rear door, in full uniform of blue and buff, sword at his side. Over six feet tall, solid, the commander-in-chief made an impressive figure.

Two members of Congress escorted him to President Hanson. General Washington leaned over and shook the seated president's hand.

The president looked up at the commander-in-chief. "Congress is always pleased to see Your Excellency, particularly now after the glorious success of the allies in Virginia. We intend to call on the states in the strongest of terms to make the most vigorous exertions at this important time. Sir, if you remain for some time in Philadelphia, you could both assist the committee to improve the army in their work and permit yourself a rest from the labors of war."

General Washington, his voice clear, controlled, answered, "I deeply appreciate the wishes of Congress, especially those that encourage the states to vigorous exertions. Their compliance will yield the most happy results. I am pleased to provide every assistance in my power to Congress's committee.

"Should I be required in service with the army I will take myself to that station with the same pleasure I hold while I remain in this city."

He bowed as the delegates clapped with approval. James sensed, again, General Washington's ability to remain in command even while attending to niceties of public appearance. An unusual man, he had to agree. *We are fortunate to have his service.*

December 4, 1781, Tuesday

"A visitor for you, sir."

James turned to the attendant. "Thank you. I will be there directly." The Assembly Room was quiet except for clerks bustling over papers piled on Secretary Thomson's tables. At the entrance of the room, he saw a familiar figure. He hastened towards the door.

"Johnny!" he gasped with surprise.

His third son, tall, hair neatly combed, dressed in an army uniform, stood at the doorway, smiling broadly. James reached him and enfolded him in a hug. "What are you doing here?"

"I am a clerk in the office of General Benjamin Lincoln." John glowed with pride.

"Yes, your mother wrote. I am just surprised to see you. How wonderful. We need to find time for a visit."

"I would like that."

It had been five years, a long time since he had seen Johnny. *So tall he is, so grown up. He is doing so well. He must be eighteen.*

"You know that General Washington meets each Monday at the office of Robert Morris, the Superintendent of Finance. The heads of all the departments are there, including General Benjamin Lincoln, Secretary of War. I assist him with note taking and other duties." John's voice was deep, confident, as he explained his work.

"I am so proud of you."

"Are you well? Do you have enough?"

"I am most well. I contemplate returning home for a visit soon."

"That is excellent news. I know, however, that funds coming from Massachusetts are slim and difficult to obtain. I hope your pay is coming through."

"As ever it has been," James said. He did not need to let John know the difficulties he had in his finances. He smiled at his son, his heart swelling with pride.

"Come to see me at my lodging soon. I stay at Mrs. Clymer's on Walnut Street." He gripped Johnny's hand in a warm grasp, patted him on the shoulder, and watched as the tall young man almost bowed in an attitude of respect, then turned to leave. *So good to see him*, he thought, as Johnny left the Assembly library. *And to think of going home, seeing all the dear family. I can hardly wait.*

That evening James thought over the state of his finances. It was becoming more and more clear to him that he must return home, at the very least for a visit. But how could he do that when to do so meant immediate cessation of income?

He smiled to himself. *This should be a familiar situation to me, more funds going out than coming in.*

Massachusetts owed him money. For years the accounts he had given the council only reckoned the bare minimum of his expenses. When he considered the sums his friends received for the same work he was doing, it seemed to him he could charge more. The luxuries and niceties which some of his friends, Elbridge Gerry and George Partridge, for example, regularly charged, brought their income to at least $9 per day, far above his own rate of compensation.

If he were to make an accounting of what was owed to him for time and services, the sum could help him pay his bills, catch up payment for his board and room, even allow him to acquire a new set of clothing and provide for his family in the coming winter.

He recalled the tantalizing suggestion made last spring by Robert Morris, now Superintendent of Finance. Morris had suggested he take a position as receiver of Continental taxes in Boston. At the time, it had not seemed he could undertake such a prospect. But now, following a victory of the most significant kind, perhaps he could. *I did aid the commander-in-chief in deciphering intelligence. And now negotiations for peace can be seriously considered. I am no longer Secretary for the Committee for Foreign Affairs. Maybe it is time I speak with Robert Morris again and revive our discussion of the position he had proposed.*

December 13, 1781, Thursday

On the 10th of December, Congress resolved that each state provide its quota of men for the troops by the 1st of March. Vigilance against the enemy would be their first priority, despite the success of the fall. President Hanson wrote a circular letter to the states, appealing to them to remember the firmness of their convictions in the present crisis.

An entire day of debate about the fisheries off the north eastern coast, a question James thought was already settled, commenced a couple of days later.

He found himself blurting out, in some exasperation, "Do you not realize the livelihood of many fishermen is greatly dependent on their right to take fish in the rich waters off the coast of New England and north, even to the Grand Banks off of Newfoundland? We spent many days clarifying that requirement in 1779. I thought the question never to arise again."

He controlled with difficulty his frustration with the newer delegates, whose knowledge of what had already transpired he found to be highly inadequate, and filed his written report of the proceedings with Secretary Thomson, relieved to have the topic placed correctly in its importance for the negotiations.

A new, disturbing, and personal difficulty weighed on James's mind. Major Burnet, General Greene's spokesperson in Philadelphia, gave him the unfortunate news that his older son, James Lovell, a major and adjutant with Lt. Col. Harry Light-Horse Lee's battalion of light dragoons, was ill. James thanked him. In his mind the fear rose that his son was suffering a recurrence of malaria.

Unexpectedly, Major Burnet stopped to introduce himself. "You deciphered messages for General Greene. What can you tell me of the British methods used?" The young officer stood ram-rod straight near James, one hand nervously twisting a thin moustache. His eagerness and determination struck James and he motioned for him to take a seat. He could not recall anyone else so interested in learning about the British cipher.

He explained to the eager young major the methods used by the British. He drew out examples while the officer listening intently.

As the sky darkened, he interrupted their talk. "We can continue this conversation later. The day is closing, and I have matters to attend to." James set his pen and ink aside.

"Certainly. I would be delighted. Thank you." Major Burnet bowed in pleasure and shook James's hand.

Back at his lodging, James wrote to General Nathanael Greene, requesting he deliver a letter from him to his son James Jr. and telling him he had had a short conversation with Major Burnet about the British cipher. *When I leave Congress, someone else might be able to work with intercepted messages.*

December 31, 1781, Monday

The business of the day concluded, James noticed Robert Morris, sitting back in his chair, reading a gazette. Today, Congress had approved the formation of a national bank, following Robert Morris's plan submitted last May. The charter of a national bank would do much, Morris insisted, to put the finances of the United States on a more even keel.

James walked up to the Superintendent of Finance and put out his hand. *It is now or never*, he thought.

"My compliments on the success of our establishing a national bank," he said.

Robert Morris shrugged, shook James's hand, eyed him with interest. "It is an institution we have long needed," he said. "Please have a seat."

"Do you remember our conversation of last April?" James asked.

"Indeed, I do."

"Does the offer still stand?"

"It does. I am most pleased with your consideration. I have had trouble finding the right individual to take the position. You, however, would be perfectly suited for it."

"It is an honor, and I find that at this time, I would be most pleased to accept it. However, I must return home first for a visit. I need to make a few necessary arrangements. Then I will return to take my final leave."

"By all means. The office is yours, when you are ready. May I offer my most sincere congratulations on your possible leave from Congress. You have served long and with merit."

"Thank you. I intend to visit my home next month. After that, I will be in a better position to undertake the office of Continental tax receiver. I hope that taking time for a leave is not inconvenient to you or the office."

Robert Morris waved his hand in dismissal. "Certainly, it is no trouble at all. The far more important matter is to put the correct person into the office. I will await your return for further information. It is a pleasure to speak with you." James shook his hand, feeling a weight slide off his shoulders as he did.

He picked up his papers and left, his mind in a tumult. The thought of leaving Congress brought up so many considerations, he was not sure which to contemplate first. Somehow, he would handle the needs, one at a time.

January 5, 1782, Saturday

James woke up each day energized. Ever since his conversation with Robert Morris, hope had nestled in his heart like a fledgling bird. He could go home to visit, perhaps receive reimbursement from Massachusetts, and, when he felt comfortable that his home and family were receptive to his return, take his final leave from Congress.

Just why did he think he needed to go home to visit before he made a final departure from Philadelphia? He wasn't quite sure. Even to himself it was difficult to explain. Perhaps he had been gone so long he wasn't sure he would fit within the family circle anymore. In any case, he knew that was what he had to do. And he needed to do it soon.

His small room contained few items that he owned. Abigail's boxes, holding a set of china and various articles shipped to her by John Adams, had been conveyed to her in a wagon with the help of General Benjamin Lincoln. He spoke with Mrs. Clymer, letting her know he would be gone for a number of weeks.

"Of course, your wife and children will be so glad to see you. And you will be home. You are from Boston, after all…. I can imagine how you must miss your home." She smiled, pulled a strand of her silver-gray hair back from her forehead, and tucked it into the pile on her head.

James agreed. "It is not so much the place as the people. I am looking forward to being with my family. And," he added, taking a chance on her good humor, "may I leave some belongings with you?"

Ann Clymer glanced down the hall at his door. "The room is yours, until you part from Congress."

He thought over the arrangements. *A winter's journey would pose problems but be manageable. The snow was thick, but the roads would be reasonably clear.* The problem of a stout horse was solved when a farmer appeared at his walkway with a sturdy gray mare. Molly, a gift from Robert Morris, would be at the stable on High Street when he was ready.

January 23, 1782, Wednesday

In the middle of the morning, at James's request, Oliver Ellsworth of Connecticut made a motion on James's behalf for him to take leave from Congress. President John Hanson looked at James sharply, before saying "Motion passed."

"I will return," James said. He gave no further information, however.

When Congress was finally adjourned, he hastened to leave. To his surprise, President John Hanson stepped down from his dais and came over to his seat, as he was about to pick up his papers.

"We look forward to your return," John Hanson said, extending his hand. Tall, determined, he spoke in clipped, precise phrases.

"As do I. But it has been long since I have been home, and it is time, indeed overdue, for a visit," James said.

"Then Godspeed. Your service is appreciated." President Hanson nodded and returned to his seat.

By the morning, his saddlebags were packed. A stable boy brought the gray mare to the back entrance to Mrs. Clymer's home. Waving farewell to Ann Clymer, who watched from inside the dining room, her granddaughter at her side, James took his leave.

The roads were as he had expected, well-traveled, snow-packed. He passed a group of Seneca Indians, on their way home from a meeting in Philadelphia. He trotted around wagons lugging merchandise. An army supply convoy trundled by, escorted by troops. Soldiers traveling on furlough walked in the countryside, singly or in pairs. *Perhaps my son James will be able to come home, when he is well enough.*

He crossed over into New Jersey and headed north. The weather remained calm, with clouds and snow flurries but absent of storms. At night he stayed in inns, some grand, some barely habitable.

Reaching the familiar house on School Street, he felt a moment of apprehension. *What if she is not glad to see me? What if I am not welcome?* He was about to reach the door when it opened from within. Mary stood in the doorway, an anxious look on her round face, her hair escaping in silver ringlets from under her white cap. Beside her stood Charles, thin and wiry at nine years old, his face lit with excitement, and the youngest, George, six, who clung to her skirts bashfully.

"Hello, my dear. I am home." James reached out his arms and she stepped into them without a sound. He enfolded her gently, as if she might break. "My dearest," he whispered, his voice cracking with emotion.

The days flew by. George and Charles gradually lost their shyness and showed him their collections of robins' eggs and snail shells. Thomas, nearly eleven, read his lessons with him, glowing under his praise. Mary, almost thirteen, brought him baked tarts, brown and sweet, of her own making, and took turns reading along with Thomas. William, at fifteen, was apprenticed at a smith's, and Joseph, eighteen, had found employment at the docks with a merchant.

He realized that in fact, as impoverished as they were, Boston was less expensive than Philadelphia. He bought a new pair of boots, the first in years.

Before long the notion crept into his mind, unfamiliar yet blissfully welcome, that he was happy, happier than he had been for a long time. The sense that he was home, was accepted, part of the family, was freeing, in a way he had not known it could be. Returning here, taking up the duties of Continental tax receiver, would be possible, even enjoyable. He had been gone for five years, and including the year and a half he had spent in British prisons, aside from a few weeks home before he had joined Congress, it had been six and a half years since he had been with his family.

He visited with Samuel Adams, busy with the Massachusetts Council. The Council invited him to be a delegate, but for once he decided against it. He had been gone too long and had been part of government too intensely to wish further service in that area.

What he most wanted was to be home and provide for his family.

Chapter 37

Continental Tax Receiver

February—April, 1782

At home he found himself busy—much busier than he thought he would be. He learned that the office of Continental tax receiver would supply some funds, but that the income would be sporadic and likely not enough for his growing family. He began making inquiries about other ways he could earn money.

He found a house on the corner of Sturgis Place and Hutchinson Street that promised more room for his family and a larger garden area. The Massachusetts Council paid him his back pay and he arranged to buy the house. Mary and he began sorting through their things, preparing for a move. The days flew by.

Towards the end of February, he threw up his hands, smiling at Mary. She was making another of numerous pleas for him to write to Abigail Adams.

"Surely you have time to write her a note?"

"Yes, Mary, I will. I have been too busy to pay her a visit. I realize she has been kind to you—that she invited you to go to visit her."

"Really, James, you owe it to her. Her friendship makes it clear that at the least you should write to her."

Laughing, he settled in his chair, took out paper, and began.

> *February 28, 1782*
>
> *"Mr. Lovell, do let me entreat you, this thirtieth time, to write a few lines to Mrs. Adams. Are you not clearly convinced that it is in vain for you to determine, as you have done, day after day, that you will go to see her? You are betrayed, by a thousand interruptions, not merely into impoliteness, but really into ingratitude to that lady. If you do not feel for yourself, I pray you to convince her that I am not*

insensible to her repeated kind invitations and other proofs of her friendly thoughtfulness of me."

Stop, pray thee, stop, Mary. I will write, this moment. Thou art indeed a good woman. What pity 'tis, as some folks think, that you have not a better husband!

And now, my esteemed friend, do you not willingly conceive that it is very difficult for me to seize hours enough to secure the great pleasure of seeing you at Braintree?

Be assured that I am not yet so finished with pressing business that I find leisure to visit at the southwest or northern parts of this town many friends of my early love or my later gratitude.

I have many things to tell; many also to ask about. I will not omit any possible opportunity of doing both within the next fortnight. In the meantime, be assured of the regard which is now jointly professed by, Madam, your obliged friends,

J. & M. Lovell

March 1782

Helping George with his Latin lesson, James thought of his friend Henry Laurens, imprisoned in the Tower of London for fifteen months. He had read in a gazette article that towards the end of February, Congress agreed to the exchange of Henry Laurens for General Cornwallis. *Freedom is so essential.* He passed his hand affectionately over the tousled brown hair of his son, who looked up at him in wonder. *What is it all for, if we do not have liberty to do what we want, spend time with those we love? Thank heavens I will have that.*

Before long he saw in a Boston gazette an article of March 2, 1782, reprinted from the *Norwich Mercury* in England. Following the House of Commons' vote in February to wage no further war with the United States, Parliament voted against continuing the American war.

James set the paper down, a wave of emotion washing over him. *The war is not over,* he reminded himself. *We still need to be vigilant, support the troops. But peace will come, as surely as light follows the dawn.*

A letter arrived from Samuel Osgood. His friend reported on matters in Congress. Reading the words "Nothing interesting has taken place since I wrote you last," James again was thankful he was no longer in that administrative body.

Congress had at length decided that Vermont must be a state independent of either New Hampshire or New York. The *Journals* for the past year had been printed through September.

Samuel Osgood ended his letter with a humorous yet insightful comment on the publication of the *Journals*.

> *This is a matter of great consequence to Congress as well as the states—as we are frequently at a loss to know what we have done. Though we might possibly understand what the Journals would have told us, still the states are totally in the dark; where perhaps some of our resolves ever ought to remain. But be this as it may, I think upon the whole Congress have done very well & great allowances must be made on account of the very different views of the delegates from the several states. This observation is needless to one who has had five years' experience. But as I am determined to fill up this large piece of paper, & nothing of material consequence to inform you of occurs to my mind, I have observed, which by the way is no observation at all & as I have but just room enough you certainly see (without the Irish Phrase Book) to sign my name. I am, very sincerely, your obedient Servt,   S. Osgood*

Left in the dark, indeed. Samuel Osgood is starting to get the gist of it. James smiled. He set the letter aside with a sigh. Such work was important, it was meaningful, it was necessary, it determined the course of the country, but for him he had had enough. He desired only to devote himself to his family and such occupations as could sustain it.

April 1, 1782, Monday

He knocked on the back door at Mrs. Clymer's on Walnut Street, then opened it cautiously. Lucy met him.

"Mr. Lovell! You have returned!"

"Indeed, I have," he said, removing his outer coat and shaking off water. The storm had hit some miles outside of Philadelphia. "I will unload and take my horse to the stable, if you will assure me my room is still available."

"It is," Lucy said. "I will let Mrs. Clymer know."

James thanked the maid, then carried in his saddlebags and saddle. Warm and dry, he sat with Mrs. Clymer to enjoy pork and beans. He told her little except that that he would be leaving before long, and to her questions about his family he answered yes, his family was well and looked forward to his return. She produced a letter that had arrived for him and he thanked her. He took leave from her early and retreated to his room, exhausted.

In his room, he opened the letter, saw the familiar handwriting. General Nathanael Greene's letter was dated January 28. The general expressed his approval of his son Major James Lovell, adjutant to Major General Henry Lee, and asked him to forward a letter he enclosed to John Adams. General Greene expressed concern that he had caused offense to John Adams, which he felt had put a stop to their correspondence. James opened his eyes wide at that. John Adams was not easily offended. He would be glad to forward the general's letter to his friend.

The following day after a late breakfast, Lucy appeared in the dining area, her face puckered with concern. "Sir, you have a visitor."

"Please show the person in, if you would be so kind."

He stood, wondering if Congress required him. Truthfully, he was hoping for one day's rest before returning. Lucy held the door open and his son John stepped in, a worried look on his handsome face.

"Father, thank heavens I found you. A rider from Boston just brought word that there has been a fire at home. Mother sends a message. She was burned, though she adds she is not too badly hurt."

James felt horrified, a shock rippling through his body. "How could that have happened?"

"Her message does not say, though she says the house sustained some damage." He held up a folded paper, unfolded it, and handed it to James. "She knew I was at the office of General Benjamin Lincoln and that I could find you, so she sent this to Samuel Adams. He located a rider coming here."

James skimmed the writing. Mary's writing was uneven, nearly illegible, the note short. "I must get back there. She will need to heal. I will leave as soon as I am able. There are some matters I must tend to. Meanwhile, your sister Mary will help her, as will the older boys there."

John nodded. His kind face, troubled as it was, relaxed. "Her message is quite brief, but you know she never asks for help unless she needs it."

"Very true. Your mother is a brave and independent person, who is capable of handling far more than we will ever know." James sighed. "I will return home soon, but affairs here must be put in order before I can leave. Thank you for bringing the message, Johnny. I am so glad you found me with no trouble. I will write to her right away so she knows I will come as soon as possible."

John shrugged. "She will do her best, I am sure. I must return to my office, but it is good to see you."

He moved closer to John and embraced his son.

"Johnny, I am proud of you. Do your best in your position and you will continue to be appreciated."

"I will, don't you fear. I leave you now to your duties." He backed away towards the door, then turned and left, his military uniform displaying his commitment with pride.

That evening, James walked through the soft spring air to Mrs. Clarke's and Miss Dalley's home. Miss Dalley opened the door and shrieked with delight. "Mr. Lovell! How good to see you!" She all but embraced him, but curtsied low instead and motioned him in. "Please come in. Mr. Partridge and Mr. Osgood will be delighted."

James entered the front parlor, where he found the two delegates reading gazettes by the fireside. He explained the message Mary had sent and his need to return soon.

"I know you were hoping to have me replace you, George. May I prevail upon you to stay, so that I may return soon?"

George Partridge, dedicated though he was to Congress, raised his dark eyebrows. But he said, "Of course. I will stay. When they find someone to replace me, then I will leave. You should return home as soon as you are able."

James nodded. "I will join you at Congress tomorrow. I do need to talk with Robert Morris about the position of Continental tax receiver in Boston. I am counting on it, though I understand it may not provide enough for me to support my family. But with that and some other prospects at home, we should be all right."

Samuel Osgood gestured to an empty chair. "Do sit down and tell us the news."

In his room, the windows open to the cool, fresh air, he wrote to General Nathanael Greene. His son James's health was on his mind, the adjutant possibly inflicted with malaria again.

He attended Congress the next day. He could not put his heart into the work, knowing he would be gone soon.

An inquiry at the office of Robert Morris gained him an appointment on April 6, and he chafed at the delay. Meanwhile, he went through personal items and packed a box to be shipped by wagon. He settled a few accounts with the stable, his tailor, the laundress. He assured Mrs. Clymer he would be leaving and paid her accordingly.

He met with the Superintendent of Finance at the new Bank of North America, in a building on Chestnut Street. Robert Morris assured him he could start the position as Continental tax receiver upon his return. The superintendent also set spurs to his leave, saying that if he did not take up those duties soon, he would be obliged to find another to fulfill them. James assured him he would leave within days.

On the 9th he wrote a letter to the president of the Massachusetts Council, John Hancock, officially announcing his retirement from Congress.

Finally, all was in readiness. He was given official leave from Congress on the 15th. President Hanson raised his eyebrows as he made the announcement but continued smoothly on to other matters, a leave taking inconspicuous as any public servant must expect when personal matters overtake the needs of government.

That night, Mrs. Clymer invited George Partridge and Samuel Osgood to dine with James. She and the cook prepared a roast beef with squash pie. The meal was quiet, subdued, despite her attempts to lighten it, the delegates each lost in their own thoughts. George Partridge and Samuel Osgood toasted James nonetheless. He tried to respond with gratitude. His heart was not in the celebration, however.

In his room, making final preparations, he was surprised by a knock at his door. It was Lucy.

"Mr. Lovell, there is a gentleman here to see you."

James followed her into the parlor, where he found a young man in uniform waiting. "Sir, Secretary Robert R. Livingston has sent you this letter, intercepted from the enemy. He requests you decipher its contents, if possible."

"I will be glad to attend to it, but I am leaving in the morning," James said.

"Secretary Livingston knows that. He would appreciate it if you copied the letter now, while I wait, then take the copy with you to work with and leave the original with me to return to him."

"That will work admirably. Please have a seat while I attend to it."

James copied out the page, puzzling over the combinations of letters and numbers. *Not an alphabetic numeric cipher,* he thought. *More like a passage cipher, one that uses a known passage to assign numbers.*

He handed the original back to the messenger, who had waited with great composure while he wrote out the letter. "Tell Mr. Livingston I will attend to it as soon as time permits."

"Thank you, sir." The young man bowed, placed the ciphered letter securely in his breast pocket, and left.

In the morning, with a sigh of relief he took Molly from the stable, loaded his saddlebags, and was off on a fair day under high drifting clouds.

On the fourth day of his journey, nearing the northern border of New Jersey, a storm blew up at noon, winds scattering tree branches across the road, rain driving like nails.

He saw the swinging sign of an inn and made for it. In a room before a warm fire, after a supper of roast chicken, he took out the intercepted letter given to him by Secretary Livingston and spread it on a table. Beside it he placed additional paper and set to work.

Several hours later, the fire low, the paper yielded its secrets. The cipher used was a passage type, one that depended on numbers being assigned to the words of a commonly known passage, or several passages, generally phrases found in a book. In that type of cipher, each letter in a phrase or sentence was assigned a number, sequentially. And, when more than one passage was used, each letter would be represented by two numbers, one indicating the passage and the other the letter.

He wrote out the message. Then, on a new sheet, he wrote the full table for passage sixteen, which assigned the numbers 1–46 to the letters in the phrase "whether a regiment of artillery or a corps of engineers." He included the table with his letter to be of help to the Secretary of Foreign Affairs.

The resulting deciphered message did not contain critical intelligence, he saw to his disappointment, but having knowledge of its cipher could benefit Robert R. Livingston.

He read over the captured message again. The name of the writer was obscured, but the surname began with *F.* Governor Robertson, to whom the writer referred, must be the British governor of New York. Otherwise, little could be deduced from the deciphered words.

> *A few days ago, I wrote more fully. This will I hope go directly to you. I have not heard from you since your letter of 2nd August, nor received any other intelligence of moment from any quarter since that time. Common reports make me anxious to hear from you: and I entreat you would let me have that pleasure not trusting to a single messenger, but by different routes. I request the same of Governor Robertson. Sent March sixteenth.*

Next, smiling, he wrote to the secretary.

> *Ringwood Iron Works, at Leisure in Storm, April 19, 1782*
> *Honorable R. R. Livingston*
> *Sir,*

> *The contents of the cyphered paper, which I copied by desire of the gentleman at my home, turn out little important in my opinion; however, the pains I have taken in the present case may lead to something important hereafter, when perhaps you will find the letters of the writer's Christian and surname. I conjecture the latter to be F—you'll observe that there is regularity of sense in the alphabets when placed by the columns of numbers from 1 upwards, which will be a great help to you in case you find any more papers cyphered by the same party. See my supplements to the first column; I made a few additions to 16 which makes that column complete.*
>
> *Accept my labors and my assurances of esteem for you.*
>
> *James Lovell*

The weather cleared the following day and he left early, intent on completing his journey. A few days later he arrived at home, safely. Mary greeted him, her right hand bound in a white cloth, her eyes shining.

Afterword

Once James Lovell had left Congress and settled with his family in their house at the corner of Sturgis Place and Hutchinson Streets, he undertook his duties as receiver of Continental taxes in Boston. His commission of one-eighth of one percent was not, however, sufficient to provide for his family. Hard times followed, until, in 1784, Massachusetts offered him the position of naval officer for the Port of Boston. Here James Lovell commissioned ships and collected fees. In 1788 he became collector of customs for the State of Massachusetts. He offered occasional service to the Continental Congress, transmitting dispatches that arrived from Europe. With his knowledge of foreign diplomacy, he wrote at their request to support individuals.

When the new government under the Constitution set up a federal system of tax collection, James Lovell, worried about retaining his position, contacted his friend John Adams, the Vice President, in April of 1789. He also wrote to Abigail, who in turn reminded her husband of the needs of "a friend of yours." He and one of his sons in their chaise joined the Vice President Elect's passage from Boston to Cambridge, giving another opportunity to remind his friend of his requests. George Washington, who generally placed those who had served faithfully in governmental positions, gave the position of collector of customs to James's friend General Benjamin Lincoln, and appointed James Lovell the naval officer for the District of Boston and Charlestown.

Lovell and Lincoln worked well together for the next twenty years. In 1814, while visiting relatives in Windham, Maine, James Lovell died, at the age of seventy-six.

We do not know that James Lovell ever went to Braintree to visit Abigail. Their friendship is shown in three letters that followed his return to Boston.

In the second of the three letters to her, written in July of 1784, James writes Abigail in his typical playful, puzzling style, telling her of his pleasure in being appointed naval officer: "…I owe the gratitude of an Information that two days ago I was most unexpectedly appointed Naval Officer of this Port, instead of that Draft of small Beer which I have told you I should want, cannot fail to afford a very competent Support to a Family whose Wellfare you have proved to be one of your tender Concerns." His last letter to her, in April of 1789, presented his worries that he would not retain his position, which in fact he did.

James Lovell, Cryptographer

The eighteenth century saw extensive use of cipher to encrypt messages, particularly during warfare. *Congress's Cryptographer: A Novel of James Lovell and the American Revolution* portrays several ciphers that James Lovell used or decrypted. The one he most often used, called "the Lovell cipher" by associates and diplomats, is an alphabet cipher, based on a keyword. The cipher used by the Lees and at times the British employs a version of *Entick's Spelling Dictionary*, called a book cipher. Seeking to offer Benjamin Franklin an easier form of encryption, James Lovell sent the commissioner directions for an alphabet square (Ch. 5). He followed that with a keyword and instructions for his alphabet cipher (Ch. 25). The British, including General Cornwallis, used a method that alternated two types of ciphers, the book cipher and the alphabet cipher (Ch. 29). The method James Lovell sent to John Adams was the alphabet cipher dependent on a keyword, as was that he sent to Elbridge Gerry (Ch. 32). General Cornwallis's message that Lovell deciphered before Yorktown used multiple alphabet ciphers. The passage cipher such as Lovell decoded in his final work for Robert R. Livingston was a form that was less frequently used (Ch. 37).

Despite his successes in the use of cipher to communicate sensitive information, James Lovell's instructions at times resulted in frustration for diplomats, who could not read at least a portion of the material he encoded.

At least two difficulties contributed to the problem. The short, written directions Lovell provided made comprehension difficult. His cryptic style of writing also caused confusion. As Abigail said, he was "enigmatical." At least once, he complicated his instructions by suggesting ways in which the user could create new keys, as when he wrote to John Adams in May 1780.

A further difficulty for those who needed to use his system was that James Lovell's cipher depended on a keyword which he communicated to the user through a clue. However, the user had to remember what the clue indicated, or the message could not be read. Francis Dana helped Benjamin Franklin to decipher a passage written in Lovell's cipher, but when John Adams asked Dana to decipher a letter from James Lovell of January 6, 1781, he was unable to do so. Here, the problem was that Francis Dana could not remember the keyword for ten days. He did eventually recall the word and then proceeded to decipher the message.

John Adams, tasked with reading instructions sent to him by James Lovell, turned to Abigail for help in deciphering them. She explained her method of using Lovell's cipher in a letter to John Adams of June 17, 1782. It is true that Abigail had success in reading the encrypted portion of the letter that James Lovell sent to her on January 30, 1781, but she first had to turn to Richard Cranch for help.

Adding to the difficulty of their use, James Lovell himself did make occasional mistakes in ciphered passages. Fortunately, perhaps, Lovell seems completely unaware of the problems his cipher caused, persisting in its use to communicate sensitive messages.

Lovell used his cipher extensively in sending written instructions to diplomats overseas. His consistent promotion of cipher for security no doubt improved secure communication for diplomats. Part of his deserved recognition as "decipherer extraordinaire," as Edmund Cody Burnett, editor of the *Letters of Members of the Continental Congress,* dubbed him, was his undoubted ability to decode British messages. His enthusiasm for and belief in the importance of encrypted messages never waned.

Accuracy in Representing Delegates to Congress

Whenever possible, accuracy in names of the members of Congress who contributed to discussion or actions has been a priority in this work. The presence of delegates or others on any given date have for the most part been verified through such records as the *Journals of the Continental Congress,* the *Letters of Delegates to the Continental Congress,* diaries, and other sources. In representing events that cannot be ascertained, for example when individuals dine together or live together, the best information that can be obtained offers a picture as to what might have happened. This work of fiction intends to present in lively manner the complex thoughts, actions, and dealings of those men and women of the tumultuous and vital years of the American Revolution.

A Note About Letters and Quotations

Letters taken from original sources, such as those by Abigail Adams and James Lovell, are paraphrased and shortened in *Congress's Cryptographer: A Novel of James Lovell and the American Revolution.* Spelling, punctuation, and grammar, including capitalization, are modernized for easier reading; additional paragraphing is provided for clarity. See the Source Notes to locate originals. Not every letter between James Lovell and Abigail Adams is included in *Congress's Cryptographer.* Read more in *Adams Family Correspondence,* found within the *Adams Papers Digital Edition,* Massachusetts Historical Society, http://www.masshist.org/publications/adams-papers.

Many letters from Abigail Adams and James Lovell have been saved and are digitized. In the *Adams Family Correspondence* are sixty letters from James to Abigail, and thirty-four from Abigail to James. Since not all letters were saved, this exchange indicates a vital and healthy dialogue, one that likely sustained both correspondents in precarious and difficult times.

From his own letters it is clear that James wrote to his wife Mary frequently, as often as once a week. However, these personal letters, likely reflecting James's many concerns for his family, have not been saved.

Message in James Lovell's Cipher

To create a ciphered message in James Lovell's keyword cipher, choose a keyword, such as the word Lucky.

Write the numbers 1 through 27 in a column to the left of the alphabet square. 27 numbers are used rather than 26 since the ampersand is included at the end. Next to the number 1, write first two or three letters of the keyword at the top of columns.

1	L	U	C
2	M	V	D
3	N	W	E
4	O	X	F
5	P	Y	G
6	Q	Z	H
7	R	&	I
8	S	A	J
9	T	B	K
10	U	C	L
11	V	D	M
12	W	E	N
13	X	F	O
14	Y	G	P
15	X	H	Q
16	&	I	R
17	A	J	S
18	B	K	T
19	C	L	U
20	D	M	V
21	E	N	W
22	F	O	X
23	G	P	Y
24	H	Q	Z
25	I	R	&
26	J	S	A
27	K	T	B

Then, under each letter, write the alphabet in order, proceeding from the letter and continuing after the ampersand is given, starting the alphabet over again.

To encipher, in the first alphabet column locate the number to the left of the first letter in the word and write that number down, then write the number to the left of the second letter in the word in the second alphabet column, then write the number of the third letter in the word in the third alphabet column, and then back to the first alphabet column, continuing on until the word is completed.

An important rule is that when ciphered words are followed by words that are not ciphered, then the next ciphered word must start over with the column under the first letter.

28, 29, and 30 may act to separate words. These are called "nulls."

What does this message say in Lovell's keyword cipher?

19.16.14.24.12.16.29.22.22.16.30.22.1.12.

Deciphered Words Within Quotations

Deciphered words written within the original cipher used in a quotation are placed within brackets: { }.

Acknowledgments

Many researchers, colleagues, friends, and family members encouraged and helped me through the process of researching and writing *Congress's Cryptographer*, all of whom deserve my wholehearted thanks: Colleen Hansen, colleague and author; Beverly Chin, Professor of English at the University of Montana and former President of the National Council of Teachers of English; writing group members Lorna, Connie, and Heather; my sister Barbara Talbot; and the publisher of my first historical fiction novel, *The Remarkable Cause: A Novel of James Lovell and the Crucible of the Revolution*, Roger Williams. Researchers and experts also contributed significantly to this novel: Karie Diethorn of Independence National Historical Park, Philadelphia, offered resources, advice, and scholarly suggestions; June Lloyd, Librarian Emerita at the York County History Center, sent me a map of early York and answered questions; Jane Ptolemy of the William L. Clements Library in Ann Arbor, Michigan, provided material to me even though at the time the library was closed due to the pandemic; Gerry Daumiller kindly stepped in and with his expertise completed the Revolutionary War Map; and Sara Martin, Editor-in-Chief of the Adams Papers at the Massachusetts Historical Society, encouraged me to use the letters from Abigail Adams and James Lovell, paraphrased, shortened, and modernized. I am ever amazed at the kind responses I receive when I send questions to libraries and reference centers.

The Remarkable Cause: A Novel of James Lovell and the Crucible of the Revolution

Read about the first part of James Lovell's life in *The Remarkable Cause: A Novel of James Lovell and the Crucible of the Revolution* (Knox Press, 2021), by Jean C. O'Connor. A teacher at the Boston Latin School, he presents the first annual oration for the town following the Boston Massacre, and is imprisoned for spying. Find out more about *The Remarkable Cause* at jeanoconnor.com.

Source Notes

Primary Source Material

Almon, J. *The Remembrancer, Or, Impartial Repository of Public Events.* United Kingdom, 1778, p. 229. Google eBooks. "About the Chevalier de la Luzerne."

American Archives: Consisting of a Collection of Authentick Records, State Papers, Debates, and Letters and Other Notices of Publick Affairs, the Whole Forming a Documentary History of the Origin and Progress of the North American Colonies; of the Causes and Accomplishment of the American Revolution; and of the Constitution of Government for the United States, to the Final Ratification Thereof. "Correspondence, Proceedings, etc., December, 1776," Google eBook.

Andrlik, Todd. *Reporting the Revolutionary War: Before It Was History, It Was News.* Sourcebooks, 2012.

Austin, James T. *The Life of Elbridge Gerry*, vol. 1. Boston: Wells & Lilly, 1828, pp. 324–344.

The Complete Writings of Thomas Paine, vol. 2. The Citadel Press, New York, 1945, Mises Institute, mises.org/library/complete-writings-thomas-paine-volume-2.

Diary and Autobiography of John Adams, Vols. 1–4. L.H. Butterfield, editor, Leonard C. Faber and Wendell D. Garrett, assistant editors. The Belknap Press of Harvard University Press, 1961.

"The Expenses of a Congressman in 1777." *The Connecticut Magazine* 10, January-March 1906, pp. 28–32, Google eBook.

Faden, William. "The course of Delaware River from Philadelphia to Chester, with the several forts and stackadoes raised by the rebels, and the attacks made by His Majesty's land and sea forces." Map, 1779. *Norman B. Leventhal Map & Education Center,* collections.leventhalmap.org/search/commonwealth:z603vn36d.

Founders Online. National Historical Publications & Records Commission, National Archives and Records Administration, www.founders.archives.gov.

The Freeman's Journal or The North-American Intelligencer, p. 3, Philadelphia, Pennsylvania, 31 Oct 1781, Wed. "Description of Celebration in Philadelphia after American Victory at Yorktown," Oct. 24, 1781. www.newspapers.com/clip/32317810/description-of-celebrations-in.

Hogan, Margaret A. and C. James Taylor, eds. *My Dearest Friend: Letters of Abigail and John Adams.* The Belknap Press of Harvard University Press, 2007.

Journals of the Continental Congress, 1774–1789, ed. Worthington C. Ford et al. Washington, D.C., 1904–37, vols. 7–22, memory.loc.gov/ammem/amlaw/lwjclink.html.

Lafayette, Marie Joseph Paul Yves Roch Gilbert Du Motier, marquis de, 1757–1834. *Memoirs, Correspondence And Manuscripts of General Lafayette.* New York,

Saunders and Otley, 1837, pp. 36–41, HathiTrust,
www.catalog.hathitrust.org/Record/006591600/Home.

Laurens, Henry. "A Narrative of the Capture of Henry Laurens, of His
Confinement in the Tower of London, &c., 1780, 1781, 1782." *Collections of The
Historical Society of South Carolina,* Vol. 1., 46 & 57–8. Charleston, SC: S.G.
Courtney & Co for the South Carolina Historical Society, 1857. Internet
Archive, archive.org/details/collectionsofsou01sout.

The Pennsylvania Packet, p. 3, Philadelphia, Pennsylvania. "Congress thanks George
Washington for the victory in the siege of Yorktown,"
www.newspapers.com/clip/32315138/Congress-thanks-george-washington-for.

Shipton, Clifford Kenyon, John Langdon Sibley, and Massachusetts Historical
Society, *Sibley's Harvard Graduates,* vol. 14, Boston, Mass. Harvard University
Press, 1933, HathiTrust, catalog.hathitrust.org/.

Smith, Paul H., et al., eds. *Letters of Delegates to Congress, 1774–1789.* 25 volumes,
Washington, D.C., Library of Congress, 1976–2000,
www.memory.loc.gov/ammem/amlaw/lwdg.html.

Thicknesse, Philip. "A Treatise on the Art of Decyphering and of Writing in
Cypher with an Harmonic Alphabet." 1772,
www.archive.org/details/atreatiseonartd00thicgoog/page/n6.

Upham, William P., William Phineas. "Letters written at the time of the occupation
of Boston by the British, 1775–6, communicated by Wm. P. Upham." Salem,
Mass., Salem Press, 1876, www.hdl.handle.net/2027/loc.ark:/13960/t88g92g6q.

Wharton, Francis et al. *The Revolutionary Diplomatic Correspondence of the United States,
under direction of Congress, with preliminary index, and notes historical and legal,* 1889.
HathiTrust, www.catalog.hathitrust.org/Record/000872440.

Secondary Source Material

Allen, Thomas B. *George Washington, Spymaster: How the Americans Outspied the British
and Won the Revolutionary War.* National Geographic, 2004.

"The American Revolution's One-Man National Security Agency." *NSA,* 1
December 2011. www.nsa.gov/Portals/70/documents/news-
features/declassified-documents/crypto-almanac-50th/the-american-
revolution.pdf.

Bendiner, Alfred. *Bendiner's Philadelphia.* A.S. Barnes and Co., 1964.

Bevan, Edith Rossiter, "The Continental Congress in Baltimore, Dec. 20, 1776 to
Feb. 27, 1777." *Maryland Historical Magazine,* 42, pp. 21–28, March 1947.

Billias, George A. *Elbridge Gerry, Founding Father and Republican Statesman.* McGraw-
Hill, 1976, pp. 130–134, *Internet Archive,* archive.org.

Brandow, John H. "Horatio Gates." *Proceedings of the New York State Historical
Association,* Vol. 3, 1903, Fenimore Art Museum, pp. 9–19. *JSTOR,*
www.jstor.org/stable/42889819.

Burnett, Edmund C. *Ciphers of the Revolutionary Period. The American Historical Review*, James J. Franklin, John Franklin; Bourne, et. al., American Historical Association, 1895, pp. 339–324, Internet Archive, archive.org.

Cashin, Edward J. "Nathanael Greene's Campaign for Georgia in 1781." *The Georgia Historical Quarterly*, Spring, 1977, Vol. 61, No. 1, pp. 43–58, Georgia Historical Society. *JSTOR*, www.jstor.org/stable/40580342.

Cohen, Fred. *A Short History of Cryptography.* www.all.net/edu/curr/ip/Chap2-1.html.

Conkling, Howard. *Le Chevalier de la Luzerne: Short Biography by Howard Conkling.* United States, n.p, 1908, Google eBooks.

Crary, Catherine Snell. "The Tory and the Spy: The Double Life of James Rivington." *The William and Mary Quarterly*, Vol. 16, No. 1, Jan., 1959, pp. 61–72, Omohundro Institute of Early American History and Culture, www.jstor.org/stable/1918851.

Ellis, Joseph J. *Founding Brothers: The Revolutionary Generation.* Vintage Books, 2000.

Ferling, John. *The Ascent of George Washington: The Hidden Political Genius of an American Icon.* Bloomsbury Press, 2009.

Ferling, John. *A Leap in the Dark: The Struggle to Create the American Republic.* Oxford University Press, 2003.

Fortenbaugh, Robert. "York as the Continental Capital: September 30, 1777—June 27, 1778." *Pennsylvania History: A Journal of Mid-Atlantic Studies*, vol. 20, no. 4, Oct. 1953, pp. 399–408. *JSTOR*, www.jstor.org/stable/27769456.

Frazier, Paul. "Mining for Victory: Daniel Roberdeau's Lead Mine and Fort." *Journal of Western Pennsylvania History*, Summer 2001, www.journals.psu.edu/wph/article/view/5040.

Friedenwald, Herbert, *The Journals and Papers of the Continental Congress. The Pennsylvania Magazine of History and Biography*, 1897, Vol. 21, No. 2, 1897, pp. 161–184, University of Pennsylvania Press. *JSTOR*, www.jstor.com/stable/20085740.

Gelles, Edith B. "A Virtuous Affair: The Correspondence Between Abigail Adams and James Lovell." *American Quarterly*, vol. 39, no. 2, 1987, pp. 252–269. *JSTOR*, www.jstor.org/stable/2712912.

Genealogy of the Roberdeau family: including a biography of General Daniel Roberdeau, of the revolutionary army, and the Continental Congress; and signer of the Articles of Confederation, 1876, pp. 15–16, Internet Archive, archive.org.

George, Alice L. *Old City Philadelphia: Cradle of American Democracy,* Arcadia Publishing, 2003.

Greene, Jack P. and J.R. Pole, eds. *The Blackwell Encyclopedia of the American Revolution,* Blackwell, 1994.

Hamer, Philip M. "Henry Laurens of South Carolina: The Man and His Papers." *Proceedings of the Massachusetts Historical Society*, Third Series, Vol. 77, 1965, pp.

3–14, Massachusetts Historical Society. *JSTOR*,
www.jstor.org/stable/25080598.

Holton, Woody. *Abigail Adams: A Life*. Free Press, 2009.

Irvin, Benjamin H. *Clothed in Robes of Sovereignty: The Continental Congress and the People Out of Doors*. United Kingdom, Oxford University Press, 2014, pp. 169–174, Google eBook.

Jones, Helen. *James Lovell in the Continental Congress 1777–1782*. University Microfilms, Ann Arbor, Michigan, 1969. Courtesy Boston Public Library.

Kelley, Joseph J. Jr. *Life and Times in Colonial Philadelphia*. Stackpole Books, 1973.

Kidder, William L. *Ten Crucial Days: Washington's Vision for Victory Unfolds*. Knox Press, 2018.

Lee, Senator Mike, *Written Out of History: The Forgotten Founders Who Fought Big Government*. Sentinel, New York, 2017.

Lloyd, June, Librarian Emerita at the York County History Center. Blog, www.yorkblog.com/universal/.

Lossing, Benson John. *The Life and Times of Philip Schuyler*, vol. 2, pp. 170–172. Originally published 1860. 2009. Google eBook.

Mack, Ebenezer, *The Life of Gen. Gilbert Motier de Lafayette: The Compatriot and Friend of Washington; the Champion of American Independence, and of the Rights and Liberties of Mankind, from Numerous and Authentic Sources*. United States, Brooks, 1859. Google eBook.

McCullough, David. *1776*. Simon & Schuster, 2005.

McCullough, David. *John Adams*. Simon & Schuster, 2001.

Miller, John C. *The First Frontier: Life in Colonial America*. Laurel, 1966.

Mintz, Max. *The Generals of Saratoga: John Burgoyne & Horatio Gates*. Yale University Press, 1990.

Morton, Brian, and Ira M. Schwartz, Donald C. Spinelli. *Beaumarchais and the American Revolution*, Lexington Books, 2003, Google eBooks.

Nagy, John A. *George Washington's Secret Spy War: The Making of America's First Spymaster*. St. Martin's Press, 2016.

Nagy, John A. *Invisible Ink: Spycraft of the American Revolution*. Westholme, 2010.

Pearl, Christopher R. "Review of Clothed in Robes of Sovereignty." *Pennsylvania History: A Journal of Mid-Atlantic Studies*, vol. 79, no. 3, 2012, pp. 317–320. *JSTOR*, www.jstor.org/stable/10.5325/pennhistory.79.3.0317.

Peckham, Howard H. "British Secret Writing in the Revolution," *Michigan Alumnus XLIV*, February 1938, 126–131.

Philbrick, Nathaniel. *In the Hurricane's Eye: The Genius of George Washington and the Victory at Yorktown*. Penguin Books, 2018.

Philbrick, Nathaniel. *Valiant Ambition: George Washington, Benedict Arnold, and the Fate of the American Revolution*. Penguin Books, 2016.

Prowell, George Reeser. *The City of York, Past and Present*, Gazette Print, 1904, Library of Congress Digitized Books, www.lccn.loc.gov/05035981.

Riley, Edward M. *Independence National Historical Park, Philadelphia, Pa.* United States, U.S. Department of the Interior, National Park Service, 1954, Google eBook.

Rappleye, Charles. *Robert Morris, Financier of the Revolution*, Simon & Schuster, 2010.

Schaeper, Thomas J. *Edward Bancroft: Scientist, Author, Spy.* Yale University Press, 2011.

Schneider, Gregory S., "The Fake News that Haunted General Washington." *Washington Post*, 10 April 2017, www.washingtonpost.com.

Schouler, James. *Americans of 1776: Daily Life in Revolutionary America.* Heritage Books, 2007.

Skaler, Robert Morris. *Images of America: Society Hill and Old City.* Arcadia Publishing, 2005.

Slauter, Will. "Forward-Looking Statements: News and Speculation in the Age of the American Revolution." *The Journal of Modern History*, vol. 81, no. 4, 2009, pp. 759–792. *JSTOR*, www.jstor.org/stable/10.1086/605485.

Stoll, Ira. *Samuel Adams: A Life.* Free Press, 2008.

Tower, Charlemagne. *The Marquis de La Fayette in the American Revolution: With Some Account of the Attitude of France Toward the War of Independence*, Volume 1, 1894, pp. 176–181, Google eBook.

Weber, Ralph E. "James Lovell and Secret Ciphers During the American Revolution." *Cryptologia* 2, no. 1, Jan. 1978, pp. 75–89.

Weber, Ralph E. *Masked Dispatches: Cryptograms and Cryptology in American History, 1775–1900.* Center for Cryptologic History, National Security Agency, 2013.

Wilcox, Jennifer. *Revolutionary Secrets: Cryptology in the American Revolution. Center for Cryptologic History*, National Security Agency, 2012.

Zucker, A.E. *General De Kalb, Lafayette's Mentor.* Chapter 10, "A Cold Reception by Congress and Its Favorable Outcome," University of North Carolina Press, 1966. *JSTOR*, www.jstor.org/stable/10.5149/9781469658759_zucker.14.

Sources

Abbreviations:

APDE – Adams Papers Digital Edition

JCC – *Journals of the Continental Congress*

LDC – *Letters of Delegates to Congress*

LOC – Library of Congress

PGW – *Papers of George Washington*, Project at the University of Virginia

Foreword

"I was put upon a deciphering Business respecting some of the intercepted Letters of Cornwallis…." James Lovell to Nathaniel Peabody, LDC vol. 16, 3 November 1780.

Chapter 1. Congress in Baltimore

"These are the times that try men's souls…." Paine, Thomas. *The American Crisis*, No. 1, p. 50, *The Complete Writings of Thomas Paine*, Vol. 1. Mises Institute, www.mises.org/library/complete-writings-thomas-paine-volume-1.

"This year will cost nearer forty million…." "Executive Committee to John Hancock, 4 February 1777. Smith, Paul H., et al., eds. *Letters of Delegates to Congress, 1774-1789*, Vol. 6. Washington, D.C.: LOC, 1976-2000.

Chapter 2. Coming to Philadelphia

"Great talkers, little doers." Benjamin Franklin, qtd. in George, Alice L. *Old City Philadelphia: Cradle of American Democracy*. Arcadia Publishing, 2003, p. 39.

"Twenty dollars a Cord for Wood…." "From John Adams to James Warren, 6 March 1777," *Founders Online*, National Archives, https://www.founders.archives.gov/documents/Adams/06-05-02-0055. [Original source: *The Adams Papers, Papers of John Adams*, vol. 5, August 1776–March 1778, ed. Robert J. Taylor. Cambridge, MA: Harvard University Press, 2006, pp. 100–101.]

Chapter 3. The Pennsylvania State House

"prudence and policy require that it should be avoided." "From George Washington to John Hancock, 1 March 1777," *Founders Online*, National Archives, www.founders.archives.gov/documents/Washington/03-08-02-0500. [Original source: *The Papers of George Washington*, Revolutionary War Series, vol. 8, 6 January 1777–27 March 1777, ed. Frank E. Grizzard, Jr. Charlottesville: University Press of Virginia, 1998, pp. 472–474.]

Chapter 4. Sabers Rattling

"its sovereignty, freedom, and independence…." JCC 9:908.

Chapter 5. *Parlez-vous Anglais?*

"Should this letter arrive unbroken…" "To Benjamin Franklin from James Lovell, [after 26 May 1777]," *Founders Online*, National Archives, www.founders.archives.gov/documents/Franklin/01-24-02-0060. [Original source: *The Papers of Benjamin Franklin*, vol. 24, May 1 through September 30, 1777, ed. William B. Willcox. New Haven and London: Yale University Press, 1984, pp. 86–88.]

Chapter 6. The Problem of Foreign Officers

"these Frenchmen have used me quite up." James Lovell to Joseph Trumbull, LDC vol. 7, 30 June 1777.

Chapter 7. First Independence Day

"Philadelphia, July 4, 1777. Sir, I think it my duty as an individual...." "To Benjamin Franklin from James Lovell, 4[-9] July 1777," *Founders Online*, National Archives, www.founders.archives.gov/documents/Franklin/01-24-02-0203. [Original source: *The Papers of Benjamin Franklin*, vol. 24, May 1 through September 30, 1777, ed. William B. Willcox. New Haven and London: Yale University Press, 1984, pp. 266–268.]

"Congress considers these letters an attempt... they may resign." Paraphrased from JCC 8:537.

"But I have thought it my duty to inform Congress of these Facts...." "From George Washington to John Hancock, 22 July 1777," *Founders Online*, National Archives, www.founders.archives.gov/documents/Washington/03-10-02-0347. [Original source: *The Papers of George Washington*, Revolutionary War Series, vol. 10, 11 June 1777–18 August 1777, ed. Frank E. Grizzard, Jr. Charlottesville: University Press of Virginia, 2000, pp. 356–357.]

"It seems French officers have a great fancy to enter our service...." James Lovell qtd. in Tower, Charlemagne. *The Marquis de Lafayette in the American Revolution: With Some Account of the Attitude of France Toward the War of Independence*, by Charlemagne Tower, vol. 1, p. 180, Google eBook.

"After the sacrifices that I have made in this cause...." Mack, Ebenezer, et al. *The Life of Gen. Gilbert Motier de Lafayette.... From Numerous and Authentic Sources*. 1843, p. 40, Google eBook.

Chapter 8. Dear Madam

"August 29, 1777. Dear Madam, More than likely General Howe will waste...." James Lovell to Abigail Adams, LDC, vol. 7, 29 August 1777.

Chapter 11. A New Board of War

"Your professions of esteem, Sir, are very flattering...." Abigail Adams to James Lovell, 17? September 1777, *Adams Family Correspondence*, vol. 2, APDE, Massachusetts Historical Society. www.masshist.org/publications/adams-papers.

"a well meant but indiscreetly-managed compliment...." James Lovell to Abigail Adams, 10 November 1777, *Adams Family Correspondence*, vol. 2, APDE, Massachusetts Historical Society. www.masshist.org/publications/adams-papers.

"To form a permanent Union, accommodated...." JCC 9:933.

"Elbridge Gerry would have penned a letter...." James Lovell to John Adams, LDC, vol. 8, 28 November 1777.

Chapter 12. Valley Forge

"December 8, 1777. Sir, By accident I find myself called upon...." Committee for Foreign Affairs to Silas Deane, LDC, vol. 8, 8 December 1777.

"a weak general and bad counselors." "From George Washington to Brigadier General Thomas Conway, 5 November 1777," *Founders Online*, National Archives, www.founders.archives.gov/documents/Washington/03-12-02-0118. [Original source: *The Papers of George Washington*, Revolutionary War Series, vol. 12, 26 October 1777–25 December 1777, ed. Frank E. Grizzard, Jr. and David R. Hoth. Charlottesville: University Press of Virginia, 2002, pp. 129–130.]

Chapter 13. Reason and Clarity Should Rule

"Grotius, Puffendorf, and Vattel, or Da, Du, and Dy." Paraphrased from "Grotius, Puffendorf, Vattel &c &c &c…." James Lovell to John Adams, LDC, vol. 8, 1 January 1778.

"You can have no conception of the arts and interest…." "From Benjamin Franklin to James Lovell, 7 October 1777," *Founders Online*, National Archives, www.founders.archives.gov/documents/Franklin/01-25-02-0017. [Original source: *The Papers of Benjamin Franklin*, vol. 25, October 1, 1777, through February 28, 1778, ed. William B. Willcox. New Haven and London: Yale University Press, 1986, pp. 44–45.]

"That if the army is not…." Fleming, Thomas. "Valley Forge," *Journal of the American Revolution*, 2013, www.mountvernon.org/george-washington/the-revolutionary-war/valley-forge/.

Chapter 14. A Toast to the Commander-in-Chief

"Yet being naturally desirous of gain, King Louis will lend us the sine qua non…." James Lovell to Samuel Adams, LDC, vol. 9, 19 February 1778.

Chapter 15. The French Will Support Us

"Mr. Dana, Congress does not trust me. I cannot go on thus." Fleming, Thomas. "Valley Forge," *Journal of the American Revolution*, 2013, www.mountvernon.org/george-washington/the-revolutionary-war/valley-forge/.

"large share of Grandmother Eve's curiosity," "very indulgent partner." Abigail Adams to John Thaxter, *Adams Family Correspondence*, vol. 2, APDE, 15 February 1778, www.masshist.org/publications/adams-papers.

"April 1, 1778. Dear Ma'am,   I tell you that the report of the assassination…." James Lovell to Abigail Adams, LDC vol 9, 1 April 1778.

Chapter 16. An Alliance!

"Louis, by the grace of God king…." JCC 11:419.

"You can have no conception how we are still beseiged and worried on this head…." From Benjamin Franklin to James Lovell, 21 December 1777, *Founders Online*, National Archives, www.founders.archives.gov/documents/Franklin/01-25-02-0250. [Original source: *The Papers of Benjamin Franklin*, vol. 25, October 1, 1777, through February 28, 1778, ed. William B. Willcox. New Haven and London: Yale University Press, 1986, pp. 329–330.]

"June 13, 1778, York. Friendly though unjust Portia…." James Lovell to Abigail Adams, LDC, vol. 10, 13 June 1778.

Chapter 17. Return to Philadelphia

"Braintree, June 30, 1778. Dear Sir, I have often written to you expressing my fears…." Abigail Adams to James Lovell, 30 June 1778, *Adams Family Correspondence*, vol. 3, APDE, Massachusetts Historical Society. www.masshist.org/publications/adams-papers.

"I always make the best of every mishap." James Lovell to Horatio Gates, LDC, vol. 10, 18 September 1778.

Chapter 19. A Rift Among the Commissioners

"Braintree, 24 June 1778. Dear Sir, I do not know whether I should…." Abigail Adams to James Lovell, 24 June 1778, *Adams Family Correspondence*, vol. 3, APDE, Massachusetts Historical Society, www.masshist.org/publications/adams-papers.

"Braintree, 19 August, 1778. My dear Sir, I just received your letter of August…." Abigail Adams to James Lovell 19 August 1778, *Adams Family Correspondence*, vol. 3, APDE, Massachusetts Historical Society, www.masshist.org/publications/adams-papers.

Chapter 20. The Newspaper War Heats Up

"This book is better than the last I sent you. It is to decipher…." Arthur Lee to the Committee of Secret Correspondence, 3 June 1776. The paragraph is the last from 6 Force's Archives, fourth series, 686. *Wharton's Diplomatic Correspondence*, vol. 2, p. 96. www.babel.hathitrust.org/cgi/pt?id=nyp.33433081773636&view=image& seq=104.

"coarse and vehement." Complete Writings of Thomas Paine, vol. 2, p. 98, Mises Institute, www.mises.org/library/complete-writings-thomas-paine-volume-2.

Chapter 21. Can You Tell Me of Mr. Adams?

"January 4, 1779. Dear Sir, May I be permitted to call your attention…." Abigail Adams to James Lovell, 19 January 1779, *Adams Family Correspondence*, vol. 3, APDE, Massachusetts Historical Society, www.masshist.org/publications/adams-papers.

"Jan. 19, 1779. Yes, lovely Portia, you have written to one who lives…." James Lovell to Abigail Adams, LDC, vol. 11, 19 January 1779.

Chapter 22. The Dept Owing to M. Beaumarchais

"Braintree, February–March 1779. Since I last wrote I have been relieved …." Abigail Adams to James Lovell, 1 February 1779, *Adams Family*

Correspondence, vol. 3, APDE, Massachusetts Historical Society, www.masshist.org/publications/adams-papers.

"lickspittle does not fall to the ground" James Lovell to Horatio Gates, LDC vol. 12, 13 April 1779.

"June 18–26, 1779. Do you love the natural sentiments of the heart?" Abigail Adams to James Lovell, 18 June 1779, *Adams Family Correspondence*, vol. 3, APDE, Massachusetts Historical Society, www.masshist.org/publications/adams-papers.

"July 19, 1779. Your favor of June 18/26 is this hour come to hand...." James Lovell to Abigail Adams, LDC vol 13, 19 July 1779.

Chapter 23. "A Wild Part to My Brain."

"August 27, 1779. Talking about friendship and other classes of affection...." James Lovell to Abigail Adams, LDC, vol. 13, 27 August 1779.

"engaged in a severe wrestling match with a chap who had successfully...." James Lovell to John Adams, LDC, vol. 13, 31 August 1779.

Chapter 24. Military Governor Benedict Arnold

"Braintree, November 18, 1779. In a letter from my dear absent Friend...." Abigail Adams to James Lovell, 18 November 1779, *Adams Family Correspondence*, vol. 3, APDE, Massachusetts Historical Society, www.masshist.org/publications/adams-papers.

Chapter 25. A Cipher for Dr. Franklin

"I wish you to be persuaded...." James Lovell to George Washington, LDC vol. 14, 23 February 1780.

"Let the alphabet be regularly squared. Agree upon...." James Lovell to Benjamin Franklin, LDC vol. 14, 24 February 1780.

Chapter 26. The Keyword—Cranch

"Our Affairs at the Southward are to be judged of by the Gazettes...." "To Benjamin Franklin from James Lovell, 4 May 1780," *Founders Online*, National Archives, www.founders.archives.gov/documents/Franklin/01-32-02-0245. [Original source: *The Papers of Benjamin Franklin*, vol. 32, March 1 through June 30, 1780, ed. Barbara B. Oberg. New Haven and London: Yale University Press, 1996, pp. 354–355.]

"May 4, 1780. Dear Sir, The bearer, Mr. Mease, is brother to the late Clothier General...." James Lovell to John Adams, LDC vol 15, 4 May 1780.

Chapter 27. Losses in the South

"June 13, 1780 [the RC is June 13, but in Adams Papers it is June 11]. Dear Sir, Your repeated favors...." Abigail Adams to James Lovell, 11 June 1780, *Adams Family Correspondence*, vol. 3, APDE, Massachusetts Historical Society, www.masshist.org/publications/adams-papers.

"In the deepest distress and anxiety of mind, I am...." Horatio Gates to Congress, 20 August 1780, *Emerging Revolutionary War Era*, www.emergingrevolutionarywar.org/2018/08/16/in-the-deepest-distress-and-anxiety-of-mind-gen-gates-letter-to-Congress-on-the-battle-of-camden, PCC, item 154, 2:234-37.

Chapter 28. A Traitor in Our Midst

"26 September 1780, Robinson's House in the Highlands. Sir, I have the honor to inform Congress…." "From George Washington to Samuel Huntington, 26 September 1780," *Founders Online*, National Archives, PGW.

Chapter 29. Reconciled to Ciphers

"Dear Balfour, Charlestown, Oct. 7, 1780. I yesterday received yours of the 27th and the contents of the letter are unpleasant. I have ordered Wymmes…." Cornwallis to Balfour, 7 October 1780. William L. Clements Library, University of Michigan, Ann Arbor.

"Popular beyond all description." James Lovell to Elbridge Gerry, LDC vol. 16, 20 November 1780.

"Is it not time…." James Lovell to Elbridge Gerry, LDC vol. 16, 20 November 1780.

"I shall call on Nanny Cl…." James Lovell to Elbridge Gerry, LDC vol. 16, 20 November 1780.

"I can only say that we are { bankrupt with a mutinous army } The latter owing very much…." James Lovell to John Adams, LDC vol. 16, 2 January 1781.

"Braintree, January 3, 1781. Your favor of December 19 was delivered to me today…." James Lovell to Abigail Adams, LDC vol. 16, 30 January 1781.

Chapter 30. The United States in Congress Assembled

"I must particularly acquaint Miss that, though the fans stuck…." James Lovell to Abigail Adams, LDC vol. 16, 27 February 1781.

"The said states hereby severally enter …." JCC 19:214.

Chapter 31. Close Call to Disaster

"Cornwallis has retreated quite out of Greene's reach…." James Lovell to Samuel Holten, LDC vol. 17, 17 April 1781.

Chapter 32. They Must Confess They Cannot Conquer Us

"Braintree, 10 May, 1781. Upon opening your favor of April 17, my heart beat a double stroke…." Abigail Adams to James Lovell, 17 March 1781, *Adams Family Correspondence*, vol. 4, APDE, Massachusetts Historical Society, www.masshist.org/publications/adams-papers.

"…consider certain names addressed to a Lady…." Abigail Adams to James Lovell, 10 May 1781, *Adams Family Correspondence*, vol. 4, APDE, Massachusetts Historical Society, www.masshist.org/publications/adams-papers.

"May 29, 1781. Yesterday's post brought me your letters…." James Lovell to Abigail Adams, LDC vol. 17, 29 May 1781.

"You would be made very happy by such an event being grounded...." "To John Adams from James Lovell, 21 June 1781," *Founders Online*, National Archives, https://www.founders.archives.gov/documents/Adams/06-11-02-0282. [Original source: *The Adams Papers, Papers of John Adams*, vol. 11, January–September 1781, ed. Gregg L. Lint, Richard Alan Ryerson, Anne Decker Cecere, Celeste Walker, Jennifer Shea, and C. James Taylor. Cambridge, MA: Harvard University Press, 2003, pp. 381–383.]

Chapter 33. My Humble Desire to Serve You

"23 June 1781. And is there no medium, Sir, between terms...." Abigail Adams to James Lovell, 23 June 1781, *Adams Family Correspondence*, vol. 4, APDE, Massachusetts Historical Society, www.masshist.org/publications/adams-papers.

"Led astray by Cornelia's fancy...." James Lovell to Abigail Adams, LDC vol. 17, 13 July 1781.

"July 14th, 1781. My dear Sir, Your favor by General Ward was not delivered to me...." Abigail Adams to James Lovell, 14 July 1781, *Adams Family Correspondence*, vol. 4, APDE, Massachusetts Historical Society, www.masshist.org/publications/adams-papers.

"I feared moths—have opened your goods—aired...." James Lovell to Abigail Adams, LDC vol. 17, 23 August 1781.

Chapter 34. French and Americans March to Yorktown

"If ever America stood in need of wise heads...." Abigail Adams to James Lovell, Abigail Adams to James Lovell, July 20–August 6, 1781, *Adams Family Correspondence*, vol. 4, APDE, Massachusetts Historical Society, www.masshist.org/publications/adams-papers.

"September 4, 1781. I found Colonel Laurens had landed at Boston...." James Lovell to Abigail Adams, LDC vol. 18, 4 September 1781.

"decipherer extraordinaire." Elias Boudinot's report, Burnett Letters VI: 239–240, fn. 2 to #349, Thomas McKean to WA, 14 October 1781, VI #349, p. 239–240. Edmund Cody Burnett, who compiled the *Letters of Members of the Continental Congress*, used this phrase to describe James Lovell.

"As a variety of insignificant figures are interspersed...." James Lovell to Nathanael Greene, LDC vol. 18, 21 September 1781.

"Philadelphia. September 21st, 1781. Sir, You once sent some papers to Congress which no one about you...." James Lovell to Nathanael Greene, LDC vol. 18, 21 September 1781.

"Philadelphia. September 21st, 1781. Sir, It is not improbable that the enemy...." James Lovell to George Washington, LDC vol. 18, 21 September 1781.

Chapter 35. Cornwallis's Message

"September 26, 1781. In truth, friend, thou art a Queer Being—laugh where I must…." Abigail Adams to James Lovell, 20 September 1781, *Adams Family Correspondence,* vol. 4, APDE, Massachusetts Historical Society, www.masshist.org/publications/adams-papers.

Note: Abigail dated the letter September 20. *The Adams Papers Digital Edition*'s note indicates that date is probably not correct and suggests it might have been written on the 26th; therefore, I have changed the date to the 26th for its inclusion, but it is listed here as 20 September in this Source Note, since that is how it is found in the Digital Edition.

"Philadelphia. October 9, 1781. Yesterday's post brought me your favor…." James Lovell to Abigail Adams, LDC vol. 18, 9 October 1781.

"York Town Virginia. 8 Sept. 1781. Sir I have made several attempts…." Wilcox, Jennifer. *Revolutionary Secrets: Cryptology in the American Revolution.* Center for Cryptologic History, National Security Agency, 2012, pp. 35–38. Original message and deciphered message.

"York Town Virginia. 8 Sept. 1781. Sir I have made several attempts…." *George Washington Papers*, Series 4, General Correspondence: Charles Cornwallis to Henry Clinton, September 8. 8 September 1781. Manuscript/Mixed Material. *The Library of Congress,* www.loc.gov/item/mgw429368/.

"Head Quarters before York. 6th Oct. 1781. Sir, I am much obliged by the communication…." "From George Washington to James Lovell, 6 October 1781." *Founders Online*, National Archives, PGW.

"As my works were not in a state of defence I have taken…." Wilcox, Jennifer. *Revolutionary Secrets: Cryptology in the American Revolution.* Center for Cryptologic History, National Security Agency, 2012, pp. 35–38. Original message and deciphered message.

"October 14th, 1781. Evening. I gave a letter for your Excellency this morning…." "To George Washington from James Lovell, 14 October 1781." *Founders Online*, National Archives, PGW.

"Head Quarters near York. 19th Oct. 1781. Sir, I have the honor to inform Congress…." "From George Washington to Thomas McKean, 19 October 1781," *Founders Online*, National Archives, PGW.

Chapter 36. The Firmness of Our Convictions

"Should I be required in service with the army I will take myself…." George Washington's speech, paraphrased from JCC 21: 1143.

Chapter 37. Continental Tax Receiver

"February 28, 1782. Mr. Lovell, do let me entreat you, this thirtieth time…." James Lovell to Abigail Adams, LDC vol. 18, 28 February 1782.

"This is a matter of great consequence to Congress…." Samuel Osgood to James Lovell, LDC vol. 18, 2 March 1782.

"A few days ago, I wrote more fully. This will I hope…." Transcription from original, captured message to Governor Robertson. Enclosure to James Lovell to R. Livingston, Ringwood Iron Works, at Leisure in Storm, 19 April 1782. www.fold3.com/image/408455 M247, r65, v2, p. 225. Via William L. Clements Library, University of Michigan, Ann Arbor.

"Ringwood Iron Works, at Leisure in Storm, April 19, 1782. Honorable R. R. Livingston. Sir, The contents of the cyphered paper, which I copied…." James Lovell to R. Livingston, Ringwood Iron Works, at Leisure in Storm, 19 April 1782. M247, r65, v2, p. 221, www.fold3.com/image/408452.

Afterword

"decipherer extraordinaire." Elias Boudinot's report, *Burnett Letters* VI: 239–240, fn. 2 to #349, Thomas McKean to General Washington, 14 October 1781, VI #349, pp. 239–240. Edmund Cody Burnett, editor of the *Letters of Members of the Continental Congress*, used this phrase to describe James Lovell.

"…I owe the gratitude of an Information…." James Lovell to Abigail Adams, 5 July 1784, *Adams Family Correspondence*, vol. 5, APDE, Massachusetts Historical Society, www.masshist.org/publications/adams-papers.

Images

Preface.

"The Revolutionary War Eastern North America." Map by Gerry Daumiller.

Chapter 2.

"Independence Hall." Independence National Historical Park, Philadelphia, Pa., p. 2, Riley, Edward M., 1954, U.S. Department of the Interior, National Park Service, Google eBook. Courtesy of Independence National Historical Park.

Chapter 5.

"James Lovell's Cipher, for Benjamin Franklin." James Lovell to Benjamin Franklin, after 24 May 1777, American Philosophical Society.

Chapter 8.

"James Lovell's Map of the 'Seat of War' in the Fall of 1777." Enclosure, James Lovell to John Adams, 29 August 1777, Massachusetts Historical Society.

Chapter 9.

"York County's First Courthouse." From the collection of the York County History Center, York, PA.

Chapter 10.

"The First County Courthouse and Adjournment of Continental Congress at York, Pa., November, 1777, on the Reception of the News of Burgoyne's Surrender." Bonham, Horace, Esq. Prowell, George Reeser, *The City of York*,

Past and Present. York, Pa., Gazettee print, 1904. p. 5, LOC,
www.loc.gov/item/05035981.

Chapter 12.

"Valley Forge, 1777. Gen. Washington and Lafayette visiting the suffering part of
the army." ID pga 06988, LC-DIG-pga-06988 (digital file from original item),
LC-USZ62-819 (b&w film copy neg.), *LOC*, Washington, D.C. 20540 USA,
hdl.loc.gov/loc.pnp/pga.06988.

Chapter 18.

Ozanne, Pierre, 1737–1813. *"Le vaisseau le Languedoc rematé en pleine mer ainsi que le
Marseillois avec des mats d'hunes rejoints par tous les vaisseaux et les frégates de l'escadre, le
vaisseau le César excepté; et faisant route le 17 Aoust 1778."* [The Languedoc vessel
remade in the open sea as well as the Marseillois with upper masts joined by
all the vessels and frigates of the squadron, the Caesar vessel excepted; and
going on August 17, 1778.] 1778–1779, Photo of Wash Drawing. Library of
Congress Prints and Photographs.
www.loc.gov/pictures/item/2004670064/resource/. Image from the group,
"Expedition of the French fleet to the United States and the West Indies
under Charles Henri Theodat, Comte d'Estaing, 1778-79."
www.loc.gov/pictures/item/2005687936.

Chapter 25.

"Combat memorable entre le Pearson et Paul Jones." Leizelt, Balthasar Friedrich, engraver,
between 1779 and 1790. Print. cph 3a04101, Library of Congress Prints and
Photographs, http://hdl.loc.gov/loc.pnp/cph.3a04101.

"Benjamin Franklin's COR Cipher." James Lovell to Benjamin Franklin, 24
February 1780, American Philosophical Society.

Chapter 26.

"James Lovell to Benjamin Franklin, 4 May 1780." *American Philosophical Society.*

"Letter from James Lovell to John Adams Using CR Key." James Lovell to John
Adams, 4 May 1780, Massachusetts Historical Society.

Chapter 29.

"Intercepted Letter, General Cornwallis to General Balfour."
Cornwallis to Balfour, 7 October 1780. William L. Clements Library, University
of Michigan, Ann Arbor.

"Explanation of British Cipher, Cornwallis to Wymmes and Balfour."
James Lovell to Nathanael Greene, 3 November 1780. William L. Clements
Library, University of Michigan, Ann Arbor.

"Substitution Tables for James Lovell's Polyalphabetic Cipher System, Keywords:
John Adams—CR; Henry Laurens—YO; Benjamin Franklin—COR; William
Palfrey—UNT; John Jay—BY." PCC, Fold3: M247, r72, i59, p. 144,
www.fold3.com/image/172707?terms=144,cipher,page.

"James Lovell to John Adams, 2 January 1781." Massachusetts Historical Society.

Chapter 32.

"James Lovell to Elbridge Gerry, 5 June 1781." Massachusetts Historical Society.

"James Lovell to John Adams, 21 June 1781." Massachusetts Historical Society.

Chapter 34.

"George Washington Visits the French Fleet." Moran, Percy. NH 2278, *Naval History and Heritage Command.* history.navy.mil/content/history/nhhc/our-collections/photography/numerical-list-of-images/nhhc-series/nh-series/NH-02000/NH-2278.html.

"James Lovell to Major General Nathanael Greene, September 21, 1781." William Clements Library.

Faden, William. *A Plan of the entrance of Chesapeak Bay, with James and York rivers; wherein are shewn the respective positions in the beginning of October 1.⁰ of the British Army commanded by Lord Cornwallis at Gloucester and York in Virginia; 2.⁰ of the American and French forces under General Washington; 3.⁰ and of the French Fleet under Count de Grasse.* London, Wm. Faden, 1781. Map. The Library of Congress, <www.loc.gov/item/74692131/>.

Chapter 35.

"Charles Cornwallis to Henry Clinton, September 8." *George Washington Papers,* Series 4, General Correspondence: September 8, 1781. Manuscript/Mixed Material, Library of Congress. www.loc.gov/item/mgw429368/.

About the Author

Jean C. O'Connor is the author of two historical fiction novels based on primary sources about a "forgotten founder," James Lovell, a teacher at the Boston Latin School, prisoner of the British, and congressman, known as "the Revolution's one-man National Security Agency:" *The Remarkable Cause: A Novel of James Lovell and the Crucible of the American Revolution* (Knox Press, 2021) and *Congress's Cryptographer: A Novel of James Lovell and the American Revolution* (Mountain Pine Press, 2024). Growing up in New England, Jean developed a fascination with the American history evident in so many landmarks there. Her enjoyment of history as well as literature led to a teaching career of thirty-seven years in Montana, particularly in Helena, the capital. As an educator, she received the NCTE High School Teacher of Excellence Award. A few lines in her grandmother's journal inspired her interest in James Lovell, her five times great-grandfather and inductee into the National Security Agency's Cryptologic Hall of Honor for his work during the Revolution.

Visit jeanoconnor.com, for more information or to contact her.